PENGUIN BOOKS

# THE FUTURES

Anna Pitoniak is an editor of fiction and non-fiction at Random House in New York. She graduated from Yale in 2010, where she majored in English and was an editor at the *Yale Daily News*. *The Futures* is her first novel.

# THE FUTURES

## Anna Pitoniak

PENGUIN BOOKS

PENGUIN BOOKS

UK | USA | Canada | Ireland | Australia
India | New Zealand | South Africa

Penguin Books is part of the Penguin Random House group of companies
whose addresses can be found at global.penguinrandomhouse.com.

First published by Lee Boudreaux Books,
an imprint of Little, Brown and Company 2017
First published in Great Britain by Michael Joseph 2017
Published in Penguin Books 2018
001

Set in 13/15.75 pt Bembo Book MT Std
Typeset by Jouve (UK), Milton Keynes
Printed in Great Britain by Clays Ltd, St Ives plc

A CIP catalogue record for this book is available from the British Library

PAPERBACK ISBN: 978-1-405-92747-5

www.greenpenguin.co.uk

MIX
Paper from
responsible sources
FSC® C018179

Penguin Random House is committed to a
sustainable future for our business, our readers
and our planet. This book is made from Forest
Stewardship Council® certified paper.

*For Andrew*

# PROLOGUE

## *Julia*

It was a story that made sense. An old story, but one that felt truer for it. Young love goes stale and slackens. You change, and you shed what you no longer need. It's just part of growing up.

I thought I had understood. It seemed so simple at the time.

We moved in on a humid morning in June. Our suitcases bumped and scuffed the walls as we climbed three flights of stairs, the rest of the boxes and furniture waiting unguarded in the foyer. The locks were clunky and finicky, resistant on the first few attempts. Sunlight streamed through the smudged windows, and the floorboards creaked beneath our weight. The apartment looked smaller than it had before, on the day we signed our lease. 'I'm going down for some boxes,' Evan said, holding the door open with one foot. 'You coming?'

'I'll be there in a minute,' I said. I stood in the center of the room, alone, finding that I couldn't breathe.

What else was I going to do? He had a job and a place

to be. I didn't, but I had him. I could feel the tremors of change even before we graduated, growing more pronounced as the date approached: time to get serious. We'd been dating for more than three years, and we loved each other, and my friends already had roommates, and I couldn't afford to live by myself. So we signed a lease. We packed our things in shared boxes. It felt sensible and grown-up. And maybe taking this plunge would repair whatever hairline crack had already appeared between us, in the late months of senior year. Double or nothing.

In New York, we settled into a routine along with our friends, accruing habit fast. We all endured the same things: shoe-box apartments, crowded subways, overpriced groceries, indifferent bosses. What kept everyone going was the dream: store windows on Madison Avenue, brownstones lit golden in the night, town cars gliding across the park. Imagining what it would be like when you got there, someday. Manhattan was like a dazzling life-size diorama. A motivation to work harder, stay later, wake earlier. Fantasy is the only escape valve – what's all the pain worth without it? But not for me. I'd screw my eyes shut and try to imagine it, what the future would look like, what alchemy might transform our current situation. But nothing came. There was no thread of hope. Who was this man next to me, his body curled up against mine? What was this feeling of vertigo that sometimes came with the blurry edge before sleep? I realized that I had made a mistake. Evan wasn't the one. We weren't meant to be.

And so my life in New York grew smaller and smaller, a thorny tangle of dead ends. I rattled around in the tiny apartment. I hated my job. Evan was too busy. My friends were too busy. I was lonelier than ever. The problem was obvious. I was trapped in an airless bubble, with no plan to get out. My life lacked any escape.

Until, against my better instincts, I went looking for it in the wrong place.

# PART I

# Chapter 1

## Evan

I could hear footsteps and murmurs from the other room. The creak of the door opening finally dissolved the last shards of sleep. When I opened my eyes, there was a pale face peering through the crack.

'Who is *that?*' somebody whispered.

The door slammed shut. The alarm clock said it was a little past 9:00 a.m. It took me a minute to remember where I was: on the third floor of an old stone building in New Haven, still wearing my clothes from the night before. I found a half-melted stick of gum in the back pocket of my shorts, tugged my T-shirt straight, and pressed my palms against my hair. When I opened the door to the common room, a plump woman was surveying the scene with a look of dismay. Empty Bud Light cans were scattered across the floor, and dirty clothes were heaped in one corner. She started fanning the stale air toward an open window. It was move-in day, late August, the first real day of college. This had to be my assigned roommate, Arthur Ziegler, and his family. I'd meant to clean up that morning, but I'd forgotten to set the alarm last night when I stumbled into bed.

Arthur was crouched in the corner, fiddling with a nest of wires. Arthur's father, a bald man in a polo shirt and khakis, was humming to himself as he peered down at the street. Arthur's mother was sniffing the air, her frown deepening. The room was quiet except for the car honks and shouts from outside. I cleared my throat. The three of them turned in unison.

Arthur's mother forced a smile. 'Well – hello,' she said, stepping over. She was small, round and doll-like, with a tartan headband and sensible shoes. 'I'm Elaine Ziegler, Arthur's mother. This is Gary.' Gary waved. 'And this is Arthur. Arthur, what – what are you doing?'

'Hang on,' he said, peering at a plastic box. A row of green lights blinked to life. 'Got it.' He stood up, dusting his hands on his jeans, then he followed my gaze. 'Oh. The router. Setting up the wireless connection. Figured it was the most important thing to start with, right?'

'Yeah. It's, uh, nice to meet you all.'

Elaine Ziegler kept staring. Maybe she was trying to reconcile it, the polite young man suddenly emerging from the shell of a passed-out lunk. Then she clapped her hands together. 'Well, let's get to work. Gary, you make the bed. Arthur, why don't you start unpacking those suitcases? And I'm just going to . . . here we go.'

She shook open a black garbage bag and bent over, reaching for the empty beer cans on the floor, crinkling her nose at the smell. I felt a hot bubble of guilt.

'Mrs Ziegler, I'm sorry. Let me . . .' I hurried to start gathering the cans.

'Well . . .' She paused, then handed me the bag. 'All right. Thank you, dear.'

When I was done, I announced that I was taking out the trash. Elaine and Gary were absorbed in a discussion with Arthur about where to hang a poster. The door creaked on its hinges when I opened it, but they didn't notice.

The captains had given us the morning off from practice. There was a diner on Broadway that I'd passed before, a place that served breakfast all day. The room was packed and buzzing, new students chattering excitedly with their families, utensils ringing against china while waiters wove through the crowds with plates aloft. I was about to give up when the hostess finally caught my eye and led me to an empty stool at the counter.

After, while I was waiting to pay at the register, a girl walked in. Other heads turned too, taking in her tanned legs, her cutoff shorts, her scoop-neck T-shirt. She had a blond ponytail sticking out from a faded Red Sox cap and a freckled nose. She leaned into the counter and said something inaudible in the din, and even that – the shape of her mouth forming silent words – carried some kind of promise. I tried to edge closer, but it was too crowded. A waiter handed her two cups of coffee. She pushed the door open with her shoulder. I craned my neck but lost sight of her on the sidewalk.

I wandered for a while, only returning to the dorm when I knew Arthur and his parents would be at lunch. I changed and jogged up to the rink for afternoon practice. I was the first to arrive, which was what I'd been hoping for. The burn of the laces against my fingertips as I tightened my skates, the smell of the locker room, the wet reflection left behind by the Zamboni, the sound of the blade carving into the ice, the wind and echo of the empty rink — it was like slipping back into a native tongue. This was the best part. It only took a second, in that first push away from the boards, to feel the transformation. From a bulky heaviness to a lighter kind of motion. The friction of the blade melted the ice just enough, sending me flying forward on threads of invisible water. I was in a different country, a different side of the continent, but in those moments at the rink, home came with me. The ice was a reminder of the world I had left behind just a week earlier: long winters, frozen ponds, snowbanks, pine trees. It had always seemed like a decent enough reward for life in a cold, forbidding land: the gift of speed, as close as a person like me could come to flight.

I grew up in the kind of small town that isn't easy to get to and isn't easy to leave. It started as a gold-rush settlement, and while no one got rich from the land, a handful of prospectors liked it enough to stay. It's in a mountain valley in the interior of British Columbia, surrounded by wilderness, defined mostly by its distance from other places: seven hours to Vancouver, two hours to the border, an hour to the nearest hospital.

In a small town like ours, where there is only one of everything – one school, one grocery store, one restaurant – it's expected that there is only one of you. People aren't allowed to change much. I was held back in kindergarten – I'd had some trouble with reading comprehension – and it marked me well into the next decade. I was big for my age, always a year older, and I think people liked me more because of it. It made the picture snap into focus: I was a hockey player; I was a born-and-bred local; I was a hard worker even if I wasn't the brightest. An image easily understood, one as solid and reliable as the mountains in the distance. I grew up with boys like me, most of us hockey players. We were friends, but I sometimes wondered how alike we really were. The things they loved most, the things that made them whoop and holler with glee – keg parties and bonfires, shooting at cans on a mossy log, drunken joyrides in a souped-up F-150 – only gave me a vague, itchy desire for more. I could imitate easily enough, like following an outline through tracing paper, but it never felt like the thing I was meant to be doing. I got good at faking laughter.

Maybe the girls at school sensed this difference. It happened fast: one day puberty arrived, and they all started paying attention to me. From then on, there was always someone waiting at my locker when the last bell rang, twirling her hair, holding her textbooks tight to her chest. I genuinely loved those girls, loved that they banished the loneliness, but it was a generalized feeling; it didn't matter who was next to me, whose bed or musty basement carpet we were lying on. I had sex for the first time with a girl a year older than I was, eleventh grade to my ninth. After she had coached me through our first short but glorious session, she started telling me her plan. She was going to drop out at the end of the year and move to the Yukon, where she'd work as a chef at a logging camp. The pay was good, and the setting was wild. She propped herself up on one elbow, resting a hand on my bare chest. She hadn't told anyone, but she was telling me. She kissed me in conclusion. 'You're a good listener, Evan,' she said, then she moved lower beneath the duvet.

A pattern emerged from the filmstrip of tanned faces and soft bodies. All the girls liked to talk dreamy – about the jobs they'd get, what they'd name their kids someday. We became blank screens for each other, desire reflected into a hall of mirrors. It solved a problem for me, but sometimes it left me wondering if that was it – if love was always so easily caught and released. I realized after a while that I gave these girls something very specific. They knew it even before I did, that I would be gone someday. I wouldn't be there to hold them accountable when their dreams eventually fell short. I wasn't like everyone else, wasn't meant to stay in this town.

Not that people didn't attempt to leave. They'd go for a few years of community college or university, but a small town like ours possesses a strange gravity, and they always came back. A few of my teammates were going to escape by leaving school early to play hockey in the Major Juniors, a path that would lead some of them to the NHL. I might have done the same. But I'd heard about someone from town, a decade ago, who'd played for an American college instead. He was rich and successful and living in New York by that time. He came back occasionally to visit, and I glimpsed him once at the gas station, filling the tank of a shiny high-end rental car. Even in that split second, I saw that he carried himself in a different way, and something within me latched on. I'd known that the world was bigger than Carlton, British Columbia, but I'd never really thought about just how big it was. I was fourteen years old, and I made up my mind. I played in Junior A and kept my college eligibility. Despite my reputation, I was smart, or at least I wanted to be smart, and I studied hard in school. In spare hours I shot tennis balls into the street hockey net, did squats and flipped tires and jogged the dirt roads around our house. On a Saturday morning, I drove two hours to take the SATs at a town on the border. In the fall of senior year, I finally got the call. The one I'd been hoping for. A new door, swinging wide open.

On the afternoon before my flight east, I stood with my parents in the driveway as the sun slipped behind the mountains, casting an early twilight over the yard. My parents owned the town's grocery store, and they couldn't afford the vacation time or the cost of the plane tickets. My mom would drive me to Vancouver, where we'd spend the night in an airport motel before my flight the following morning. My dad was staying at home to work. I'd said good-bye to my friends at a party the night before, truck headlights illuminating the clearing in the woods where we always gathered, squat kegs and foamy cups of beer clutched in the semidarkness.

It was quiet during the car ride out of town. 'Music?' my mom asked, and I shook my head. The trees along the highway blurred together.

'Evan,' she said after a long silence. 'It's okay to be nervous.' She looked over at me, her face tanned from the summer. A long salt-and-pepper braid fell down her back. Her bare arms were lean from years of carrying boxes from delivery trucks to the loading dock. It was her hands on the steering wheel, their familiar age spots and creases, her thin gold wedding band, that made me understand that I was really leaving.

But I shook my head again. 'I'm fine.'

'Well,' she said. 'I guess you're probably pretty excited about it.'

I was. I still was. But the anticipation had been building up for so long, and now that it was actually here, the moment felt disappointingly ordinary. We could have been driving anywhere, on a family trip, or en route to some hockey tournament. I had the feeling that eventually we'd turn back in the other direction, toward home. It seemed impossible that this was how life transformed itself: a drive down a road you'd driven so many times before.

'Only a hundred more kilometers,' she said an hour

later, as we whizzed past another road marker. I felt like I should make conversation – it was the last time I'd see her for months – but I couldn't think of anything to say.

'Checking in?' the clerk at the motel asked.

'The reservation is under Peck. Two rooms,' my mom said, digging through her wallet. I raised my eyebrows at her, my eternally frugal mother. Only when we were wheeling our bags down the hallway, away from the lobby, did she lean over and whisper: 'You're a grown-up now, honey. I think you deserve your own room, don't you?'

I was on campus early. Every year a rich alum from the hockey team paid for the team to have use of the rink for one week in late August. The captains would run the practice, skirting the NCAA rules that prevented us from officially beginning practice until October. Most of the players lived off campus and could move in early. After my flight – the longest I'd ever taken, the first one out of the country – I caught a shuttle bus to New Haven. I was going to crash at the hockey house for the week, along with the other freshmen. The door was unlocked when I arrived.

'Hello?' I called into the empty living room. I followed the sound of voices to the back of the house, where I found two guys sitting in the kitchen, eating dinner.

'Hey. I'm Evan Peck. I just got here.' I held out my hand.

'Hey, man. I'm Sebi. And this is Paul. We're new, too.'

'Where are you guys from?'

'Medicine Hat,' Sebi said.

'Kelowna,' Paul said.

Our team was mostly composed of guys like that, guys like me – Canadians from the prairies and the western provinces, some New Englanders, a few boys from Minnesota. It made settling in easy. The routine was familiar, the intensity turned up: twice-a-day practices, runs and lifts, team dinners. I was exhausted, not so much falling asleep every night as passing out, too tired to feel homesick. On the second-to-last day of that week, toward the end of afternoon practice, I noticed a man sitting in the stands, watching us scrimmage. He wore a crisp suit and tie, which seemed incongruous with both the August heat outside and the manufactured cold inside the rink.

'Did anyone else notice that guy?' I asked in the locker room.

'The guy in the stands?' one of the seniors replied. 'That's Reynolds. He's paying for all this.'

The same man was waiting outside the rink when we emerged in the late afternoon light. He wore mirrored sunglasses and leaned against a bright yellow sports car. One of the captains went over and shook his hand, and they spoke briefly.

'Guys,' the captain called out to the rest of us. 'We're going over to Liffey's for beers. Mr Reynolds is treating.'

'I still don't really get who this guy is,' I said to Sebi as we trailed the group down Whitney Avenue. At the bar, quiet on a weekday evening when the campus was still empty, Reynolds took off his jacket, rolled up his sleeves, and slapped his card down to open the tab.

I thought of the dwindling contents of my wallet as I reached for the pitcher. I was planning to find a job on campus, but until then, I was spending the last of the money saved from my summer job. At least the beer was free. A little later, Reynolds came over to our table and pulled up a chair. 'You're all new, huh?' he said, reaching to pour himself a beer. 'I don't recognize any of you from last year.'

We nodded. 'Yes, sir,' I said.

'Well, this is my favorite time of year, getting you guys together for the first time. The main thing is you get to know each other. These early days are the best, let me tell you. When everything's still up for grabs.'

Reynolds had the build of an athlete in retirement, muscles gone soft, a cushiony midsection. His mirrored sunglasses shone like an extra pair of eyes from the top of his head. He squinted at us. 'Not that I don't expect a return on my investment.' He laughed. 'I'm paying for this because I expect you guys might be able to bring home a national championship in your time here.'

We sipped beer in silence. 'Did you play at all after college, Mr Reynolds?' Sebi finally asked.

'It's Peter. No. No, I wasn't good enough to go pro, never expected to. But there's another game, you know. It pays better and it lasts longer.' He laughed again, his teeth glowing white. 'Moved to New York, started in

17

banking, and now I'm running a hedge fund. You know how hedge funds work?'

He talked and talked, going into more detail than any of us could absorb. I tried to pay attention, but I kept drifting, noticing instead the embroidered monogram of his shirt, the gold wristwatch peeking from beneath his cuff. His accent still had the last traces of a childhood spent somewhere in Canada's sprawling interior. He was rich and young. He'd done everything right. But he looked tired beneath it all.

The sky outside had darkened. Reynolds waved down the waitress to close out his tab. 'Have to head back,' he said, draining his beer. He passed around business cards. 'I know you guys are good, but odds are you're not going to the pros after college. Call me if you ever want advice.'

Earlier that day, before afternoon practice, I'd finally moved my things into my dorm room. The other students would be arriving the following morning. That night, after Reynolds left, I wanted to forget what I was about to face: the people who had earned their place at this school through different means – through more *legitimate* means. I'd spent the previous week pretending that this place belonged to me, but it was only that – pretending. After leaving the bar, a few of us picked up a case of beer and a handle of whiskey and brought it back to my room, drinking until late. By the end of the night, it had done the trick. I'd almost forgotten. I kicked the empty cans aside and collapsed onto the bare bed.

★

In the dim basement of a frat house, in a room that smelled like beer and dirt, a girl pressed her body against mine. She kept laughing at everything I said. It was that first night after everyone arrived, the first real night, and my teammates and I ventured in a pack from party to party. I moved my hand down her waist, over her T-shirt, and she drew closer. *Okay,* I thought. It still worked. We danced for a while, and then we were kissing. She tasted like tequila and salt. A few songs later, she pushed closer with impatience. She was cute, with a great body, and both of us were the right amount of buzzed. But in that moment sex seemed only marginally appealing, not worth all the trouble. I felt a little melancholy. My teammates were scattered throughout the room, distracted by other girls or games of beer pong, so I extracted myself and left the party unnoticed.

Back at the dorm, the light coming through the door to my entryway caught a figure in silhouette. It was a girl, tall and long-legged. Blond. She looked familiar. As I got closer, I recognized her from the diner that morning. Her hair was loose and long, and she'd changed into a dress. She was looking for something in her purse and didn't see me until I was right behind her, reaching for my key card.

'Oh! God, you scared me,' she said.

'You need to get in?'

She laughed. 'I think I managed to lose my card already.'

'You live here, too?'

19

'On the fourth floor. I'm Julia.'

'I'm Evan. Third floor.'

I stepped aside to usher her through the open door. 'After you.'

'Oh – thanks.'

The door fell shut with a loud bang.

'So, Evan.' She smiled. 'Where are you from?'

'Canada.'

'Really? That's cool. Where in Canada?'

'The middle of nowhere. You've never heard of it.'

'Try me.'

'Carlton. It's in British Columbia, the interior.' She shrugged, and I laughed. 'I knew it. What about you?'

'Boston. Well, just outside Boston. Brookline.'

I was tempted to say something about the Red Sox, remembering the hat from that morning, then I reminded myself that she didn't know I'd been looking.

'Did you go out tonight?'

'Yeah, with my teammates. Hockey,' I added.

'That explains the Canadian thing. You must get that a lot. Or you will.'

I laughed. My beery buzz had vanished. The way she was looking at me wasn't the way the other girls looked at me back home. Her face was like an image firmly fixed on canvas where the other girls' had been slippery glass. Right here in the present, breathing the same air, not off in some imagined future. Midnight wasn't late. The night was just starting. 'Hey, are you hungry?' I asked.

'Starving, actually.'

We walked to the pizza place on Broadway. Up at the counter, she reached for her purse, but I waved her money away. I could give her this, at least. On the way home, we sat on a low stone wall, waiting for the pizza to cool. I watched as she plucked a piece of pepperoni from her slice. Her kind of beauty snuck up on you. You had to look a little closer to really get it. Someone called her name from across the street. She waved back at him.

'That was fast,' I said.

'What was?'

'You made friends already.'

'No, we went to high school together. There are a bunch of us here.'

'Oh. That must be nice.'

'I guess. What about you? What do you think of it so far?'

'This place?' I swiveled, taking in the panorama. 'Just like the brochure. But more drunk people.' She laughed. 'It's about what I expected. Or not. I don't know. I'm still taking it in.'

'Different from home?'

'Are you kidding?'

She smiled. 'It must be an adjustment.'

'That's an understatement. What about you? What do you think of it?'

'It's just like the brochure.'

'Touché.' I laughed. 'So, Julia. How was your summer?'

She blinked once, staring down at the sidewalk. She blinked again.

'I'm sorry. Wrong question?'

'No, no, it's just – long story. I don't need to burden you with it.'

'You can tell me.' A beat. 'People like to tell me things.'

'You'd better be careful. I might never shut up.'

Eventually she took the last bite of her pizza, and then she held the crust out toward me. 'Do you want it? I never eat the crust.'

'Sure?'

'I wouldn't offer it to just anyone,' she said in mock solemnity. 'But I can tell we're going to be good friends.'

Back in the dorm, we stood in the hallway outside her room. It was late, 3:00 a.m., then 4:00 a.m. Other students tripped up the stairs to bed, but we kept talking and talking, and whenever I thought maybe the conversation had reached its natural end, one of us fired off in a new direction, bringing the other along. She didn't invite me inside. Mostly I was glad for that. Finally, when she started yawning uncontrollably, I said that I should probably get to bed.

'Yeah. Me, too.' She paused, hand on doorknob. 'Thanks for the pizza, Evan.'

'Anytime.'

She smiled. 'See you in the morning?'

Julia had a boyfriend. Of course she did. A guy named Rob, from her boarding school. They'd been together for almost two years. But by mid-September, she was barely mentioning Rob. Usually I was the one to ask about him, as a way of making sure he did in fact still exist. I wondered how much she and Rob actually spoke, how much she told him about her new life at college.

It turned out to be easy enough: making friends, fitting in. It didn't seem to matter how different two people might be or how different their lives had been before college. That was true for me and my roommate, Arthur. We fit together like puzzle pieces, a big one and a small one. And it was true for me and Julia. She took my hand at parties, leading me through the crowd. She came and went through our unlocked door like another roommate. She helped me cram for midterms; she read my papers. I needed the help. That was what surprised me most – how hard the work was. It was like the other students saw English where I saw hieroglyphs, even in the most basic, introductory courses. Maybe that hometown feeling had been right all along; maybe I *was* the same as the Evan Peck who'd failed kindergarten way back. I couldn't admit this to anyone, not even to Julia, although she probably saw it anyway. She saw everything about me.

One night in late October, coming home from practice, I passed her in the courtyard, where she was on the phone, pacing back and forth. I pointed to the door, but she shook her head. Then she snapped: 'Rob, listen to me – no, just listen. Why are you so pissed? Seriously? What do you want me to say?' She rolled her eyes at me and mimed holding a gun to her head. She cupped her hand over the phone. 'Sorry. He's ranting. I'll see you up there in a minute.'

I spent Thanksgiving with Arthur's family in Ohio. On Sunday afternoon, we got back to campus. Every time I heard footsteps on the stairs from the other students trickling back, I wondered whether it was Julia. We hadn't spoken during the weeklong break. I fiddled with my cell phone – I'd finally gotten one, after a few months of working on campus – but something stopped me from calling. The neediness of it, maybe. Later on Sunday night, Julia's roommate, Abby, knocked on our door. They had liquor leftover from before the break and were having people over that night.

My stomach twisted as we climbed the stairs. There were about a dozen people crammed in Abby and Julia's small common room. Julia was across the room, talking to Patrick, another guy from our entryway. She looked different, but it was hard to say why. She tossed her head back when she laughed and kept resting her hand on Patrick's forearm.

'Evan,' Abby said, pulling me aside. '*Evan*. I have to tell you something. She might kill me for telling you first, but I don't care.'

'What is it?'

Her eyes sparkled. 'Julia and Rob. They broke up.'

The rolling eyes, the mimed pistol. Julia had started to hint that the end was imminent. Abby laughed. 'Oh, come on. Don't act like you're not totally overjoyed.'

'I'm not. I mean, I am. But –'

She shoved me. 'Go.'

The mantelpiece served as the makeshift bar. I went over and poured myself a drink, willing my heart to slow down. I glanced at Julia, but she was still talking to Patrick. She hadn't seen me, or she was pretending she hadn't. It seemed strange.

'Hey,' I said to Arthur when he wandered over. 'Hey, Arthur, guess what.'

'Julia and her boyfriend broke up. I know. Abby told me, too.'

'Yeah. Big news, right?'

'So this is it, then? You guys are gonna be together now?'

I shrugged, but I liked the suggestion of inevitability. Julia. It *did* seem inevitable. It always had. 'I haven't even said hi to her yet.'

'You sure it's such a good idea?'

'What do you mean?'

But at that moment, an arm slipped through mine. 'Hey, stranger,' Julia said, kissing me on the cheek.

'Hey, you,' I said. Arthur was slinking away toward the door.

'How was your first-ever American Thanksgiving?'

'You people really like your football.'

'Do you want to know how mine was?' Her cheeks were flushed, her eyebrows arched. She was drunk.

'I do. You wanna get out of here?' I slipped my hand into hers, which was warm and familiar, and it flooded me with hope. 'Let's get something to eat.'

'No.' She pulled her hand away. Yanked it, almost. 'Come on, stay! Don't you want another drink?' She started to refill my empty cup. Then Patrick called her name from across the room, asking for another beer.

'You got it,' she called back. She handed me my cup and went back over to Patrick, who ruffled her hair. She avoided me for the rest of the night. When the last of the liquor was gone, Julia and Abby announced they were going to the deli on Broadway for sandwiches. Julia didn't seem to notice or care when I didn't come along.

But I wasn't tired yet. Back in our room, I stared at a muted rerun of *SportsCenter*. I couldn't make sense of it – of her. What explained her sudden distance, her caginess? Julia didn't bother playing games, not usually. I liked that about her.

Later I felt a hand on my shoulder, someone saying my name. I opened my eyes, and Julia was standing in front of me.

'You came back,' I said.

'I'm sorry,' she said. 'I got this for you.'

She held it out like an offering: a sandwich from the deli. My favorite kind, the one I always ordered. I never realized that she'd been paying such close attention. The heft of the paper-wrapped mass in my hand sparked the strangest feeling, or, really, two feelings at once. A homesickness I hadn't realized that I'd been feeling all along, and a sudden cure for it. 'Can I sit?' she asked.

I patted the couch, and she folded herself around me, resting her head on my shoulder, draping her legs across my lap. She was always so at ease in the world. Taking my hand at a party, resting her head on my shoulder: those gestures made the world feel big and small at the same time. It was just me and Julia, but what lay before us stretched so far you couldn't see the end.

'How was your Thanksgiving?' I said. 'I never asked.'

'Abby told you, right?'

'Yeah. Do you want to talk about it?'

'Not really. There's not much to say.'

She lifted her head to look at me. The sparkle and flush I'd seen earlier that night were gone, replaced by the old steadiness. 'Abby went home with that guy,' she said. 'Patrick. That guy I was talking to. She's not going to be back until morning.' She took my hand and led me upstairs.

One week later, we were walking back from dinner, Julia's hand in mine. It was a cold December night, our breath clouding white in the air, and she slipped our twined hands into my jacket pocket for warmth. I'd been thinking about it all week, and I wanted to say it.

'Julia,' I said. I stopped and pulled her closer. 'I love you.'

We stood together for a long time. She wrapped her arms around me inside my jacket, my chin resting on top of her head, the night dark and still. She was silent except for the sound of her breath, dampening my shirt. It had been only a week. Maybe this was too soon, too fast. Maybe I was alone in feeling this way.

But then: 'I love you, too. Evan. I love you.'

The heavy certainty of it, like a smooth stone in your pocket. We stood there for a long time, rooted to the ground by what we'd just said. When we started walking again, I realized my toes had gone numb from the cold.

---

The years went fast. We had our separate lives, but they were lived in parallel, and we ended every day the way it began: together. I couldn't untangle the feeling of my new life – the one I'd always imagined having – from the feeling of being with Julia.

Spring of our junior year, Julia went abroad, to Paris. She said that she'd always regret it if she didn't. And, she added, it might do us good to have some time apart. To become our own people. I didn't disagree. Occasionally I wondered whether there was some chance I was passing up in being with Julia, some mistake in committing to one person so early on. I missed her when she was away, but the hockey season didn't give me much time to be lonely. And it wasn't loneliness, in any case, that I felt in those rare moments of quiet. I didn't feel particularly different when Julia wasn't there – but the world felt different. The horizon drew nearer, the colors grew paler. That semester was when I realized how much I needed her.

'I can't wait to see you,' she said, her voice scratchy over Skype. It was late May; I hadn't seen her since January. 'I miss you.'

'Me, too.'

'I'm going to meet you at the airport, okay? Right near baggage claim.'

The crowds ebbed and flowed beneath the bright lights of Charles de Gaulle Airport, and then I saw Julia. She wore a loose black dress that skimmed her tan thighs, a bright scarf, her hair in a bun. She looked older, and more beautiful. That summer we traveled across Europe, living out of our backpacks and surviving on bread and wine. It was my first time abroad, and I was self-conscious about my unstamped passport. Julia had traveled a lot on family trips to London, Paris, Venice, Barcelona, Athens. She knew her way around these cities intuitively. One afternoon in Rome, she led me to the top of the Aventine Hill. 'Where are we going?' I asked.

'You'll see,' she said, walking with purpose.

At the top of the hill was an orange grove overlooking the city. The sky was soft and golden, and couples took turns posing for pictures in front of the sprawling sunset view. I figured this must be the place she'd meant to lead us. But Julia kept walking. She led me past the grove, down a paved road, to a plain-looking green wooden door. 'What is it?' I said.

'Okay.' She pointed at a small keyhole. 'Look through that.'

I found out later that it was a famous thing to do: to peer through this keyhole and see the framed view of the basilica in the distance. But at that moment it felt like she was giving me something just discovered, something I never would have found for myself. A new way of looking at the world. There was a stillness as the image came into focus.

We got back to campus senior year, and it was different. It was better. We were happy. I felt more certain about all of it. It made sense to me, for the first time, how one thing flowed into another; that there was a logic to the way life unfolded. We never did wind up winning a national championship, the one Reynolds had hinted at back in freshman year. I was a solid player, up and down my wing with discipline, but I wasn't good enough to play forever. Gone were the days when I'd cram my hours with extra squats and lifts and sprints. It didn't matter anymore, because that wasn't what I wanted. I was done with hockey. What I wanted was a life with Julia.

I still had one of the business cards from four years earlier. Reynolds must have passed out hundreds of those over the years. Finance was a well-trod path for other guys from the hockey team. *I could do that,* I thought. And it felt in keeping with a certain vision, an answer to the question that I'd been chasing ever since I was a kid. The jobs in finance flowed through campus like a wide, swift river. I wound up getting an offer from the most competitive place I applied to – Spire Management, a hedge fund in New York.

And when I asked Julia to move in with me, she said what I knew she would say. She smiled and threw her arms around me. 'Yes,' she said. 'Yes. I will.'

# CHAPTER 2

## *Julia*

Abby and I were at a party at Jake Fletcher's apartment on the night of the opening ceremonies for the Beijing Olympics. The flat-screen TV in the living room showed a massive stadium filled with glittering lights. Jake shared this apartment, at the top of a high-rise building in the financial district, with three of his friends from Dartmouth.

'Holy shit. Look at that view,' Abby said. The Statue of Liberty was visible in the distance, through the window. 'How much do you think they're paying?'

'A couple thousand each.' The wraparound terrace, the sunken living room: Jake and his roommates may have been pulling down banker salaries, but this was above and beyond. 'Right? At least. I'm sure they're getting help from their parents.'

'You think any of them are single?'

I grimaced. 'Ugh. Don't even joke.'

'Hello? You've seen my shit-hole apartment, right? It might be worth it.'

She turned, expecting a laugh, but instead she saw me scanning the room again, frowning at my phone. She waved her hand in front of me. 'Earth to Julia?'

'He's two hours late. He hasn't even texted.'

'Oh, don't be such a mope. Come with me.' She grabbed my hand. Abby always knew how to turn things around. She was the youngest of five, and the Darwinian pressures of a crowded childhood had made her resourceful. She was like the stone soup of friends. Give her twenty bucks and a room and you'll get a great party.

'Hold this,' she said, handing me her cup. We found an empty corner on the terrace, forty stories above the street. A constellation of cigarettes moved through the night air. Music thumped from the built-in speakers.

'Where'd you get that?' I asked as she lit the end of the joint.

'Here. We're splitting this.'

'I haven't smoked since graduation.'

'That's no way to live,' she said in a choked voice, holding the smoke in her lungs. Then she exhaled. 'See? This party is awesome.'

We'd smoked half the joint when I saw Jake Fletcher across the terrace. I waved him over.

'Hey, Jake,' I said. 'This is my friend Abby. My roommate from college.'

Abby held up the joint, but he shook his head. 'I wish. They drug-test us at work.'

'Where do you work?' Abby said.

'Lehman.'

'Oh, well, sorry about that,' she said. 'Great party, by the way.'

Abby got even friendlier when she was high. She and Jake started talking. My attention slipped loose, which didn't take much to happen these days. There was a pause in the music, and the next song that played was one of the big hits from the previous summer, a song I'd heard a million times on campus in the past year. I leaned out over the railing. We were at the edge of the island, where the East River curves into the harbor. The shorter, darker skyline of Brooklyn sat across the water like another city.

I could close my eyes, and the sounds of the party weren't so different from those in college, but I wasn't tricking myself. The feeling in the air had changed. There was a whole world out there, beyond wherever we were gathered. It didn't matter whether it was a cramped walk-up or a tar rooftop or a weedy backyard strung with lights. How you spent your time was suddenly up to you. There were other options. Infinite, terrifying options opening up like a crevasse and no one to tell you which way to go. I think everyone was wondering, through the haze of weed and beer pong and tequila shots, whether this – right here, right now – was in fact what they were supposed to be doing. I suspected I wasn't alone in detecting a desperation in the muggy air, people laughing too loudly, drinking beer that hadn't been chilled long enough.

My reverie was interrupted by the sound of my name. I turned and saw Evan pushing through the crowd. Evan, who was more than two hours late, his tie in a straggly knot and dark circles under his eyes.

'Nice of you to join us,' I said, more sharply than I'd intended.

'I'm sorry, Jules. I got held up at work. There's this big new project, and –'

'It's fine.' My cup was empty, and that suddenly seemed like the most pressing thing. I pointed at the kitchen. 'Let's go get a drink.'

We took a cab home that night, up the FDR. The old Crown Vic groaned as the driver hunched over the wheel, his foot pressed down hard, swerving between lanes and urging the car to go faster. The meter ticked higher, and I felt a prick of guilt for taking a cab instead of the subway. I leaned my forehead against the cool glass of the window and saw the Pepsi-Cola sign glimmering up ahead like a lighthouse. I'd been unfairly terse with Evan all night. We both knew what he was signing up for when he took the job at Spire. I turned back toward him, intending to apologize and to ask him about the new project he'd mentioned. But his eyes were closed. He was already asleep.

———

I guess I'm having trouble knowing where to begin. It's true, that summer was when the feeling descended. Those hot, humid New York City days and nights when I was nervy and jumpy all the time, a constant thrum underneath ordinary movements, a startled sensation like taking one too many steps up the stairs in the dark. It seemed obvious enough, the source of it. I had just graduated. I was trying to become an adult, trying to navigate the real world. Trying to find an answer to the question of what came next. Who wouldn't be made anxious by that? The problem existed in the present tense. But sometimes I wonder whether I got it all wrong. I wonder how far back it really goes.

---

Junior year of college, Christmas break. I was home earlier than everyone else because I had a light exam schedule that semester. My parents were out, and I was wandering around the house with nothing to do. I pulled out an old hardcover copy of *The Wapshot Chronicle* from one of the bookshelves in the living room. A frail, yellowed photograph slipped from the pages. It was a picture of my mother as a young woman, wearing a loose paisley dress, her long hair parted down the middle. She was sitting on a flight of steps with a group of girls flashing peace signs at the camera. On the back of the photograph, in her delicate handwriting, was the inscription: REPRODUCTIVE RIGHTS RALLY, WELLESLEY COLLEGE, 1975.

I shivered. Her hair, her smile: it was like looking at a picture of myself dressed up as a tourist from another era. I closed the book, put it back on the shelf. Then I took the book out again, removed the picture, and put it in my pocket. I kept thinking about it, all through that week, that month. How different my mother looked back then. She was the exact same age in that photograph – a junior in college – as I was in that moment. She never spoke about college. When she occasionally talked about the past, the stories always began in law school, never further back than that. Law school was where she and my father met. Both of them graduated near the top of their class and took jobs at high-powered firms before my mother left to raise me and my sister. I don't think she ever stopped comparing herself to my father, who is a senior partner and a widely admired attorney. She excels in other ways instead: charity boards, meetings and lunches, a perfectly slender physique. Her energy is always channeled to productive ends. But maybe that wasn't how she originally intended her life to turn out. Maybe there was another trajectory, one she'd been careful not to reveal to us.

But how would I know that? She doesn't complain or wax nostalgic. She doesn't tolerate moping – not in herself and certainly not in us. She was too busy shaping us into the best versions of ourselves. That was her job, and she was good at it. I turned out right. I fit smoothly into the world around me. My teachers liked me. I fell into a comfortable position within the social hierarchy: near the top of the pyramid, but not so high as to wind up a target of scheming usurpers. I never had a problem getting a date. I checked every box there was to check: friends, boys, sports, school.

It's only now I see the red flags along the way. Cracks in the armor. I remember a writing assignment in English class, the year before I left for boarding school. Our class filed outside, notebooks in hand, and sat down on the grassy hill behind the gym. Our teacher told us to describe the scene around us in any way we wanted – to be creative, to free-associate. I never liked English as a subject. I never got what was so great about it. Still, I was surprised to find a bright red C on my essay and a note from the teacher asking me to come see him. He inquired, eyes full of concern, whether I'd understood the purpose of this assignment. I'd always done okay in his class before, even though I hated it. I could string together insightful statements about *Hamlet, Lord of the Flies,* you name it. But somehow, I couldn't manage such an open-ended task. I struggled to fill those two pages. I had described the sights, the sounds, the smells. What else was I supposed to do? My stomach roiled with humiliation. What else did he want me to say?

But that was just one essay. One bad grade evened out by many good ones. The next year, I went away to boarding school, and I had never been happier. I started dating Rob. I played volleyball in the fall and lacrosse in the spring. I snuck cigarettes in the woods on Friday nights and sipped spiked hot chocolate at football games on Saturday mornings. I got straight As. Rob was recruited to play soccer at Harvard, and I was going to Yale. We agreed to try long distance, although I think both of us knew it wouldn't last. And it didn't matter, because on the very first day of school, I met Evan.

Three weeks after I found that photograph of my mother, I left for a semester abroad. She had been the one to persuade me to go. I'd lamented the idea of leaving, of missing Evan, of missing Abby and my other friends. 'Don't be silly,' my mother said. 'They'll be there when you get back.' She framed it as a decision to be made for practical reasons. When else would I get the chance to live in Paris? Why wouldn't I take advantage of this opportunity? She was right, of course, but I had different reasons for going. Sophomore year had been a difficult one, a bad year capped by a particularly bad incident. I needed a change. I sent in my application the first week of the new school year.

That January, I flew to Paris on a red-eye and took a bleary taxi ride to a crooked street in the 11th arrondissement. That old picture of my mother at Wellesley came with me in my suitcase, and I tacked it to the wall above my narrow bed in my homestay. My host was young and gamine, with bad teeth and great hair. She was a costume designer for the national theater. She hosted students in her spare bedroom to make extra money, she explained, so that she could spend her summers traveling with her boyfriend. Her hours ran long and late, and I rarely saw her, but the apartment always smelled like her – strong coffee and clove cigarettes.

Except during our weekly Skype dates, I didn't think about Evan much. I was too consumed by what was in front of me: the bottles of wine on the banks of the Seine, the afternoons in the Luxembourg Gardens, the yeasty scent of the bakeries when we rambled home from the clubs at dawn. I sank into it, like a deep bath, and I felt myself letting go of something for the first time. Evan and I planned that he would meet me in Paris after the semester ended. But when that day arrived, on the Metro ride to the airport, I felt sweaty and nervous. What if, these past months, I had changed – or he had changed – so much that we wouldn't have anything to say to each other? I scanned the crowds at baggage claim, anxious not to miss him; he didn't have a phone that worked in Europe. We'd spent time apart before, the previous two summers, when he'd gone back to Canada and I'd gone back to Boston. But this stretch was different. I'd learned to live in another country. He'd learned to live without me. Suddenly our plan – traveling through Europe for two months before senior year – struck me as foolish. What if he arrived and everything was all wrong? What if it was over?

Then I spotted him, towering above the rest of the crowd, in a ball cap and T-shirt. He saw me and smiled. I'd forgotten what it felt like to be wrapped in his arms, to feel the vibration of his laughter in his chest. Things did feel different. Evan felt like an old friend, an old lover, one whose reappearance in my life was sweeter for giving me a link between past and present. I was known; I was remembered, even far from home.

We flew back to Boston in August, pausing for a night, and then we got on a plane to British Columbia. It was my first time out there, my first time meeting his parents after more than two years of dating. His hometown was tiny, like a grain of sand on the map. That first night, in Evan's childhood bedroom beneath the slanted rafters, in the modest house tucked among the tall pine trees, I realized that I had never experienced so much quiet in my life.

'Have fun, kids!' His mother saluted us with her thermos as his parents drove to work the next morning. She leaned through the window as they backed out of the driveway. 'Oh, and Julia, my bike's out back if you want to borrow it.'

We rode through town that first day, Evan pointing out the landmarks of his childhood: the high school, his first girlfriend's house, the hockey rink where he'd spent so many hours practicing. Weeks, months, years of practice. Someone called his name as we were pedaling away from the rink. 'Peck? Is that you?'

'Coach Wheeler?' Evan called back. The two of them hugged, the coach clapping him hard on the back. 'Julia, this is my old coach, Mr Wheeler. Coach, this is my girlfriend, Julia Edwards.'

'Where are you from, Julia?' He knew right away I wasn't a local.

'Boston,' I said. 'Evan and I go to college together.'

'How is it out there? Been meaning to ask your folks how your season was. He was the best player I ever had.' He winked at me. 'No one ever worked as hard as Evan Peck. I knew this guy would go places.'

Evan beamed from the praise. They talked for a long time, catching up on Evan's college career, on how close Yale had come to winning the championship that year. His coach asked whether he knew what he was going to do after graduation. 'You going to try and play in the minors, maybe?' he said. 'Or you could go over to Europe. You're good enough for it.' Evan shrugged, his smile slackening, the light dimmed. I couldn't read the expression on his face.

The next day, we biked over to the river to meet up with some of his friends. Most of them had stayed put, working construction or other odd jobs in town, still living in the houses they grew up in. They brought along beer and a waterproof boom box, and we went tubing down the river. It felt like something out of a movie. We floated with our inner tubes lashed together, our toes trailing in the cold water, the beer light and fizzy on our tongues. Evan traced circles on the back of my hand. He tilted his head back to look at the summer sky, a bright blue banner framed by the soft green fringe of the pine trees. 'God, I love it here,' he said.

'Why did you ever want to leave?' I asked, with genuine curiosity. He seemed so happy, so comfortable.

'I don't know,' he said. 'I guess it never seemed like enough.'

His mother picked us up downriver, and we strapped our bikes to the roof rack of the car. Evan offered me the front seat, but I shook my head and slid into the back. His mother turned around. 'What did you think?'

'I loved it,' I said, and I meant it. We were silent for the rest of the ride home. I could see where Evan had inherited his tranquillity, the ease he could find in just about any setting. I imagined car rides from years before, his mother shuttling him to early morning practices, each of them silently content in the other's presence. The landscape out here had a way of shutting your mind off. We were all tired and happy, warm from the sun, hungry for dinner, and that was all that mattered.

The two weeks went quickly. His parents hosted a barbecue the night before we left. Nights there were cold, and by the time the burgers were sizzling on the grill, everyone had donned sweaters and sweatshirts. I borrowed an old crewneck emblazoned with Evan's high school mascot. 'Look at that,' his dad said, pointing at the sweatshirt with a pair of tongs when I approached the grill. 'Julia, you could be a local. You fit right in.' Evan's mother leaned over and said, 'He means that as a compliment, hon.'

The next morning, on the bus that would take us back to the Vancouver airport, I waved good-bye to his parents through the window with a dull ache behind my eyes. How was it possible to be homesick for a place that I couldn't call home, a place I'd only known for a handful of days? The previous two weeks had felt like an escape, different in aesthetic but not so different in essence from the way I'd felt in Paris. I realized, at that moment, that I had no idea what I wanted. There was so much out there. The bus shuddered and heaved into motion, and I blinked back a few tears. I was going to be okay. I had Evan, no matter what happened.

By senior year, my commitments had dwindled. Club sports, volunteering, writing for the magazine: the extra-curriculars I had taken up with such diligent dedication as an underclassman were finally finished. I was working on my thesis, about Turner's influence on Monet, and Monet's London paintings. Other than that and a few seminars that met once a week, I took it easy – everyone did. Abby and I went out almost every night; someone was always throwing a party. The nights we didn't, we smoked pot and ordered Chinese and watched bad TV. Things didn't matter so much. The hurdles had been cleared, and we'd earned our break.

One night during the fall of senior year, I was sitting on the futon in our common room when Evan let himself in. He slept in my room almost every night.

'Hey,' I said, muting the TV. Then I looked up. 'Hey. Whoa. What's with the suit?'

He tugged at the cuff. It was short on him. 'I borrowed it from one of the guys on the team.'

'Yeah, but why are you wearing it?'

'Oh. I went to a recruiting session. Didn't I tell you?'

I had become vaguely aware of it a few weeks earlier – the flyers and e-mails from the finance and consulting recruiters. They made it easy, hosting happy hours and on-campus interviews, promising an automatic solution. I hadn't pegged Evan for this path, and maybe that's why it caught me so off guard. I thought I knew him too well to ever be surprised. That night, when he showed up in his borrowed suit, I didn't say anything more. This phase would pass. I couldn't imagine him actually going through with it.

But a month later, he told me he'd gotten called back for several interviews. We had just had sex, and we were spooned together in bed. He mentioned it in the same tone he might remark about the weather, but beneath that was evidence of a certain pride. Validation at being selected to interview. The thrill of success, even if it wasn't permanent yet.

'That's, um, great.' I hoped I sounded normal.

'Jules, I'm really excited. I think this might be what I'm meant to do.'

'When's the interview?'

'And you know the best part?' He hadn't heard my question, or didn't care. 'A job like this could get me the visa I'd need to stay after graduation. Wouldn't that be great? To know that I could stay and not have to worry about it?'

In January, he had an interview with Spire Management, the famous hedge fund in New York. Even I had heard of Spire. Evan kept insisting it was a long shot, it was too competitive. People *killed* for jobs at Spire. But he got the offer in March. Suddenly he had an answer to that question everyone was asking: *What are you doing next?* Evan, working in finance in New York City. I don't know what I'd imagined for him, exactly, but it wasn't this. Evan, who was so old-fashioned in his decency, who was so patient and kind. Maybe he'd be a teacher, or a hockey coach in some small town. Or he'd start a company, or he'd go to grad school – but this? It almost gave me whiplash, but I seemed to be alone in this reaction. Evan was happy. Our friends were happy for him. I was the only one who struggled to adjust to this new idea of him.

'Julia,' Abby said a few days later. We were sitting around watching reruns of reality TV. 'You know what? We should throw a party. For Evan. Tonight.'

'Don't you have that essay due?'

A long bleep obscured a string of cursing from the real housewife on screen. Abby shrugged. 'The class is pass-fail.'

'Okay. I'm in,' I said. 'What else do we have to do tonight?'

But as we lugged cheap booze back from the liquor store, a nasty voice in my head, dormant for so long, started to resurface. *What are you doing, Julia? What do you want? Why don't you make up your mind?* I had made absolutely no plans for the future, and that seemed okay, as long as I wasn't alone. But as I looked around the party, I realized that I was the only person left. The only one without a job. Abby was going to be a teacher. Evan's roommate Arthur was working for the Obama campaign. And Evan had secured one of the most competitive jobs in finance. Only then did I see it clearly: everyone was figuring it out. Everyone except me. I had no passion, no plan, nothing that made me stand out from the crowd. I had absolutely no idea what kind of job I was supposed to get.

Later that night, at the party, I overheard Evan talking to a friend of ours, Patrick, a tall guy from Connecticut who rowed crew. The guy Abby had slept with, freshman year, expressly to give me and Evan the room. Patrick still pined after Abby, but she had long ago moved on. She never kept a guy longer than a few weeks.

'You followed the news about Bear over spring break?' Patrick asked.

'Yeah,' Evan said.

I was standing several feet away, but they didn't notice me.

'That was nuts. Feel bad for all those guys who got their offers rescinded.'

'I know. Jesus. What a mess.'

'Close call, too. My dad works at a hedge fund, and he was jumpy as hell. You know I was interviewing with Bear back in the fall? I'm so glad I didn't go with them. Shit. Can you imagine?'

'Seriously. You're going to Goldman, right?'

'Yup. By the way, congrats, man. You must be stoked about Spire.'

Evan's eyes suddenly lit with anticipation. 'So stoked.'

That expression on his face: a huge, satisfied grin. He didn't know I could see it from where I stood. He had big plans for the future. He was going places. The system had deemed him exceptional. Why shouldn't he feel a little cocky? When he told me about the offer earlier that week, he had insisted it was just a job like any other. 'The main thing,' he said, 'is that now I'll be able to stay. Isn't that great?' He didn't want me to feel bad. And I didn't. I didn't really care. It hadn't sunk in that there was something I had forgotten to do.

But when I saw that expression on his face, talking with Patrick about their jobs and the money and the city and the future, I realized that the way he was looking at me was different from the way I was looking at myself. Evan saw someone who wasn't keeping up. Someone he had to tiptoe around. I felt a shift that night, when I overheard their conversation. It was also the first time I was aware that Evan had concealed something from me, that he had been anything less than totally honest.

A week later, he asked me to move in with him.

———

We didn't bring much with us when we moved to New York: clothes, books, lamps, my futon and coffee table. It all fit into a handful of boxes and suitcases. We unpacked everything that first day. I even managed to hang our meager art – a few prints I'd gotten in Paris, my favorite Rothko poster from MoMA – strategically covering up the cracks and stains that showed through the landlord's cheap paint job.

'Wow,' Evan said, grinning as he surveyed our tiny apartment, our new home. 'This is awesome. I can't believe we're *unpacked*.'

He went into the bathroom to brush his teeth before bed, and a sob caught in my throat. The only thing that had kept me from losing it that day was the relentless distraction of unpacking. I caught a glimpse of myself in a window turned mirrorlike by the darkness. This was where I was: in a shitty fourth-floor walk-up in the shitty part of the Upper East Side. Tired, sweaty, dirty, and what was the point? Why was I even here? I didn't have a job. I didn't even have prospects. Evan and I would both wake up in the morning with nothing to do, with a day to spend however we wanted. Evan could enjoy it because it was sanctioned, an acceptable length of idle time before his job started. But this freedom, for me, came with a different weight. With the knowledge that every moment I wasted was another moment I wasn't looking for a job. My breath grew fast and short. What was I *doing?*

Evan emerged from the bathroom, wiping away the remains of toothpaste. He saw me frozen in place. 'Jules?' he said. 'Jules, are you okay?'

'I'm fine,' I said, but the tears had started spilling over. 'I'm . . .'

Evan led me to the futon, where we would sleep that night; we'd chosen the cheapest possible delivery option, and our mattress wasn't going to arrive for another week. 'Hey,' he said, rubbing my back. 'Julia. Hey. What's wrong?'

'I don't know,' I said, tears flowing, trying to choke back the waves I felt rising through my chest. 'It's just – I don't know – I'm tired, that's all.'

We sat in silence for a long time. That's one thing I'd

always loved about Evan. He knew when it was enough just to be there; when nothing had to be said or asked. Several minutes later, my pulse slowed down, my breathing steadied. I felt like such an idiot. What was I crying about? If I didn't have a job, that was my own fault, and it wouldn't help to sit there and whine about it.

'Well,' I said, finally. 'I bet you're regretting this, huh? Asking me to move in. You're stuck sharing a lease with some blubbering crazy person.'

I thought Evan might smile or laugh. The call-and-response of our relationship. But his eyes were sad. It was a pity I'd never seen from him before.

'Julia,' he said quietly. 'Don't say that. Don't even think that, okay?'

Later, I got up to brush my teeth in our closet-size bathroom. Evan had kept an extra toothbrush in my room for years, but when I lined mine up against his that night, it felt different. A permanent version of what we'd only been pretending to do before.

———

By late June, three weeks into my joblessness, my mother was ready to intervene.

'Julia,' she said, already sounding harried and annoyed, even though she was the one who called me. 'I only have a few minutes – we have to make this flight – but listen, sweetheart. I'm calling about the job situation. There *has* to be something more you can do. I can't bear the thought of you just sitting in that apartment all day.'

Which was pretty much what I'd been doing that summer afternoon. I'd been feeling okay about the day up to that point – I'd already sent out applications for assistant openings at a small museum, a PR firm, and a publishing house – but my mother's words punctured any feeling of progress. I was standing directly in front of our newly installed air conditioner, enjoying the luxury of the cold, and I reached out to turn the air up a notch, in a gesture that felt like spite. My mother, father, and sister were all flying to Nantucket that day. This was the first summer I wasn't invited on the family vacation. My mother thought my finding a job ought to take priority.

'Mom,' I said with a sigh. 'I get it.'

'Have you thought any more about what we discussed last week?'

'You mean taking the LSATs?'

'I'm not saying you have to *go* to law school, Julia. It's just not such a terrible idea to have that in your back pocket.'

'*Mom*. I'm trying, okay? Trying isn't the problem.' That was true, but it was an aimless kind of trying. I had applied for all sorts of jobs, anything that seemed remotely likely, but there was no unifying theme. The HR departments could probably sense the dispassion in my cover letters. That feeling had set in, and I couldn't shake it: *What was wrong with me?*

My mother called back the next day, the roar of the Atlantic in the background. She told me that she had spoken with Mrs Fletcher, a friend from Boston. The

Fletcher Foundation was looking for an assistant, and I should send my résumé right away. 'I don't think it pays much, but Julia, you should take this job if it's offered to you. I mean it. You really need to get going.'

The next day, I was in the office of Laurie Silver, the president of the Fletcher Foundation. 'So you're friends with the Fletchers?' she asked, peering at me over her glasses. She was small and birdlike, dressed in black, with silver jewelry that jangled and clanked every time she moved. 'Yes, that's right,' I said. 'My mother and Mrs Fletcher are involved in some of the same charities in Boston. And my father is one of Mr Fletcher's attorneys.' Laurie nodded, scribbling a note in the margin of my résumé. I had also entangled myself, briefly, with their son Jake Fletcher the summer before freshman year of college, but that wasn't a topic for discussion. The Fletchers were extremely wealthy – he made a fortune in venture capital, and she came from an aristocratic southern family – and their foundation provided grants to artists, museums, and other worthy recipients.

'Well, Julia,' Laurie said. 'You've come along at a good time. I'm in need of an assistant rather urgently. It's paperwork and record keeping, running errands, basically pitching in wherever you're needed. Does that sound okay by you?'

'Absolutely.'

'Then I'd like to offer you the job. We'd need you to start next week. The salary is twenty-five thousand dollars, plus health insurance.'

I nodded vigorously. 'Thank you, Laurie. Yes. I'd be thrilled. Thank you.'

She stood up and shook my hand. 'You can find your way out okay?'

It was the lunch hour, and the office was abandoned. I wound up looping the perimeter of the floor before eventually finding my way back to the elevator. I was dizzy with relief. Someone was willing to pay me for my time! No matter how paltry the money, no matter how humble the work might be – this was exactly what I needed. Balance had been restored between me and everyone I knew.

On my first day at the Fletcher Foundation, I found a list awaiting me, sitting in the middle of my new desk. The list, from Laurie's former assistant, outlined in neurotically perfect handwriting all the tasks I would have to, in her words, 'learn how to perform immediately.' By the end of the first day, I had them down pat. I wondered whether my predecessor was just not very smart. Maybe she had been fired, based on how challenging she seemed to find these tasks.

On my second day, I had an early morning e-mail from Laurie asking me to brew the coffee when I arrived. There was a small kitchenette with a sink and a microwave and an old drip machine. It seemed easy enough. When Laurie arrived twenty minutes later, I delivered a mug of coffee to her desk with two Splendas, as requested. She was on the phone. A minute later, she called for me to come in.

'Julia, thank you for the coffee, but I'm afraid – well . . . you didn't use soap on the machine, did you?'

I had to think about that one for a minute. Soap? 'Oh – oh, I'm sorry, Laurie. I washed out the basket in the sink and I used the sponge on it. Maybe the sponge had soap on it. I thought I should clean out the basket, and –'

Laurie sighed. 'Yes, you're right, you *should* clean it, but don't use soap on it. Just use very hot water to rinse it, then dry it off with paper towels. You see, it makes the coffee taste like soap. I can't drink this. Why don't you ask Eleanor to show you what I mean? And if you wouldn't mind making a new batch.' She slid the mug across the desk.

I rinsed the basket several times with near-scalding water. I wasn't going to ask Eleanor for help. I had met Eleanor the day before, and she scared me. She was the foundation's one-woman publicity department. She had red hair and a porcelain complexion and dressed like a *Vogue* editor. She had started five years earlier as Laurie's assistant. I was sure she didn't have the time to help me with coffee brewing. Meanwhile, I began to reevaluate my feelings about my predecessor. Maybe she hadn't been fired. Maybe she had gotten fed up and quit.

Eleanor walked past the kitchen as I was very, very carefully drying out the filter basket. She stopped and stared at me from her towering stilettos.

'Oh, no. Let me guess. You used soap on the machine.'

I laughed nervously. 'Yeah.'

'Don't worry. It's just one of her pet peeves. How's it going otherwise?'

'It's good. I think I'm getting the hang of –'

'Good,' she said, then glanced at her watch, which was large and gold and glinted in the light. 'I have to get on a call, but why don't we have lunch sometime? We should get to know each other. Next week, okay? Let's say next Friday at twelve thirty.'

'Sure – yeah – yeah, twelve thirty is great,' I stammered.

'See you then,' she said.

That week and the next passed uneventfully. I kept minutes at the meetings: the fall deadline for grant applications was September 15; plans were on track for the gala in November. I answered Laurie's phone, filed her paperwork, made polite small talk while I waited to use the copy machine. On Friday morning, at the end of my second week of work, the phone rang. 'Julia, it's Eleanor.' Her voice crackled from a bad connection. 'I'm off-site this morning, so I'll meet you at the restaurant, okay?'

The maître d' sat me outside. Eleanor arrived ten minutes late. She tossed her long red hair over her shoulder and dropped her bag onto the seat next to her. She kept her sunglasses on. I wondered how she managed to afford all of it, the watch and the bag and finely made clothing. Surely the foundation didn't pay her *that* much. She waved to get the waiter's attention. 'Iced tea, please. Julia?'

'I'm okay with water.'

'And an ashtray, too. Thanks.'

She pulled out a pack of Camel Lights and a silver Zippo. 'So,' she said, leaning back in her chair, directing a stream of smoke from the side of her mouth. 'Laurie tells me you're friends with Henry and Dot.'

'I guess so. Really it's more my parents. They're friends with the Fletchers.'

'Close friends?'

'Kind of. My dad is one of Henry Fletcher's lawyers. They go way back. My mom is involved in some of the same organizations as Dot. You've met the Fletchers, too?'

She smiled, like she knew something I didn't. 'Oh, of course. Henry and I do a lot of work together. I do all the publicity – which I guess you know by now – so I'm really the gatekeeper when people want to talk to Henry. We're very close. And they are quite involved in the event planning. This gala might drive me mad, actually. Henry is as sweet as they come, but Dot can be a total control freak.' Eleanor ashed her cigarette. 'She's so *stubborn*. I swear, everything I suggest, she wants to do the opposite of. I don't know what it is about her. You know what I mean?'

So this was why she had asked me to lunch. Even behind her sunglasses, I could see the hunger for gossip. Truth be told, I didn't really know much about the Fletchers. Not at that point, at least. I'd said hello to them at parties for years, but that was it. They were rich, that was the main thing to know. I mumbled some assent, and Eleanor's gleam faded to indifference, as fast as a scudding cloud. She glanced at her watch, calculating how much longer she'd have to endure with me.

We passed the time with empty back-and-forth. She perked up when I mentioned that Evan worked at Spire. 'Oh, they're great. Their CEO, David Kleinman, he bought a table at our gala last year. Those guys are legendary.' She laughed. 'So I guess you're doing well for yourself, then.'

After our plates had been cleared and we were awaiting the check – she kept looking over her shoulder to hurry the waiter – someone called her name from down the sidewalk. She pushed back her sunglasses, and she smiled for the first time.

I turned in my seat. Then I went cold, despite the sunshine. I turned back, and reached for my water to erase the dryness in my throat, my hand shaking. The person waving at her was Adam McCard.

Eleanor kissed him on the cheek. He turned to introduce himself to me just as I was standing up and trying in vain to smooth the wrinkles from my dress. Before I could remind him who I was, his mouth fell open.

'Julia Edwards!' he shouted.

He remembered me. Of course he did. He laughed, then hugged me. 'I can't believe it! It's been – how long? Two years?'

'Something like that.' I smiled. Then I exhaled. My nerves were already fading. I felt shy, empty of anything to say, but a little part of me felt an old comfort return. Adam could always make me feel like I belonged, which in those tricky months after graduation was the most important and elusive feeling of all.

I saw Eleanor watching us – watching me – with unconcealed disdain.

'How do you two know each other?' she said.

'Wow. I can't get over it.' He shook his head. 'El, Julia and I went to college together. We both wrote for the same magazine on campus. Shit, we go way back. Wait – how do you guys know each other?'

'We work together,' Eleanor said. 'Julia's an assistant at the Fletcher Foundation.' She pronounced the word *assistant* with a distancing sneer.

'Man. This is crazy.' Adam looked at his watch. 'Shoot, I'm actually late for something. Jules, I'm so glad I ran into you. I didn't even know you were in New York. I'll give you a call, okay? Eleanor, beautiful, you look as amazing as ever.' He walked backwards down the sidewalk, waving before he continued on his way.

'Well,' Eleanor said, donning her sunglasses again and reaching for the check, which had arrived at last. 'You just know *everyone*, don't you?'

# CHAPTER 3

## *Evan*

'Do you want to ride in together tomorrow?' Julia had asked the night before. We were lying in bed, her blond hair fanned out across my chest. It was the first day of work the next morning, for both of us.

'Nah, that's okay. I have to get there early.'

'Evan.' She turned to look at me, like she could sense the anxious jump in my stomach. 'You're going to be great. You know that, right?'

I drank my coffee too fast on the subway ride down and burned my tongue. My pace quickened on the sidewalk in midtown, to keep up with the other workers hurrying toward their air-conditioned refuges. Outside my building, I caught a glimpse of my reflection in the glass and started – I wasn't used to seeing myself in a suit. Up on the thirty-ninth floor, a receptionist typed rapidly behind an imposing front desk branded with Spire's logo. She sized me up in one glance. 'First day?' she said.

I'd gone through several rounds of interviews back in the spring. My third and final interview had been with

Michael Casey, the second in command at Spire. Back in March, he'd come to fetch me himself from the thirty-ninth-floor lobby, jerking his head for me to follow. He was on the short side, and his hair was going salty from gray. Other people stepped back as Michael walked past with an impatient stride, giving him a wide berth. In his office, he pointed for me to sit. He looked pissed off. He hadn't even shaken my hand. He must hate this part, I thought – sifting through résumés, trying to discern some difference among us. It was all a big waste of his time. The interview was doomed. It was stupid of me to ever think I'd get the job. But then Michael picked up my résumé, and at that moment his expression changed. Softened. He looked up at me, back down at the résumé, and nodded carefully.

'You're from Canada,' he said.

'Yes, sir.'

'British Columbia – near Vancouver?'

'In the interior, actually, about seven hours away.'

'Small town?'

'Yes, sir.'

Michael crumpled up the résumé. 'Tell me about yourself.'

I launched into the routine I'd been perfecting the previous few months. My experience was thin, with none of the internships that everyone else had done, but I had other talking points. An economics major interested in the efficiency of the free market. A varsity athlete who knows the value of teamwork and discipline. So on and so forth. But Michael interrupted me before I was even halfway done.

'No, no, I already got all that from your résumé. Tell me more about where you're from. Your hometown. How's the economy doing out there?'

'My hometown?' I said, scrambling to rearrange the words in my head. Michael nodded. 'Well. It's really small. There's not much to do. We like to joke that there are more bears than people.'

Michael smiled. He nodded again for me to continue.

'Everyone who can plays hockey. That's the main source of entertainment.'

'You played? You must have been pretty good to get to Yale.'

'I'm all right.'

Michael barked a short laugh. 'You're all right,' he repeated. 'That might be the first humble sentence ever spoken in this office. What do people do for work?'

'My parents run a grocery store. There's some tourism a few towns over, so some people commute to that. And logging is pretty big in the region.'

We went on like that for a while. To my surprise, Michael seemed engaged. Some transformation had happened. Maybe my lack of experience wasn't such a bad thing.

They didn't seem to think it was, in any case. Two days later, I got the call from Spire. The job paid more than any of the others I'd applied to, a six-figure sum that I couldn't quite believe. I accepted on the spot. I'd be the only person from Yale joining Spire that year. I was certain the old small-town Evan Peck was gone, once and for all.

I was assigned to sit next to Roger, another analyst, a former tight end at Stanford with a thick Alabama drawl. We didn't have much to do early on. When we weren't in training sessions, we wasted a lot of time on ESPN or skimming the news, only jumping into action when the higher-ups staffed us on something. But it looked bad to leave before 10:00 p.m., so none of us did, no matter what. There were five analysts in total that year, all of us men, which wasn't that remarkable – Spire overall was mostly male. Roger was our ringleader, the one who stayed latest and arrived earliest and generally assumed authority. He led the charge every night for postwork drinks at a bar called McGuigan's near the office, and already it felt like a mandatory part of the routine.

'So how was the first week?' Julia asked. This was Saturday morning. We'd brought bagels to the park along the East River. Every night that first week, Julia was already asleep when I got home. It annoyed me a little, that she couldn't bother to stay awake. Her job ended many hours before mine did. This was the first time we'd really seen each other since the weekend before.

'Good,' I said. 'I think. I don't know. It's hard to tell what it's really going to be like. It's all just training sessions for now.'

'What about that guy – Michael? The one who interviewed you. Have you seen him yet?'

'I passed him in the hall, but he was talking to some-one else. We didn't say anything.' Truthfully, I wasn't sure whether he even recognized me.

Julia nodded. She was quieter than usual. She seemed to be gazing at the buildings across the river in Astoria, but her eyes had that glassy quality of staring at nothing in particular. There was a poppy seed stuck to the tip of her nose. I leaned over and brushed it away. She turned and then smiled. Back to normal.

'Everything okay?'

'Fine,' she said. 'Just distracted. Thinking about work.'

'What's up?'

'Nothing worth talking about. Tell me more about your week.'

It was a relief to have Julia there, to have a partner in the minor struggles: how to decipher the Con Ed bill, where to find the nearest Laundromat, what to do about the noisy neighbors and the leaky faucet. She always knew exactly what to do. I was acutely aware, that summer, of how alone I was in the world. My parents had gone back to Canada right after the graduation ceremony, and I wouldn't see them again for months. This never bothered me in college, when the proximity of your family only mattered when it was time to travel back and forth. But being in the real world seemed to emphasize how far I was from home – something I hadn't felt in a long time. And moving to New York had highlighted certain differences between me and Julia, too, things I'd never noticed before. The advice and money and connections she took for granted. How she was never limited to this place. She could always take the train to Boston, or hop on a plane to Nantucket. Even though she made less than a fifth of what I did, she had money from her parents. We'd agreed to divide the rent in line with our salary discrepancy, so I paid two-thirds, although sometimes I wondered how fair that was. My money came like water from a pump, flowing only as long as I kept working. Hers came like a spring whose source was bountiful and deep. We never talked about this.

The truth was that I missed my friends, my teammates, the ones who hadn't come to New York. I especially missed Arthur, who was working in the Obama campaign's field office in Ohio. We'd traded a few stiff e-mails since graduation, but I couldn't say what I was really thinking, not in stark black-and-white text. I didn't even *know* what I was really thinking. And we hadn't acknowledged the fight we'd had right at the end. I wondered if we ever would.

The shower was already running when my alarm went off on Monday morning, at the beginning of the second week of work. Julia's bathrobe was hanging on the hook, the steam drifting through the open door.

'You're up early,' I called into the bathroom.

'I figured we could go in together,' Julia said over the weak sound of the shower. Our water pressure was pathetic. 'You have to be in by eight thirty, right?'

We walked to the subway hand in hand, stopping for

an iced coffee at the cart on the corner of 3rd Avenue. The train was packed, and I got on last. Julia was crammed next to me, the front of our bodies pressed together. I felt an incongruous longing for her in the chaos of the train car. The smell of her perfume, the tender paleness of the part in her hair. We hadn't had sex all week, not even on the weekend; I'd been too exhausted. I was an idiot for not appreciating what was right in front of me. I slipped my hands down her waist, pulling her closer, and kissed her on the forehead. She smiled up at me. She seemed to know what I was thinking.

We commuted together all that week. I liked the routine. Alternating turns in the shower, Julia drying her hair while I shaved in front of the speckled mirror. The coffee cart, the descent into the hot subway, the kiss good-bye. On Thursday night of that week, Julia had plans to get dinner with her parents, who were passing through town. 'Bummer you have to work so late,' she said as we walked to the subway on Thursday morning. 'They'll miss you.'

'Your parents? I doubt that.'

She laughed. 'You know what I mean. Their version of missing.'

Later that night, as I was riding the elevator down to the lobby to pick up my dinner delivery, I thought of Julia and her parents. I pulled out my phone and texted her: Sorry I couldn't make it. Tell them hi.

She texted me back a few hours later. Just finished. I'm nearby. Meet me outside your building in a few?

It was almost 10:00 p.m., and the office was dead.

There was no one left to impress. I stood up and turned off my computer. Roger raised an eyebrow. 'No McGuigan's tonight?'

'Nah, not tonight. Other plans.'

Julia was waiting outside. She was more dressed up than usual, probably for her mother's sake. Had she been wearing that dress this morning? I couldn't remember. She was clutching a funny-looking silvery thing.

'What is that?'

'Leftovers,' she said. 'It's for you.'

'Weird-looking leftovers.'

'You've never seen this before? No, see, look. It's a swan. See? That's the neck, and those are the wings.'

It was made of aluminum foil. 'That's a thing?'

'I ordered the biggest steak so I'd have extra. My mom almost had a fit – she thought I was going to eat the whole thing. Oh, and guess what else I got?' She opened her tote bag and pointed inside, but it was too dark to see. 'Come on, I've got a plan.'

We walked up Broadway, the crowds gradually thinning as we left behind Times Square. Julia was chattering happily with news from home, from work. She was having lunch the next day with her coworker Eleanor. She was hopeful that they might become friends. This stretch of midtown at this hour was strange and abandoned, like the aftermath of a hurricane. Julia tugged me across the intersection. We stopped, and she swept her arm across the mostly empty plaza. 'Voilà. It's like our very own Campo de' Fiori.'

'Columbus Circle, you mean?'

'Come on, play along. You remember that night, right? It was almost a year ago exactly.' She sat down on the stone steps next to the fountain and pulled two cups from her tote bag, then a half-empty bottle of wine. She split the remaining wine between the two cups, handed one to me, and stashed the empty bottle in her bag.

'Where'd you get all this?'

'We got the wine to go with dessert, but we couldn't finish it, so I took it with me. And the cups are courtesy of Starbucks.'

We touched the paper cups together. 'What are we toasting to?' I said.

She tilted her head, her blond hair catching a shimmer from the lamps at the edge of Central Park. The stoplights changed from red to green, and the yellow taxis swept forward in unison, peeling off at various points around the traffic circle. If you squinted, the color blurred into one mass, and it looked like the same ring of taxis going around and around, forever. Julia smiled at me and said, 'Whatever we want, I guess.'

I wanted this feeling to last. To fix it in place.

We kept commuting together. On Wednesday morning, our third week of work, the subway was messed up, even worse than usual. Several trains went by, the doors opening and closing on packed cars from which no one disembarked. It was hot and sticky, and frustration was mounting on the platform. People jostled, leaning into the tunnel to look for the next train. Someone stepped on Julia's sandaled foot. 'Ow!' she said. 'Fuck. That hurt.' When the third and fourth and fifth trains passed by, Julia muttered, 'This is fucking ridiculous.' The sixth train pulled up, and she said, 'I'm getting on this one, I don't care.' We both squeezed ourselves in, but Julia slipped farther into the train than I did, finding a pocket of space in the middle of the car. She gave me a halfhearted shrug, then looked away.

It was a strange thing to watch her from this distance. To realize what a difference a few meters could make. The way she glanced at her watch, as if to make the train move faster; the way she stared vacantly at the ads for dermatologists and vocational schools. She seemed frustrated and grumpy, but underneath was something harder. An irritation that had nothing to do with the sick passenger or the signal malfunction or whatever had caused this train backup. Something that had been there before we'd even left the apartment that morning. It was like I was looking at Julia from a different angle and seeing something I hadn't seen before.

The next morning, she was still asleep when I left for work.

---

August arrived, and the city grew quiet. Our neighborhood was a ghost town on weekends. It had become a way of marking time, the Hampton Jitney pulling up on Sunday evenings, the seep of sunburned passengers back to the crosshatch of numbered streets. Everyone who could afford to had fled for the beach.

Work was quiet, too. I checked everything two or three times, guarding myself against boneheaded mistakes. The bosses accepted the work I was doing with a clipped thank-you. I tried to see this as a positive – the models and decks must have been good enough to make it across their desks without comment – but I felt a crackling undercurrent of worry. The sluggish market, rumors about layoffs. There were still long stretches of hours, sometimes days, when I didn't have much to do. Maybe it had been rash to jump at this job. Maybe I should have thought more about trying to play hockey after college – in Europe or the minors. My life at that moment would have been totally different.

Until one Friday night in early August, when my luck changed.

It was early evening. The higher-ups had left around lunchtime to beat the beach traffic. The other analysts were already at McGuigan's. I was getting ready to leave when my phone rang.

'Could you stop by?' Michael Casey asked in a flat, untelling tone.

When I arrived, he looked up from a stack of papers and gestured me inside. I hadn't been in there since the interview back in March. His office was bare of decoration except for a few pictures of him and a younger blond woman who had to be his wife, the two of them smiling against Caribbean sunsets and snowy ski hills.

She looked a bit like Julia, though not as pretty. No kids, I noticed. Michael was unsmiling. 'So, Evan. How have things been? What are you working on?'

'Good. Great. Things have been great. I've, um, been working on a few projects for Steve. He's had me run some models for the macro group. And, uh . . .'

Michael nodded briskly. 'Fine. And are you liking it? Is the work engaging?'

'Well, um, yeah, I would say it is.' Shit. This was exactly what I'd feared, coming across as some inarticulate hick with nothing to say. 'It's been really interesting, learning about these new markets, and —'

'All right. It's okay, Evan. Relax. We don't have to skirt around this. I know what it's like, your first month on the job. It's boring. You can admit that, okay?'

I laughed. I hoped it sounded confident, not nervous. 'I guess.'

'I was impressed with you in our interview, Evan. I was. I admire your ambition. It's not easy to get yourself out of a small town. Trust me, I know. What I want to know is what you're looking to get out of this. Don't get me wrong. Some people just want to do their two years, go to business school. They'll do fine for themselves. Dip their toe in, then do the next thing. For some people, that's just fine.'

Michael leaned back in his chair, his evening stubble catching in the light.

'You know, I grew up in South Dakota, on a farm in the middle of nowhere. Where I came from, people never left. You understand what I'm talking about.'

I sat up a little straighter. 'I do.'

'People like us, we actually have an advantage. We remember where we came from. We work that much harder. Now, Spire gets its pick of who to hire. The best and the brightest. But it's not often I have the chance to hire someone like you. Someone who reminds me a little of myself.'

A few blocks away, my coworkers were already drinking and laughing, off duty for the night. I felt a buzz and pop of adrenaline near the point where my spine met my brain. Just like at the beginning of a game, right before the puck drops.

'Evan. I think you're smart. I think you've got huge potential. My question is, what are you looking for? Do you want to try for something bigger?'

'Yes,' I said. 'I do.'


The tone shifted. Faster, more relentless. I was trying to keep up.

'I'll tell you, first of all, there are no sure things. We always have to bear that in mind. Nothing is certain. But this is the closest thing to certainty that I've ever seen in this world. So. What's the most important thing you learned about hedge funds when you decided you wanted to work here?'

'How to – how to exploit inefficiencies in the market?'

'That's one thing. And some people may agree with

you that it's the most important thing, but that's not the answer. The *most important* thing you need to know is the art of timing. Being first. Knowing when to get in and when to get out. Knowing the inefficiencies does you no good if you screw up the timing.'

'Right. Timing. I see.'

'And what does the right timing allow you to do? What's the primary rule of arbitrage?'

'Buy low, sell high?'

'Exactly. If you can get it cheap and find a market for it at a higher price, then that's all there is. Simple, right? And if you can time it perfectly, then you're golden. So what's the cheapest thing you can buy right now in this country?'

'Well, um . . .'

'You read the news. You see what's happening with the housing market. We're right on the edge of a complete collapse.'

'Housing? So buying up cheap housing? And then find –'

'No. Right track, though. Break it down into components, make it liquid. What do you need to build houses? What's in demand when the market is booming? I'm talking physical resources. Something you can count and measure and ship.'

'Lumber?'

'You would think this would be a terrible time to bet on lumber, with the housing market cratering, right?'

71

'Right.'

'No one is going to touch it. No one with an ounce of sense. People go looking for an ark in a flood. Who goes looking for more water? So what does that mean, Evan?'

'It's cheap.'

'Dirt cheap. And that's where we come in.'

'You guys celebrating something?' Maria asked as she brought over another round, later that same night. We were at McGuigan's, at our usual booth in the corner. Maria, our regular bartender, was just a few years older than we were. 'The weekend,' Roger said loudly. 'Why don't you join us for a round, gorgeous?' Maria smiled with cool tolerance while she stacked our empty glasses. Roger had been leering at her for weeks. 'That one's mine, fellas. I call dibs,' he said when she was barely out of earshot.

I felt my phone buzz with yet another text from Julia. I was supposed to meet her at a party downtown, and my time was up. I went to the bar to pay for my drinks. Roger often laid down his card at the end of the night, picking up the tab like he was some big shot, but I didn't like the feeling that I owed him something.

'Leaving already?' Maria said. She counted out my change, but I waved it away.

'Yeah. A party downtown. I'm already late.' I wondered why I didn't mention anything about Julia – that I was meeting my girlfriend at the party, that my girlfriend was the one pestering me to get going. I hadn't yet found a way to work Julia into any of my conversations with Maria. I wasn't sure I needed to, or wanted to.

'Have fun, Evan,' she said. 'See you next week, right?'

I called her name from across the room. Julia was out on the balcony, staring at the Brooklyn skyline with that same vacant look I'd noticed her slipping into on occasion.

There was a pulse of relief across her face when she saw me, and then her expression clouded back into annoyance. Maybe it would have been better to make up some lie about work and skip the party entirely. But she had insisted I come along. 'Jake Fletcher is having a party for the opening ceremonies tonight,' she said that morning, calling after me as I was about to leave. 'We have to go. Remember? It's his parents' foundation I'm working for, after all.'

The television in the corner showed a massive stadium filled with flag-bearing marchers. I squinted and moved closer through the packed living room. I thought of Michael's abrupt departure a few hours earlier, and it finally made sense.

A ding had sounded from Michael's BlackBerry as we were talking. He glanced at the screen and stood up sharply. 'I have to go,' he said. 'I've got a flight to catch. I had one of our researchers pull this material together' — he indicated a blue binder on the desk — 'and I want you to get up to speed. We'll convene when I'm back.' He started down the hallway, and I had to jog to keep up.

Before Michael stepped into the elevator, I asked where he was going.

He looked up from his phone, brow furrowed. Then he smiled. 'China.'

'Oh,' I said. 'That's great. For business, or –' but the doors slid closed.

I'd forgotten about the Olympics until then, but the scene on the TV explained it. He and his wife were probably reclined in their first-class seats at that moment, en route to Beijing. I still hadn't quite absorbed it – Michael, the legendary and fearsome Michael, had just handpicked *me* for this big new project. At the party, I tried to pull Julia aside to tell her the news. But she kept shaking herself free of my grasp. She knew everybody there: friends from Boston, from prep school, from college. Most of the time she remembered to introduce me – 'Oh, do you know my boyfriend, Evan? Evan, this is so-and-so' – and I'd nod and they'd continue talking. Anyway, I suspected that I had served my purpose the moment I'd walked through the door. I'd proved to Julia that I was a loyal boyfriend who would answer her call, and Julia had proved the same thing to her friends. A lot of them worked in finance, like me, but it didn't give us anything to talk about. Everyone worked in finance.

As the party ended, I climbed into the cab while she was saying good-bye to someone on the sidewalk. I closed my eyes, and when I opened them we were almost home. Julia was at the other side of the backseat, legs crossed, staring out the window. I felt a jolt at that moment.

Annoyed with how the night had gone, with this sour distance between us, that stupid party. Things were about to change for the better, beginning right then.

'Leave it off,' I said, when Julia went to turn on the lights in our apartment. I kicked the door closed and pushed her up against the wall. She tasted like sweet white wine, and that made me even harder, knowing that she was drunk. She snaked her fingers through my hair. She was yanking loose my tie, unbuttoning my shirt, unbuckling my belt. I hitched up her dress and we had sex against the living room wall, her legs wrapped around me. 'Oh, God, Evan,' she said, her fingertips digging into my scalp, our bodies slamming into the wall. 'Oh, my God.'

We collapsed on the bed afterward. We hadn't had sex like that in a long time. Later, I realized that I never told Julia what happened at work. It was the whole reason I'd been trying to get her attention, but when I finally had it, I'd completely forgotten about it.

The blue binder from Michael was waiting right where I'd left it the night before. I'd woken up without an alarm that morning, showered, and gone straight to the office. While I was waiting for my computer to warm up, I pulled out my cell phone and flipped it open and shut, considering whether to call Arthur. Maybe I was making too big a deal about our fight. But it wasn't even 10:00 a.m., and Arthur liked to sleep late. I put the phone back in my pocket and opened the binder.

It contained a massive sheaf of information about the state of the North American lumber markets: quarterly reports, stock trends, charts and graphs of historical data, analyst predictions for the coming years. The recommendation was unanimously bleak. The rest of 2008 into 2009 and 2010 and beyond was terrible. In our conversation the night before, Michael had hinted about a new source of demand, but what new source of demand? I couldn't see it. My optimism started to evaporate. Suddenly someone was paying attention to my work. This might be the thing that exposed me as a fraud once and for all.

Roger sauntered in later. 'Whatcha working on there, Peck?' he drawled.

'Just something for Michael,' I said. The last thing Michael had told me was to keep quiet about this new assignment, for the time being. Roger stared for a beat before he sat down. He made a point, later that day, of not inviting me to lunch. He didn't say good-bye that night, either. But I didn't care. I was going to have bigger problems than Roger if I didn't figure this out fast.

It was only at the very end of the day, when the office had emptied again, that I finally saw it. The page was headlined BRITISH COLUMBIA PRODUCERS – PACIFIC WESTCORP. The number I'd been focusing on was 'Growth Forecast 2009.' It was a useful indicator, and for the most part that number had been negative, often double-digit negative. Flat at the very best. But Pacific WestCorp was predicting 200 percent growth for the next fiscal year.

Two hundred percent growth. I reached for a highlighter.

There was a line in fine print that broke out the predicted revenue for 2009 in terms of North American versus international markets. Nearly all of next year's revenue for Pacific WestCorp was predicted to come from international markets. And below that was an analyst's note: *Pacific WestCorp predicts exports to China in FY 2009 will increase tenfold, to $500 million CAD.*

I sighed in relief, letting the yellow highlighter bleed through the paper. But a series of questions sprang to life in the back of my mind, like popcorn popping in the microwave. Why weren't these predictions making news all over the Street? Why wasn't everyone lining up behind this company? If this held true, it would be the easiest decision anyone ever had to make – Pacific WestCorp was going to make a fortune. But the answers sprang up, too, like echoes to the popping questions. Investors were often skittish about exports to China. It was a risky game, and the taxes and tariffs and unpredictable barriers to entry were enough to dissuade most people. There were far saner ways to make money. The Chinese didn't always play by the same rules as we did, and that was a dangerous proposition when hundreds of millions of dollars were at stake.

'China,' Michael had said with a smile, just before the elevator door closed.

As the market sunk deeper, the numbers that had been hovering in the back of my mind started to loop obsessively: my student loans and my share of the rent on one side, the comforting and hefty regularity of my paychecks on the other. I couldn't admit my worry aloud. No one at work talked much about the crisis as it escalated. It was too big to put words to; too abstract, too unknown, but mostly too frightening.

But, finally, on the morning of Monday, September 15, our CEO, David Kleinman, summoned the entire office to the fortieth-floor boardroom before the markets opened. Lehman was about to go under, and Merrill was on the edge. What Michael had been talking about was finally here, the water lapping at our doorstep.

Roger hummed the death march as we walked up the fire stairs. 'A hundred bucks says at least ten people go home today,' he said.

'Jesus, Roger, don't say that.'

'Is that a bet?'

'Hell, no. If I'm fired, I'm gonna need all the money I can get.'

'*You're* not getting fired, teacher's pet.'

We continued trudging. I'd been wondering when Roger was going to say something. There was no way he hadn't noticed my increased tempo, the early mornings and late nights and busy weekends, all of it because of the budding WestCorp deal. But he'd kept his mouth shut over the previous month, concealing what was almost certainly jealousy.

Kleinman walked into the boardroom. 'Everyone here?' he asked. His bald pate shone under the lights. Michael, to his right, nodded at him. 'Good,' Kleinman continued. 'The reason I've called you here this morning – well, you know the reason. It's a shitstorm out there, and today's only going to get worse. Now, let me make this clear from the start. Spire is healthy and profitable, and we are well equipped to weather this. No one is being let go. I repeat, no one is being let go. Not today, not for the fore-seeable future.'

He paused. 'You can all relax, you know. Christ. Loosen up, people.'

Someone laughed, then another person. Someone started clapping.

'See, that's what I want.' Kleinman smiled. 'We're smarter and faster and better than the other guys. I'm not saying this isn't serious – you all know people who will lose their jobs, people whose companies might even go under. But if you keep doing what you're doing, you can sleep at night knowing that your future at Spire is secure.

'So. That begs the question: Why am I taking up your very valuable time? Right now there's a helicopter sitting on the roof of this building that will take me to Teter-boro, where I'm getting on a plane to DC. I'm joining the government advisory team until we get through this crisis. I got the call early this morning, and I wasn't given much time to decide. But it was clear to me what I had to do.'

Kleinman glanced around the silent room for reactions.

'This means that for the next few weeks or the next few months, or however long this takes to settle down, I'm handing over the reins to Michael Casey. Michael will lead you through this just as well as I could myself. And we didn't get to where we are today by caving under pressure. So don't fuck this up.' Another small wave of laughter, and he smiled again. 'I'll see you all on the other side.'

Kleinman stood up. The rest of the executives followed suit, nodding at him crisply, ready to do battle. He turned on his heel and strode out of the room, his secretary chasing him with a pen and one last piece of paper to sign. Everyone started to file out. Only Michael remained seated. Running his hands over the finely grained wood of the table, and smiling to himself.

# CHAPTER 4

## *Julia*

I'd taken to having the news on in the background while I got ready for work to dispel the constant quiet. Since he'd started working on this WestCorp deal, Evan had been out the door before my alarm had even gone off, every day for weeks.

I was clicking through channels while I brushed my teeth and stopped on CNBC as it returned from a commercial. I sat down on the futon, the minty toothpaste tingling in my mouth. It was Monday morning, and a situation that had looked uncertain before the weekend had exploded into full-blown apocalyptic chaos. Weeks earlier, Evan had explained to me how the housing slump would actually help Spire's position on this WestCorp deal – the further the market sunk, the more Spire eventually stood to gain – but at that moment, even he seemed worried about how fast it was happening. We had watched the news the previous night: enormous firms shuttering, thousands of people losing their jobs, billions of dollars vanishing overnight. Friends of ours saddled with apartment leases they could no longer afford. I knew I shouldn't enjoy it too much, but I couldn't help it: part of me felt a weird thrill at our positions suddenly flipping. I was employed while they were adrift.

Evan had been pacing in front of the TV the previous night, Sunday night, worrying about what might happen. This panic was new; I'd never known him like this. 'But Spire's going to be fine, right?' I said. That's what he'd been saying to me all along. 'They're not going to fire you. Right?'

'They're not going to fire you,' I'd said with more conviction earlier that summer, before either of us had started work. We were standing in the Brooks Brothers on Madison Avenue, the afternoon sun flaring through the windows. I was drinking a Pellegrino and watching Evan in the mirror in the fitting area.

He laughed. 'I hope not.'

'So why worry whether they're returnable? You'll be wearing these for years.'

He adjusted his tie. 'Habit, I guess.'

'You look great. I think you should get both.'

He'd never owned a suit before. That morning in early July, he had been looking up the address for a discount retailer downtown. 'You still have all of your signing bonus?' I'd asked, and he nodded. 'Okay. Come with me.' There was a Brooks Brothers near our apartment. He'd guffawed at the price tag on the suit I pointed out, but I pushed him toward the dressing room. 'Could you help us?' I asked a salesman. 'He's probably a forty-two long. He needs one in blue and one in gray. And some shirts and ties.' When the salesman went to get his pincushion, Evan looked at the price again, whistled, and wondered out loud whether he could return them.

But I think he knew, even then, even if they were nicer than what he needed, that he looked too good not to keep them. When he stood on the raised block to let the salesman adjust the hem of his pants, it was like a time-fuzzed image snapping back into focus. I could appreciate just how handsome he was, as I had at the beginning. His sandy brown hair, his light blue eyes. Wearing the trappings of adulthood like a natural. Our gazes met in the mirror, and he smiled at me.

'I'm glad you made me get them,' Evan said. We were walking back to the apartment, a bag with his new shirts and ties swinging from one hand. He'd pick up the altered suits in a few days. He kissed me. 'I don't know what I'd do without you.'

I was proud of him. Really, I was. He was a boy from the middle of nowhere who had gotten himself to Yale. He was working at the most famous hedge fund in New York, leaving for work every morning in his finely made suits. He'd said it to me more than once that summer. *I don't know what I'd do without you.* I knew he meant it as a compliment. But Evan was always better at taking direction from others than he was at taking direction from himself. It could have been anyone prodding him to get a better suit, and his gratitude would have come out sounding the same. My being the prodder was only incidental.

I suppose, at the time, I didn't understand how rapidly my feelings toward Evan were evolving. Maybe I didn't want to admit how little it took to dismantle what we'd built. It wasn't that our relationship had been perfect before. We'd fought in college, but those fights always felt specific: fireworks that faded into smoke as fast as they arrived. But in New York, in the real world, every annoyance and disagreement felt like a referendum on our relationship. The bitterness started to linger. I was seeing growing evidence of why this was never going to work. A sickening suspicion that Evan and I were, in fact, all wrong for each other.

On the surface, my life seemed normal enough. I went to work, I jogged in the park, I saw my friends at crowded bars and brunches. Evan and I would try to have a late dinner on Friday or Saturday, compressing a week's worth of intimacy into a few hours, but more and more often he didn't even have time for that. Every night, I came home to a quiet apartment. My brain crackled with excess energy. I'd pace. I'd toss aside books, unable to concentrate. I'd sit in silence, ears pricked, hearing every flush of the toilet and clacking of heels echo through our building. Sometimes I'd try to stay up late for Evan, but those were always the nights I fell asleep with the lamp burning. Or, instead, I'd decide to go to bed early and wake up for a long run before work. Those were inevitably the nights I tossed and turned in our too-hot bedroom, unable to sleep, and when the alarm went off at 6:00 a.m., I'd rise like a zombie and jog through the empty streets.

What had happened? Looking back at those early weeks in New York, as we were wading into the shallows of our new lives, I realized that everything had changed so quickly. Earlier in the summer, things hadn't been perfect, but they'd been okay: late nights out, long walks home, lingering over the last glass of wine. But something had changed soon after we started working. I was plagued with a new dissatisfaction. Was this it, was this everything? Was this my life from now on? Something was wrong, but I couldn't put my finger on it – until suddenly, it seemed obvious what the problem was.

One August weekend, Evan and I were having a hurried brunch before he went back to the office. He had a new habit of keeping both his phones, flip phone and Black-Berry, on the table while we ate. I was telling a story when his BlackBerry vibrated. He picked it up immediately and started reading the e-mail that had just come in. 'Oh, man,' he said loudly. I couldn't tell whether it was good news or bad. Then he smiled at the screen. A big, wide, face-cracking grin. 'Jules, this is awesome. Oh, man. So I was telling you about this WestCorp deal, right? Well . . .'

And he launched into the details, forgetting entirely that I'd been in the middle of a story. But I wasn't listening. Instead I was thinking that I was such an idiot. It was so obvious – how had I not seen it before? That night in March, when I'd overhead his conversation with Patrick. That smile, that big grin. It was the exact same grin he was wearing at brunch, chattering away about the WestCorp deal. It was the blossoming of the seed I'd first glimpsed months earlier. Evan was more excited about his future than I was about mine. He had been all along. More alive with energy, with possibility, thinking about a million things other than me. I'd seen it before, how Evan threw himself into something he cared about. It happened in the most intense parts of the hockey season, back in college, and it was happening now, only now it wasn't finite. This wasn't just a season. This was real life. Our life – my life.

I had a suspicion. I started administering silent tests. Evan would get home, dropping his briefcase to the floor with a sigh. 'You wouldn't *believe* what happened at work,' he'd say, flopping down on the futon. He told me everything about Michael Casey, about the WestCorp deal. On and on and on. I'd keep perfectly quiet, waiting for him to finish, to turn his attention to me – to anyone but himself. Waiting for him to ask how my work was going, what I'd eaten for dinner, the people I'd been hanging out with in his absence. Anything. But he never asked, not once.

This new Evan didn't have anything left for me. Evan needed me to affirm his existence, to nod and smile and say the right thing at the right time. He failed the test, and my suspicion was confirmed. He wasn't really thinking about me. He never was. *I don't know what I'd do without you.* He seemed to forget that it was supposed to be reciprocal.

At work, later that September day, there was nervous chatter in the hallways. I imagine that was true everywhere in New York that afternoon – watercooler speculation about how far it would go, if we were witnessing the end of one era and the beginning of the next – but we had particular reason to be concerned. Organizations like ours formed an appendage to the financial industry, rising and falling along with the market. It was symbiotic, our minnow cleaning the gills of the whale that swam around lower Manhattan. We relied on the largesse of the Fletchers and others like them to keep us alive.

Had I started thinking of the foundation as *ours*? Had I started thinking of myself as *us*? I guess I had. I was beginning to understand why people sometimes stayed in jobs they hated. It wasn't just about the paycheck. It was about the structure, contributing to the hum of civilized society. My own contribution was almost invisible, but I liked the accoutrements. The nameplate on my desk; the security guard in the lobby who knew me by sight. Even if the job wasn't much, it was something. I'd complain about it to Evan, but all he said was how lucky I was to have such easy hours; cutting, even if true.

I thought of Evan pacing the apartment the night before, of what he must be going through at work. After lunch, I sent him a text. He didn't respond until hours later, when I was getting ready to leave. All good. Probably gonna be here late.

Can you take a break for dinner? I wrote.

I'll go out around 6:30 to get something, he replied.

I glanced at my watch – it was approaching 5:30 p.m. I thought of one night from earlier that summer, from better days. This was a chance to get back what we'd lost

87

track of. I walked north from my office and found a deli a few blocks from Evan's office. His favorite sandwich, the same since college: a chicken cutlet with mozzarella and bacon. I took two sodas from the cooler, draped with strips of dusty plastic that reminded me of tentacles at a car wash.

I thought about calling, but I liked the notion of surprising him. Maybe it was the air of doom making me alert, but I felt optimistic. Renewed with hope. I leaned against the side of his building, my eyes closed against the sun, two sandwiches and two cans of soda in hand. Maybe we both just needed to try a little harder. This was a phase, and it would pass. I checked my watch. It was 6:30, then it was 6:45, then it was almost 7:00 p.m. Well. I couldn't be upset with him. He didn't know I was waiting.

A group finally emerged from the building, spit out of the revolving door like pinballs. Evan came out last, jogging to catch up with his coworkers. They all had their jackets off, their sleeves rolled up, and they were laughing about something.

'Evan!' I called, waving at him.

He looked confused when he saw me. The group kept walking, slower now, giving him the chance to catch up. A few of the guys stared at me.

'Hey,' he said, walking over. 'What are you doing here?'

'I brought dinner.' I lifted the deli bag. 'I thought we could eat together. Like the old days, you know.'

'Oh. That's nice of you, Jules.'

'I got your favorite. Chicken cutlet with bacon and mozzarella.'

'The thing is,' he said, glancing over his shoulder, 'I was going to get dinner with the guys. We're going to this new Indian place on Ninth. You understand, right?'

I squinted. I couldn't see. The sun was right in my eyes.

He laughed, then took the sandwich from me. 'I can have it for lunch tomorrow, okay? Don't worry about it.'

'But what about – how was your day? I was watching the news at work.'

'We're fine. Our CEO had to leave for Washington. He's joining the government advisory team. So Michael's in charge now. Acting CEO.'

'Is that a good thing?'

'It's a great thing. It means the WestCorp deal becomes a top priority. Pretty cool, right? Hey, I should really catch up with the other guys.' He rested his hand on my shoulder for a moment. 'Thanks again, Jules.'

'You're welcome.' I didn't mean it.

He started to walk away, then paused. 'Oh. I forgot to tell you. Guess whose byline I saw today?'

'*What?*' A truck was rushing past, blaring its horn.

'I said, "Adam McCard."'

My heart sped up. My hands went clammy. I was suddenly glad Evan was already several feet away. My brain couldn't think up a reply.

'He's on the business beat at the *Observer*. He was

writing about the crash. Small world.' Evan smiled. This time, he walked away for good.

Was it possible that he knew? Through the rest of that week, I waited for Evan to bring up Adam's name again. I was certain he was going to test for my reaction, to watch for the fluttering pulse in my neck or the nervous twist of my hands – damning proof of how much that name still meant to me.

But that wasn't Evan. I was the one who thought like that, not him. I could never decide whether Evan sensed those concealed parts of me and chose to leave them alone, or whether he thought that what he saw was everything there was to see. And the harder problem was – I could never decide which of those possibilities I wanted to be true.

———

A memory, from freshman year, from the time when Evan and I were just friends. A few months, that's all it was, a ratio that diminishes as the years go by. But those days were intense and heady, when our affection was waxing like the moon, when the uncertainty electrified the air between us. In an odd way, those feel like our purest days. When we were truly ourselves, before we started bending and changing to accommodate each other.

But that's not quite right. Because even then, even before we were together, I was hiding certain aspects of myself from Evan.

That night, in early October, we were on the couch in Evan's common room. Evan was sitting upright at one end, and I was lying with my head in his lap, the TV low in the background. Evan would occasionally brush a piece of hair from my forehead, but he couldn't see the expression on my face from where he sat. At the time, I was still dating Rob, my high school boyfriend. Evan didn't mind talking about Rob, which surprised me. Maybe he knew it was only a matter of time before Rob would cease to be an obstacle.

'So you and Rob,' he said. 'Do you ever worry that he might cheat on you?'

'Not really. We have too many friends who could report back to me if he did.'

'Even if he was secretive about it?'

'Rob thinks too highly of himself to cheat. Like, he doesn't see himself as that kind of guy. He's too proud.'

'Do you think he worries about you? That you might ever cheat on him?'

'I don't know. Maybe.'

'Were you guys always faithful to each other?'

My face must have tightened when Evan asked that last question, but he didn't notice. He just kept running his fingers through my hair, tracing the ridge of my ear. I thought before answering. This was the second time a chance had arisen to make my confession. The first had been the very first night of school, while we were eating pizza. He'd asked me about my summer, and I'd almost said it – the look on his face had been so warm and trusting, and I wanted to tell him everything. He was just a friend at that point, and there was no reason not to be truthful. But even at that first moment – and at that second moment, too – I wanted Evan to think of me a certain way.

'Yes,' I lied. 'I mean, I always was, and he was, too, as far as I know.'

'Mmm,' Evan said. 'Did I tell you about what happened at practice? So one of my teammates said . . .'

It never came up again. He never knew the difference. Perhaps he hadn't been administering any kind of test, or perhaps he had been, but only unconsciously. As the night wore on I began to feel a certain relief – that I had passed – but there was guilt, too. Did I think it was okay to lie because it was never going to happen again? Or did I know, even then, that it was an error destined to be repeated?

———————

I tried not to think about Adam. I really tried. Our encounter that summer had lasted barely two minutes, capped with an empty promise to stay in touch. How many times did that happen in a given day in Manhattan? Hello and good-bye, a hundred heartbeats. I did everything to force Adam McCard out of my mind. I focused on whatever was in front of me: Evan, work, friends. But there was too much time in between. Too many empty hours, alone with nothing but my thoughts. I scanned the faces of everyone I passed in the street. I jumped every time my phone rang. While I was waiting for sleep, I found myself thinking about him. Adam McCard, Adam McCard, repeating billboards at the side of the highway. It seemed impossible he wasn't thinking about me, too.

And then, just as September was about to turn into October, I heard my phone ringing over the weak dribble of our shower. How did I know? But somehow I did: I knew that this time it would be him. His voice on the message was deep and smooth, an answer to an unasked question.

'Julia, gorgeous, it's me, Adam. If you're screening my calls, I don't blame you. God, I was so happy to run into you this summer. My only excuse for not calling is how busy work has been. Original, huh? But let me buy you a drink some night and tell you all about it. Please. I'd love to see you. Call me back. Same number.'

We planned to meet for drinks the next night at a bar downtown. From the outside, it looked like a very Adam place. A wooden door, no visible sign. The kind of place easily passed without notice. I'd dressed carefully, pulling my hair back and putting on lipstick, and earrings that dangled against my neck. My palms were sweaty, and my mind was jumbled. I had to remind myself it didn't matter. He was the one who called me. There was nothing to lose. I walked into the bar a few minutes late and didn't see him. Lots of young men with dark hair and deep voices, but no Adam. Maybe he was standing me up. Maybe it was for the best. Maybe it was better to go back to my own life and listen to that instinct flaring in the back of my mind – to stay away.

Then I felt the hand on my shoulder.

Adam kissed me on the cheek in greeting, the scent of his aftershave something that I'd never realized I'd memorized.

'Julia. You look amazing.'

'Thanks.' I tried not to blush.

We found a small, rickety table next to an open window at the front of the bar, where the breeze from the sidewalk drifted in. It was still warm, the last of an Indian summer. Adam picked out a bottle of wine for us to share. A Friday night, and the bar was full of people laughing off the week with pints of beer and platters of oysters on ice.

'This place looks great,' I said.

'It used to be a dive bar. We'd come here sometimes in high school. You could bribe the bouncer to let you in without ID.'

'Doesn't seem like that would work anymore.' There were exposed bulbs, framed prints, cocktails, craft beers, the prices high enough to make me wince.

He lifted his glass. 'Then it's a good thing we're so old,' he said. 'Cheers.'

It was like days had passed, not years. Adam's voice had that unchanged quality to it, a baritone depth that made me feel like we were actors on a stage, exchanging lines. Something about the way he leaned forward and cocked his head: it was like a cue, and the words that emerged from my mouth were more eloquent and interesting and right. The evening light came in at a low angle, casting a long shadow behind my wineglass on the table, warming my shoulders. I crossed one leg over the other, and my sandal dangled from my big toe.

I had a second glass of wine, a third. I'd been nervous and hesitant walking into the bar, but even an hour with Adam put me at ease. I was more relaxed than I'd felt in months. I was flirting, but just a little. I was still waiting for a signal that it was okay to keep going down this road.

The sun finally slipped behind the building across the street, and Adam's face sharpened in the dimmed light. In the previous few years, since I'd last seen him, he'd acquired an appealing patina of experience. The conversation lulled, and in that moment I felt the night changing cadences. A deepening, the wine sinking in, the dinner hour upon us. The silence flustered me, and I didn't know where to direct my gaze. A long second ticked by. When I looked up at Adam, his smile had disappeared.

This was it.

'Jules,' he said. He took a breath. 'I can't – I feel like I have to say something.'

I shook my head. I wanted – needed – this moment to happen, but I wanted the outcome without the procedure. Wake me up when the surgery is over.

'About last time, I guess. It was a long time ago. But I was a jerk. It was totally inappropriate. I should never have said or done those things. I'd like to think I'm a different person now, and I want to say –'

'Adam, it's okay. We don't have to talk about it.'

'No, I want to say it. I'm sorry, Julia. It's been

weighing on me, especially since – I guess that's the real reason I never called. I was worried you wouldn't want to talk to me again. I wouldn't blame you for that.'

'It was just a misunderstanding.'

He tilted his head and smiled sadly. Apologies didn't come naturally to Adam. 'I'm not sure I deserve to get off so easy.'

'It's fine. We're fine.' A pause – could I say it? 'I missed you.'

We talked about my job, about the last two years of school. Adam was the first person since graduation who actually seemed curious about my life. I didn't realize how much I'd been holding back until he started asking questions.

'Well, she sounds like a character,' Adam said after I told him about Laurie's soap-in-the-coffee bit. 'I know the type. Probably spent too many years living alone.'

'It's so strange. She's smart – I can see that. I respect her. I want to like her. But it's like I'm not there. It's like she doesn't even see me as a real person. I don't get it.'

'That's her mistake, Jules. It sounds like you're too good for that place.'

I'd forgotten how much I loved the sound of Adam's voice. 'I guess I should stop whining,' I said, reaching to refill my glass. 'At least I have a job, right?'

'What about Evan?' he asked. 'What's he up to these days?'

96

'Oh.' I was surprised that Adam had even remembered Evan's name. 'Evan.'

'You guys are still together?'

'Yeah. Yeah, he's working at a hedge fund. Spire Management.'

'Spire? That's a tough place to crack. He must be good.'

Relief washed over me. Back in college, Adam usually dismissed guys like Evan, if he noticed them at all. But now he was genuinely interested in Evan, in what he was working on. There was a warmth to his questions. Adam *had* changed. He wasn't the same person he'd been the last time we'd seen each other. Evan was my boyfriend, and Adam respected what I'd chosen. It felt good. This, maybe, was the signal I'd been waiting for. I nodded vigorously when he suggested a second bottle.

'So you're a reporter?' I said later. 'How long have you been there?'

'It's boring. You don't want to hear about it.'

'No, I do.' He grimaced, and I laughed. 'Come on. It can't be as bad as my job.'

'About a year and a half now. I started as a stringer, and then they had an opening on the business desk. The editor said he would move me to politics before the election.'

'That sounds promising.'

'He changed his mind. Once the housing bubble started heating up, he decided he needed me to stay where I was. So.' He sipped his wine. 'It's annoying. I don't like what I'm writing about. It's the same news everyone else is reporting. I'm putting out feelers for other jobs.' He shrugged, looking resigned. 'Not much else to say about it.'

---

In the following days, this gave me comfort. Even *Adam* didn't have everything figured out? Unfathomable, a few years earlier. In college I was certain he was going to be famous. Adam McCard – people would know that name.

We knew each other from the campus magazine at Yale. In the first weeks of fall, freshman year, I crammed into a musty old office with two dozen other freshmen, lured by the promise of free pizza. The editors of the magazine made their pitch, telling us that joining the magazine would be the best decision we ever made. I thought I'd never go back. Me, the girl who hated English class, the girl who still recoiled from the memory of that bright red C on that stupid essay? But the next week, I returned. Already the people around me were finding their niches: Evan with his hockey, Abby with her volunteer work. I knew that I needed to hurry up and find my thing. I was assigned to write a short profile of the new football coach. I didn't know the first thing about football. 'I'm sorry. This is probably awful. I'm a terrible writer,' I told my editor, an older girl named Viv, when I turned in that assignment. 'That's okay,' Viv said. 'That's what I'm here for.'

My next assignment was to review a new show at the campus art gallery. 'Julia,' Viv said as she read my draft.

'This is really nice. Your descriptions are great. You must know a lot about this stuff.' The rest of my assignments from Viv were, thankfully, in that vein. I wrote several more pieces for the magazine that year. I wasn't gung-ho about it, wasn't angling to be an editor. But I liked walking into the office and feeling that I belonged. I liked the satisfaction that came from Viv telling me I had done a good job.

As a sophomore, I wrote more. I had a regular beat by then, on the arts and culture desk, and I was getting ready to declare an art history major. Those moments when I was starting a new piece – blank document, blinking cursor – were a rare reliable pleasure in my life. Writing for the magazine was one of the only things I had control over. Sophomore year was proving to be strange. Bad strange. Compared to freshman year, everything felt precarious. The landscape of friendships had shifted, thrown off by different dorms and new roommates. Classes seemed harder. Parties seemed duller. Everyone was sinking deeper into their own worlds. Evan was consumed by hockey and didn't have much time for me. When we were together, we bickered frequently. Our relationship didn't seem so fated or so satisfying anymore. I felt restless, in search of something new.

'I've noticed you around a lot,' Adam said, dropping into the chair next to mine one midwinter afternoon. He extended his hand. 'Remind me of your name.'

'Julia Edwards.'

'Nice to meet you, Julia Edwards. Adam McCard.'

I knew who he was, of course. He was the editor in chief, a senior. Adam had never before paid attention to me.

'Are you new?' he asked.

'I'm a sophomore. I wrote a few pieces last year. I'm doing more this year.'

'What are you working on?' He peered at my computer.

'Oh,' I said, tempted to cover the screen with my hands. 'It's just a little thing. It's stupid. A review of a new show at the Center for British Art.'

'Aha. Julia. Of course. You're the genius art critic. I love your stuff.' Someone called his name, and he stood up. The issue was about to close, and the editors would work well into the morning hours. Before he walked away, Adam put his hand on my shoulder. 'Hey, Julia. Let's grab coffee this week. Get to know each other. Sound good?'

A few months later, in the spring, I arrived at the magazine offices one night, ready to go over an article with Viv. But I was told she was sick, at home in bed. We still had a few days before the issue closed, so I put my laptop back in my bag. Adam spotted me just as I was about to leave. We had been having coffee every week. I'd admitted to Abby that I was developing a little crush on him, but it was innocent. It was nothing compared to what I felt for Evan, obviously.

'Julia. Leaving already?'

'Yeah. Viv's out sick.'

'I have half an hour until my next meeting. Why don't we give Viv a pass on this one? I'll edit it for you.'

My hands were shaking as I pulled out my laptop and opened the file. This was a terrible development. I had written this piece quickly, to meet Viv's deadline, and it was full of holes. Viv was exacting, finding the flaws in my work with merciless rigor, but she actually made me feel okay about that. It was never going to be right the first time; I knew that by now. I was fine with Viv seeing a rough draft of my work, but not Adam. I liked Adam, I liked spending time with Adam, but I wasn't ready for him to see an unedited version of my thoughts. This was going to be a disaster.

'Let's see,' he said, squinting as he read. A few minutes later, he looked up from the laptop. 'This is great.'

'Really?' I thought he was joking, but then he nodded. 'Wait, really? Do you think so? I know I need a better opening, and —'

'No, it's great. Yeah, the lede could be punchier, but once you've nailed that I think you're basically done.' He leaned back in his chair, hands folded behind his head. 'So. What should we do for the next twenty-four minutes?'

I laughed, closing my computer. 'Did you turn in your thesis? Or theses, I guess?' Adam was a double major in English and history. He'd spent the previous year writing about the Weimar Republic for the history department and working on a novel to fulfill the requirements for his writing concentration in English. His novel was also about the Weimar Republic. I'm not sure the English and history departments were, respectively, aware of this.

'I handed in history last week. And I'll hand in the novel next week.'

'And that's it, right? You're done? I'm so jealous.'

'Don't be. You're the lucky one. Two years left until shit gets real.'

I rolled my eyes. He knew my complaints. Adam often took the train into the city on weekends, forgoing campus parties for the more glamorous options of New York, where he'd grown up. I was envious. Did he not get how constricted, how stifling this life felt? Class, study, party, Evan. Over and over and over.

He smiled. 'You know I'd take you with me if I could. Start our own magazine or something.'

'Ha. I'd just be deadweight.'

'No way. I'm going to miss you, Jules.'

'Shucks.'

'I mean it.' He nudged my foot with his. 'I really like you. You're special.'

That was the thing about Adam. You believed everything he said. He said that he was going to be a writer after he graduated. I never imagined that he wouldn't succeed. He would go to New York after graduation and find a job at the *New Yorker* or *Harper's* or the *Paris Review*. In a few years he would have published his novel, and his picture would be gracing the cover of the arts section in the *Times*. There was no question about it. Adam would succeed at whatever he chose to do.

I took the subway home that night, after Adam and I said good-bye. The man sitting next to me on the uptown train was flipping through a copy of that morning's *Observer,* scanning each page for a few seconds before moving on. Until he stopped and pulled the paper a little closer. Adam's byline. The man read Adam's article slowly, nodding to himself. The train reached Grand Central. The man stayed in his seat, eyes glued to the page. It wasn't until the car had emptied and refilled that he looked up and jumped to his feet, elbowing his way out before the doors closed, sprinting to catch the late train back to Rye or Greenwich.

I'd wanted to lean over and tell him: I know Adam McCard. More than that: he's my friend. He'd liked me, once upon a time. He told me I was special. That night was the very first time, that year in New York, that I felt like I knew something that the people around me didn't. That I felt like I had a reason to be there. I sat back in my seat, flooded with a warm feeling of satisfaction.

He called me again the next week and the week after. October dawned chilly and clean. The whole planet was tilting on its axis in a new direction, a better direction.

The New York I'd been living in went from dull sepia to vibrant color. As Adam and I spent more time together, I felt a distant pity for Evan, for the narrow constraints of his world. In Chinatown Adam and I ate strange, spicy food in fluorescent-lit dives. We drank wine at sidewalk tables in SoHo. We went to gallery openings, to readings, to jazz shows in West Village basements. Adam took me to secret bookstores; he lent me his favorite novels. He was so confident, so comfortable. He wasn't running around in search of an identity, the way so many of my classmates were. He already knew who he was, and that was intoxicating. Adam would sometimes slip his arm through mine as we walked, or place a hand on my shoulder as he stood behind me at the museum, or brush a stray leaf from the sleeve of my jacket when we sat in the park. Women looked at him with envy. I craved the intimacy, every little touch. I so badly wanted more.

One night, at a French bistro in the West Village, the remains of steak frites on the table between us, he asked me the exact question I'd avoided asking myself.

'So what does Evan think of us spending all this time together?'

I toyed with my napkin. 'He doesn't mind. He's working on this deal all the time, anyway.'

He sipped his wine, watching me. He must have realized the truth, that I hadn't said a word about this to Evan. Adam always knew how to read me.

Evan was still a factor in this equation, much as I wished otherwise. We kept up the charade at our weekly dinners, when he talked in a monologue about work. He'd seemed tired lately, worn down by the demands of the deal. For some reason, Michael wouldn't staff anyone else on it. It was Evan and Evan alone. 'But,' he said in early October, his voice straining with a forced optimism, 'it's really starting to come together. Michael had me run a model this week. The numbers are dynamite. You wouldn't believe how huge the upside is.'

Evan's hours only grew more extreme as the fall progressed, and our date nights became rarer and rarer, until eventually I was left with the life of a single woman. The turning point came when I started taking advantage of this instead of resenting it. It was a new stage in our relationship, that was all; a phase where I could be more independent than ever before. A weight had lifted from my shoulders. I was free. There was a different kind of sadness in my life now, but it was a sweeter kind of sadness, easier to bear, because I had never accepted that falling for Adam was in fact such a hopeless mistake.

'What did you do?' Abby squinted at me. 'Did you change something? Your hair?'

I shook my head. Nothing had happened between Adam and me, but still, I didn't know what to say about it. Even Abby's sympathy only went so far. For the time being, I kept my mouth shut.

It was a Saturday night in October, and we were at her apartment in Harlem, a run-down and homey old railroad setup she shared with a friend. Her super had turned on the radiators early, so Abby kept the windows open to let out the heat. She used the gas burner on her stove to light the end of a joint. We smoked it sitting cross-legged on the living room floor while we waited for our Chinese food.

'Don't you miss this?' she said, exhaling. 'It's almost like we're back in school.'

'You never told me who you've been getting this from.'

'Why? Are you in the market for some? Evan need something to take the edge off?'

'It just seems so *real*. Buying weed from a real drug dealer.'

'A *drug* dealer!' She yelped in laughter, collapsing to the floor. 'You sound like Mister Rogers. No. No. Actually, I just got it from another teacher.'

'That is terrible.'

'Where the hell is our food?' She stood up and wandered into the kitchen, opening and shutting all the cabinets. 'I'm starving.'

The end of the joint smoldered like a jewel. I slipped a bobby pin from my hair to hold the burned nub. 'You're done?' I asked Abby. She waved, and I pulled the last of it into my lungs. It was pungent and stronger than what we had smoked in college.

'How were your parents?' I said. They had visited her the week before. Abby wandered back in, eating Froot Loops from the box. 'You know dinner's going to be here in, like, five minutes.'

'Appetizer. They were good. We went to Ikea, and I talked them into buying me a nightstand, so success.'

'Had they seen your apartment yet? Did they like it?'

'They did.' Abby paused, her hand full of brightly colored cereal, and tilted her head in contemplation. 'They did, except my mom got sort of teary. I don't know. I think it was too real for her. Seeing me all grown up and everything.'

I threw a pillow at her. 'You are *not* that grown up.'

'Well, my mom cries at everything.' It was true. I'd taken a picture of them at graduation, Abby and her parents, and her mother had been sobbing before I even turned on the camera. She was sentimental. Their other four kids were already grown and scattered, with careers and marriages and children and at least one divorce. But Abby had always been the baby, and suddenly she was gone, too.

After dinner, when we had devoured the sesame beef and kung pao shrimp and cold noodles, I felt myself sliding into a familiar jelly-limbed mellowness. Our thoughts were moving slowly enough for us to observe them, like glassy orbs in the air.

'Do you know that feeling?' Abby said, her voice thin and distant. 'When you wake up in the middle of the night and don't recognize the room you're in? Like, the shadows on the ceiling are all weird, and you're like, where the fuck am I?'

'Yeah.'

'I hate it.'

She was lying on her back, arms and legs splayed out, gazing up at the ceiling. She was quieter than usual. I nudged her with my foot.

'You okay?'

She rolled to her side and curled into a fetal ball. 'It was sort of weird. When my parents visited. I couldn't figure it out. And then my mom told me, on their last night, when the two of us went to get ice cream after dinner. It's my dad's job.'

When I got high, my emotions always felt slow to catch up, thickened like honey left in the fridge. 'What happened?' I said, belatedly registering the heaviness in Abby's voice.

'Nothing. Nothing yet. But you know, he works at a bank. This year has been brutal. He thinks he's going to be laid off soon. Which explains – well, like, every time we went out to eat, he'd sigh and roll his eyes at the prices. He and my mom got in a big fight, I guess, and he told her she needs to go back to work. But I mean, who the hell is going to hire her right now?'

'Oh, Abby. That sucks.'

'The whole thing is a disaster.'

A few days earlier, the president had signed a massive bailout into law. A few weeks before that, the Republican nominee had suspended his campaign, announcing that he had to return to Washington to address the crisis. I followed the developments with a shallow curiosity, but lately I'd been caring less about all of it. Maybe this was going to be the headline for the era when the historians had their turn. Maybe the market crash would emerge as the defining moment of the year, of the decade. But I'd been thinking about other things. I'd been thinking about Adam, the sound of his voice, the color of his eyes. Talk of the NAS-DAQ and the Dow was so abstract. The world still looked the same. The sun still set and rose; the moon still pulled the tides in patterns around the globe. My mind was aloft, scattered among the stars. I squeezed my eyes shut and tried to snap out of it. Other people were hurting, even if I wasn't.

'I'm so sorry,' I said.

'At least I'm off the dole, right? Last kid. No more tuition.' She tried to smile. 'I don't know. I mean, maybe he won't even lose his job. Maybe everything will be fine. But it's so weird. These are my parents. It's weird to have to worry about *them*. Aren't they supposed to worry about me?'

I lowered myself to the floor and curled up behind Abby, a big spoon to her little one. It was rare for me in our friendship, offering comfort to her. To Abby, who always knew what to do. 'You want to sleep over?' she said. I had started spending the night occasionally, when the quiet of my apartment was too much. I texted Evan to tell him. We lay in her bed, talking until late, when we finally drifted off.

The next morning, we went to the diner on the corner for breakfast. I emptied the tiny plastic cup of cream into my coffee, watching it swirl into spidery threads. I still felt a little high. Abby scrolled through her phone while eating a piece of buttered toast. She had cheered up considerably.

'Guess who texted me last night,' she said. 'Jake Fletcher.'

'You guys know each other?'

'Remember? You introduced us at his party. I've bumped into him a few times. He asked for my number last week.'

'Wow. Small world.'

'I think I'm gonna do it. I have gone *way* too long without any action.'

I laughed weakly, signaling to the waiter for more coffee. Abby looked at me.

'Wait. Wait – what is it? Do you guys have a history?'

'No! God, no. I've just known him since forever. I still think of him as, like, the bratty five-year-old he once was. That's all.'

She raised an eyebrow. I wasn't sure whether she bought it. But that was the nice thing about us. Abby knew the difference between big lies and little ones. She might guess at what I was leaving out: a game of spin the bottle in middle school, or maybe a tipsy kiss in the backyard during one of his parents' big parties in Boston. A stupid kid thing that wasn't even worth the energy to mention. Something you could skate past because you were so certain it was meaningless, that it had nothing to do with what you were actually talking about.

# CHAPTER 5

## *Evan*

'What the fuck, man?' Roger said, shaking his head. 'It's a bloodbath out there.'

Despite Kleinman's rousing speech that morning, there was not much to be done that day. The top executives were in damage-control mode, on the phone with our investors, conveying to them the same confident lines we'd just heard. But everyone else had too much time on their hands. Taking slow walks around the floor, calling their wives in the middle of the day. Roger staring, slack-jawed, at the computer screen. The eerie quiet was only punctured by his occasional declarations of disbelief, which I did my best to tune out, because I was the anomaly. I actually had work to do. This lumber deal was taking up every second of my time.

Roger noticed me studying a model and chewing on a thumbnail. 'What is that?' he said. '*Peck*. Are you actually working right now?'

'Just something, um, something leftover from a few days ago.'

Keep it light and vague, those were my orders. 'Not till we're ready to push the button,' Michael had said. 'Soon. I know how hard you've been working on this, Evan. I've seen how late you're staying and how early you're coming in. I'm impressed. You're handling this very well.'

This was the previous week, in Michael's office, the beginning of September. I had stopped by to go over the latest numbers. I'd been working up the nerve to say something to Michael about the workload, which I could barely handle. In a bathroom stall that morning, I practiced the sentence in a whisper. My stomach was a watery mess. *Michael, I wonder whether we want to think about bringing someone else on board. Couldn't the deal use a fresh pair of eyes?* That seemed a fair enough rationale.

But Michael had preempted me with praise before I had a chance to open my mouth. It was a cornering tactic. A dare. What was I going to do, tell Michael that his confidence was misplaced? That I actually *wasn't* as capable as he thought I was? And risk getting kicked off the deal entirely? So instead I mumbled a thank-you.

'And I appreciate it,' Michael went on. 'How discreet you've been. That's the best way to handle a deal like this. Stay quiet. Just focus and do what you're doing. Keep up the good work, Evan.'

So that was it. I was just going to put my head down and get through it. Just as I'd done in the past, taking it one predawn practice at a time, inching closer to the end. By eleven that Monday morning, the morning of

Kleinman's departure to DC, I had finished the latest component of the model. I walked the papers over to Michael's office. There was an assumption in the formula that needed clarifying, the one part of the deal that still didn't make sense to me. I was a little worried, actually. It was the last factor that seemed liable to screw everything up.

Michael's secretary, Wanda, halted me outside his office. She was all sassy middle-age curves: blown-out hair, chair-wide hips, bright red lipstick. 'Uh-uh,' she said in her Jersey accent. 'I don't think so, honey. You're not getting in there today. You wanna give that to me, I'll try to get it to him.'

I peered over Wanda's shoulder, trying to see through the open door. She'd been with Michael for years, and she could be excessively protective. 'What's he doing?'

'Trying to run the company — what do you think? He's been on the line all morning.' The phone on Wanda's desk rang. She tapped her Bluetooth headset and jerked her head to dismiss me. 'O-*kay?* Stop by tomorrow. Maybe I can fit you in.'

I couldn't go any further on this model without Michael answering my question. So I spent the rest of the morning as Roger and the other analysts did, trolling the Internet for updates, killing time in an uneasy boredom, the same things I had done at the beginning of the summer. The TVs in the lounge were tuned to CNBC and Bloomberg Business. People lingered there, watching, looking for any excuse to stay away from their desks. Late

in the afternoon, I walked past and found myself hypno-
tized by the mounting intensity of the coverage.

WALL STREET'S WORST DAY SINCE 9/11
DOW DOWN OVER 500 POINTS
LEHMAN DECLARES BANKRUPTCY
MERRILL BOUGHT BY BANK OF AMERICA
IS YOUR MONEY SAFE?
FORCED LIQUIDATION — HISTORIC VOLUME
EVERYTHING CALLED INTO QUESTION

One of the managing directors, a petite brunette
woman, had her hands steepled over her mouth and
tears in her eyes. Another woman put her arm around
her shoulders. 'Her husband works at AIG,' I heard
someone whisper. 'Three kids. Just bought a house in
Quogue.'

Roger, standing across the lounge, caught my eye and
waved me over. 'Let's go to the roof,' he said.

'What? Now?'

'Come on. It's dead. No one's gonna notice.'

We took the elevator to the top of the building, where
Roger propped open the door with a loose brick. It was
a beautiful day, a bluebird September sky. The city
stretched out far below us, metal and glass glittering in
the sunlight.

'Holy shit,' I said.

'You never been up here?'

'I had no idea we could get up here.'

'We're not supposed to.' Roger pulled a crumpled pack of cigarettes from his pocket. 'You want one?'

'I'm okay.'

I wandered out toward the edge. The roof was covered with tar paper and gravel. Only a low wall and a flimsy metal bar stood between me and the sixty-story drop. On the other side of the roof was the area where David Kleinman's helicopter had taken off that morning.

From this vantage point, life down below was proceeding normally. Taxis and trucks flowed up 8th Avenue in waves. Tiny pedestrians drifted down the sidewalk, their motion smooth and toylike. Sounds echoed up from the street: honking horns, a jackhammer, the rattle of a loose manhole cover, a siren in the distance. I could almost pretend the crisis was contained within the walls of our building, the babble of the TV irrelevant beyond its perimeter. The numbers were plummeting, the market was in a frenzy, but for the moment, it didn't result in any visible change. No fires, no earthquakes, no violence or bloodshed. But it would take time for the real world to catch up to what was happening on our screens, and in a situation like this, the worst lay ahead. I understood that.

That woman downstairs, trying not to show her panic: her husband would lose his job, and she would probably keep hers, but it didn't matter. The balance would be upset. I knew that feeling, of living exactly within your means. Their life was fancier than mine – children in private school, a second house in the Hamptons – but that feeling didn't change. The precarious flow of incoming and outgoing gave you a toehold in this world, but it was one that would vanish if the paychecks stopped. Numbers had always felt realer to me than anything else. Days like this reminded you of that.

To the rest of America, to the rest of the world, I was indisputably one of them, even if I hadn't been pushing shady CDOs. A bad guy. A practitioner of the dark arts who had suddenly lost control of his slippery magic. Why didn't this bother me more? In the past, I think it would have. But my mind kept going back to the numbers. You could talk in generalities: Wall Street *bad*, Main Street *good*. It didn't really mean anything. I liked the economy of action. A goal scored before the third-period buzzer, a clean and precise pass, an airtight model. You didn't need words to complicate it. There were winners, and there were losers. The game bore it out. At first this job seemed more practical than anything else: a way to stay in New York with Julia, to make money and pay off student loans quickly. But it had transformed into something else. The thing I was *meant* to be doing.

I shoved my hands in my pockets and turned, taking in the panorama. The city was sparkling and alive, taking up every inch it could. I looked back at Roger, leaning against the wall. He was moving his lips as he read something on his BlackBerry.

'What is it?' I asked, walking over.

'Shit. This is crazy.' Roger thrust his phone toward

me. 'You see that picture? No, scroll down. There. That short guy in the blue tie? That's my old roommate from Stanford. What are the odds, man?'

'What is this?'

'He works at Lehman, I guess. The little shit is famous.'

'Actually, it looks like he just got fired.' I scrolled to the top, where the headline read: LEHMAN GOES UNDER. It was from the *Observer*. The picture showed several bewildered-looking young men standing on the sidewalk, clutching cardboard boxes while pedestrians streamed around them.

'Whatever. He was a tool.'

'How did you find this?'

'I always read the *Observer*. Just for their finance guy. He's good. You never read him?'

'What's his name?'

Roger reached for his phone, checking the byline. 'Adam McCard.'

'Adam McCard?'

'What, are you deaf?'

'No. No, it's just that I *know* Adam McCard.'

Roger raised an eyebrow. 'How?'

'He was a friend of Julia's in college. Really? Adam McCard?'

'He's a good reporter. Better than anyone else. He actually seems to get it.'

'Shit. If you say so.'

Roger took a final drag of his cigarette. Adam McCard.

I hadn't thought about him in months – in years. 'Ready?' Roger kicked the brick away and held the door open.

'Right behind you,' I said.

---

Sophomore year, Julia dragged me along to a party off campus. I was hungover and stiff from the night before, from the hockey team's end-of-season rager, but Julia insisted I come. She was in one of those moods. The party was on a dark, tree-lined street, in a crumbling old Victorian with a sagging porch. She had given a vague explanation of the occasion – for the magazine she worked on? Something like that – but when we walked through the front door, I saw the real reason.

Adam McCard was leaning against the wall, arms crossed, one foot hitched up. He waved at Julia, then shook my hand, gripping it too tightly. He told us to help ourselves to the beer in the kitchen, *his* kitchen. I realized belatedly, stupidly, that this was his house. Julia had been mentioning Adam's name a lot in the preceding weeks. I'd decided, a while earlier, that I hated him.

We joined a group in the kitchen gathered around a keg. They gave me curious looks. 'Are you an *athlete?*' one girl asked. She was scrawny, black-clad, with a cigarette smoldering between her pale fingers and an expression of surprised wonder.

'I'm on the hockey team.'

'Oh,' Julia said. 'Oh, that reminds me of something. So last night . . .'

I tuned out quickly. I was thinking, mostly, how hungry I was. Maybe I could slip out for a slice of pizza and get back before she noticed. But a minute later, Julia said my name. I turned to face her. She leaned against me, briefly, in recognition.

'So Sebi finally finishes the bottle,' she continued. 'We're upstairs, in his room, and he goes over to the window. Then he pulls down his pants and starts pissing all over the crowd at the frat next door. Just, like, so casual about it.'

The group laughed. Julia's eyes were glittering.

'Some of the guys from next door get really mad. They come over, trying to start a fight. They're threatening to call the cops, all that stuff. We're downstairs at that point, too. Sebi had passed out in his bed. They keep asking who it was, who did it, no one's going to tell. But then Sebi strolls up to the front door himself and asks what the problem is. And he's totally buck naked.'

They laughed louder. 'So funny,' the scrawny girl said flatly.

'So the frat guys are backing away, they don't know what to think, and Sebi offers to walk them home, throws his arms around their shoulders, being all friendly. He was completely blacked out at that point. He tried to pull one of the guys in for a hug, and that's when they all finally ran away. No one wants to fight a naked dude.'

Julia was grossed out when this happened the previous night, at the party at the hockey house, grimacing at the sight of Sebi's bare ass. But not anymore. She was beaming, clearly thrilled with the story's reception.

Later, when we were finally alone, I asked her what that had been about.

'What the hell, Jules? That was embarrassing.'

'Oh, come on. It was hilarious. You're never going to let Sebi live it down.'

'Yeah, but we're his friends. These people don't know him.'

'Relax.' She rolled her eyes. 'It's not a big deal.'

*Relax?* She wouldn't even look at me. I felt a smoldering curl of disgust. 'What's with this attitude?' I snapped. I wanted to grab her by the shoulders, shake her until she listened. How did she not get it? 'Jules. Why are you being like this?'

'*God.*' She rolled her eyes again. 'Whatever. I'm going to the bathroom.'

She walked away. In those days our fights seemed to come out of nowhere, and with more and more frequency. They were about stupid, meaningless things, but Julia could so easily turn vicious, like an animal baring her teeth. I never knew what to say. I just wanted it to be over. It always seemed easiest to concede before things escalated. I was good at apologizing, even if I didn't know what I was apologizing for.

I pushed through the living room, which was tight with bodies. The bathroom door was locked. When the door finally opened, some other girl emerged, her expression smeary with drink. She gave me a hazy smile. I went back to the kitchen, then to the backyard, then again to the living room. Julia was nowhere. I pulled out my phone and texted her, then I opened the front door to check the porch. Nothing. I called, but she didn't pick up. Five minutes passed, then six, seven. Ten minutes. Fifteen. Where was she? Maybe this was some kind of punishment, forcing me to navigate this awful party alone. She probably enjoyed the thought of it.

Then, just as I was about to call again, I saw her coming down the stairs from the second floor. She pushed her way past the crowds. Her cheeks were flushed, her hair messy. She was staring straight ahead. She noticed me and came over, but she was still avoiding my gaze. 'Had to use the bathroom upstairs,' she muttered. Then I noticed Adam McCard behind her, bouncing down the stairs two at a time.

She walked several paces ahead of me the whole way home. She wouldn't even let me come close. As good as an admission of guilt, in my mind. When we got back to the dorm, I was going to tell her that I'd sleep in my own room that night. But outside her door, when Julia turned to face me and looked up at me for what felt like the first time all night, her eyes were brimming with tears. Her lower lip quavered, and she burst into a sob. 'I'm sorry,' she gasped. 'I'm sorry, Evan. I'm so sorry.'

———————

I checked my cell phone when I got back to my desk that afternoon. Julia had texted, asking me how my day was. It was sweet. I smiled to myself.

We usually ordered dinner from a regular rotation of

places in the neighborhood: Italian, Chinese, Thai, Vietnamese, Turkish. Roger always took charge, dictating what everyone was going to order so we could share, and he calculated the tab ahead of time so that we could maximize our thirty-dollar per diem. That night, around seven, he threw a balled-up piece of paper at my head to get my attention.

'Peck,' he said. 'Let's go. We're going out for dinner.'

'Picking up? Or out out?'

'Out out. It's deader than a doornail around here. Hurry up,' he drawled, standing. 'I made a reservation. A new Indian place on Ninth.'

My stomach rumbled as we walked to the elevator. Roger had that slightly satanic ability to discern your desires with perfect accuracy. Going out for dinner, eating at a table with real tablecloths, hot and spicy food washed down with frosty beer – it was, in fact, exactly what we needed in that moment. And so, by the time we emerged into the last of the day's sunlight, I was actually in a pretty good mood.

'Evan!' I turned and saw her squinting against the lowering sun. Julia.

'Hey.' I felt the guys staring as I walked over. 'What are you doing here?'

She lifted up a plastic bag, a logo I recognized from a deli around the corner. I went there for lunch when I was too impatient for delivery. 'I brought dinner. I thought we could eat together. Like the old days, you know.'

'Oh. That's nice of you, Jules.'

'I got your favorite. Chicken cutlet with bacon and mozzarella.'

Which I'd ordered many times before. The bread was usually stale. The chicken cold and tough. That sandwich was always a last resort. Roger and the others were walking away without me. I just needed a break. The thought of it was unbearable, eating that terrible sandwich, forced to talk about my day, to fake it with Julia. I just wanted to *be* for one minute. With people who understood. I told her the truth, partially. 'The thing is, I was going to get dinner with the guys. We're going to this new Indian place on Ninth. You understand, right?'

She was quiet, the bag drooping from her wrist. But just because she could saunter out of her job whenever she liked didn't mean that I could. I was annoyed. I was a little pissed, actually. She could have called ahead. Roger had made a reservation and everything. Her mopey silence was unfair. This didn't seem like it could be *my* fault.

After I took the bag from her, promising I'd eat it for lunch the next day, but already planning to let it molder in the refrigerator until I was forced to throw it out, I thought of something. I'd meant to text her earlier.

'Oh,' I called as she walked away. 'Guess whose byline I saw today?'

'Another round?' the waiter asked. The empty beer glasses were speckled with our greasy fingerprints from the paratha.

'Absolutely,' Roger said. I still had an inch of beer left, which Roger pointed at. 'Keep up, Peck.'

We went out together a lot. Dinner, the bar after work almost every night, clubs on the weekends. In better moments, it reminded me of the hockey team. It was something even more comfortable than friendship. I drained my glass and handed it to the waiter.

'Who was that?' one of the other analysts asked me.

'Who was who?'

'That girl you were talking to back there.'

'Oh,' I said. I'd already forgotten. 'Right. That was Julia. My girlfriend.'

'What was she doing here?'

Roger laughed, reaching for the last piece of paratha. 'You didn't know?' he said loudly. 'Peck is completely whipped. Does whatever his girlfriend tells him to.'

I rolled my eyes. 'She was just saying hi.'

'Hey, Roger,' one of the other analysts said. 'So what happened to that chick from Saturday night?'

'Which one? Can't keep track.'

'The blonde. The one from the club.'

'Her? She won't stop calling.' He gestured at his phone. All of us kept our BlackBerrys faceup on the table, alert to the buzz of incoming e-mails through dinner. He tipped back in his chair. 'She was all right. I'm worried she's gonna be a clinger.'

The waiter delivered our entrées. Roger made another lewd crack about the girl he'd brought home on Saturday night. I ate my lamb curry and let myself dissolve into the banter. Something about that time of year had been making me homesick. Fall had always meant a turnover in routine, a new year of school, the beginning of the hockey season. I missed it, even the miserable parts: muscles that screamed in pain, bruises blackening under pads, sticks slamming into legs. Maybe *homesick* wasn't the right word. It was more like a part of me had been put away in a dusty old box, and I missed it. But moments like this were a relief. Another beer, and another. In those moments, I'd forget.

At McGuigan's later that Monday night, I slipped out of our booth while Roger was in the middle of a story, and waited at the bar for Maria to look up.

'Hey,' she said, finally. She smiled. 'How long have you been sitting there?'

'Busy night?'

'You have no idea. Hang on a second.' She delivered a brimming tray of bourbons to a waiter, who carried it over to a table. Not our table, but it might as well have been. You could tell they were bankers from a mile away. Almost everyone in there was. Young guys in loosened ties, getting bombed with an end-of-the-world abandon.

'That'll keep them busy for about five minutes,' she said. 'The usual?'

After several weeks of going to McGuigan's almost every night, I had befriended Maria. She felt like someone I'd known for a long time. In a strange way, even longer than Julia. Like someone from back home. I liked her company, especially when I'd had too much of my coworkers. One night she let me buy her a drink and told me her story. She was putting herself through law school at Fordham with loans and bartending wages. As a girl, she had dreamed of becoming a ballerina, of studying at Juilliard. Her teachers at home all said she had the talent, and she'd moved to the city for it. When I asked what happened, she shrugged. 'Flat feet.' She was tall and gorgeous, had thought about modeling, she said, but realized that if her body could let her down once, it could do it twice.

'So why law school?'

'I want to be taken seriously, I guess. I find it interesting. Mostly I don't want to end up like my mom.' She paused. 'I sound like an asshole.'

'Not an asshole. I get it.'

'Well. You're nice, Evan. You're not like those other guys, you know?'

Guilt twinged in my chest occasionally during those hours we spent talking, sometimes till the end of her shift. Hours I should have been spending with Julia. I worried Julia could smell the bar on me when I got home, stale beer and smoky whiskey clinging to my shirt before I stuffed it into the laundry pile. I found myself daydreaming about Maria. It reminded me of high school – a girl waiting by your locker after the last bell. Consistent pleasures: the same familiar face, day in and day out.

Maria drew a Guinness for me. 'What's going on tonight?'

'What do you mean?'

'You guys are all worked up. All of you.'

'Oh. It's the market. This could be the end for a lot of companies.'

'Okay, but you'll be fine, though.'

'But that's the thing. Nobody knows. There's never been anything like this. Nobody knows what could happen to Spire.'

'Well, I don't mean Spire. I mean *you*. Say you get fired, go bankrupt, whatever. *You* aren't going to have a problem getting a job. I mean, look at you.'

I raised an eyebrow.

'Not like that.' She laughed. 'I mean you're smart, you're polite, you look like a guy anyone could trust. You fit right in. Guys like you don't stay unemployed for long.'

Someone was waving her down. She rested her hand on mine before she walked away. Maria was good at her job. 'Don't worry too much about it, Evan. You're just one of those people. It's all going to work out, you know?'

'Evan. Come on in.'

This was the following evening, Tuesday night. It was the first time Michael's door had been open and unguarded in almost two days.

'Is this an okay time?' Michael was typing fast, glancing over his shoulder at a chart, ignoring the blinking messages on his phone. His office looked like a war zone.

'Fine, fine. I sent Wanda home. What do you have there?'

'The WestCorp models. They're almost finished, but I need to check an assumption with you before running it.'

'What is it?'

I took a deep breath. 'The exports to the Chinese market. I wasn't sure what tariffs they're subject to and how much that's going to affect us. I've done some research, and there's a lot of variation in the taxes on lumber exported to China, so I thought I'd go with a rough average, something like –'

'Zero.'

'Pardon?'

'Your number is zero. The WestCorp exports won't be subject to any tariffs or taxes. Is that all?'

'Well – yes. Yeah, that's it.'

'Good.' Michael turned back to his computer. I started toward the door, but I couldn't help myself. It had been puzzling me for so long. And it still didn't quite make sense.

'Michael, just want to be sure – no tariffs or taxes at all for these exports, none? It's just that I've seen a lot of –'

He spun in his chair and stared at me, anger flaring in his eyes. 'No,' he said sharply. 'No tariffs. *None*. Put that in the model and run it. E-mail me the numbers when you have them. Then go home.'

Back at my desk, as I plugged the last numbers into the model, I felt a hot flush spread under my collar. I shouldn't have questioned Michael like that. In all my research, I'd never seen a scenario in which the trade barriers had been dropped completely. But he was the boss after all. Maybe I hadn't looked hard enough.

After the model was finished, I checked everything over slowly. The papers were still warm in my hands when I walked over to Michael's office, a stupid-big grin stuck to my face. Assuming we took even a conservative position on WestCorp, the money we stood to make was staggering. I had to read it twice, three times to be sure. This kind of good news ought to be delivered in person. When I got there, the door was nearly closed. Michael was on the phone. I almost didn't recognize him – his voice was strange, different. It quieted. I edged a little closer.

Then Michael spoke again. Another language. It sounded familiar.

Then I remembered: in his usual overly ambitious way, Arthur had decided to take up a new language junior year, even though he already spoke French and Spanish. He stayed up late every night, practicing his tones and inflections. This was the fluent version of those efforts. Michael was speaking Mandarin.

A prickle ran up my spine. Odd. Michael had always asked one of the third-year analysts, a Princeton grad who spoke flawless Mandarin, to translate on conference calls with the Chinese. Michael never spoke on those calls, not once.

It went silent again. I was about to leave the model in

the in-box on Wanda's desk, but I hesitated. I'd e-mail it instead. Better not to have evidence that I'd been hanging around. Overhearing things that I strongly suspected I wasn't supposed to overhear.

The apartment was dark when I got home. It was early for me, just past eleven, but Julia was already asleep.

I sat on the futon and opened my computer. I found myself typing Michael Casey's name in the search bar. Strangely, it had never occurred to me before, to do this. I didn't even know what I was looking for. Maybe an explanation for what I'd overheard. The creepy feeling that I couldn't shake.

I hit Enter.

The top search results were from Spire's website, Michael's official company biography. Undergrad at South Dakota, wildcatting for oil in West Texas for a year, MBA completed in 1983. He started at Spire in 1986. Michael never said anything about working any-place but Spire. I wondered about that three-year window after his MBA.

I kept clicking through the results. A few pages in, there was a link to an archived article in the *New York Times*. A profile from the business section, dated 1985. There was a grainy photo on the page. I squinted. It was Michael, twenty-odd years earlier.

I scanned through the article. Michael had worked at another hedge fund called Millworth Capital. In the summer of 1985, he made upwards of $400 million for

Millworth, shorting foreign currencies. The profile described his unlikely success: a farm boy, the first in his family to go to college, a rising star on Wall Street at age twenty-six. The reporter asked Michael what he thought he could attribute his success to.

Mr Casey tilts back in his chair, resting his feet on the desk. There are no traces of his former life in his office: no family pictures, no college diploma.

'I don't think there's any one way to answer that question,' he says. 'You could point to any number of things. But I think there was a moment when I got hooked on this. My first big trade. I cleared $50 million in one day. I was twenty-four years old. I wasn't going to look back after that.'

'Evan? Evan? Hello?'

Julia was standing in front of me, hair rumpled and eyes scrunched against the glow of the computer screen. I twitched, my hand slamming the laptop shut. 'Oh,' I said. 'Hi. I didn't hear you get up.'

'I said, what are you doing? Work?'

'Uh, just some e-mails. I'm done now.'

She padded over to the kitchen sink, her bare legs sticking out from beneath her T-shirt. She took a glass from the cabinet, turned on the tap, held her finger in the stream of water, waiting for it to get cold. Mundane gestures I'd seen a hundred times before, but at that moment, they felt too private for me to witness. Part of a separate life. I wanted something from Julia that it felt impossible to ask for. A silence different from the one that had grown between us.

'I'm coming to bed,' I said. She waved a hand to show that she'd heard before disappearing into the darkness of the bedroom.

# Chapter 6

## *Julia*

I looked up from the donor database I was updating to see Eleanor march into Laurie's office. Others maintained a certain deference around Laurie, asking me in a whisper if she was available before approaching her door, but not Eleanor. Not this day, not any day. She slammed the door shut behind her, but her voice vibrated through the wall.

'Laurie, I don't know how you expect me to pull this gala off. Not with this shitty budget. This is pathetic.'

'It's the best we can do. You know things have been tight around here.'

'But this is *ridiculous*. This is less than half our budget from last year. Do you expect me to cook the food myself? There's no way this is going to work.'

This conversation kept repeating itself. Each week, Eleanor secured a few more dollars for the November gala. Then she turned right back around and cajoled Laurie for more. And, strangely, Laurie never lost her patience with Eleanor. It was clear that the crash was creating a strain. Laurie had taken to sighing a lot and rubbing her temple. She grew brittle with the rest of us. But never once did she shout back at Eleanor. It baffled me, but then again, almost everything about Laurie baffled me. I answered her phone and kept her schedule, but I had no insight into what she was thinking. Her remove seemed deliberate. She must have seen me as just one more link in a chain – another assistant, another year. I wondered if I could ever prove I was different. But then what? I didn't want to work there. I didn't want to be Eleanor in five years. Eleanor, who breezed in and out of the office when she felt like it, who threw temper tantrums, who'd barely spoken to me since our lunch over the summer.

In late October, Eleanor declared that she would be leaving town to 'recharge' before the gala. She would be unreachable for the next five days, on some tropical island. The following day, a Thursday, Laurie told me to get Henry Fletcher on the phone. His secretary said he wasn't available, but she could pass along a message. 'I don't want to leave a message,' Laurie yelled from inside her office. 'I'll try him this afternoon.'

He remained unavailable that afternoon, and Friday morning, and Friday afternoon. Laurie swirled around her office, slamming file drawers, throwing out papers, rearranging furniture. I wanted to help – it was distressing to witness – but I wasn't going to put myself directly in her line of fire. She seemed ready to snap at any moment. And as much as I disliked the job, it was still the only job I had.

*

I wonder. Could I see it at the time? My life crystallizing into a new pattern. Evan and I drifting, each of us caught in different currents. Adam and I had grown closer, and I contemplated what I had ever done without him. I was never good at skepticism, at questioning what was happening to me. And besides, nothing had even happened – nothing that couldn't be explained away in innocence. Until one specific night, the weekend at the end of October. When imagination hardened into reality.

Abby called me that Saturday afternoon. 'Come to this party with me,' she said. 'I'm schlepping all the way to Brooklyn. I need a buddy for the subway.'

The party was in the garden-level apartment of a brownstone near Prospect Park, hosted by a girl from college, someone Abby knew better than I did. She and her roommate both worked in publishing. We picked up a bottle of wine on the way over, and when I set it down on the kitchen counter, I saw that someone else had brought the same bottle of wine, down to the identical $8.99 price sticker on the neck.

Tall bookshelves, track lighting, dusty Oriental rugs. It was a nice party. Lively, not too crowded, the conversation earnest and serious. A lot of the parties Abby and I went to that year felt like an ardent imitation of college: twenty-two-year-olds spending their salaries on light beer, blasting hip-hop, puking out the cab door. This pulled in the other direction: people acting older than they really were. It surprised me how rarely those two worlds ever overlapped. There wasn't any middle ground.

'So Jake's coming by,' Abby said as we helped ourselves to the wine. 'Later. Is that weird? I'm not sure he's ever been to Brooklyn before.'

'Wow. So are you –'

'Kind of. I don't know. It's nothing serious yet.'

'But you like him?'

'I like him enough to sleep with him.' She shrugged. But she was blushing a little.

I finished my wine and had another, then another, drifting from conversation to conversation. The night passed easily, without friction. After a while, Jake arrived. I saw Abby kiss him and lead him to the kitchen. I turned back to my companion, who was critiquing a recent article in the *New York Review of Books*. Out of the corner of my eye I saw Jake slip his arm around Abby's waist and draw her in.

*Stop it,* I thought. I had no right to be jealous. In fact, I should have been happy for them. That would be definitive proof of just how meaningless my own encounter with Jake had been.

The drink crashed over me like a wave, stronger than it had been a minute earlier. It was past midnight, and the group I was standing with was gone. The party had thinned, and the music was louder without the muffling of voices. Jake was kissing Abby, pulling back to whisper in her ear, making her laugh. I had to admit he was cute. And Abby looked so happy. He tugged her closer. I could tell they were having great sex, probably twice a day.

And I felt like I was going to be sick. I went outside to the garden and sunk into a dented plastic chair, lowering my head between my knees. Then I noticed another couple in the corner of the patio, snuggled close, sharing a cigarette.

'Fuck,' I said. They looked at me, startled. Couples everywhere, reminding me of what I didn't have. It was horrible. For so many years, I'd been one half of a whole. I knew that the wine was making it worse, but I couldn't help it. All this affection, this electric desire zipping through the air – it made me feel unloved and worthless. I was twenty-two years old, for God's sake. When was the last time someone had kissed me like that?

On Thursday night, two nights earlier, Evan had gotten home just after I'd returned from dinner with Adam. He dropped his briefcase and coat on the floor, went to the kitchen, opened the door to the refrigerator, and stared into the chilly blue light.

'We have nothing to eat,' he said. That was his greeting. 'What did you eat?'

'I, uh, picked up a slice of pizza on the way home.'

He sighed and shut the refrigerator. Then he collapsed on the futon next to me.

'Is everything okay at work? You're home pretty early.'

'Fine. Things are slow this week. Should be back to normal soon.' He stared at his hands, picking at a cuticle. He didn't know what to do, or where to look.

'Okay. Well, I'm going to go to bed.'

Eventually he slid into bed next to me. I switched off my lamp, and we lay there in the darkness. It had been nearly a month since we'd had sex. Evan's leg brushed against mine, and he left it there. My pulse accelerated. A minute later, I rested my fingertips on the back of his hand. He was perfectly still, and then he rolled over, away from me. From his breathing, I could tell he was already asleep.

Maybe that was the power Evan wielded in our relationship. I was so used to his presence that when he pulled away, it left me spinning. I took it for granted, like the subways running regularly or the water coming out of the faucet. Even then, even with everything, Evan gave me what I hadn't yet learned to provide for myself.

──────

Sophomore year, one rainy night in March, Adam and his housemates threw a party. I was insistent that Evan come, which should have been a red flag. I'd gone to plenty of parties without him. Was I trying to protect myself from what awaited? It seems obvious now.

'Jules, seriously. I don't want to go.' Evan was slumped on his couch, playing a video game. 'Just go by yourself. It's not like I'm going to know anyone there. And I'm still beat from last night. And it's pouring.'

'I don't care,' I said. I felt like stamping my feet. He'd been consumed by the hockey season for the previous four months. He needed to care about *me* for a change. 'Evan, *come on*. You said last night that you would.'

'*Fine.*' He tossed aside the controller. 'I don't remember saying that, though.'

Adam was in the foyer when we arrived. A fizz of excitement: I'd never been inside his house before. In the kitchen, I stood where I had a view of the living room and the rest of the party. I hoped that I'd catch Adam again later in the night. The beer had already loosened me. I just wanted to talk to Adam: that was it. Nothing was going to happen.

'Are you an athlete?' one girl was asking Evan.

'I'm on the hockey team.'

'Oh,' I said, thinking of something. 'Oh, I have to tell you guys the funniest thing. So last night –' I looked over at Evan, but he was staring off, not listening. Evan's teammate Sebi had made a fool of himself at the party the previous night, pissing on the crowd next door from an upstairs window. Everyone laughed uproariously at the end of the story. I couldn't help laughing, too. It was funnier in the retelling.

Later, as the group disbanded and I started to wonder where Adam was, Evan grabbed me by the wrist.

'Ow. Jesus.'

'What the hell, Jules? That was embarrassing.'

I rubbed my wrist, though it didn't hurt that much. It was more the surprise. Evan had a look on his face. Not anger – disappointment. Scolding. *What the fuck is wrong with him?* I thought. After months of ignoring me, this was what I get? I snapped at him, then pushed through the living room. The bathroom door was locked. I made my way upstairs instead and found another bathroom door ajar. I locked it behind me, lowered the toilet lid, and sat down, pressing my palms into my closed eyes.

The night before, at the hockey party, Evan left me with his teammates and said he was going to get us another drink. That night they had played the last game of their season. Toward the end of the third period, Evan swooped down the wing and scored the winning goal. The team never got as far as the preseason polls had predicted, but the season ended on a happy note. They piled on Evan, thumping him on the back. He was only a sophomore; there was always next year.

In the living room of the hockey house, I glanced at my watch. He'd been gone for a while. It was late, hours after the Sebi incident, and the party had died down. I made my way into the kitchen, which led to the back porch, where they were keeping the keg. Someone had propped open the back door. A strong breeze swept through the kitchen, making music of the plastic cups scattered across the floor. Outside, the porch light illuminated the keg like a piece of scenery on a stage.

Evan was standing there, talking to a girl I didn't recognize. She wore a low-cut tank top, her blond hair dark at the roots. Trashy. Maybe she went to one of the community colleges near New Haven. Sometimes those girls crashed our parties. She was shivering. Evan removed his sweatshirt and draped it around her shoulders. She pulled it tight and smiled at him. He smiled back. She reached out and touched him on the forearm, and then –

'Evan,' I shouted from inside the kitchen. They both jumped, like they'd been caught at something. 'What are you doing?'

'Hey. Um, Julia,' he said, floundering. 'This is –'

'Are you ready to go? Let's go,' I said, turning on my heel.

Later, while we were lying in bed, he asked me why I was so mad. They had just been talking. She was dating another guy on the team. She had forgotten her jacket. Et cetera. He gave me an opening to explain myself. 'Jules, are you jealous? Is that it? Because –' But I cut him off. 'I'm not *jealous*,' I snapped. 'Of her? Please.'

I opened my eyes. I was in the bathroom in Adam's house, the sound of the party thumping below. Why was everything so difficult? One party, another party, and things kept going wrong between us. What gave Evan the right to be so judgmental, so *disappointed* in me? His teammate was the one who had acted like an idiot, who had broken at least one law. All I had done was repeat what I had witnessed. 'Tell the truth,' Adam liked to say at the magazine. 'The truth always makes for a more interesting story.' I looked in the mirror. Screw it. Maybe I didn't need to care so much about what Evan thought. What did he really know about me?

When I opened the door, there was another girl waiting outside. One of Adam's cooler, older friends. Probably an art or theater major. A messy bun atop her head, willowy limbs, a small tattoo inside her wrist. She winked at me like we were both in the know, using the upstairs bathroom.

'Julia?' Adam was down the hallway, pulling a door closed. His bedroom, I guessed. Probably where the other girl had just come from. 'Is everything okay?'

I wanted to cry, but didn't. 'Yeah. Everything's fine.'

He kept his hand on the doorknob, watching me carefully. I felt like he understood everything I was thinking, everything I yearned for. He had all the answers to all my questions. Adam pushed the door open and gestured at the room behind him. 'You want to come in for a minute?'

---

At the party in Brooklyn, I went back inside, in search of my coat. But when I turned into the hallway to leave, I slammed directly into the one person who could fix this black mood. The person who always managed to find me at exactly the right moments.

'Hey!' Adam said. 'Julia. Are you leaving already?'

'I was thinking about it.'

'Have a drink with me. Come on, I just got here.'

I let Adam lead me back into the kitchen. Abby shrieked when she saw him. They had been friends in college, too — she was friends with just about everyone — but she hadn't seen him since he graduated. 'Where have you been hiding?' she said, hitting him on the shoulder. Adam just winked and slung his arm around me. She raised an eyebrow at me. I shook my head: *just flirting,* nothing more. Abby knew that I had had a little crush on Adam in college, but I never told her what had happened between us that night. We chatted, and they caught up. Adam kept handing me drinks.

Little things. New intimacies. Slipping his hand down my back, pressing his hip against mine. Adam was debating with Jake about some recent development in the Lehman bankruptcy. They kept talking, talking. I couldn't follow the conversation, but it didn't matter. Adam was at my side, and I was certain I was the only thing he was thinking about. He never even bothered to say hello to the girls hosting the party.

After a while, Abby rested her head against Jake's shoulder. 'What do you think – should we get going?' she said. 'We have to get up early tomorrow.'

She said to me and Adam, 'We're meeting his parents for brunch.'

I raised my eyebrows. *We?* Parents? Brunch?

She shook her head to dismiss my implication, but again – that blush. They were a couple. A real couple, no matter what she said.

'Oh, shit,' Jake said. 'I forgot to tell you. My dad canceled. My mom thinks we should wait till he's back. She said maybe in a few weeks.'

Abby's smile wilted. 'Why?'

'Some business meeting, I guess. He's off in the Caribbean for something.'

I coughed, almost choking on my wine. It finally added up. Eleanor's rocketing ascent at the foundation.

Her power over Laurie. Her possessive smile at the sound of Henry's name. *We're very close*. An image of Henry and Eleanor under a dark sky and a tropical moon. Drinking Champagne, sex on smooth white sheets, the ocean crashing against the shore outside their villa. Tall palm trees dramatically lit from below. Each one of them an aphrodisiac to the other.

'Tough life,' Adam said heartily.

'Well,' Abby said, more subdued. 'We should go, anyway. It's late.'

The black mood descended again, magnified by the fact that I was by that point blazingly drunk. I couldn't believe it – *this* was what my life looked like? My best friend was sleeping with my secret ex, whose father was sleeping with my coworker. My boyfriend was ignoring me, in love with his job instead. And I was treading water in a pool of dead-end nothingness. What the hell had happened? When did it all go so wrong?

Adam got us a cab and told the driver to stop at my place first. It was the gentlemanly thing to do, but I knew what it meant. Adam lived alone. If he wanted to sleep with me, he would have brought me back to his place on the Upper West Side. The flirting meant nothing at the end of the night. I wasn't pretty or cool or charming or sophisticated enough. Everyone was moving forward, and I was getting left behind.

I was quiet and sullen, finally too drunk to conceal it. Adam noticed.

'You okay, Jules?'

'I'm *fine*. It's just . . . I don't know. Ugh.'

'What is it?'

'I don't know.'

'You can tell me.'

'God. Adam.' I snapped. 'This sucks. I'm all by myself. Completely alone. Everywhere I go.'

He reached for my hand. 'Don't say that. You have me. I'm right here.'

'I *don't* have you, though. I have this lousy boyfriend who doesn't give two shits about me because he's too busy with this fucking lumber deal.'

'Maybe it'll be over soon,' Adam said carefully. It wasn't the first time I had complained about Evan's devotion to his work. 'It can't last forever.'

'I mean, Jesus, the way he talks about it. It's like the universe revolves around this fucking middle-of-nowhere Canadian lumber company. Pacific WestCorp. It's so *important*. They're gonna make so much *money* off it. They're gonna be rich and famous. You know, I can't remember the last time he even asked me how my day was. How work is. None of it. He's an asshole. He doesn't think about anyone but himself.'

I was ranting, but I couldn't help myself. Abby and Jake, Henry and Eleanor. I couldn't complain about any of them, so my anger funneled toward Evan instead. *'WestCorp Timber is gonna make Spire more money than any deal on Wall Street.'* I imitated Evan's voice in a snide tone. *'People's heads are gonna turn.* Him and Michael Casey, at the top of the fucking world. Fuck all of it.'

The lights of Manhattan glittered up ahead. We were zooming across the bridge, the East River rippling below like black velvet.

'It's disgusting,' I added. The torrent wouldn't stop. 'They're so fucking arrogant. He's saying this trade is foolproof. It's like they didn't even notice what's been happening. How fucked up everything is. How screwed the rest of us are.'

Adam was silent, probably dreading the rest of the ride. Even through my drunken haze, I saw what an idiot I was, complaining about my boyfriend, like *that* was a turn-on. Great. He was never going to call me again.

But then he slid close and put his arm around my waist. I closed my eyes and turned my face away, trying not to cry. The cab accelerated into a curve on the FDR, pulling me into the corner. 'Jules,' he said softly. 'Jules, it's okay.' Adam took my chin in his hand and turned my face toward him, and then he kissed me.

We broke away a moment later, pausing. Then we kept going. He slid his hand under my shirt, and I felt him go hard through his jeans. He kissed my neck, ran his fingers through my hair. The solid heft of his body, the pressure of affection – I'd been missing this for so long. The feeling of someone else's hands showing me what to do next. My body had almost forgotten how to do this.

Too soon, the cab had stopped. 'Miss?' the driver said.

'I –' I stopped, looked at Adam. Both of us were breathing hard.

He glanced down at his lap. 'You should go in, Jules. It's late.'

'I don't have to. You know.'

'Let's just say goodnight for now. I'll call you in the morning, okay? I promise.'

He kissed me good-bye, less urgent and more tender. Then he reached across the seat and opened the door. I watched the cab pull away, heading west toward the park. I shivered and pulled my coat tighter around me.

When I lay in bed that night, next to an already sleeping Evan, I was aware of something. After Jake Fletcher, I had been racked with guilt. It had happened the summer before freshman year of college, while we were on Nantucket with our families. Rob was my boyfriend at the time. I didn't have to face him for another two weeks afterward, which gave me time to collect myself, to replay the memory – Jake and I, high and drunk, sneaking down to the nighttime beach, him tugging down my shorts, me not wanting him to stop, so helpless in the face of his attention – over and over and over, until eventually it became something that happened to a different version of me. I decided, on the ferry ride home, letting the wind tangle my hair and the salt spray sting my eyes, that I didn't have to tell Rob. It was a stupid mistake, but it was just sex. As soon as it was over, when Jake rolled away from me and I was aware again of the cold sand sticking to the back of my legs, I realized that it was never going to happen again. The guilt formed a high wall in my mind, and the memory lived behind it, drying and shriveling with age. Sometimes I almost managed to forget it entirely.

But this, with Adam. The feeling that washed over me as I lay there next to Evan — it wasn't guilt. It was more like a beginning than an ending. A book cracked open to the very first page. How could I feel guilty about something that was so clearly meant to happen?

# PART II

# CHAPTER 7

## *Evan*

In mid-November, Michael stopped by my desk.

'You're coming with me and the rest of the team to the conference in Vegas. The flight is at five. Go home and get your stuff and take a car to the airport, terminal four. Travel is e-mailing your ticket now.'

I glanced at my watch – 2:34 p.m. – and started shoving things into my bag. 'So I'll see you –' I started to say to Roger, but he had his headphones in and refused to meet my eyes. Uptown, I packed as fast as I could, then sprinted down the stairs to the waiting town car. I called Julia from the car and told her I wouldn't be able to make dinner – it was her birthday that night, but she seemed to understand, which was a relief. They were calling my name on the PA when I ran up to the gate.

'Right over there, Mr Peck,' a chirpy flight attendant said, pointing at the remaining empty seat in the business-class cabin, next to Roger.

'Too bad,' Roger said without looking up from his

BlackBerry. 'Thought this train was going to leave the station without you.'

'Sorry to disappoint you.'

'Sir?' the flight attendant said, offering a tray with a flute of Champagne. 'Just let me know if I can get you anything else. We'll be taking off shortly.'

The flight attendant was cute and perky and available, exactly Roger's type, and I expected him to make some crack about it. But he kept his eyes locked on his phone, his mouth shut. Roger had been bragging about this for weeks. Spire was sending a small team to a global investing conference in Las Vegas, and Steve, the head of our macro group, had been so impressed with Roger's work that he invited him along, too. A first-year analyst had never gone to one of these conferences before. You didn't get to jump the line like this, not unless you were exceptional. My stomach had churned at the thought. Well, I was working on a deal that would dwarf a trip to Vegas soon enough. Let Roger brag all he wanted.

But there I was. Ruining Roger's week, to boot. I counted six people from Spire, scattered through the cabin: Steve, Brad, and Chuck, all from Spire's macro group, plus Roger, Michael, and myself. This had nothing to do with my work, but I supposed that Michael would fill me in eventually. I finished my Champagne, settled in, and closed my eyes. Business class. I could get used to this.

*

A hand on my shoulder shook me awake, and Brad's face came into focus. I'd only spoken to him in passing before. He was Korean American, in his thirties, had a PhD in applied mathematics from MIT, a mind like a thousand-horsepower engine. He'd made the company an enormous amount of money over the years.

'So here's the deal,' Brad said, addressing me and Roger while he scanned his phone screen. 'Travel tried to get new rooms, but the hotel is sold out because of the conference. So Evan, you're going to be in Roger's room.'

'The hell?' Roger snarled. 'Are you serious?'

'Suck it up, sweetheart. Chuck and I have to share a suite, too. Michael took Steve's suite, and Steve is taking mine.'

'There better be separate beds,' Roger said. When Brad left, Roger finally snapped. 'What the fuck, Peck? Why are you even here?'

'I don't know. You heard it. Michael only told me a few hours ago.'

Roger looked like he wanted to punch me in the face. The plane's engines hummed in the background. 'Whatever it is y'all are up to,' he said, clenching his fists on his armrests, 'you sure have a way of pissing other people off.'

---

More than a month earlier, as the market panic was reaching its climax, I'd put the final touches on the WestCorp deal. The numbers were dazzling. Michael had said it right: this was a check just waiting to be cashed. Early

153

one October morning, after working straight through the night, I was finally done. The very last piece was in place. This was the deal that would permanently cement Spire's dominance, during the most volatile moment of our lifetime – and I was right in the middle of it. I left the folder on Michael's chair and went for a walk in the cool dawn, stopping at a bench in an empty Times Square with a coffee and Danish in hand, watching the city wake, the taxis and pedestrians flowing up and down the streets, the conclusion vibrating through me like a note struck on a piano.

Back in the office that morning, I shaved and changed into the spare shirt I kept in my desk drawer. I sat, calmly, waiting for the call from Michael. But morning passed, then afternoon, without a word from him. I went past his office around 8:00 p.m., but his door was closed.

Nothing the following day, either. Or the day after that. When I couldn't stand it any longer, I went by his office. He ignored me while I hovered in the doorway. I cleared my throat. 'Michael. Just checking – what's the latest on the WestCorp deal?'

That got his attention. He turned to look at me.

'Something's come up,' he said. 'It's on hold until I iron out a few more details.'

'Oh. Okay. So –'

'So I'll let you know.' He turned back to his computer.

Panic rose as I walked back to my desk. What did he mean? Iron *what* out? But there had been a finality in his tone. I was just a low-level analyst, after all. He didn't owe me any explanation. These kinds of things happened. Deals were called off all the time, for all sorts of reasons.

But it made me feel sick, physically sick, the thought of so many days and nights disappearing with nothing to show for it. Who was I? What was I doing there? I'd always had an answer before. I was a boy from British Columbia. A student. A hockey player, most of all. When graduation erased that, I found a new scaffolding. I was an analyst at Spire Management; that was the life I was building for myself. Everything else that was fading into the background – Julia, my friends – was made bearable by this. The sureness of my work and the nearness of success. Without that, I started to come loose.

My solution: I'd keep busy, so busy I wouldn't have time to think. I jumped at every assignment, tried to fill the hours, insurance against the worst outcome. Roger and the other analysts must have sensed the change – my constant volunteering, joining them for lunch when before I'd been too busy. Julia could sense it, too. She was cooler and quieter than ever in the moments we overlapped at home. She sat there looking at me, but her mind was somewhere else. It was like she could tell how desperately I was faking my way through it, and it disgusted her.

Until just a few days before the trip to Las Vegas, when something had changed. I got home early and found Julia standing at the stove. Stirring a pot, flipping through a magazine, one bare foot lifted to scratch the back of her calf. 'It smells amazing,' I said. When she turned, it was the old Julia who was looking at me: the spill of blond hair over her shoulder, her eyes crinkled at the corners from her smile. 'There'll be enough for both of us,' she offered. After we ate, I led her into the bedroom. The sex was good, not the best ever, but it was what I had needed: the two of us, finally in the same place again. It was so sad that this tiny moment of tenderness was even worth remarking on.

The next night, I stopped by McGuigan's with the guys after work. Just for a drink, one drink. It was a weeknight, and I wanted to get home early again. To get things back on track with Julia. I sat at the bar, waiting for Maria. I was going to end this flirtation, or whatever it was, before it went any further. I'd slip in a mention of *my girlfriend,* which would do the trick. A clean break.

Maria came over and drew a pint of Guinness without needing to ask. Part of me wished that we'd gotten our chance – that I'd made a move one of those late nights, saying good-bye on the sidewalk outside the bar, a one-time slip that could be forgiven. I sipped my beer, feeling nostalgic. I'd finish the drink before I said anything.

Another man came into the bar and sat a few stools down, a tanned guy in a leather jacket. Maria said something to him, then poured him a generous whiskey. I lifted my glass to get her attention. She came back over and placed another pint of Guinness on the bar, then said,

'This is it for me tonight. Cathy'll take care of your tab.'

'Where are you going? Actually, I wanted to talk to you about –'

'I'm off early,' she said. 'I've got plans.'

A minute later, she emerged from the back with her coat on. The guy in the leather jacket stood and gestured at her to go ahead. They passed me on their way out, and as an afterthought, Maria turned on her heel.

'Oops. I should introduce you. Evan, this is Wyeth. Wyeth, Evan.'

I was used to towering over other people, but Wyeth was the same height as me. 'Hey. Maria's favorite customer,' I said, extending a hand and forcing a smile.

'Hey. Maria's boyfriend,' he said.

Maria smiled, then tugged on Wyeth's sleeve. 'See you later, Evan,' she called over her shoulder. Through the window, I watched them pause on the sidewalk. Maria stood on her toes and kissed him, for a long time.

I sat back down, disoriented. Cathy, the other bartender, came over a few minutes later. 'Another?' she said, pointing at my empty pint glass. I shook my head. 'I'll have a Scotch. Straight up.' The other analysts were going out to a club in the Meatpacking District where Roger knew the promoter, and I went along. We got a table and ordered bottle service. A group of lithe, glittery women floated toward us. I poured myself a vodka on the rocks, one after another. This feeling could only be scoured out by something strong. Music – deep house with a thumping beat – vibrated through every pore. After a while I looked up and realized a petite Asian girl was sitting on my lap. She leaned in and said something inaudible. *'What?'* I shouted back, over the music. She leaned in again and this time licked the edge of my earlobe, and finally – finally – my mind went empty. We wound up pressed against a wall at the edge of the room. Her tongue in my mouth, her tiny body, my hands sliding up her sequined miniskirt, it was all I was aware of. I wanted this nameless girl more than anything I'd wanted before. I'd fuck her right there in public if I had to.

The next day, I got up from my desk several times to go retch in the bathroom. *You asshole,* I thought, staring at my sweaty and sallow reflection under the fluorescent lights. I'd managed to tear myself away from the girl and get a cab before any of my coworkers noticed. I passed out on the futon at home. At an early morning hour, I dragged myself to the sink for a glass of water and took a scalding shower. Eventually I crawled into bed next to Julia, my hair wet, feeling like a teenager sneaking in after curfew.

Two black town cars were waiting for us at McCarran. They whisked us straight to the expensive steak-and-red-wine restaurant in the hotel, our luggage sent up to our rooms without us. A private room in the back of the restaurant was walled in by ceiling-high racks of wine bottles. Chuck and Brad and Roger started getting drunk and rowdy. Steve was supervising in a bemused way, and I was just trying to roll with it. I drank my wine slowly, still feeling my bender from a few days earlier. Michael was distracted, answering e-mails, stepping out to take calls. When he left the room to take his third call of the night, Chuck rolled his eyes and said, 'Why the hell is he even here?'

Roger shot me an accusatory look.

'I mean,' Chuck continued, looking at Steve for an answer, 'doesn't he have better things to be doing? Like running the company?'

Steve shrugged. 'He's the boss. He can do what he wants.'

'Probably just wants to get laid,' Brad said sullenly. Chuck hooted in laughter, and Roger joined in. Chuck was slightly older, had a fiancée, owned rather than rented, but in every other way, he and Roger were practically twins. They were, of course, hitting it off.

Michael walked back in, eyes still glued to his screen. In that moment, between songs on the restaurant speakers, the clicking of Michael's BlackBerry keys was the only sound to be heard. Chuck, in a fit of flushed boldness, balled up his napkin and lobbed it across the table at Michael's shoulder.

Michael looked up, as surprised as the rest of us.

'Hey, Michael,' Chuck said. 'I know you're the CEO, but you're in Vegas, man. Drink up. We're going out tonight.'

Michael stared at him. 'What did you say?'

'I said, "Drink up."'

Silence. Then Michael broke out in a smug grin. 'You're right,' he said finally. 'Someone get me a real drink.'

Chuck hooted again, calling for the waitress to bring a bottle of their best Scotch, and I relaxed a little. Michael drank a double in one smooth swig, then another after that. A limo was idling outside, waiting to take us to a high-end nightclub where Chuck had reserved a table. In the limo, I sat next to Michael, who kept refilling my glass and clapping me on the knee when I downed my Scotch straight, in one macho gulp.

Liquid courage helped. I was careful to keep my tone light, not ruining the mood. 'Michael,' I said. 'I just wanted to ask, before everything starts tomorrow – what's, uh, what's the agenda for this weekend?'

'Oh, you know. Keynotes and panels, networking, the usual. Most of it will be interminably dull. These things always are.'

'Right. So I've heard.' I nodded. 'But the focus is on global macro, isn't it? I'm just wondering if there's any-thing you wanted me to – or what the angle . . . or I guess takeaway, you could call it –'

Michael clapped me on the knee again, refilling my glass. 'Evan, don't worry. You're asking why I invited you, aren't you? Just watch and listen, and you'll see. You could learn a lot these next few days.'

We pulled up at the entrance of another hotel-casino

monolith. Chuck led the way down the long, plushly carpeted hallway toward the club. The Scotch in the limo had been too much for me. The night began to blur and spin when we entered the club. The whole room seemed to rattle from the collective frenzy: drinking, dancing, snorting, vibrating. Women in thongs and pasties shimmied on platforms around the dance floor. High up in his booth, the DJ lifted his arms, and the crowd responded with a deafening roar. Smoke and confetti poured from the ceiling. Our waitress was wearing a tight scoop-neck minidress that displayed her cleavage, which bounced vigorously whenever she mixed a drink in the cocktail shaker. I had shot after shot handed to me. I was drunker than I'd been in months, drunker even than a few nights ago in Meatpacking. I had long slipped past the point of enjoyment. What time was it? Would this night ever end? Nothing seemed to exist except for this club, the gyrations of the people around me. A slow-motion orgy: Michael getting closer and closer to a blond woman on the banquette, Chuck kissing a woman — then two at once — sitting on his lap. Steve had turned in earlier, his wedding ring glinting in the strobe lights. Brad had his hand at the small of our waitress's back, his eyes traveling toward her chest. Roger was off somewhere else.

Our limo driver was, miraculously, still outside when I got up to leave. I pulled the hotel-room key card out of my pocket, where the room number had been written on the card's paper envelope: 3605. Back in the hotel, I stumbled toward the elevator bank and leaned my forehead against the cool marble wall while I waited. It felt so good. I could have fallen asleep there. I found myself wandering down a long hallway, red carpets and golden wallpaper. Such a long hallway. How had I gotten there? I studied the paper envelope again: 3605. I looked up, and there I was – our room at last.

I swiped my card, and the light turned green, but the door banged abruptly and wouldn't open more than an inch. I pulled the door closed and tried again. The light turned green, and I pushed the door open, but again it banged up against something. I squinted, trying to right my vision, and saw that the security flip bar had been latched into place.

I propped the door open with my foot and shouted through the opening, 'Roger. Roger! Come on, it's me.'

Silence at first, and then came the sounds of female giggling. 'Ocupado, amigo,' Roger said from within the room.

The door closed with a bang, and I slumped against the wall, my legs splayed out across the floor. Sexiled. I needed some kind of plan. Focus. I closed my eyes. My head jerked up – had I fallen asleep? – and I slapped my forehead several times. I hated being this drunk. I couldn't stay out in the hallway. Everyone from Spire was staying on this floor. I couldn't let them see me like this. No way.

Back at the elevator bank, I pushed the Down button. I'd explain myself at the front desk. Maybe they'd had a cancellation. Or I'd take a cab to one of the motels I'd seen between the airport and the Strip. They had to have something, a bed where I could sleep for a few hours before morning came.

A small ding sounded as the car arrived. I kept my eyes down and didn't see the dark-suited figure striding out until we nearly collided.

'Evan? Whoa, what are you doing?'

It was Chuck, looking rumpled and sweaty but in better shape than I was, and thoroughly pleased with how the night had gone.

'Yeah. Hi – hey, Chuck. How are you?'

'How are *you*? What, you didn't get enough? Going back out for more?'

'No.' I shook my head with effort. 'I'm locked out. Roger is – he has . . . company.'

Chuck laughed. 'Shit. Well, come on, you can crash in our room for now. Roger's gonna be done soon. Trust me, he's paying her by the hour.'

I followed Chuck to his suite at the other end of the hallway. Even through my blurring vision, I could see that it was enormous. Bigger than any New York apartment I'd ever seen. Steps led down to a sunken living room with floor-to-ceiling windows. The skyline sparkled against the desert night. I could make out a bar on one side of the living room and a huge soaking tub on the other. A spiral staircase, half hidden in the darkness, twisted up to a second floor.

'Nice, huh?' Chuck said, his voice echoing in the room. 'Would've had the place to myself, too. The beds are spoken for, but I think there's a foldout in that corner near the kitchen. Brad's still out. He'll be back soon.'

Chuck's footsteps retreated up the spiral stairs. I found the bathroom, flipped on the light, and hurled the contents of my stomach into the toilet. I paused, gulping for air, then puked again. After the nausea receded, I splashed water on my face and rinsed my mouth. I felt better. More in control. I'd sleep a little, get back to my room, be fine in the morning. Hungover, but fine.

Something woke me. The sound of the air-conditioning turning on or off. I'd passed out on the couch without bothering to unfold it. I was shivering, and I had a kink in my neck.

It was tempting to stay there, to close my eyes and let the drunken fog tug me back under. I knew I ought to get up, go back to my room, get some real sleep. In just a few minutes. My mind swam with the soothing hum of the AC.

Then, how much later I didn't know, there was the sound of laughter and high heels on the marble floor. The high-pitched, breathy voice of a woman.

The lights went on. Suddenly I was wide awake, my heart hammering and blood rushing to my head. Brad was back, with company. I felt a preemptive embarrassment at being discovered here.

There were more than two voices. One woman and another. Brad muttering something. Then:

'I'm going to have a drink. Ladies?' Michael.

The two women chorused a yes.

The sound of liquid splashing into glasses, bodies sinking into leather sofas. I turned onto my stomach and peered over the arm of the couch. My view was mostly obscured by the dining table and the oak-paneled bar. They hadn't seen me, and the window for making myself known without humiliation was closing rapidly. No, I realized. It had closed already.

Brad was on one couch, Michael and the two women on another. One woman, the blond from the club, was hunched over the glass-topped coffee table. When she sat up, she handed a rolled-up dollar bill to Michael.

'This is good shit, Brad,' Michael said, wiping the coke from his nose.

Brad was silent. It looked like he was reading something on his phone.

'So,' Michael said. 'What do you ladies think of my friend here?'

The second woman – a redhead – giggled. 'I think he's handsome.'

'I think *you're* handsome,' the blond purred, nestling up to Michael.

'I think you have better taste than your friend.' He ran his hand up her bare arm. I grimaced. She was at least thirty years younger than he was.

The redhead stood up, dress slipped off her shoulder to expose a lacy black bra, and went to the other couch. She snuggled up to Brad, but Brad just kept his eyes on his phone.

'So what do you guys do?' one of the women asked. 'You must be big shots with a room like this.'

'You should see my room, honey. We'll take a field trip later.'

'We're in finance,' Brad said abruptly. 'Hedge funds.'

Silence, then one ventured, 'Hedge funds. What does that mean?'

'It's a way of investing designed to mitigate risk,' Brad said, alert again. 'Hedging your bets. At any given point in time, we're betting on a number of different scenarios, so no matter which way the market goes, we're protected. So an example would be – if I met a woman out at a club, but I wasn't sure how she felt about me, maybe I'd bring her friend along, too. See? I've hedged my bets. In case one says no, I have a backup.'

Michael snorted. 'Brad's a nerd, in case you couldn't tell. Don't get him started. But this is boring. Let's talk about something else.'

'Actually.' Brad's voice was rising. 'Actually, I don't think it's boring at all. It's interesting, in fact. I was going through the books this week, and there was some *fascinating* stuff in there.'

'Not now. We have company.' Michael slid his hand up the blond's skirt and kissed her neck. She was giggling and blushing. Her friend attempted the same with Brad, but he pushed her away impatiently.

'I think we do, Michael. I think we want to talk about this right now. We can do it alone, or we can do it in front of these two. Up to you.'

Michael laughed. 'Ladies, I'm sorry. I apologize for him. No manners at all.' He tucked several crisp-looking bills into the blond's dress. 'Some other time.'

The high heels obediently clacked their way back across the marble foyer, and the doors opened and closed a moment later. Michael turned to Brad.

'You mind telling me what the fuck that was about?'

'I need to talk to you about this, Michael. Right now. We have a big problem on our hands.'

'What? For God's sake, what is it?'

Brad took a deep breath. 'I was looking at the books, getting ready for the conference. I noticed something wasn't lining up. So I went deeper into the numbers, and I saw we have a lot of exposure – a *lot* of exposure – in one particular area. Which I'd heard nothing about. The lumber markets.'

'And?'

'Do you know about this? All the money we have tied up in lumber futures?'

'Of course I know about it. I'm running this company. It's my deal.'

'Well, then explain it to me. Because I'm sure as hell not seeing it. The housing market is the worst it's ever been. And yet we're betting that the demand for lumber is going to go *up?* For there to be massive, imminent *growth?*'

'Correct.'

'What the hell, Michael?' Brad stood up and started pacing. 'This isn't some murky situation where we don't know what the economy is going to look like next year. We *do* know. No one in their right mind is going to be building.'

'In North America, maybe. But before you get any more worked up, Brad, I suggest you look at the bigger picture. We're not betting on there being demand here.'

'Where, then?'

'China.'

'*China?* Are you serious? We have no idea what the Chinese are going to do *tomorrow,* let alone next year. Since when do we make predictions about their market with *any* kind of confidence?'

Michael chuckled. 'Brad. Are you sure this isn't some kind of personal animosity? I know the Koreans aren't big fans of the Chinese, but –'

'Stop. Just stop. Does Kleinman know about this?'

'It doesn't matter. Kleinman put me in charge, and frankly it would look bad for him to be overseeing every little deal while he's in Washington.'

'Every *little* deal? Michael, are you even listening? Our exposure on this is *massive*. If it goes the wrong way, we are totally fucked.'

'You're getting hysterical about something that's going to make us a lot of money. Will you listen for a minute, *please?*'

Brad stood in place, quivering with anger. He seemed on the verge of shouting, but he clamped his mouth shut and crossed his arms over his chest.

'Thank you. Sit down, too. You're acting like a lunatic. We've been working on this position for a long time. Months and months. Demand from the Chinese market for North American lumber has already gone up this year. Every single one of our predictions has played out, and I guarantee you that demand is going to continue to skyrocket in 2009. Our calls on WestCorp are going to make you a very rich man.'

My mind was racing. So the deal wasn't dead. Not at all. It was very much alive.

'What I don't get,' Brad said, 'what I don't understand, Michael, is that if this bet is such a sure thing, why isn't everyone else all over this? We don't specialize in this. There are a dozen shops that know lumber better than we do.'

'Because it's impossible to make any real money selling anything to the Chinese, that's why. You know that. The tariffs and taxes eat into your profits like a parasite. It's byzantine. The only way to make money is to find your way through that system.'

Brad started pacing again. Michael sat back on the couch calmly, waiting.

Brad wheeled around to look at Michael. 'Your trip to China in August. For the Olympics, right? Did you go to a single event? Or was that all just a cover?'

'Of course I did. Swimming, rowing, whatever. Let me tell you, you meet all sorts of people at the Olympics. All sorts of politicians and government flunkies who are just so *eager* to rub shoulders with us Americans. The people in that country love us. They finally got a taste of capitalism, and now they can't get enough. They know how much better things are over here. They'll do just about anything to catch up.'

'Jesus Christ. Are we talking bribery, Michael? Did you bribe the fucking Chinese *government?*'

On the plane ride that day, we had encountered a particularly nasty bout of turbulence. I gripped the armrests, my jaw clenched. I *hated* turbulence. I kept counting to ten, over and over, waiting for the plane to steady again. Surely it would stop when I got to ten. That's exactly how I felt at that moment.

'Give me a little credit,' Michael said. But before I could exhale, he continued. 'Bribery. It's such an unsubtle word. You can wipe that sneer off your face. I didn't *bribe* the Chinese government. We worked out an arrangement that was mutually beneficial.'

'What arrangement?'

'Sit down. You're making yourself all agitated.'

'*What* arrangement, Michael?'

'The appropriate Chinese authorities are now inclined to look favorably upon lumber imports from certain Canadian companies. Those imports won't be subject to the usual taxes and tariffs. When WestCorp sells their lumber to Chinese buyers, they'll keep one hundred percent of the revenue.'

'And what are they getting in return?'

Michael sighed. He seemed bored by the conversation. 'WestCorp wanted the Chinese to drop the trade barriers.

The Chinese wanted a few favors that some highly placed WestCorp executives were, luckily, able to grant.'

'*What favors?*'

'Like I said. The Chinese love us. They love our lives. They love North America. They want to come here, to live here, to buy homes here – well, not *here* here, not Las Vegas, this place is a hellhole. But Vancouver? Toronto? That's a different story. These businessmen and bureaucrats, now they've got money to spare, but the one thing they still can't buy is a normal life. They want their kids to be like ours. To go to Ivy League schools. To have good careers. They need visas. And Canadian immigration moves like molasses. WestCorp was able to help them out. Speed things up through back channels. They have something we want. We have something they want. It's really not so complicated.'

'And you went to Beijing to make this happen. You decided to put the entire company at risk for this deal. I can't *believe* this.'

'Yes, I did. And I would do it again. I don't need to tell you how dismal things are. How pathetic our returns are this year. How much worse it's going to get. Do you really want to go back to New York and tell half the company that they're going to lose their jobs? China is booming. They need lumber, and the Canadians have a glut they need to unload. We're just providing liquidity. We're making a market. We applied a little pressure to make it happen, but it's happening, and it's working.'

Brad was silent for a long time.

'You're not going to be able to keep this quiet much longer, Michael,' he said at last. 'Pretty soon someone else is going to notice it, too, someone besides me, and they'll start asking questions.'

'Maybe. But what they'll notice is how much money we're making. And what they'll ask is why they didn't think of this earlier. Does anyone really care how you get from point A to point B? Did you hear a single complaint from a single banker cashing his checks during the last five years? And we're not stupid. We've been discreet for a reason. When people finally notice, the proof will be there. The profits will be there. I'm not going to apologize for doing my job.'

'You keep saying "we." Who is we?'

'Me and Peck, the analyst. That's it. A few people have pitched in occasionally, but they never really knew what they were working on.'

'And does Peck know about the arrangement you have going?'

I closed my eyes and felt an insane rage – all of it directed at Roger. Most of me realized that this was ridiculous. Roger was the least of my concerns. But were it not for him, I would have been asleep and blissfully ignorant. Yes, I'd had my suspicions along the way. The trip to China. The overheard phone call. But I'd decided, a while earlier, to trust that Michael had a plan. He was the boss. He wasn't going to do anything *illegal*. I kept my head down and did my job. It had worked, up until that moment.

'He knows I went to China,' Michael said. 'He doesn't know what I did there. I picked him for a reason. He keeps things to himself. And he's ambitious, too. He wants it to succeed. I can tell. He's perfect for this.'

'Michael, come on. He's – what? – twenty-three years old? These analysts go out drinking every night. They can't keep a secret.'

'He's different. And we have an insurance policy on him.'

'How?'

'He's Canadian. Which the WestCorp guys loved, by the way. But his visa is contingent on his remaining in our employ. If he puts this deal in jeopardy, we'll be talking layoffs. Visas don't come cheap. He'd be the first to go. So it would behoove him to keep his mouth shut.'

I could make out a green pinprick of light from the smoke detector on the ceiling above me. The rage had turned into panic. A stinging rash spread across my chest, down my arms, and under my shirt. Breathe, I reminded myself. Breathe.

'Fucking hell, Michael. This is your mess. Okay? I don't want anything to do with it. And I'd like you to leave now, if you don't *mind*.'

'You're the one who brought this up,' Michael said, standing from the couch, tugging his cuffs straight. 'I didn't ask you to get involved. And Kleinman didn't ask you to be his watchdog. I'm going to bed.' The door opened, there was a pause, and Michael said: 'And I hope you don't have trouble sleeping, because I certainly won't.'

*

'All right, Peck?'

Chuck cuffed me hard on the back. We were at the breakfast buffet outside the conference room, where the day's first panel was about to begin. Chuck popped an enormous strawberry into his mouth and winked.

When I finally returned to my room, I'd lain in bed for the next three hours, jittery and unable to sleep, while Roger snored loudly on the other bed. I'd taken a long shower, had already drunk several cups of coffee, but it didn't help. My mind was like a helium balloon. I tried to concentrate on the men on stage who were holding forth on the euro. A glossy pamphlet promised several more panels like this one before the day was out. The bland normalcy of it contradicted everything that had happened the previous night.

The conference broke for lunch around noon. On my way out, I felt a hand grab my elbow.

'I need you to do something for me,' Michael said.

Did he know? But how would he know? I followed him out of the conference center, back to the hotel elevators. Up in Michael's suite, I had to shield my eyes from the sun, blasting in full strength through the wide windows.

Michael disappeared around the corner. This room was even bigger than Chuck and Brad's. Plush cream carpeting, a dazzling glass chandelier, an urn on the hall table overflowing with tropical vines and flowers. Michael returned holding a slim leather briefcase. Black, brand new, with a small combination lock built into the top. He handed it to me. It was surprisingly light.

'I want you to walk this over to the Venetian,' he said. 'Bring this to a Mr Wenjian Chan. He's a guest there. Walk, don't take a cab. It's important that you hand it to Chan directly. Not to the concierge. Tell him you're there on my behalf. Okay?'

What had I been thinking, trusting Michael all this time? Of course he didn't care about me. He didn't give a shit.

'It's a short walk,' Michael said. 'You'll be back in time for the next panel.'

He turned and disappeared around the corner. I stood there, unsure what to do. I wanted to shout after him, tell him that I knew. Drop the briefcase and walk away forever. But I'd never do that. It must have been why Michael picked me. He saw it from the start – from the very first time I walked into his office. I wasn't brave. I never was. Obeying orders was just about the only thing I knew how to do.

At the Venetian, a young Asian girl opened the door. She inclined her head and gestured me inside. She spoke in Mandarin but stopped when she saw the look on my face.

'Michael Casey?'

'No. No, I'm Evan Peck. I work with Michael.'

'Ah. Mr Peck. My mistake. Please, come this way.' Her English was smooth and flawless, with no more of an accent than mine. She had a round and dewy face, and couldn't be more than a teenager.

I followed her down a hallway to a large sitting room.

An older man with silver hair gazed steadily at the view of the desert through the window, indifferent to the luxury of the suite, to the Champagne chilling on ice, to the mirrored walls. He turned toward me.

'Michael Casey?' He had a thick accent.

I shook my head. My shirt, soaked with sweat from the walk under the scorching noonday sun, started to chill in the air-conditioning. The girl cut in, in rapid Mandarin. The man kept his eyes on me while they spoke, then he smiled. The girl turned back to me with a respectful tilt of her head. 'This is my father, Wenjian Chan. He was expecting to speak to Mr Casey. He has asked me to stay and translate.' She paused, waiting for me to nod. I did.

'Thank you,' she continued. 'Forgive our urgency, but he asks whether he may please have the briefcase you are delivering on behalf of Mr Casey now.'

She took it from me and laid it gently on the coffee table. Her father put on reading glasses and spun the combination lock. It opened with a pop. Chan removed a slim manila folder and scanned each page in the folder carefully. Several minutes later, Chan looked up and spoke to his daughter. It was clear from his tone that he was satisfied.

The girl smiled at me. 'Thank you. My father is very pleased with this. Please convey our gratitude to Mr Casey.' She held out her arm and started to lead me to the door when Chan interrupted, barking at her.

She stiffened and turned red, then shook her head at her father. Chan was pointing at me, his voice almost at a shout.

She started speaking, but he cut her off, insistent. My heart started thudding like a muscle gone loose. The daughter drew a deep breath, glancing sideways at her father.

'My father is very pleased with the help you have offered to us. And now that you have helped us with these papers' – she was so quiet I could barely hear – 'he wonders if you might offer us help in the future, too.'

'I'm sorry?' I said. Chan was chattering excitedly. My mouth had gone dry. Michael hadn't said anything about this.

She turned a deeper shade of red. 'I'll be applying to college next fall, here in America. My father is aware that you might have useful connections. You went to Yale, yes? You know many people there?' She took another breath and added, 'He says that he would like to – as you say – keep in touch.'


The words echoed through my head. *Keep in touch.* I began walking back to the hotel, then I broke into a run, sweat dripping down my forehead and into my eyes. I had to talk to Michael. So they knew where I'd gone to college. What else did they know about me? Just exactly how far did this thing go? What were they expecting from me?

But at the conference, Michael was nowhere in sight. I ducked into a corner and dialed his number. It went directly to voice mail. I sent a frantic e-mail. I tried calling again, but his phone remained off. I refreshed my e-mail. Nothing.

The afternoon panel was about to begin, and the others were drifting back into the ballroom. Chuck waved me over. I was the last one to file into our row and wound up sitting next to Roger. He didn't seem affected by the night before. Bright-eyed, cleanly shaved, popping a stick of gum. His collar crisp and perfectly white. He raised an eyebrow, taking me in. 'You look like shit,' he said.

The panel was about to begin. There was an empty seat in the middle of the row, where Michael was supposed to be. I craned my neck, scanning the entrances to the ballroom. I had a sudden, dizzying fear.

'Oh,' Roger said. 'Who are you looking for? Michael, your boyfriend? He had to leave. Just went to the airport. He's flying back to New York right now.'

# CHAPTER 8

## *Julia*

I was standing in our tiny kitchen, humming to myself, stirring a pot of pasta and a bubbling skillet of sauce. It was Adam's recipe. He was always giving me things like this – scraps of knowledge, bits of adulthood. I wanted to make it just so I could tell him later that I'd done it.

I heard the door open, then the jangling of keys and the thunk of a briefcase dropped to the floor. 'What's this?' Evan said. He was home earlier than usual. I don't think he'd ever seen me use the stove before. 'Are you making dinner?'

He looked so disbelieving that I smiled. 'Pasta. There'll be enough for both of us.'

'It smells amazing.' He hovered a few inches away. A year earlier, he would have slipped his arms around my waist. 'I'm starving.'

We ate together on the futon. When I finished my pasta and looked up, Evan was watching me. He took my hand and pulled me to my feet. I let myself follow him.

What I felt for Adam was spilling over into the rest of my life, like some blissful pharmaceutical. When Evan was on top of me, I stared at the ceiling. I didn't want to have sex with him, but I also didn't mind. I felt easy and calm about it.

After, as Evan was catching his breath, he turned to me.

'It's your birthday on Thursday,' he said.

'Yup.'

'We should go out.'

I'd been counting on Evan having to work, leaving me free to do something with Adam instead. 'Oh. Okay,' I said.

'Unless you already have plans?'

'No. Uh, no plans. That sounds good.'

'I'll make a reservation somewhere. I'm glad I remembered.' He kissed me on the cheek, then rolled over and fell asleep.

This was part of the problem. Evan remembered my birthday; he stayed faithful to me; he paid his share of the rent on time. There had been no dramatic betrayals. Instead there was a long stretch of absence. Where I saw an accumulating string of rejections, lonely nights and questions unasked, Evan probably saw a normal relationship. He upheld his end of the bargain. He checked the boxes required of him. And if there were no further boxes to check, he probably assumed he'd done everything he needed to do.

On Thursday morning, two dozen red roses awaited me at the office, with a card that read: 'Thinking of you today – Adam.' I propped the card next to my computer. Laurie saw the flowers when she came in, paused briefly, but didn't ask about them. My phone rang later that morning, my sister calling.

'Julia?' Elizabeth said. 'Hey, happy birthday!'

'Why are you whispering?'

'I'm in the library. Studying for midterms. How's the day been?'

'Pretty good. I'm at work, so . . . you know. Boring old Thursday so far.'

'Are you and Evan going out tonight?'

'Yeah.'

'Somewhere good?'

'I hope so. He was supposed to make the reservation.'

'How's he doing?'

'He's fine.'

She was quiet for a moment. 'Jules?' she finally said. 'Is everything okay?'

'It's fine. I don't know. Yeah.'

'What's wrong?'

But that was the thing. I didn't want to talk about Evan or what was wrong; I wanted to talk about what was finally *right*. Having to muffle the good news – Adam, this new turn my life had taken – was so annoying. I couldn't do or say what I wanted, not even on my birthday. I inhaled the thick, sweet scent of Adam's roses. What was wrong with this picture? I hadn't heard a thing from Evan all day. Evan, the one who was supposed to be my boyfriend.

'Is it Evan?' she prompted, interrupting my silence.

'Kind of.' I sighed. 'Things aren't great.'

'Oh, shit. What's going on?'

'Well, for one, he works all the time. I barely even see him.'

'Poor guy.'

I laughed bitterly. 'Don't feel bad for him. He loves it.'

'Okay, then. Poor you.'

'I guess it's okay. I've been spending a lot of time with' – I came so close to blurting out Adam's name, so incredibly close – 'with, um, friends. Keeping busy, you know.'

The rest of the afternoon passed in tedium, with Laurie dropping off files and marked-up memos on my desk. Her eye kept catching on the roses, but she seemed strangely determined not to comment. Near the end of the day, my phone rang again.

'Jules,' Evan said, his voice heavy. 'I'm so sorry. I'm on my way to the airport right now. Michael just told me. Spire's sending a team to this conference in Las Vegas, and he wants me along, too. I'm there all weekend. I feel terrible.'

'A conference? Why?'

'I'm not sure. It's global macro, stuff I don't even work on. Michael said he'd fill me in later.' A loud honk sounded. I had to hold the phone away from my ear. 'Shit,' he said. 'This traffic is insane. I'm sorry, Julia. I really am. I'm on the red-eye back on Sunday, so I'll see you Monday, okay?'

'Whatever. It's fine,' I said. Evan, once again relegating me to second place, proving how little I mattered to him – a fact that was equal parts upsetting and liberating. I felt a weird mixture of anger and relief. It *was* fine. In fact, maybe it was better than fine. I'd be spared from dinner at some overpriced midtown restaurant, with mediocre food and nothing to talk about. The weekend was all mine. I put a smile back into my voice. 'See you in a few days.'

---

I began running longer, farther that fall. I could go for six miles, eight, even nine or ten without tiring. Far north along the river and back down to the Queensboro, or in long loops around Central Park. I thought maybe I'd train for a marathon. Or at least a half marathon. The miles flew by while my mind was lost in daydreams, breath steaming in the cold morning air, the rhythmic crunch of gravel under my shoes. I felt my body growing lighter, stronger. For six months my imagination had been starved of oxygen, but I was breathing at last, enormous gulps of air.

For the first week, after that kiss in the cab, Adam and I had studiedly sober interactions: brightly lit coffee shops, a walk at lunch, a gallery opening in the evening. Testing the water. That deliberateness seemed so grown-up, part of the reason I was sure it was the right thing to do. We didn't talk about what had happened in the cab, but it saturated our relationship with a new intensity. Adam would e-mail me at work to tell me a funny thing he'd overheard or share a link to a story he thought was interesting. He'd ask how a meeting went, how my day was going. Things he hadn't done before. It thrilled me, the knowledge that Adam – Adam McCard, the most dazzling man I'd ever met – was thinking about me all the time.

We made plans to have dinner on a Saturday night in early November – a week after the kiss – then stop by his friend's party afterward. Evan would be working late, as usual. We met at the restaurant, a small place in the West Village. He was waiting for me at the bar, and I could taste the liquor on his breath. I knew this was it, the night when things would go one way or another, once and for all. I was nervous. The way I imagined an actor might feel before the curtain rises for the first time.

We had a drink before dinner, then shared a bottle of wine. Adam greeted the maître d' by name. The sommelier, too. He was a regular. It skipped across my mind that he had probably brought other women here before, other girlfriends, but I didn't care. It was my turn. There was candlelight, thick linen napkins, leather armchairs. The menu, tiny type on creamy paper. Jewel-like coins of tuna tartare, halibut crusted in a bright green sleeve, a tangle of golden pasta. The wine was a rich, deep Burgundy – at least that's what Adam told me – and I was tipsy by the time we stood up to leave, my nervousness forgotten. Adam helped me on with my coat. He was so handsome up close. The dark hair, the cheekbones. He leaned forward to kiss the tip of my nose.

'Come on,' he said. 'Nick's place is right around the corner.'

The doorman nodded us inside a stately brick building on Christopher Street. Adam held my hand through the crowded apartment to the bedroom, where we added our coats and scarves to the pile heaped on the bed. It was a big room, an adult-size bedroom, with a proper four-poster, a woven rug, art on the walls, floor lamps. It looked like a room Nick must share with a girlfriend, one with good taste and plenty of money.

These were all Adam's friends. He was a few years older than me, and he ran with a crowd a few years older than him, so these people were miles beyond anyone I knew: journalists and editors and lawyers and producers, people who no longer had *assistant* in their titles. Adam steered me through the party, introducing me to everyone he knew. At one point, he bumped into a woman smoking a cigarette next to an open window. He turned to apologize, and I watched both of them light up with recognition. 'Sara,' he said, kissing her on the cheek, then tugging me forward. 'Hey. You two should meet.'

She was Japanese, her hair like a long curtain framing her face, her clothing artfully draped, her build slender and delicate. Her silhouette was like an old Al Hirschfeld sketch. 'Sara, this is Julia Edwards. She was at Yale a few years behind us. Jules, Sara runs a gallery in Tribeca.'

'Hey,' she said. Her voice was smoky and cool. 'Nice to meet you.'

Adam cast his eyes across the room. 'I just have to say hi to somebody. I'll be right back.'

I was nervous again without Adam there as a buffer. Surely Sara would dismiss me out of hand: a ditzy girl who didn't belong, too young, too naive. She'd only talk to me until she could find an excuse to leave. But after he walked away, she smiled at me. She was less intimidating when she smiled.

'When did you graduate?'

'Just this year. In May.'

'Tough year. What are you doing in the city?'

'I'm working at a nonprofit. The Fletcher Foundation. I'm just an assistant, but –'

'But you have a job? Hey, that's great. That's more than a lot of people can say.'

I laughed. 'I guess.'

'Most of my friends had to intern for, like, years before they found jobs. You're doing fine.'

'It doesn't really feel that way.'

'It will, eventually.' She had a knowing glint in her eyes. A lot of the people in this room did. I wanted that – the knowingness – more than anything. An understanding of the world and where I fit in it. Sara told me about her gallery in Tribeca, some of the artists she represented. She was going to Art Basel in Miami Beach in a few weeks. We talked for a while about the recent Turner show at the Met and the new Koons installation.

I was surprised to find I was actually having fun. Sara made me feel like myself.

'Here,' she said as she lit another cigarette. 'Here's my card. Call me sometime. We can have lunch. And if you're ever interested in leaving that job of yours, the gallery might be hiring next year.'

'Really?'

'Really. We could use someone like you. You seem smart. And nice, too. Too nice for Adam.'

She exhaled a plume of smoke. I laughed nervously. *Too nice for Adam?* I glanced down at her business card. A simple square with her name in raised black type. SARA YAMASHITA.

'There you are,' Adam said. 'Come on – let's say hi to Nick.'

'It was nice to meet you,' I said to Sara, slipping the card into my purse. 'And thank you, really. I appreciate it.'

'No problem.' She smiled serenely. 'Keep in mind what I said.'

Nick had a real kitchen, too, a separate room with marble countertops and oak cabinets and a stainless steel range. He was holding court, in the middle of some story, and he turned toward us at the sound of his name. He was just like Adam, I could see – brimming with the same confidence, tailor-made for this kind of life. Nick stepped forward and reached for my hand. 'You must be the famous Julia,' he said. 'What can I get you guys to drink?'

He was tall and tanned, with very white teeth and a

shock of blond hair. He wore a navy blue cable-knit sweater and khakis and soft brown loafers. He seemed to match his apartment: old money, old-money taste.

'I'll have a bourbon,' Adam said, 'and she'll have a vodka soda.'

'With lime, if you have it,' I added. Adam always forgot the last part.

While Nick was fixing our drinks, Adam nudged me. 'So what do you think?'

'This kitchen, holy shit. Is this guy a millionaire or something?'

'You were talking to Sara for a while.'

'Yeah. I like her. I can't believe she runs her own gallery.'

'Don't be too impressed. It's all her family. Their money, their connections. Nothing she got on her own.'

'What, are you not a fan?'

'No, nothing like that. Sara's a good person for you to know. But her dad is one of the biggest art dealers in the city. How hard do you think she had to work to get that gig?'

'She seems to be doing what she loves, at least.' I wished Nick would hurry up with the drinks. But he was distracted, greeting more people in that clubby way.

Adam laughed. 'Sara's not like that. I'm not sure love is an emotion she's capable of.'

I tried to read his expression. For Adam to criticize someone else's family connections seemed unfair. He had grown up in a Central Park West penthouse, his father a real estate mogul and his mother a society type. Adam was as privileged as they came. So what if he hadn't chosen to follow his father into real estate? It was still strange for him to belittle Sara for doing something that almost anyone in her situation would have done. It stung, too, realizing that Adam could have said the same thing about me. The job I had, at a foundation run by our family friends – nothing I got on my own.

A thought occurred to me.

'How do you know Sara again?'

'Hmm?'

'Was she in your college, or what?'

'No. We dated for a while.'

'Oh.'

'It was freshman year. We met through the magazine.'

The same way that Adam and I had met. Adam's reputation was well known. He'd slept around, a parade of flings and hookups, often a few at the same time, many drawn from the ranks of the magazine. This party had to be populated with other past conquests besides Sara. But weirdly enough, I wasn't jealous. Maybe because I had no real claim over Adam. Being with Adam had become a way for me to step outside the bounds: a minor rebellion, leaving behind the boring life I had before. This was a different world, one of sommeliers and marble kitchens and doormen. It was a world where you could be blasé about the past and the consequences of your actions. A world where envy was what other people felt, not you.

'What, are you going to Russia for that vodka?' Adam said to Nick, raising his voice over the chatter.

'Hey.' Nick flashed his white-toothed smile, cutting a lime into wedges. 'You want your drink or not?'

He handed us our glasses a moment later. Heavy cut-crystal tumblers. My hand dropped under the weight. I felt like I was at a party at my parents' house.

'So, Julia,' Nick said. 'Tell me about yourself.'

'Oh.' I hated that kind of question. What the hell was I supposed to say? What were the things that made me interesting or special? 'Well, right now I'm –'

'Nick. There you are.' A brunette woman in a red dress appeared next to Nick. She laid her left hand across his chest, and an enormous diamond flashed from her ring finger. 'Sweetheart, pass me the seltzer? Someone spilled in the living room.'

She noticed Adam and me standing there. 'Hi,' she said, turning to offer me her other, ringless hand. 'I'm Megan. Nick's fiancée.'

'Julia. Thank you so much for having us.'

'You go with him?' She pointed at Adam.

'She's my date for the night,' Adam said. 'We're old friends from college.'

'Well.' She smiled tightly. 'Welcome.'

*Fiancée?* I thought as Megan walked out of the kitchen. *Engaged?* I didn't know anyone who was engaged. When I saw that diamond sparkling on her finger, I felt the gulf that separated me from the rest of the partygoers crack wide open. It made sense. She and Nick had to be in their late twenties. Their kitchen, their artwork, their furniture, their clothes. Poised right on the cusp of bona fide adulthood. Only a handful of years separated us, but I felt further away from them than I did from my childhood self. I was about to turn twenty-three years old, and I couldn't even begin to imagine it, real adulthood.

The thing was, it hadn't always been so impossible to imagine. We had never actually talked about it, never said the word *marriage,* but that summer Evan and I spent in Europe – hot nights walking around Rome, sunny days on the Greek coast, afternoons in Paris – I thought about it more than once. I held his hand in mine, wrapped my arms around his neck, and felt myself consumed by love. A love that could endure anything. A love that had changed me. I grew dizzy from it sometimes. Of course we would be together forever. Of course we would get married someday.

But then everything changed. I regarded the Julia from a year and a half earlier with pity. That girl had known so little about what was to come – had been so naive about what it took for a relationship to work in the real world. I could never marry Evan. Never, ever. Evan wasn't someone I could have a life with. We were too different, and he didn't care about me. That's why it felt so natural, sliding into this new thing with Adam. Evan and I were clearly headed for a breakup. It was only a question of time.

So why didn't I rip the bandage off? Why keep living with someone for whom I felt nothing? Ending things would have kept me from cheating on Evan. It would have prevented so much of the collateral damage. But that decision would have taken conviction. Planning and execution. And, frankly, it would have required that I find my own place to live, which was annoying and prohibitively expensive. And in that moment, I liked the *doing*. Abandoning myself to impulse. Besides, I thought. The coming holidays might precipitate a breakup. They always had a way of throwing gasoline on the fire. Evan wasn't any happier in this relationship than I was. If I waited, he might just do it himself.

'Let's mingle a little longer, and then we can go,' Adam said.

We talked to more of his friends. They were so different from the people at parties I'd gone to with Abby and Evan. A filmmaker working on an indie documentary. A consultant traveling four days a week to Omaha. A literary agent who had just sold a novel for seven figures. But even in this crowd, I could sense that Adam was exceptional. People were drawn to where he stood like iron filings to a magnet. He was as charming and commanding as he'd been in college. In this apartment, in this room full of people, Adam was still the brightest star in the universe.

And he had chosen me. In the cab afterward, he took my hand.

'You're so beautiful. You know that, right?'

'Come on. Stop.'

'I mean it. I adore you.'

He leaned over and kissed me. We were sailing up 8th Avenue, no sign that the cab was going to go across town. Adam must have given the driver his address. My heart sped up. This was it. We stopped at a brick building at the corner of 80th and Riverside Drive. 'You have to come up for a drink, at least,' Adam said, giving me an excuse that I didn't need. 'I have a great view.'

Adam's apartment was on the twelfth floor. He tossed our coats on an upholstered chair in the foyer and led me to the far end of the living room. Family money: there was no way he could afford this on a journalist's salary. He steered me to the window and slipped his arms around me from behind. The Palisades looked dark and velvety across the river, and the lights of Weehawken and Hoboken sparkled in the southern distance.

'Amazing, right?' he said, brushing his lips along my neck.

'Mmm.'

'I've wanted you to see this for a long time.'

'It's beautiful.'

He turned me around, sliding his arms down my back, keeping me tight against him. He kissed me, and for a second it ran through my head like a siren, the last time we'd been here – but then it disappeared. I wanted this. There was no hesitation this time.

Afterward, we lay facing each other. Naked, sweat cooling, the room dim except for the glow from the streetlamps outside. He had one arm behind his head, and with his other hand he traced a line along my waist.

'I can't tell you how long I've thought about that,' he said.

'Me, too.' I moved closer and buried my face in his chest, breathing him in.

'We fit together,' Adam said. 'Look at that.' And it was true. Our bodies were made to be in this very position. He kissed me on the forehead and said, 'Do you want to stay over? I make a mean breakfast.'

'I think I'd better get home. What time is it?'

'A little after one.'

'Can I use the bathroom?'

'Out the door and to your left.'

I showered, my hair pulled back in a bun to keep it dry. I opened my mouth and tipped my head back, letting the hot water run in. I had to stifle a laugh. Adam McCard. It had finally happened. The steam drifted through the bathroom, and the glass door of the stall fogged over, and everything else disappeared.

---

Monday, more than two weeks later. A few days after my birthday. I went for a particularly long run that cold November morning. As I came down our block, I remember thinking it strange that there was someone sitting on our stoop. Who had time to linger at this hour? It might be one of the homeless men who sometimes slept in the alcove outside the drugstore. I dreaded having to squeeze past him on my way inside.

As I got closer, I felt a prickle on my neck. It was Evan.

Sitting there, on the stoop. How had I not recognized him sooner? He was staring at his phone and jiggling his knees in a fast bounce, his duffel bag beside him. I'd forgotten that he was getting back from Las Vegas that morning. Adam and I had spent the weekend at his apartment, which was the best birthday present I could have asked for. He cooked, we listened to jazz, and I sat on the couch reading and watching the Hudson flow past. 'Evan should go out of town more,' he said when I emerged from the shower wearing one of his button-downs. 'Where did you say he was again?' He was in bed, shirtless, wearing his reading glasses. He looked like Clark Kent. It was a Saturday night, and we were staying in. I slid under the covers. 'Some conference in Las Vegas. It's weird. Michael wanted him to go along at the last minute. It has nothing to do with what he's working on.' Adam nodded, his brow furrowed. Then he relaxed. 'Well, it works for me.' I'd finally gone home late on Sunday night. The creaking floorboards in our dark apartment filled me with a wretched loneliness.

I stopped a dozen yards short of our door. Evan still hadn't seen me. He stood up, picked up the duffel bag, then put it down. He tilted his head to look up at the sky. He checked his watch, then paced a few yards before reversing course. Something was off. I suddenly saw him as any stranger might: unshaved, tired, puffy, anonymous. It's an odd trick, to consider how different someone looks when you strip away the forgiveness of familiarity. I had always known Evan up close. I encountered him all at once, and that's what I had always liked about him: no hidden tricks or trip wires. But right then, that November morning, I had the feeling of traveling back in time. Evan was becoming a stranger in front of my eyes. This man sitting on my doorstep was someone I had never met before.

I shivered. This was how bad it had gotten: I considered turning around to do another lap in the park, waiting for Evan to leave for work. But then he finally looked up and saw me.

'Julia,' he said, springing to his feet.

'Hey. How was the trip?'

He glanced over his shoulder, then up the street behind me. His eyes, when they landed on mine, were brimming with a new emotion. Panic? Fear?

'I have to tell you something,' he said, and he pulled me inside.

---

The long-awaited Fletcher Foundation gala had been the week before. I got there early, in charge of checking guests in upon arrival. I peered through the doors into the ballroom, which glowed softly, with white roses and candlelight on every table. Up on stage was Eleanor, clipboard and BlackBerry in hand. She wore a long black gown. Her skin had the slightest dusting of a tan.

Laurie arrived, looking exhausted. I had overheard snatches of her conversation with Henry Fletcher earlier that day. She was explaining that the gala had cost more than anticipated. Donations had dried up, returns from the endowment were down, and we were tight on cash for the rest of the year. The conversation seemed to go badly. 'Yes, of course,' she had said, raising her voice. 'Of course I *know* how bad the market is right now. But I'm telling you that we're at real risk of —'

She paused, apparently listening to him. She spoke more quietly, and I couldn't make out what she was saying. She sighed after she hung up. Then she shut her door, and it stayed shut for the rest of the afternoon.

'Oh, hello, Julia,' she said distractedly. She dumped her bag and coat on the check-in table. 'Can you find somewhere to put these?'

The guests started arriving in a trickle, then all at once. I kept a smile plastered on my face, answering questions, directing traffic. A corner of my mind worried over Laurie's mood. If things were as bad as she said, I wondered whether my job might be in jeopardy. A little later, Abby and Jake walked through the door. 'Julia!' Abby said, coming over to give me a hug. 'Holy crap. Woman in charge.'

'Hey,' Jake said, jerking his chin in greeting.

'Hi, guys. Let's see . . . you're at table one. No surprise there, I guess.'

'You look great,' Abby said.

'Stop. *You* look great.' She did, too. I had never seen her so radiant. 'Hey, Jake, are your parents here? Laurie is eagerly awaiting them.'

'Yeah,' Jake said, rubbing his chin and looking bored. 'They're outside. My dad got stopped by some reporter.'

*Adam,* I thought, and my heart fluttered.

'Are we sitting together?' Abby said.

'What? Oh, no. Laurie is probably at your table, though.'

Abby and Jake drifted toward the coat check. There was a lull in the arrivals. I took the chance to scoot out from behind the table and survey the red-carpeted sidewalk. Henry and Dot Fletcher were talking to the reporter, a man in jeans and a parka. He held a recorder up toward Henry Fletcher. The parka man turned, catching the light on his face. It wasn't Adam. Of course it wasn't. I went back to the table, smoothed my skirt, and resumed my smile. The Fletchers approached the table. Dot, to her credit, remembered who I was.

'Julia, dear! It's so wonderful to see you. How are you?'

'I'm well, thank you. I'm so –'

She clutched my hand to cut me off. 'I was just talking with your mother the other day. You look lovely. So grown up. Doesn't she, Henry?'

He turned, distracted, rubbing his chin. He and Jake were so much alike.

'Of course. Nice to see you.'

Dot smiled sweetly at me, waving her fingers as they walked away to join the party. Henry, I noticed, had a tan, too.

★

Eleanor swept through to check on me as the guests started filing into the ballroom for dinner, after the cocktail hour ended.

'What time is it?' she said.

There was a clock on the wall. 'Ten past eight.'

'Good. Stay here till eight thirty, in case anyone trickles in.' She tossed her hair back over her shoulders. 'Oh, and Julia, I forgot to say. Laurie doesn't like junior staff to drink at work events. It's always been her policy. So just be aware of that.'

She emphasized the *junior* in 'junior staff' with particular care. I gave the finger to her back as she walked into the ballroom. The event had started at 6:30. Nobody else was going to show up at this point. This was pure spite – Eleanor wanting to remind me that she was the one in charge.

I texted Adam. How's the deadline coming?

It was quiet in the entrance hall, just the muted sound of traffic on Park Avenue and the occasional clatter of silverware from the ballroom. I started counting the number of no-shows for the final tally when I felt my phone buzz.

Still trying to get this piece done. I don't suppose you have any comment on the AIG bailout? Or insight into what the Fed is thinking?

I laughed. No comment. And no insight. Sorry, I'm useless.

A minute later, another buzz. Not useless. You're my motivation to get this done. Meet me later for a drink?

★

I found my seat in the back as the waiters were delivering the entrées. Everyone was already paired off in conversation, raising their voices against the echo of the big room. My arrival went unnoticed. I cut my chicken and asparagus into small, careful bites, taking up as much time as I could. I buttered a roll and ate it, then buttered and ate another one.

*Thank God,* I thought when the waiters cleared our dishes and Henry Fletcher approached the podium on stage. He cleared his throat, and the microphone screeched with feedback. He rattled off a list of thank-yous, then droned on about the importance of supporting young and emerging artists. That during these trying economic times, it was crucial to ensure that arts programs retained funding. It was very dreary. Half the room was checking e-mail by the time he was finished.

At the end of his speech, Mr Fletcher paused. He folded up the piece of paper he had been reading from, removed his glasses, and returned both to his pocket. Then he cleared his throat again. 'And now, before I turn it over to the formidable Laurie Silver, I'd like to make an announcement.'

This was a surprise.

'I'm pleased to say here, for the first time, that Dot and I are making a donation of ten million dollars to the Fletcher Foundation to establish a new series of grants for next year and future years. And for all donations made in the next six months, we will personally match your gifts dollar for dollar.'

The room erupted in applause. Mr Fletcher smiled a stiff smile.

'We want to show our commitment to the vitality and endurance of the great achievements of the foundation during the past decade, and we hope you'll join us in doing so. And, without further ado, Laurie Silver, president of the Fletcher Foundation.'

The room rose to its feet, the applause swelling as Laurie ascended the stage. I was relieved. Even if I hated it, I would be able to keep my job until I found something better. Laurie and Mr Fletcher embraced. She was smiling, but she looked less exuberant than I expected. From the snatches I'd overheard, Laurie had asked for another three or four million to keep things running. Henry Fletcher had just thrown us a lifeline above and beyond what we needed, I was sure of it.

After Laurie's speech, I found Abby and Jake by the bar. I ordered a double vodka on the rocks. Eleanor's rule probably wasn't real, and I didn't care. Something about the news of the donation, and Laurie's reaction, had unsettled me. I suspected that I had very little understanding of what was really happening. It was all occurring under the surface, where I couldn't see. But a minute later, after the drink, I felt better. Calmer.

'That was nice, right?' Abby said to Jake. 'It's great that your parents are doing that.'

Jake shrugged. 'Yeah. It's good.'

'Did you have fun?' Abby asked me.

'Sure. It was fine.' I tipped back my drink, the ice rattling in my glass.

'Let's get you another one of those.' She waved at the bartender.

'We're going out after this, right?'

'Not me. My alarm is going off tomorrow at six whether I like it or not.'

'What? Abby!'

'Do you know what it's like teaching kindergarten with a hangover? Fucking miserable is what. I learned my lesson the first time. Sorry, Jules, I can't.'

'It's just been so long since we went out together.' I sounded whiny.

Jake faked a yawn, slipping his arm around Abby's waist. 'Yeah. I've got an early day tomorrow, too. Should we go get a cab?'

'Sorry, sorry.' Abby hugged me. 'You look great, though, you really do.'

When the bartender came over, I ordered another drink. The ballroom was emptying fast, the guests bolting for the coat check and their black cars. I noticed Laurie and Dot Fletcher by the side of the stage. The vodka emboldened me. I ought to go and thank Mrs Fletcher for the donation. Laurie sometimes seemed to forget that I was a real person, equipped to handle more than the most basic administrative work. This – a chance to sound articulate and thoughtful – might help remind her of that. I was smart, I was interesting, I was capable of intelligent conversation. I deserved more than I was getting. Maybe I just had to take it for myself.

I touched Mrs Fletcher on the elbow. She looked startled to see me. 'Oh, hello, Julia. Laurie's speech was wonderful, wasn't it?'

'Yes, it was. Mrs Fletcher,' I said, glancing over at Laurie. Her lips were drawn in a tight line. 'I just wanted to say thank you, so much, for your and Mr Fletcher's show of support tonight. It was inspiring, really.'

Dot and Laurie made brief eye contact, something passing between them. 'There's no need to thank us, dear. We see this foundation as our responsibility. It bears our name, after all.'

'Of course. Well, I thought it was very nice.'

'Yes,' Laurie said. 'In fact, we were just talking about what this donation is going to allow us to do in the upcoming year.'

Laurie looked more annoyed than anything else. She and Dot tilted their shoulders to indicate I was no longer welcome. But I was distracted anyway by the sight, behind them and out of their field of vision, of Henry and Eleanor.

It looked innocuous enough. Their heads were awfully close together, but it was noisy in the ballroom. I stepped aside and took my phone out, pretending to check something. Then I glanced back up at Henry and Eleanor. He slipped his hand to the small of her back, leaning in closer. She looked over her shoulder, then nodded. From my pretending-to-be-on-the-phone post a few feet away, I heard Mr Fletcher approach Laurie and Dot. 'Honey,' he said to Dot. 'I just got a call from the office. I need to go in tonight. Something urgent's come up.'

'Now? Henry, it's so late.'

'Turmoil in the Asian markets. I should only be a few hours. You take the car, and I'll see you back at the hotel.' He exited the ballroom with long and loping strides. Eleanor had already disappeared.

Outside, the sidewalk held a few lingering couples. It was a little after 10:00 p.m. I was less than twenty blocks from our apartment. I could go home, wash my face, put on my pajamas, and wake up early and fresh the next morning. Be responsible. It didn't sound so bad. I started walking north on Park, past the empty office lobbies strung through the night like square golden beads. Some of the lobbies had oversize sculptures in the center, like exotic flowers suspended in a high-ceilinged terrarium. They looked so strange, alone in the night, on display for no one.

I was getting closer to home, and Park had gradually turned residential, the big glass lobbies replaced by solid limestone and brick. I felt my phone buzzing and saw Adam's name on the screen.

'Hey. Where are you?'

'Walking home. I just left the gala.'

'I'm only going to be a few more minutes. Meet me at my place?'

'Well . . . I really am almost home. It's getting kind of late.'

'I have a good bottle of wine. I've been saving it. In the cabinet next to the fridge. The doorman will let you in. I'll be right behind you.'

This was my fourth visit to Adam's apartment in as many days. Upstairs, I flipped the lights on and wandered through the living room, running my fingertips along the spines of the books on his bookshelf. It was the first time I'd been alone with Adam's things. I went into the bedroom. He had a desk at one end of the room. I noticed the bookshelf next to his desk was filled with books on finance. Histories, economic theory, *Barbarians at the Gate, When Genius Failed, Liar's Poker*. Curious. It was his beat at the *Observer*, but he'd always described it as a way station. Not something he was genuinely interested in. I pulled the copy of *When Genius Failed* from the shelf. The pages were dog-eared and bristling with Post-it notes. I fanned through it. There were pencil marks and underlines on nearly every page. It had the look of something obsessive.

I jumped when the door slammed. 'Hello?' Adam called. I shoved the book back onto the shelf and hurried out to the living room, where he was shrugging off his coat. 'There you are,' he said.

'How was work?'

'I'm glad it's over.' He ran his eyes over me. 'That is one hell of a dress.'

'You think so?' I glanced down, tugged at the fabric. 'I was just about to take it off, actually. But if you'd prefer I keep it on . . .'

Afterward, in bed, he rolled over and pulled a pack of Marlboros from his nightstand drawer. He lit the cigarette, inhaled, then exhaled with a sigh. He always looked more pensive in profile.

'You smoke?'

'Sometimes.'

'I don't think I knew that.'

He blew a smoke ring that floated briefly in the air above him. The room was almost unnaturally quiet. The constant thumps and squeaks and rattles that I'd come to expect in our walk-up apartment were absent here. Thick walls, double-glazed windows, the rugs and the floor-to-ceiling bookshelves: we were in a womb of money and culture. 'There's a lot you don't know about me.' Then he laughed. 'You want one?'

'Sure,' I said. I didn't want it, not really, but it felt like the right thing to do.

———

In our apartment, that morning of his return, I sat on the futon while Evan paced.

Back and forth, back and forth. I'd never seen him like this.

'Evan, what is it?' I said. 'Just tell me.'

He stopped abruptly. 'Michael. It's Michael. The thing has been rigged all along. And he made me deliver the papers, so the blood is on my hands, too. They trapped me. I can't go anywhere. It's totally fucked.'

'Slow down,' I said. 'What? What are you talking about?'

'The WestCorp deal. It's fixed.'

'What do you mean?'

He took a deep breath. He started talking about the mechanics of the deal, Spire betting that WestCorp was going to skyrocket because of their exports to China. I nodded. I knew all that. Then he explained that China had agreed to loosen the trade barriers, to drop the taxes and tariffs. Again, old news.

'Evan,' I said. 'I don't –'

He held up a hand, kept talking. He'd gotten locked out of his hotel room by his coworker. So he'd crashed on the couch in another suite. Michael and someone else from Spire came back to the room in the middle of the night.

'Did they know you were there?' I interrupted. Evan shook his head. 'Why didn't you say something? Like, hey, guys, I'm right over here?'

'I couldn't, Jules. I just couldn't. It was too late.' There was a sheen of sweat on his forehead. The other person in the room confronted Michael while Evan was listening. He'd spotted something in the books. Michael admitted that the deal was rigged. Michael and WestCorp had arranged for immigration papers for the Chinese officials and their families. The next day, Michael asked Evan to deliver a briefcase to a Mr Wenjian Chan at the Venetian.

'And you did it? You agreed to deliver the briefcase?'

He nodded, looking pale and sick.

'Evan. You had just overheard all that and you *went along* with it?'

'What else was I going to say? He didn't know that I'd overheard them. So I deliver the briefcase, and Chan seems happy. But before I walk out, his daughter stops me. Translating what her father's saying. They want to keep in touch, she says. She's applying to college in the States, and they want my help. They seem to think I have the right connections. Like, she can blackmail her way in through me.'

'Did you tell Michael this?'

'He was already gone by the time I got back. I haven't talked to him yet. I don't know what to do.' He stopped his pacing and sank down onto the futon next to me. He dropped his head in his hands. 'Jesus. What the fuck am I supposed to do?'

I was silent. I waited for him to look up at me, but he wouldn't. He kept his palms pressed up against his eyes, like a child willing a monster to disappear. After a minute, he said it again. 'Julia. What should I do?'

He finally looked up. I flinched when he reached for my hand, when his gaze locked on mine. My heart was hammering. Evan had been ignoring me for so long. He hadn't asked a single question in all that time. How was I? How was my day? How was I feeling? What was I thinking? And, finally, this was what he came up with. He wanted my help. I was only there to solve his problems, and then he'd go right back to ignoring me.

I was also thinking: how had he not figured this out? His pretending at innocence made me queasy. He *wasn't* innocent. He'd done this, too. He let himself become blinded by it. *We're going to make billions. Spire is going to crush the rest of Wall Street.* But when the truth finally became too uncomfortable, he wanted out. He wanted an escape. I was angry, but part of me felt relieved, too. Validated. I wasn't the one who had fucked up our relationship. I'd been duped. Evan had betrayed me – had betrayed us. And whatever was happening, whatever person Evan was becoming, I wanted no part of it. This was a waste of my time. I was done.

'I don't know, Evan.' I stood up, walked over to the kitchen. 'I don't know what you should do. You need to figure this out on your own.'

'What do you mean?' He looked confused. He hadn't even considered that I would be anything but sympathetic. That confirmed it. He really *wasn't* thinking about me.

I reached for a glass and filled it with water. I was just realizing how thirsty I was. 'I mean that I don't have the answer for you. This is *your* problem. You need to fix it.'

He said nothing for a long minute. My pulse was pounding in my ears. I hated this person in front of me, hated what he made me feel. I felt it boiling up, the blood in my body primed for a fight. Shouts, slammed doors, permanent words. *Get out. The end.*

But he just said, quietly, nodding to himself, 'Okay.'

'Fine,' I said. 'I'm late for work.' I put my glass down loudly on the kitchen counter and went into the bathroom, slamming the door behind me. The shower took a long time to get hot, and as it did, I felt the sharp edge of my anger dulling. This was how it always went. Evan was always waiting for me to cool down, to come to my senses. He never let our fights escalate, never shouted back. His patience knew no bounds.

It didn't have to be this way. Our relationship deserved a better ending than this. I wrapped myself in my towel and opened the bathroom door. I could apologize, tell him I was sorry for snapping like that. I would.

But Evan was already gone, his duffel bag left behind on the floor, the imprint of his body slowly fading from the cushions on the futon. I was too late.

# CHAPTER 9

## *Evan*

Paranoia was a disease whose symptoms I didn't recognize right away. Or maybe that's the essence of it: nothing is as it seems. The world rearranges itself while you aren't looking. You never know you're suffering from it.

'Evan? Honey, are you there?'

'Yeah. Yeah, sorry, Mom, I'm here.'

My parents often called to catch up after their workday ended. I'd stepped outside the office to take the call, pacing for warmth in the chilly November night. Until I noticed a dark figure sitting in the front seat of a car parked down the block. Just sitting there, unmoving. He'd been there for at least fifteen minutes. Watching me.

'I said, how was your weekend? It was Julia's birthday, right?'

'Yeah. Um, it was good.'

'I hope you two did something nice.'

I hadn't told them I'd gone to Las Vegas. It felt like a jinx, telling them even that, spreading any aspect of the story further than it needed to go. A family of tourists was walking down the block in an unwieldy ameba, arguing about the best way to get back to their hotel. I ducked behind them, trying to blend in and get a better look at the figure in the car without his seeing me. We got closer and closer, and finally I could see clear through the window. It was a chauffeur, his cap pulled low over his forehead. Asleep.

'Hey!' One of the kids glared at me. I'd stepped on his heel.

'Shit. Sorry,' I said.

'What?'

'Nothing, Mom. I should go.'

The same thing kept happening all week. The towel hanging crooked when I was sure I'd left it straight. My desk chair spinning in slow circles when I returned from lunch. And a hot flare of panic until I eventually realized the explanation. Julia wiping the toothpaste from her mouth in the morning, leaving the towel askew. Roger pushing past my chair on his way to the bathroom. Chan and his colleagues were businessmen, not thugs. They weren't going to corner me and press a gun to my head in some dark alley. Whatever they did was going to be more subtle than that.

We got to the airport in Las Vegas on Sunday evening for the red-eye home. I stood in front of the departures board. The destination cities were organized alphabetically, and near the end of the list was Vancouver. The flight was leaving a few minutes after ours.

I could do it. I could afford the ticket. I had my passport with me as ID – my British Columbia license had
expired a few months earlier – and I had my duffel bag in
hand. I'd arrive near midnight, get a room in an airport
motel. There was a Greyhound that headed east out of
Vancouver in the morning. My hometown sat near the
end of the line. I imagined walking into the grocery
store, near where the bus dropped me off. Finding my
parents in the back, doing inventory or reviewing the
accounts at the end of the day. They would be surprised
to see me, but maybe not that surprised. I could sleep in
my own bed, with the familiar rush of wind through the
tall pine trees outside. I could be doing all that *tomorrow*.
It was right within my reach – a chance to run away and
pretend this never happened.

'Evan?' Chuck emerged from the airline's first-class
lounge and caught me staring at the board. 'They're calling our flight. Come on, let's go.'

———

'I'm sorry, hon,' Wanda said. It was Monday morning.
I'd gone home to change after the flight, then went
straight to Michael's office. Wanda could probably tell
that I was underslept and in desperate need of a shower.
I hadn't had time to wait for Julia to finish hers. 'He's
completely jammed today. I can't fit you in anywhere.
You want me to get him a message?'

'You can just tell him that I'd like to see him. *Need* to
see him.'

'What's it regarding?'

I shook my head. 'He'll know.'

I tried again on Tuesday, on Wednesday, on Thursday. It was the same story. Door shut. Wanda shaking her head. It had been almost a full week since I'd found out, and the knowledge was starting to solidify within me. Telling Julia had done no good. I knew I owed her the truth – I couldn't just flee to Canada, if only for that reason: the thought of telling her what I'd done over the phone or in an e-mail had made me too sick to go through with it – but she seemed utterly uninterested in it. The sting of her cold reaction only lasted for a few moments. So Julia was in a bitchy mood – I still had bigger problems. I decided to try to use this mess to my advantage. There was more than one way that I could have theoretically discovered the truth. Maybe Chan had let something slip, and I'd put two and two together. I'd show Michael that I knew exactly what he was up to. Show him that I wasn't so easily duped after all.

Late on Friday afternoon, I tried one more time. Wanda sighed. 'I'm sorry, Evan, but you'll have to wait until Monday. Mr Casey is about to leave for the weekend.'

'Who is that?' Michael strode into the hallway, pulling on his coat. 'Oh, Evan. Wanda, you know you can always send Evan straight in.'

'That's okay.' I stepped back. 'I don't want to interrupt.'

'I have an appointment, but we can talk along the way.

That'll be better, in fact. Get your coat and meet me at the elevator.'

Downstairs, Michael and I climbed into the back of a town car idling by the curb. It sped off, heading west. 'Just give me another minute,' Michael said, his thumbs punching the keys of his BlackBerry. Then he glanced up, saw the look on my face, and grinned unnervingly. 'Relax, Evan. This is going to be fun.'

The car came to a stop.

'My favorite place in the city,' Michael said, climbing out. We were out past the wasteland of 11th Avenue, in front of a nondescript building. The elegant silver lettering above the door was so discreet that you had to know what to look for.

'Mr Casey,' a voice boomed as we walked inside. A man in a dark green suit shook Michael's hand. He had slicked-back hair, a signet ring on his pinkie, a big barrel chest, and spindly legs. Like a toad with a very good personal shopper. 'We're so glad you could make it in this evening.'

'Bruno, this is one of my associates, Evan Peck.'

He extended a hand. Soft, pink, recently moisturized. 'Bruno Bernacchi. It's a pleasure to meet you.'

I glanced around the room. The cars gleamed under the bright lighting like sleeping animals. Maserati of Manhattan. It was empty except for the three of us. Bruno noticed me looking. He had a quick, darting gaze that didn't miss a thing.

'We normally close at five o'clock,' Bruno said to me in a conspiratorial tone. 'But we're always open for Mr Casey. One of our very best customers.'

'Your message said it was delivered today?'

'Just this afternoon. It's the newest model, a beauty. They aren't officially available until next year. There's a waiting list already, but you're at the top of the list, of course, Mr Casey.'

'I'd like to take it for a test drive.'

'Of course. I have in mind a route through Westchester. Wait until you see how this one handles the curves.'

'Actually, I'd like to take Evan along. This is the only time I can give him all week. So the two of us need to talk during the drive – multitask, you know what I mean?'

Bruno's smile wilted. His pink hands fluttered, his fingertips pressed together.

'I know you have your rules,' Michael said. 'But Bruno, I've given you a lot of business over the years. Surely we can take it out for a spin.'

I could see the calculation ricocheting through Bruno's eyes. Michael was smiling, but he was dead serious. A man whose wishes were dangerous to deny.

'You'll be here when we get back?' Michael said through the open window on the driver's side. It was a two-seater sports car, as precise and elegant in design as a piece of sculpture. I was in the passenger seat. For the first time, I understood why people liked to describe an engine as purring. The vibration felt like a warm heartbeat. 'We'll be a few hours.'

Bruno started to open his mouth, then swallowed. He looked severely pained, but he nodded. 'Of course, Mr Casey. I'll be here.'

'Ready?' Michael said after he'd rolled the window up. 'Don't forget to buckle up.'

We drove in silence for a long while up the West Side Highway.

'I'm going to take us over the bridge,' Michael finally said. He glanced over his shoulder, pulling into the right lane and then onto the exit for the George Washington Bridge. 'You can't really get a feel for it in the city. What do you think so far?'

'It's . . . uh, nice.' *Nice?* That was a stupid thing to say. But I was silently panicking, and it was making me dumb. We were headed to New Jersey. The Pine Barrens. Michael was taking me out there to kill me – or worse. It was insane, but it was all I could think.

'Wait until you see it on the open road.'

Friday evening, and the bridge was predictably jammed. Michael answered e-mails on his BlackBerry, glancing up whenever the traffic inched forward. I stared out the window, frantic but numb. Trapped. It was winter dark outside, and the caramel leather interior of the car was lit with a golden glow. What was I going to do, get out of the car and make a run for it? That seemed like the stupidest option of all.

Finally we made it off the bridge and into New Jersey. Michael turned onto the Palisades Parkway. There was a physical relief when we accelerated onto the highway, the engine finally flexing its muscles, opening up the way it was intended to.

'So Evan,' Michael said. 'I have good news. We're going live with the WestCorp deal.'

'That's – that's great.'

'I've reallocated the fund's capital, and I'm doubling our position on WestCorp. This is going to be one for the books.'

He looked at me. The speedometer was steadily climbing. He was weaving from lane to lane without signaling, and I felt my pulse accelerating along with the car. 'You should be proud, Evan,' Michael said. I wished he would look at the road. 'It's extremely rare to work on a deal like this. At any point in your career. You've done a stellar job. The fact that you're so young only makes it more impressive.'

He glanced ahead. 'That's our exit,' he said. 'Next one.'

The sign said we were entering Alpine, New Jersey. We swung around the bending off-ramp, the car handling the curves as beautifully as Bruno had promised. The busy highway vanished, and moments later we were driving down quiet streets. There were high, manicured hedges and towering old trees, wrought-iron gates at the end of every driveway. You couldn't even see the houses. These were rich people. I wondered if this was where Michael lived.

We came to a dead end, a cul-de-sac. Michael stopped the car in front of a gate, one even higher and grander than the others we'd passed. 'We're here,' he said, turning off the engine. 'Get out of the car.'

My legs were shaking as I climbed out. Michael stood in front of the gate, hands in his pockets. It was dark – cloudy, no moon, no streetlights – but Michael seemed to know what he was looking at. I stood next to him, and after my eyes adjusted to the darkness, it materialized. The shape of a house in the distance, down the long driveway.

'A few years ago,' Michael said, 'my wife told me she was tired of the city. She was sick of all the noise, the honking, the traffic. She wanted a yard. She wanted to be able to go outside in the morning and look at trees and flowers. She said she missed having nature around her.'

He shook his head. 'I grew up on a farm. You knew that, right? In the middle of South Dakota. You want nature? That's all there is out there. I had to get up every morning at dawn. Milking the cows, shoveling manure, waist-deep in shit before the sun came up. And after school, there was more. There was always more. It was mud and dirt and hay and shit everywhere. This' – he gestured at the boxy hedges and clipped grass – 'isn't nature. Not to me.'

'But my wife . . .' He laughed, shook his head again. 'My wife grew up in the suburbs. This is practically the wilderness to her. Me, I like the city. I like taxis and elevators and restaurants. But she wanted to move. She said she wasn't going to raise our kids in some *apartment*. So we bought this place a few years ago. Renovated, fixed it up, redid the yard. You want to see it?'

It took me a second to realize the question wasn't rhetorical. 'Oh, um, sure,' I said.

Michael punched a four-digit code into the keypad next to the gate. A moment later, it opened with a mechanical screech. He'd left the keys in the Maserati, in the cul-de-sac. I guess the chances of it getting stolen were low in this neighborhood. People here already had their own fancy sports cars. Michael kept talking.

'When she first raised the issue, I shut it down. I told her no: it's my money, I'm going to spend it the way I want. And we have a penthouse, for Christ's sake. It's not like the kid would be deprived. But she pushed and she pushed. And then I realized – it's like when you have something and it doesn't mean too much to you. But it means a lot to the other person. It means an enormous amount to them. And if you give it to them, maybe it's a little sacrifice for you, but they are going to owe you for the rest of your life. You let them have their way now, and you'll have the upper hand on everything else. Leverage, right? So I told my wife okay. Let's pick out a house.'

We were finally there. The house was enormous: a circular driveway with a fountain in the middle, a grand entrance flanked by tall columns. It looked like one of the old French castles that Julia and I saw during our summer in Europe – the same kind of expensive-looking stonework and old-fashioned architecture. But the fountain in the driveway was empty and dry. Every window in the house was dark.

'That's the thing, Evan.' Michael turned to face me.

'Sometimes you have to do things in life that you don't really want to do. But you have to bear in mind that there's a bigger picture. Do you understand what I mean?'

I was newly aware of how quiet it was. How we hadn't seen a single person since we exited the highway. At least the dark concealed the nervous swallow in my throat. But if Michael was going to do something to me, I realized, he would have done it by then. 'Yes,' I said. 'I think I do.'

He gestured at me to follow him down a path around the side of the house, which opened out to the backyard. Actually, it wasn't a backyard. It was more like the grounds of a country club: tennis courts, a pool, terraced stone patios. The yard was immaculate, but it was obvious that no one was living there. There should have been some sign of life. A chair on the patio, a toy or a ball left in the middle of the lawn. A smudge on the windowpane from a curious hand pressed against it. Anything.

'What do you think of it?'

'It's really nice.'

'I never even spent a single night out here. My wife didn't, either. It was a good thing we didn't sell our place in the city.'

'Why didn't you move in?'

He shrugged. Michael looked human-size, for the first time, like an ordinary man. One whose life contained mistakes, maybe even regret. 'Like I said. She wanted to live out here to raise our kids. When that didn't materialize, we didn't have any reason.'

He stared at the back of the house. A long moment

passed. The wind rustled the nearly bare branches of the trees. It felt like we were a thousand miles from Manhattan. Then Michael smiled that disturbing grin of his. 'Well, I got my way in the end.'

As we skirted the side of the house, back toward the driveway, I slowed my pace to look through one of the windows. Gradually the room came into focus, like a darkened fishbowl. It was completely empty. The walls blank, the floor bare and uncovered. There was one lonely drop cloth in the corner of the room. A ladder and a bucket of paint. It looked like the job had been abandoned halfway through. Like whoever it was couldn't get out of there fast enough.

Back at the car, I moved toward the passenger side. Michael put his hand on my shoulder.

'Why don't you take over for a while?' he said. 'You ever driven a Maserati?'

This was the old Michael, back again. The Michael whose orders you obeyed without question. He opened the passenger door and climbed in. 'Come on, Peck. It'll be fun. You don't get to do this every day.'

My knees were shaking again as I walked to the driver's side. I turned the key in the ignition, and I remembered that my driver's license had expired. Test-driving a car like this without a license seemed idiotic. I wondered if I should tell Michael. But he interpreted my pause as something else.

'You *do* know how to drive stick, don't you?'

'Yes.'

'Good. Let's go. Take us back the way we came.'

I'd only driven stick in my parents' old truck, the one they used when our newer car was in the shop. This was nothing like that. But soon enough, I got the hang of it. All you needed was a light touch. Not to control the car but to meld with it. Feel the acceleration and the curves within your own body. Trust that it was going to be okay. From the corner of my eye, I saw Michael smiling.

'Feels good, doesn't it?'

'Yeah, it does.'

'They're addictive. I have two already. Never get the chance to drive them. Just don't have the time. But I felt like we needed to celebrate. It's been a big couple of weeks. Take a right up here. We want to head back to the bridge.'

I nodded.

'So Wanda said you were trying to get an appointment all week. What did you want to talk to me about?'

I was trying to merge onto the southbound Palisades Parkway, glancing over my shoulder for an opening. It was one thing driving the Maserati on the empty streets of Alpine, New Jersey. It was another driving it in thick highway traffic. A single scratch on this car would probably send me into bankruptcy. I hadn't really been listening. 'I'm sorry, Michael. What did you say?'

'What did you want to talk to me about?'

'Oh.' The steering wheel went slick under my palms. 'The, um. I wanted to talk to you about the Las Vegas trip.'

'What about it?'

The traffic was even heavier than it had been an hour earlier, coming out. I could feel the Maserati bucking underneath me, growling at the speed I was forcing it to hold to. Part of me wanted to drop this, move on. But I couldn't. I had to do it, now or never. I took a deep breath. 'Well, when I delivered the papers –'

'Yes, Chan was very happy with them.'

'Well, as I was about to leave, he told me that he wanted to stay in touch with me. Chan's daughter was there, too, translating for us. She's applying to colleges in the fall. I think they want my help with it. They know I went to Yale.'

Michael laughed. 'Typical. Greedy bastards.'

'I guess I'm just not sure what I'm supposed to do. Or what they're expecting me to do. I don't have connections like that.'

'Of course you don't. You can't buy your way into Harvard or Yale.'

I felt a surge of relief. 'Exactly.'

'Listen, Evan. These guys think everything has a price tag. They want more, more, more. We've held up our end of the bargain. It's done. Anything else is icing on the cake, and they'll have to pay extra for that. So Chan's daughter will apply next year. By that point, this deal will be wrapped up. There won't be anything they can do.'

I was processing. 'So you want me to –'

'No. Evan. I don't *want* you to do anything. I'm not

224

*asking* you to do anything. Do you understand? You handle this as you see fit. Right?'

A low-riding Camaro swerved in front of me. I slammed on the brakes.

'Jesus,' Michael said. 'Be careful.'

I could feel the sweat gathering between my shoulders.

'Listen,' he said. 'Evan. You know how to play this game. That's one of the reasons I hired you. You've got the right instincts. You're sharp. You see things clearly. I don't have to tell you what to do. You were *made* to do this kind of work. And there's no higher compliment than that.'

We drove the rest of the way in silence, down the parkway, back across the George Washington Bridge. I thought about what Michael was saying. The confidence he'd had in me all along. He'd said as much to Brad that night in Las Vegas. Ambitious. A hard worker. Perfect for this project. He had no reason to lie to Brad, no way of knowing I was listening. He was telling the truth that night. Michael really did see something in me. And maybe it was something that I was only just starting to see in myself.

We drove down the West Side Highway, approaching midtown. The sign for West 54th Street loomed in the distance. I signaled and started to move into the left lane.

'No,' Michael said. 'Keep going.'

'Isn't the dealer on Fifty-fourth Street?'

'You're going to drop me off downtown first. Take it to West Twelfth Street.'

Michael was back on his BlackBerry, squinting at the screen and responding to e-mails. As we passed the Lincoln Tunnel, his phone rang.

'Babe,' he answered. 'Yes. Yes. I'm almost there. Ten minutes, okay?'

He had me take West 12th to Bleecker, then hang a right and loop down to West 11th. Finally, on a street lined with town houses and trees, Michael had me pull over.

'Up there, on the right,' he said. 'The house with the green door.'

Before he climbed out of the car, he leaned over and pressed on the horn. The sound blared through the quiet. Michael paused outside the car, one hand on the door, then ducked through the frame to look at me. 'Good talk, Evan,' he said. 'See you on Monday.' The door closed with a satisfying thump.

The door of the town house swung open. A figure, silhouetted by the light from the front hall, moved out on the stoop. She was petite and curvy, with wavy hair. Brown hair. I remembered the pictures of his wife from his office: a cool blonde, sleek and slender. Michael kissed this other woman, reaching down to grab her ass. She smiled and swatted his hand away, a joke they shared. Then they stepped inside and closed the door.

# CHAPTER 10

## *Julia*

'Is Evan going to join us this year?' my father asked. He and my mother were on speakerphone in the car, driving back from an event in Boston. It was the week before Thanksgiving.

'I'm not sure.' Evan had spent the previous three Thanksgivings with us, so it was only natural they assumed he'd come this year, too. 'He's been so busy. He might not be able to take the time.'

'Julia,' my mother chimed in. 'We really need to know. Jasmine is planning the menu and doing the shopping now.'

'Yeah, I know, but his schedule is so unpredictable.'

'We understand, sweetheart,' my father said. I could picture him shooting my mother a look. She didn't understand the world of men and their work, and the precedence it took. Lately, strangely, Evan's stock had gone up with my parents; he had a job at Spire, therefore he was a person of substance. 'Evan has to do what he has to do,' my father said, respect in his voice. 'Good for him. Give him our best.'

'Ask him again tonight, Julia,' my mother persisted. My father sighed in the background. 'This makes things complicated.'

Didn't I know it. The truth was I hadn't asked yet. To not invite Evan seemed cruel, but having him there seemed even worse. I hoped, in the days leading up to the holiday, that the obvious solution would present itself. Evan would preempt my question and tell me he had to stay in New York and work. I just couldn't get up the nerve to ask. We'd barely spoken since his return from Las Vegas. Our silences had grown denser, colder. I'd been surprised it had gone on so long – a day or two, maybe, for Evan to gather himself and save face, but a whole week? I had underestimated Evan. Or maybe I overestimated him. Why should I have been surprised that he had a breaking point, just like everyone else? A point at which he no longer wanted to bother – a point at which he stopped caring, as I already had, weeks earlier?

On Monday night, four days before Thanksgiving, Adam cooked dinner for me at his apartment. I had stopped being coy, stopped pretending at early mornings and other excuses. I wanted him all the time. It was the best sex of my life – in the shower, on the dining-room table, in every corner of his beautiful apartment. Sometimes I worried about the loss of control. I was in too deep; I was getting sloppy. Making all the clichéd mistakes that people make when they have affairs. But then I fell for the biggest cliché of all: I thought I was different. It was going to be different with us. What Adam and I had ran deeper than the physical, I was sure of it. I felt like I was finally beginning to understand myself, that I was finally seeing in myself what Adam had seen all along. Potential. Something bigger and better. A chance to live a different kind of life.

I got home around midnight on Monday, figuring I had a few hours to spare. Evan didn't usually leave work until two or three in the morning. But as I approached, I noticed the light shining from beneath our door and the dull garble of the television coming from inside. I smoothed my hair, tugged my clothes straight, wiped away the last traces of lipstick. I'd been putting more effort into my appearance lately, but Evan didn't notice.

He was sitting on the futon, staring at the TV. Among the beer cans dotted across the coffee table, there was a plain manila envelope. Evan reached for the remote to mute the TV. Then he turned to look at me, like an afterthought.

'Where were you?'

'Out with coworkers.' I hung my coat on the back of the door. I'd had the excuse ready to go for weeks. It was the first time I'd had to use it. 'We got a late dinner afterward.'

The room smelled like beer. Evan shifted forward in his seat, tenting his fingertips over his mouth for a moment. Then he reached for the envelope on the coffee table and held it between his two hands.

'What is that?' I asked, my curiosity getting the better of me.

He cleared his throat. 'Michael and I finally talked about Vegas.'

He turned the envelope over, examining the other side. There was no postage, no writing or marking on it. I wondered what he was looking for.

'No one's getting bonuses this year,' he said. 'We'd all known that for a while. Some of the guys were pissed. They were counting on it. But it wouldn't look right, not in this economy. Bad optics, you know.'

*Optics*. This was not the Evan I knew.

'Michael reiterated that today. No bonuses. But, he said, he wanted me to have this. As a token of his appreciation. He said he was proud of the work that I'd done on this WestCorp deal.'

He handed me the envelope, nodding at me to open it. Inside were several stacks of crisp new hundred-dollar bills wrapped in paper bands.

'How much is this?'

'Twenty thousand dollars.'

'Jesus. But Evan, what are you – you can't keep this, can you?'

'I don't know.'

He stood up, taking the envelope back. On his way to the bedroom, he dropped it on top of the bookshelf, like he was tossing aside a pile of junk mail. A gesture of indifference that both frightened and disgusted me. Evan couldn't feign innocence any longer, not like before Las Vegas. He knew exactly what Michael had done – what he *himself* had done. They were breaking the law. And this time, he hadn't asked my advice. He was acting like this was the most normal thing in the world. The Evan I knew was never coming back. So then what was his deal? It was so obvious he didn't care about me anymore. Why was he still here?

Later, in bed, wide awake. 'When are you leaving for Boston?' he asked.

'Oh. Uh, Wednesday afternoon.'

He was silent. I wanted to sit up, turn on the light, ask him what the hell he was thinking. But we were past that point. Whatever words we might once have said had nowhere left to land.

'Are you . . .' I started to say. 'For Thanksgiving, are you –'

'I'm staying here. Work.'

'Right. That makes sense.'

He rolled over, away from me. Our cheap mattress bounced and sagged from the shift in weight. 'Goodnight,' he said. A few minutes later, he was asleep.

———

Elizabeth was waiting for me at the train station. It was colder in Boston than in New York, and she wore a huge parka with a fur-lined hood. She was the small one in our family – a delicate build, a foxy face – and the parka made her look even tinier.

'This is weird,' I said, climbing into the front seat of

her old silver Saab. Hot air blasted from the vents. I kicked aside the empty Dunkin' Donuts cups rolling around in the footwell.

'What?'

'I should be the one driving. I'm your big sister.'

She laughed. 'You're a bad driver. I wouldn't let you.'

'You got home today?'

'Yeah. The roads were terrible. It snowed last night. Can you believe that? In November.'

Elizabeth went to a small college in Maine. She had been at the top of her class in high school and would have had her pick, but she decided to forgo the most competitive schools – no Ivy League for her. She was majoring in studio art. She wrote poetry on the side, and she developed her own photographs. My parents had expressed concern about the path she seemed to be headed down, but Elizabeth kept telling them this was what she wanted to do. Eventually it sank in, and for the most part, they left her alone.

'Plus I barely slept,' she said. 'I was in the studio until four in the morning. So how's New York? No Evan this year?'

I grimaced inwardly at his name. 'He couldn't take the time.'

'Are things any better between you guys?'

'Actually, there's this guy I sort of reconnected with. From college.'

'What?' She whipped around to look at me. 'A guy? Like, romantically?'

I saw the disapproval written across Elizabeth's face,

and I changed tack. The urge to confess came so strongly, but the lie came easily, too. 'Oh . . . um, no. Not like that. We've just been spending time together. Friends. I don't know what it is.'

Elizabeth nodded, turning back to the road. She had always liked Evan, and I felt bad dumping this on her. But she was also my sister, and she knew me better than anyone did. She may not have liked what I was saying, what I was implying, but I think she understood what lay behind it.

After a long silence, she piped up again. 'Hey, can you let Pepper out? Mom asked me to walk him.'

'So why don't you walk him?'

'I'm just dropping you off. This girl from school is having a thing. Mom and Dad are at that party at the Fletchers'. I didn't know I was going to have to pick you up.'

'Well, thanks for squeezing me in.'

'I'm just saying. I have other plans.'

'Yeah, well, so do I.'

'Really?'

'Really.' Well, I had the option to have plans. One of my boarding-school friends had started an e-mail chain suggesting that anyone in Boston for the holidays meet up at a local bar on Wednesday night. It seemed better than sitting alone in our empty house, waiting for everyone else to return. I'd been doing that too much this past summer in New York. 'I'm meeting up with some Andover people at Finnegan's.'

'Finnegan's! Yikes. Have fun with that.'

Elizabeth dropped me off, and I found the spare key under the planter. Pepper, our black Lab, was in his crate in the mudroom off the kitchen. His tail thumped as I fiddled with the latch, then he burst out and collided with me. He nuzzled his wet snout into my palms.

'I love you, too, Pepper,' I said. 'Let's go outside, okay?'

Pepper had been my and Elizabeth's dog. When we were younger, we alternated taking him on short, lazy walks. Suddenly I was thirteen years old again: the cold air, the sparkle of the stars overhead, the warm glow of windows in the dark, walking Pepper between home-work and bed. Running through dates of battles or lines of Shakespeare or base pairs of DNA. Worrying about grades. Worrying about getting into a good college. I had never bothered to worry about what came after that. No one *told* me to worry. Surely another rung on the ladder awaited, and wouldn't that next part be just like every other part? Pepper sniffed around the base of a tree. He didn't tug at his leash the way he used to. He was an old dog, I realized, almost ten. He only had a few good years left.

Tears pricked the corners of my eyes when we got back inside. I'd been feeling strange all week. 'You want a treat, Peps?' I said, brightening my voice. He wagged his tail. The clock on the microwave in the kitchen said it was just after 8:30 p.m. The group had planned to meet at Finnegan's by eight.

My parents had taken my dad's car to the party at the

Fletchers', which left me with my mother's Volvo. I wondered, for a moment, whether I wanted to do this. Drink bad beer and eat greasy food with people I didn't really care about. Maybe for once I'd be better off at home, by myself. Put on a pot of tea, curl up with a book, run a bath. Embracing instead of fleeing the solitude. I hesitated, about to switch off the ignition. Then my phone buzzed with a text from one of the lacrosse girls: Great! See you in a few! I put the car into drive and headed for the bar.

---

I thought things at work might have improved after the gala, but the only person altered by the news was Eleanor. She floated in late every morning, smugger than ever, leaving for lunch and often not returning. But Laurie was the same as always. A heavy cloud trailed her as she passed back and forth in front of my desk.

Laurie was on the phone around ten days before Thanksgiving. It was a quiet afternoon, and if I stopped the clatter of my typing, I could just make out what she was saying to the person on the other end.

'Well, I can't get in the middle of this. It's not my place.'

Silence. I squinted at my computer screen in case someone walked by.

'I'm trying.' She was nearly whispering. 'I'm just trying to keep this place running. What else can I do?'

Laurie hung up, sighed loudly, and walked out of her

office. She flung her coat over her shoulders. 'Julia, I'm leaving for the day,' she said. 'If anything comes up, call my cell.' When she disappeared into the lobby, I reached for my wallet. I still had Sara Yamashita's business card from the night of Nick's party. I ran my finger along the edge of the thick card stock, thinking.

'Are you kidding?' Abby said to me. This was a few days later, the weekend before Thanksgiving. We were at a Mexican place on the Upper East Side. She swiped a tortilla chip through the guacamole. 'You should call her. Absolutely.'

'It doesn't seem too pushy?'

'Jules. She wouldn't have told you to call unless she actually wanted you to call. Come on! Quit that miserable job of yours. It's what I keep telling Jake.'

'Things are still bad?'

Abby rolled her eyes. When Lehman went under, Henry Fletcher called in a favor with a friend at Barclays, which was absorbing certain Lehman assets. He ensured that his son would have a place in the new organization. But it had all been a waste. According to Abby, Jake's grumpy dislike of the work had morphed into outright hatred.

'Poor guy,' she said. 'He's miserable. I mean, he never liked banking to begin with. The Barclays people are assholes, apparently. He wishes he'd just been laid off, like everyone else. He's going to take the GMAT next year.'

'Wow. Has he told his parents?'

'Hah. You know what they're like. He can't talk to them about this stuff.'

She went quiet, staring down at the table. A week earlier, Abby's father had finally lost his job. She delivered the news with a shrug, a what-can-you-do resignation, but there was a catch in her voice. The value of their house had plummeted by half. Her mom had started looking for work. They were pretending that everything was going to be fine. But Abby, as the youngest, had spent many years learning to decipher the language of her parents. She saw right through them.

'I'm sorry, Abby. That's really shitty.'

'Oy vey,' she said with a sigh. Then she tried for brightness again. 'Hey, could we get two more margaritas? And some more chips?' she said to our waiter as he walked past. She picked up her fork and scooped a bite of guacamole. 'This stuff is seriously like crack. So wait a second: how do you know this girl again? This Sara girl?'

'She went to Yale. She was a few years ahead of us.'

'Funny. Her name doesn't ring a bell.'

'Well, actually – I met her through Adam. Recently.'

'Adam?' She raised one eyebrow. 'Where was this?'

'Some party. He used to know her from the magazine. We sort of hit it off.'

The waiter arrived with a fresh basket of chips and two new drinks. After he took our order, Abby lifted her margarita toward me.

'I think this is great, Jules. Do it. Call her. To new

beginnings.' We clinked our glasses, and I took a sip of my drink – the salty and sweet tang of artificial lime. The restaurant was loud and chaotic, with colorful Christmas lights strung across the mirrored walls and pocked wooden tables. Saturday night in New York City. Moments like this I felt lucky, almost happy.

After dinner, Abby headed toward the subway, and I pretended to walk back to my apartment. But I pulled out my phone and called Adam instead. He was at a dinner party that night hosted by a classmate of his from high school, a downtown party girl who lived in an enormous SoHo loft. 'She's a brat,' he'd said. 'Trust fund when she turned eighteen. Never had to lift a finger.' Adam's critical streak was something I was still learning to navigate. He was suspicious of people who had it too easy, but at the same time he seemed suspicious of people who hustled too hard for their success. That's what I thought at the time, at least. Although later I realized I was wrong about the latter: it was jealousy, not suspicion.

I did sometimes wonder why he acted so friendly toward the people whom he claimed to dislike. I'd asked him why he was going to the dinner party if he hated this girl, and he shrugged. 'She knows a lot of people. Her parties are good for networking.' He grazed his hand along the back of my head. 'I'd have more fun with you, though.'

When he picked up the phone, there was a swell of sound in the room behind him, conjuring a picture in my mind: the beautiful people, the expensive clothing, the perfect decor. I felt a sharp pang of loneliness. 'Hey, you just finish dinner with Abby?'

'Yeah. You're still there?'

'They just cleared the main course. Maybe another hour or so?'

I took a cab to his apartment. The happiness of dinner with Abby had vanished, and I was in a maudlin mood. I wandered around Adam's apartment with an enormous glass of red wine, tempted to let it slosh over the rim onto his pristine carpet. But Adam hadn't done anything wrong; there was nothing I was allowed to be mad about. At some point I lay down on the couch and later woke to the sound of the front door opening. The glowing read-out on the cable box said it was 2:00 a.m. I'd been in his apartment for more than four hours.

'Where were you?' I said, rubbing my eyes.

Adam sank onto the couch, slung his arm around me. 'Sorry. It went later than I thought. I called. Your phone must be on vibrate.'

I rested my head on his chest. He smelled like bourbon and a sugary dessert. The faint scent of tobacco, which I had gradually grown to like. I ran my hand over his shirt, down to his belt buckle, and turned my head to kiss his neck. My addiction was kicking in despite my bad mood, despite the beginnings of a red-wine headache. I pulled him toward me. We had sex on the couch, my dress hiked up and his pants tugged down, fast and hard and mechanical. But something seemed different in Adam. He hadn't needed this the way I had. He was going through the motions, sating my hunger without needing to sate his.

Afterward I told him what Abby and I had talked about over dinner.

'I think I'm going to call Sara. You know, Sara Yamashita, from the party. I'm going to ask her to lunch.'

'You are?'

'She told me to keep in touch.'

'Sara's a lot of talk. I wouldn't get your hopes up.'

'But it's worth a shot, right? It can't hurt.'

Adam reached for my hand. 'Trust me, babe. I know Sara better than you do. It might not be such a great idea. All I'm saying is don't rush into it. You want to be deliberate about your next move, right?'

'I guess.' I glanced again at the cable box – it was almost 3:00 a.m. I started gathering my things, the scarf and boots and coat I'd scattered around the apartment like an animal marking its territory. 'I should get going.' Adam sat back on the couch, taking a beat too long before he stood up to walk me to the door. I wondered how much longer we were going to have to do this – saying good-bye in the middle of the night, sneaking back to our own lives. I was already getting sick of it. In the cab ride home, I checked my phone. There were no missed calls or texts from Adam, despite what he'd said – nothing, from anyone, all night. I was annoyed all over again.

When had I lost the power to control my own moods? I felt so porous that fall, so absorbent of whatever the people around me were doing. There was nothing to keep me tied to the earth. I scudded in whatever direction the wind decided to blow. My mistake was that I kept interpreting it as a good thing, confusing that lightness for spontaneity.

---

'Julia! Hey!'

Someone waved at me from the sidewalk outside the entrance to the bar. It was Camilla, a girl from the lacrosse team. We had lived in the same dorm for my three years of boarding school. She had arrived at school with glasses and curly hair and prissy sweater sets. But after a few months around the older girls, she'd learned the ways of experience – hair straighteners, tight jeans, push-up bras, contact lenses. She started sneaking boys back to her room in the middle of the night. She was legendary by senior year. Camilla stubbed out her cigarette as I approached and gave me a hug.

'Oh, my God, I am *so* glad you came. It's fucking freezing. How can you stand this place?'

'Yeah, sorry. Not exactly sunshine and palm trees. When'd you get home?'

'I flew in on Sunday. I decided to make a week of it.' Camilla had gone to USC and was working as an assistant to some big-shot movie agent in Los Angeles. She had a tan, and her hair smelled like coconut oil. I was vividly aware of how different her life was from mine. 'Let's go inside,' she said, tugging my hand.

I followed Camilla toward the corner of the bar where the other lacrosse girls were standing. Most of them worked in consulting or in finance or as paralegals. A few of the finance girls joked blackly about how much time they had left – the bosses were just waiting for the holidays to pass before they brought down the ax. There were one or two outliers who, like Camilla and me, had found low-paying assistant jobs in more 'creative' industries. 'That sounds . . . interesting,' one girl said after I told her about my job at the Fletcher Foundation. She was an analyst at Goldman Sachs, and we quickly ran out of things to talk about. I was about to use my empty glass as an excuse to leave when I felt a hand on my shoulder.

'Julia?' he said. The dark wavy hair; the aquiline nose. His voice.

'Rob,' I said. 'Wow. Hi.'

'It's been a while, huh?'

'Wow. What, like, four years or something?' But, really, I knew: it had been almost four years to the day since we'd broken up at Thanksgiving, freshman year of college. We hadn't seen each other since.

'You look great.'

'So do you.' He did. Energized, happy. Rob at his best. 'I was just about to get another drink. Do you want to . . . ?'

After we got our drinks, he pointed at an empty booth. 'You want to catch up for a minute?' he said.

In the booth, our knees touched for a brief moment. 'Wow. It's so strange. You look the same,' I said.

He laughed. 'In a good way, I hope.'

'Where are you living?'

'Here, in Cambridge. I'm applying to med school. Working in one of my professor's labs for the year.'

'Med school! Right. I'd forgotten about that.'

'You thought I'd changed my mind?' He smiled.

Later, a waitress came by and brought us another round. Rob could still make me laugh. He was still that boy he'd been in high school, the one who made the younger girls blush when he talked to them in the cafeteria. Whose confidence and affability extended to everyone. He would make a great doctor. For the first time in four years, I found myself thinking about him as a real person. Not as a footnote to my history, a static piece of the past. As a living possibility, right in front of me.

'Are you still with that guy?' he asked. 'What was his name again?'

'Evan,' I said. I could feel the effects of my two and a half drinks. A looseness in my limbs, a narrowing of my mind. 'Evan Peck. Yeah. I mean, sort of.'

'Sort of?'

'Things aren't great. I'm not sure how much longer it's going to last.'

'Really.' His leg brushed against mine. 'That's too bad.'

'What about you? Girlfriend?'

'There was this girl, but we broke up at graduation. It wasn't going anywhere. Honestly, of all the girls in college, I'm not sure any of them really came close to you.'

He moved nearer, resting his hand on my knee. I was almost overwhelmed by nostalgia, by the rush of memories: fall afternoons on the sidelines of the soccer field, cheering for Rob after he scored a goal. Study hall, kissing in the dusty back corner of the library. The way he would sometimes catch my eye in the middle of class, backlit by the morning sun, and wink as our teacher droned on about mitochondria. Life opening up before us. That moment bursting with possibility – a feeling that now seemed light-years away. I never thought things could get so complicated. I didn't think I was capable of feeling so uncertain, so confused. Rob leaned closer, and so did I.

'Julia!' Camilla was yelling from the bar. 'Get your ass over here!'

The spell broke. We took a group picture. The band, back together again. Camilla ordered a round of tequila shots, but I demurred. I had to drive home. On my way out, I waved good-bye to Rob. He mouthed, *I'll call you.*

The next morning, I went downstairs and found my mother in the kitchen, hands on her hips, staring at a casserole dish. The turkey was already in the oven. The pies were lined up neatly on the counter. Jasmine, our housekeeper, had made everything days in advance.

'Well, there you are. Happy Thanksgiving, sweetheart.' She kissed me on the cheek, then resumed staring at the casserole. She poked it and frowned. 'I can't for the life of me understand what Jasmine did to these potatoes.'

'The same thing she does every year?'

'She's trying something new. That's what she said. It smells' – she leaned forward, sniffing – 'I don't know. It smells *off*.'

'I think that's just garlic.'

'Garlic.' She sighed. 'Why does everything need to have garlic in it?'

She came and sat next to me at the kitchen table. She was wearing what she called her 'work clothes' – faded jeans, an old cardigan – what a normal person might wear to the grocery store but what my mother only wore within the confines of the house. She wouldn't be caught dead looking like this in front of her friends. She was sipping her coffee and watching me while I peeled a banana.

'Mom. What?'

'Your hair is getting so long.'

'I haven't found a place in New York yet.'

'Why don't you just get it done while you're here? I can call. I'm supposed to go in tomorrow.'

'How was the party last night?'

'Oh, it was nice. The Fletchers are doing some land-scaping, so their yard is a complete mess. Your father is actually on the phone with Henry right now.'

'Is something going on?'

'Everything's fine.' She set her coffee down and rubbed at an invisible scuff on the table. 'Did I tell you? I've been asked to join the board of that new women's clinic. You remember, the one Mrs Baldwin is involved in?'

'Is that why we had to invite the Baldwins to Thanksgiving this year?'

She pursed her lips. 'We invited them because they're our friends. You've known them a long time. Don't you remember how much you loved it when Diana used to babysit for you? Anyway, it's a wonderful organization.'

Charities and nonprofits sought out my mother for many reasons. My father's firm was a generous and reliable donor; she was a lawyer herself and could perform certain legal functions; she was smart and asked the right questions. Her days had long ago become full with assorted obligations, as full as they would have been with a normal job. When I was younger, around eleven years old, she'd considered going back to work. She mused about it out loud, asking me and Elizabeth whether it would be okay by us. Until, abruptly, those musings stopped. Then she'd been brittle with us in the weeks that followed, losing her patience and snapping at us more than usual. It didn't seem fair; it wasn't our fault. I knew the reason – I'd overheard the argument – but something drove me to ask the question. Maybe I wanted her to finally lose it, to admit her anger. I felt an anticipation of shame, and a sick curiosity, as I said it: 'Mom, why *didn't* you go back to work?'

Her cheeks reddened. But that was all I would get. She had too much control.

'Because, sweetheart, I want to spend time with you and your sister. *That's* my job. That's the most important thing to me in the whole world.' She smiled, her face returning to a normal hue.

But I knew the truth. A few weeks before that, the night of the incident, I'd been setting the table for dinner when my dad got home. My mother poured a glass of wine and slid it across the kitchen counter toward him.

'I have good news,' she said.

'Oh?' My dad took a sip of wine. 'This is excellent. Is this the Bordeaux?'

'James. I got the job.'

He took another sip, slowly, then set his glass down. 'You did.'

I'd rarely seen her smile like that. Goofy, giddy. 'They met all my terms.'

'Julia,' my dad said, 'why don't you go see where your sister is?'

I held up the forks and knives, bunched in my hand. 'But I'm setting the table.'

'It can wait. Go ahead.'

As I walked out, I tried to catch my mother's eye. But she was staring at my father, and her smile had disappeared. I ran up the stairs, then along the second-floor hallway to the top of the back staircase, which led down to the kitchen. I climbed down the back staircase as quietly as possible, stopping just before the kitchen came into view. I held my breath and listened.

'But you knew this wouldn't work, Nina. I told you that *weeks* ago.'

'No. No. You said you had some concerns, and we

agreed that we'd discuss them when the time came. Okay, so now's the time. James, I had to work my *ass* off to get this job. This is an incredible opportunity. It's the best class-action group in the country.'

'This is a terrible idea. The girls need you at home. And we don't need the money.'

'I don't care about the money. It's important work. A third of my cases are going to be pro bono. Do you know how hard I had to push to get them to agree to that? Do you know how unheard of that is?'

'It's a massive conflict of interest. That firm has multiple cases pending against my clients.'

'So I recuse myself from those cases. We put up a Chinese wall. Plenty of people have done this before. You think we're the first pair of lawyers to ever run into this?'

'You cannot do this. You will not. You'd be working for a bunch of glorified ambulance chasers. You'd be embarrassing me in front of everyone we know. You'd be embarrassing *yourself*.'

I flinched at the sound of glass smashing against the wall.

'Nina, stop it.'

'It's my turn, James.' She was shouting, her voice high and hoarse.

'You're not thinking straight. You don't want this.'

'Fuck you. Don't tell me what I want.'

Shortly after that, my father came upstairs and told us that we were going to McDonald's for dinner. Elizabeth was gleeful – we never ate fast food – but the whole time I felt a sad lump forming in my throat. Those french fries were bribery. My mother's car was missing from the driveway when we left, and it was still missing when we got back from dinner. Lying in bed that night, I tried to make myself cry, but I couldn't.

In the morning, my mother was back, smiling tightly as she waved us off to the school bus. There was a ghost of a red wine stain on the kitchen wall, scrubbed but not quite erased. The next week, she announced that we were renovating the kitchen, a project she claimed she'd been thinking about for a long time. The contractors sealed off the doorways with thick plastic. They let her do the honors. She picked up the heavy crowbar and swung it against the old walls and cabinets, smashing them into dust.

---

The Baldwins were friends of my parents from the neighborhood: the husband a surgeon at Mass Gen, the wife on many of the same committees as my mother. I was seated next to Mrs Baldwin, whose earlobes were soft and stretched from her heavy pearl earrings. She took tiny, precise bites of her food and dabbed her lips with her napkin between every bite. 'So, Julia. How is life in New York? What an exciting time this must be.'

'It's good. A lot of friends from college moved down, too, so it's been fun.' I took a big swallow of my wine. 'But tell me about Diana. What's she doing in Paris?'

Mrs Baldwin beamed. She loved nothing more than talking about her perfect children. 'Oh, Diana is just wonderful. She *adores* Paris. I'm not sure she'll ever come back!' She laughed in high, tinkling tones. 'She's fluent in French – did you know that? She's working at the American Library. She has a little apartment in the Seventh. One of her best friends is the niece of the ambassador to France, so she's become friends with everyone at the embassy through her. Isn't that marvelous?'

'It sounds great,' I said, reaching for the wine.

'You studied in Paris, didn't you, Julia?'

'Yes. Spring of junior year.'

'I remember that. Your mother told me how much you loved it.'

Well, of course she did. My mother had studied in Paris during her Wellesley days, too, and she laid out the reasons why I ought to go; she was the one who pushed me from hesitation to action. At first it felt like I was just doing the sensible thing, following in her footsteps, making her happy. But I had loved it – that was true. Not instantly. It was a love that came gradually, and it felt sweeter for it.

I went in armed with a plan. My first week in the homestay, before classes began for the semester, I'd get up early and make an itinerary for the day: museums, scenic routes, famous patisseries. My hostess encountered me on one of those mornings as I was scrutinizing a guidebook over breakfast. She looked baffled when I explained: I had a long list of sights in Paris that I wanted to see. I'd use this time, before school started, to knock out as many as possible. She stubbed out her clove cigarette and sat next to me at the kitchen table.

'Julia,' she said in a thick accent, preferring her bad English to my even worse French. 'This is not what you do. You come to Paris to live. *Alors.*' She closed the guidebook firmly. 'You do not use this. You walk the city and you see it. You understand, yes?'

I took her advice, and I walked through the city for the first time with no plan and no guidebook. It was a cold, miserable, wet January day. I'd worn the wrong shoes, and my feet were soaked and freezing within five minutes. I went into a café for lunch and ordered an omelet, and the waitress smirked at my pronunciation. The food sat strangely in my stomach, and jet lag trailed me through the afternoon. When I was waiting at the crosswalk on the Rue de Rivoli, a bus roared past and soaked me with puddle spray, and that's when I lost it. I was homesick and lonely and I missed Evan so much, and I was crying, and all I wanted was to go curl up on my narrow bed in the homestay. But going back felt like admitting defeat. So I kept walking. I crossed the Pont Royal and wound up at the Musée d'Orsay. My feet were still soaked, and my clothes were, too. My eyes felt gritty and puffy, and I was so tired I thought I might pass out. This was distinctly not how I'd imagined it – my first week in Paris, my first visit to the famous Orsay.

I sat on a bench up on the fifth floor and let the crowds

slide past, obscuring then revealing the artwork on the walls. It felt good to stay in one place, to sit and get warm. The light grew dimmer from the afternoon sunset — January in northern France. I'd been sitting on the same bench for at least two hours. Eventually the crowds thinned, and I had my first uninterrupted view of the art in front of me. There was a Monet that I recognized. The Parliament building in London, silhouetted against a reddening sky, the sun reflected in the water. A painting I'd studied before, in class. That day in Paris, I stared at it for so long that it changed into something else. No longer a specific building in a specific place but a mixture of color and movement that the eye could interpret any way it wanted. It was like when you say a word over and over and it becomes strange and new, a collection of sounds you'd never thought to question before. When you learn that there is something to be gained by examining what's right in front of you.

I lingered until a security guard told me to leave. I bought a postcard of that painting in the gift shop, and when I got back to my homestay, I tacked it up on the wall next to the photograph of my mother, the one I'd found a few weeks before. My mother as a younger woman, before her life had solidified onto its current course. Every morning during that semester in Paris, those images were the first things I saw when I opened my eyes. I began to think of them as a pair, as a symmetry. The past, the present. They reminded me of the gift I'd been given: time. Time to do nothing, or time to do whatever I wanted. I didn't need to have it all figured out. The uncomfortable feeling that had plagued me through sophomore year, that had made me feel strange and restless – it had taken a while, but it had finally evaporated. I was okay, right where I was.

Mrs Baldwin was regarding me with a quizzical expression.

'I'm sorry?' I said, emerging from the undertow of memory.

'I said, you're living with your boyfriend in New York, isn't that right?'

'Right. Right, yes. We went to college together. He works in finance.'

Those data points rendered him acceptable. Mrs Baldwin didn't need to know any more. She started telling me about her son's wedding over the summer – it was just the loveliest wedding, they were married at the Cloisters, the bride's parents were famous-ish, and the mayor came. I refilled my wineglass again, then again. The memories of Paris had made me melancholy, had reignited a longing for some vanished chapter of my life. It was a feeling too big to hold on to.

'You okay?' Elizabeth said between dinner and dessert, after we had gotten up from the table to load the plates into the dishwasher.

'I had too much wine.'

She snorted. 'Sitting next to Mrs Baldwin? Next time I'd go for something stronger. Heroin, maybe.'

'How was your end of the table?'

'He kept touching my hand. Like, to make a point in conversation. But he was leaving it there a little too long.'

'Dr Baldwin? Ugh. Creepy.'

My parents waved good-bye to the Baldwins as their car backed out of the driveway. When the front door closed, I noticed a slump in both of them. The mask dropped, the smile loosened. They didn't particularly enjoy the company of the Baldwins any more than Elizabeth or I did. But they did see the utility of their company. The Baldwins were the right kind of people with the right kind of connections.

'Just leave it,' my mother said when Elizabeth and I started clearing the dessert dishes from the table. 'Let Jasmine get it in the morning. I'm going to bed.'

She trudged up the stairs. My father retreated to his study off of the kitchen; always more work to be done. Elizabeth shrugged and went up to her room, too. Pepper had been in his crate all through dinner, and no one made a move to let him out. So I unlatched the door and fed him a scrap of piecrust from Mrs Baldwin's plate, then took him for a long walk through the dark and sleepy neighborhood.

# CHAPTER 11

## *Evan*

Roger caught me earlier that day. 'Trouble in paradise?' he said, clapping me on the shoulder.

I jumped in my seat and exited the browser where I'd been looking at apartment listings, but I felt the heat rise in my face. Roger sat down across from me, grinning with glee at his discovery. 'The wife mad that you've been spending so much time in the office? She kicking you out?'

'Shut up, Roger.'

'Oh, wow. Did I hit a nerve?'

Several hours later, Roger was gone. Everyone was gone, except for me. The streets were quiet when I finally left the office around midnight. The scattering to home had begun that afternoon. The only signs of life in our neighborhood were the divey Irish bars jam-packed with city kids who were home for the holidays from college, drinking with friends.

In the bathroom, brushing my teeth, I heard a strange noise. A mechanical chirp. After a minute of confusion,

I finally saw it on the ceiling: the smoke detector, flashing a yellow warning light. I dragged a chair over and disconnected it, took the battery out, and it went silent. It was too late to go out and buy a new battery. I'd have to survive a night without it.

But I couldn't fall asleep. The whole apartment felt unsettled – it had ever since I'd gotten back from Las Vegas. I'd taken to lingering longer and longer at the office to avoid it. At least I could still feel normal at the office. Even when she wasn't around, the feeling of Julia clung to the apartment. I'd started checking online apartment listings in my spare time, furtively, clearing my browser history afterward like I'd been watching porn. The options beckoned: sexy, seductive, a fresh start. Rents were loaded with incentives, post-crash. The new glassy, high-end buildings on the far West Side were perfectly affordable for a young finance bachelor. Then I'd shake my head. I wasn't a bachelor. Julia and I were still together, after all.

I kept tossing and turning that night, thinking I was hearing the distant chirp of the dead smoke detector. I finally drifted off, but I woke a few minutes later with a start. I thought I smelled smoke, but I knew it was nothing.

The next morning, as I passed the diner on the corner, I stopped and peered through the window. A TV in the corner showed the crowds at the parade. It looked cozy inside. The jingling bell announced my arrival, and a sullen waitress showed me to a table. 'Happy Thanksgiving,' she said, slapping the laminated menu on the table. 'You want coffee?'

The coffee was sour and burned, and the eggs were runny, but it didn't matter. I'd passed the diner every morning, and I'd always wanted to stop there. When the man at the next table departed, he left behind his copy of the *New York Observer*. I grabbed it, straightening the crinkled pages. There was a story about the war in Iraq, the troops celebrating Thanksgiving in Baghdad and Basra. An item about the Detroit bailouts. At the bottom of the front page was a teaser for a story inside:

**HEDGE FUNDS DOWN IN 2008**
*Results show steep drop in earnings across industry. A12*

I flipped to page 12. It was Adam McCard's byline.

'More?' the waitress said, not bothering to wait for a response. She tipped the carafe and let the coffee splash over the sides of the mug.

I skimmed the story. Manhattan, Greenwich, Stamford — everyone was having a bad year. Negative returns, investors yanking their cash, waves of layoffs. Hundreds of funds had shut down already, and more were on the brink of collapse. Sometimes you had a bad year, everyone knew that. But this looked to be something bigger. A bad decade, or more. Even at Spire, money was tight, and there weren't going to be any bonuses that year. People grumbled, and Roger let slip, bitterly, that he'd been counting on a bonus to make up for the money he'd been wasting on bottle service. But I think most of us knew how good we had it. We still had our jobs. Spire was the one hedge fund in the industry that hadn't laid off a single person since the downturn.

The WestCorp deal had finally gone live earlier that week, on Monday, a few days before the holiday. Michael had called me into his office that morning. He gestured at me to sit, then he shut the door. He didn't mention the car ride on Friday night, what had happened, or what we'd discussed. And that was okay – I didn't need him to explain anything. I finally felt like I got it. Like everything made sense.

'Evan. I realized I never actually thanked you for coming on the Las Vegas trip the other week, on short notice. You were immensely helpful. So thank you.'

'Of course. I was glad to.'

He searched, it seemed, for a crack in my expression, a sign of sarcasm or timidity. Finding none, he reached inside a drawer and withdrew a manila envelope.

'This deal is going to make history. And 2009 is going to be a record-setting year for us because of it. But you probably know that things are tight in the interim. I debated whether I ought to give this to you. But I wanted you to have it as a token of Spire's appreciation. Of my appreciation.'

He slid the envelope across the desk. 'I doubt I need to say this,' Michael said, 'but it would be best if you kept this quiet for now.'

After I left his office, I went into a bathroom stall and sat down on the lowered toilet lid. I paused, for a moment, to make sure I was alone. I ripped open the envelope. Inside were several stacks of crisp hundred-dollar bills. I counted them slowly. It took a long time. I counted them again, to be sure.

Twenty thousand dollars in cash. There was no note.

---

I spent Thanksgiving Day at the office. I deleted old e-mails, checked over some models I'd been working on, read a backlog of market reports. I was already impatient for the holiday moratorium to be lifted, for work to resume. Around midday, my cell phone started vibrating. I smiled when I saw the name on the caller ID.

'Arthur!'

'Hey, Evan! Happy Thanksgiving.'

'You too. Jeez, man, I thought you were dead. How are you?'

Arthur was even busier than I was, and I figured my unreturned e-mails and calls were a symptom of that. A funny reversal of roles had happened by the end of college. Freshman year, Arthur lived in my shadow. Physically and metaphorically – being an athlete came with a certain amount of built-in respect. I was the one who knew about the parties on Saturday nights, whose name was recognized by other people. But by senior year, Arthur was the bigger man on campus. He'd grown into himself. He was president of the debate society, elected to Phi Beta Kappa, tapped for one of the elite senior societies. Arthur Ziegler was going places.

The noise of a full household echoed from the other end of the line. I remembered the Thanksgiving I'd spent with him, freshman year, all the cousins and aunts and uncles. The cramped dining-room table groaning under the weight of too many dishes, voices shouting to be heard over the Buckeyes game on TV. Four years had gone by: was that possible? He surely must have noticed the comparative silence coming from my end. It was the first time that day it occurred to me how depressing this must look to someone else. And then he asked:

'Hey, so where are you today? Are you up at Julia's?'

'No, actually – no. I couldn't get away from work.'

'They don't even let you have the one day off?'

'It's been crazy lately. But it's all right. You know how I feel about her parents.'

He laughed. 'How is Julia? You guys are still dating, right?'

Did he know how close to the truth he was cutting? 'She's fine.'

'Just fine?'

I felt something tightening inside. To be honest, that was the real reason Arthur and I hadn't talked much since school ended. The night before graduation, we'd run into each other at the pizza place on Broadway. We got our late-night usual: one slice of cheese for him, two pepperoni for me. We wound up in my bedroom, talking, reminiscing. I was sitting in my desk chair, and Arthur was perched on my bed, swinging his feet above the floor. I was halfway packed, posters stripped from the walls and the closet rattling with empty hangers. The next morning, in a few short hours, we would don our caps and gowns and assemble for the graduation procession. Arthur was talking about the Obama campaign, how his work would put him on the front lines of history. He sometimes turned a little grandiose when he was drunk.

'Are you nervous at all?' I asked.

'No. This is what I'm meant to be doing. I know it.' He drummed his fingers against his thighs and nodded, lost in his own thoughts. Then looked up at me, his eyes narrowing. 'But what about you?'

'What about me?'

'Are *you* nervous?'

'For what?'

'Well.' Arthur swept his hands across the room. 'Everything. New York. Your new job. But mostly, *dun-dun-dunnn* – moving in with your girlfriend.'

I laughed. 'Nah. Not really.'

Arthur went quiet. A heavy expression descended on his face.

'Well, maybe you should be.'

'What does that mean?'

'I just mean,' Arthur said, 'it's a serious step to take. Moving in together. Are you really ready for it? Sometimes I wonder whether you've thought it through.'

'Wait. Wait, what? I don't remember you saying any of this when I was actually making this decision.'

'Well, honestly, I kept hoping you'd see it on your own.'

'See what on my own?'

'What a colossal mistake this is.'

I jerked my head back and laughed. This had to be some kind of joke.

But Arthur took a deep breath. 'She's just – well. Look, I'm not trying to offend you. Maybe I shouldn't have said anything. But Julia can be difficult, right? I know how it's been with you guys. And I worry that without some space between you, some breathing room, she could drag you down into the morass with her.'

My hands were gripping the back of the desk chair. So hard that I thought the wood might splinter. 'This is my girlfriend you're talking about,' I finally said.

'I know. But I've known you a long time, Evan, and I've known her a long time, too. And she can just be so . . . well, self-pitying. You've seen what she's like when she's in a bad mood. And I know she's had a hard time finding a job –'

'Oh, come on,' I snapped. 'That is so petty. She'll get a job.'

'Right, well, that's not exactly the point. The point is whether it's a good idea to be moving in with someone so self-centered.'

'You're calling her self-centered?' I shouted.

He stared back at me. 'Yes.'

'What the fuck is your problem?'

'I wouldn't be telling you this if I didn't think it was for your own good.'

'Oh, well, in *that* case.'

Arthur sighed. 'Forget it. Forget I said anything.'

I stood up and opened the door. 'It's late. I think you should go.'

The next morning, we managed to act like nothing happened. These would be the pictures printed and framed, to be looked at years later: graduation day, all of college reduced down to a single snapshot. Julia had her camera with her, and she made us pose together, two roommates with their arms slung around each other. Still best friends, four years later, amid a sea of black polyester robes fluttering in the May breeze.

My mind snapped back to the present. The glowing, blipping computer monitor in front of me, the hum of the lights overhead. Arthur on the other end of the line.

'Julia? Uh, no, she's good. I don't see that much of her. I'm barely ever home. But she seems to keep busy.'

'That's good.'

There was a long pause. Arthur cleared his throat. 'Well, they're about to carve the turkey. I'd better get going.'

We hung up and promised, emptily, to talk again soon.

---

I had chalked it up to jealousy at the time. Arthur never warmed to Julia. When I was with her, I wasn't with him. Simple as that. I suspected that they were too much alike. Not superficially, but underneath they had that same quality. A watchfulness, a gaze that never missed a thing.

It was why I liked them both so much. They took me in whole without my needing to explain myself.

So that's all it was, I told myself while Julia and I drove a rented U-Haul down I-95 to New York the day after graduation. Arthur's words had been humming through my head since our fight. He was jealous. He thought I was picking her over him. Those nasty things he'd said – it was just envy. In our tiny new living room that first night in New York, I looked over at Julia. She had her hands on her hips, head cocked to one side, deciding where to hang the pictures. I felt such a rush of love at that moment, watching our new life become real. It wasn't a fluke, the way I felt about her. We were meant to be.

But Arthur's words were back again. Fresh and whole, like a submarine breaking through the surface. Had he been right all along? Self-centered. Self-pitying. Julia had an independent streak that I'd always liked, but since graduation, it had hardened into something else. A life so separate that I wasn't even part of it.

Had I known it, too? Julia was flawed, like anyone else. Sometimes she could be selfish, it was true. But she had so much that transcended it. When things were good, the selfishness disappeared completely. And for most of our time together, that's the way it was. I'd had glimpses of how it might be different. Our fights. The way she could snap like a sprung trap. One weekend sophomore year, when her friends from boarding school were visiting, I watched her turn into this other version of herself. They were catty and cruel, making fun of old classmates on Facebook, getting more vicious with each bottle of wine. 'Look at her dress!' Julia shrieked, mouth stained red with drink. 'God, she looks like a Russian prostitute.'

But those moods passed quickly. Mostly, college had been good to us. Julia's arc bent toward a happier version of herself. Senior year, after we got back from our summer abroad and our visit to British Columbia, she was more comfortable and relaxed than I'd ever seen her. There was one night in particular that sealed it for me, that seemed like definitive proof of the kind of person Julia had become. A Saturday in early September, near the start of senior year.

'You sure it's cool if I don't go?' I said. Abby's society was throwing a big party that night. A fancy one, with a dress code and bartenders. I sat on her bed as Julia was getting ready.

She caught my eye in the mirror. 'Of course. You already had plans.'

'It's just with the guys. I could cancel.'

'I don't mind. Hey, how do I look?'

She spun in her dress and heels. I smiled. She didn't even need me to say it.

But later that night, when I was hanging out at the hockey house, plans shifted. One of our teammates was also in Abby's society, and he texted me and some of the other guys around 11:00 p.m., begging us to come to his rescue at the party. It was a question of loyalty; we couldn't leave a teammate twisting in the wind like that.

When we arrived, ten minutes later, I saw what the problem was. This was one of those parties where the main form of interaction was conversation. The lights were too bright, the music too quiet, the whole vibe too stiff. He stood in a corner, eyes wide and terrified. Making friends with new people, especially nonathletes, was not his strong suit. The poor guy. When he saw us, he practically shouted 'Thank God.'

A few heads turned at his outburst. Julia was one of them. I felt immediately guilty. So I hadn't been willing to come to this party for her, but I had been willing to come for my friend? We lumbered in like a bunch of cavemen. I was still wearing a baseball hat and hadn't shaved in more than a week. There was no way this wasn't embarrassing for her. She spotted me and walked quickly across the room. I braced for impact. I deserved whatever I was about to get.

But instead she threw her arms around me. 'Thank God is right,' she whispered. She turned to my teammate and added, 'I am *so* glad you told them to come.'

'You're not mad?'

'Why would I be mad? This party is dead. You just saved my life. Come on, let's get a drink.'

Julia got the bartender to pour a dozen shots of whiskey. She raised her glass for the first toast. 'To bringing home that championship,' she said, and everyone cheered. One of my teammates nudged me after Julia threw her shot back without a grimace. 'She's a keeper, man.'

It was one of those long, meandering nights, the

best kind, when you don't need a plan. By senior year, all of us finally understood that we did, in fact, belong there; that we were no longer faking it. We ended the night, many hours later, lying in Julia's bed in the darkness.

'I'm so happy,' she said. 'Evan. I want you to know that.'

'I'm happy, too.'

She was quiet for a while. Then her hand drifted over, her fingers intertwining with mine. 'I'm just so glad we made it. You know?'

I leaned over and kissed her on the forehead. 'I love you, Jules.'

'Mmm,' she said, yawning, curling up in sleepiness. 'See? You always know exactly what to say.'

This was the Julia I loved the most, the person whose love meant more for having been tested, for having endured. But in the months between graduation and late fall, the story had changed. The arc I'd seen over the previous four years had vanished. Her outlying behavior became the new normal. She was spikier, crueler. Harder in every way. I considered the question from different angles. Had something happened in the world, an outside shift that set her in a new direction? Or was it inevitable, an uncovering of the person she'd always been? Maybe it wasn't that her flaws were balanced out by the good. Maybe it was that the flaws were merely one side of a two-sided coin. What made a person good also made a person bad. Confidence could easily become arrogance.

A sense of humor was only ever a few rungs away from cruelty.

———

Things were back to normal by late afternoon. E-mails started flooding in, and my BlackBerry resumed its regular buzzing. Michael told me he wanted to review the WestCorp numbers first thing the following morning.

As the sky darkened and night fell, I felt better. It was weird, actually. It was the opposite of that sick Sunday night dread I'd sometimes felt in college, the looming threat of classes in the morning. I was already thinking happily about the next day, about the office coming alive again with the sounds of work, the way it was supposed to be. I had told Julia about my bonus earlier that week, but I hadn't told anyone else. I'd stuffed the money into my sock drawer. I liked the idea of it tucked away, secret proof. On the walk home, I decided to stop for a drink. Maybe I ought to celebrate. It was Thanksgiving night, and Michael was right, after all. This was a historic deal. I ought to take a moment to savor it.

It was a cold, clear night. Along Central Park South, I passed families bundled up inside horse-drawn carriages, the hooves clopping loudly on the pavement. Christmas lights laced the awnings along the street. I saw the Plaza Hotel up ahead. I'd been to the Oak Bar once before, with Julia. We came into the city one weekend senior year to have dinner with her parents. We'd gone for a drink at the Oak Bar afterward, then caught the last train back to New Haven. At that hour, 5th Avenue had been so peaceful, just the two of us for blocks at a time as we walked down to Grand Central, the passing whoosh of a street sweeper and the silent drift of steam from an open manhole.

When I walked in, the bar looked just as I remembered – dark wood and leather and a soft glow from the chandeliers. I ordered a martini, and it slid down my throat, cold and bracing and wet. I ordered a second one. The bar was half full, a murmur of conversation and clinking ice cubes occasionally punctuated by the cocktail shaker. There was a beautiful foreign-looking couple at a table, the woman's neck dripping with diamonds. Another young woman in a black dress, a few stools down, glancing nervously at the door. A mother and father and two little boys, the parents drinking their nightcaps while the boys munched on peanuts. It was comforting, being alone in a room with other people. A floating island where we'd all happened to seek refuge in this eerily quiet city.

The door swung open, letting in the cold. A man in a dark coat and cream-colored scarf came in, peeled off his leather gloves, and ran a hand through his hair. He turned, and I felt a pulse of recognition ripple up my spine. I knew him from somewhere. He scanned the room, and his eyes landed on me.

He recognized me, too. He smiled and strode over.

'Hey – it's Evan, right? Evan Peck?' He extended his hand.

'Yeah. Hi.' I squinted. 'God, I'm sorry, you're so familiar . . .'

'Hey, don't sweat it. Adam McCard. We met a few times through Julia.'

Of course. That grin, the too-strong aftershave.

'Right. Good to see you, man.'

'You, too. You're in the city these days?'

'Yup. Yeah, Julia and I live together.'

'Oh, no shit. You two stay in town for the holiday?'

'Just me. I couldn't really get away from work.'

'So you wind up here on Thanksgiving night. Hey, things could be worse.' He laughed, showing teeth like white coins. There was something different about him. The few times I'd met Adam in college, he'd always looked past me. Always scanning the room for something else. But that night his eyes were fixed directly on mine.

'So where do you work?' he said.

'I'm in finance. Spire Management – a hedge fund, actually.'

'Wow. They're huge. You liking it there?'

'Yeah, I am.'

'Rough year to start a career in finance.'

'We've been lucky. No layoffs, knock wood.'

'Amen. What are you working on over there?'

The bartender swooped over. 'Another martini, sir?' I shook my head and asked for the check. When I turned back, Adam was still staring. 'Oh, the usual stuff,' I said.

'You know,' Adam said, lowering his voice, 'I saw that

270

Spire's taking a big position on some lumber company up in Canada. Some really ballsy play. You work on that?'

Part of me wanted to take credit for it, just to shut Adam up. *Yes, I did, and what the hell have you done lately?* But I was skittish about saying too much. The deal was public news, but it was habit by then, keeping it close to the chest, need-to-know. 'Not really,' I said lightly. 'But what about you? I've seen your articles. They're good.'

He stared for a beat longer. Then, suddenly, the old Adam was back. His gaze slackened and his eyes surfed across the room. 'Thanks,' he said in an empty tone. 'Glad you're a fan. Hey, great running into you. I'd better go join my date.'

The woman in the black dress at the bar lit up with a smile at Adam. 'See you around,' Adam said to me. He slid on the stool next to the woman and pulled her in for a long kiss. She had transformed from her nervous self and was suddenly playful as a kitten, kissing his neck and snuggling against him. Adam snapped his fingers at the bartender. I drained the last of my martini and stood up to leave, feeling slightly sick.

# CHAPTER 12

## *Julia*

The forecast called for snow – up to ten inches in the city, the first blizzard of the season. A few flakes were starting to fall when I went out for lunch that Friday afternoon in December, for a chicken-salad sandwich and a Diet Coke from the deli around the corner, where the cashier had finally started to greet me as a regular.

Laurie had spent most of the day with her door shut. Was there something unusually tense in her mood, in her heavier footsteps and louder sighs? I didn't notice it at the time. I was daydreaming about the weekend. Abby was throwing a holiday party on Saturday. I had Christmas shopping to do. For Adam, in particular. I'd saved a few hundred dollars during the previous months, bits and pieces from my paychecks. It was a good feeling, having money I had earned and could spend any way I wanted. It was the first time I could say that. I wouldn't be able to impress Adam monetarily, but maybe I could impress him with a gift that proved just how well I knew him.

Something small and perfect. More evidence that we were, in fact, meant to be together.

'Julia,' Laurie said, startling me from a consideration of whether I could afford one of the first-edition Updikes I'd seen in the window at Argosy. 'Come in and talk to me.'

She shut the door and lowered herself into the chair behind her desk. This was bound to be something annoying. We weren't just going to chitchat, that was for sure. I'd long since given up hope on that. Laurie only called me in to give dull, impersonal, demanding instructions. A new workflow procedure that needed enacting, a problem that needed fixing. I had forgotten to bring a pen and paper. *Pay attention,* I thought.

'So Julia,' she said, sweeping the papers on her desk into a neat stack, squaring the edges. 'We have to let you go.'

I waited. I wasn't even sure I'd heard her right.

Laurie cleared her throat, her eyes still fixed on her desk. 'The donation promised to us by the Fletchers has fallen through at the last minute. It's been a difficult year, you obviously know that, and with market circumstances changing so rapidly, the Fletchers didn't feel they could follow through on their initial commitment. And so without that, we have to cut costs. We're letting others go, too. I'm afraid today will be your last day.'

I blinked like a dumb animal. *Say something,* I thought. *Don't just sit here.* But I couldn't. My mouth was dry and hot and cottony. The room was too warm, the radiator groaning and clanking with steam. Laurie should open a window.

'You're awfully quiet,' Laurie said. 'Do you have any questions?'

I tried to think of something, anything, to say. This might be my only chance. 'How many others?' I managed.

'I'm not at liberty to discuss that. You're the first person we've told.'

She finally met my gaze. Didn't she feel an ounce of pity for me, the person who had sat right outside her office for the past five months, answering her phone and making her coffee every goddamn morning? Didn't she feel *anything*? I wanted her to explain it, to apologize, to lessen the blow somehow. To say *something,* anything. It's not personal. We're so sorry to do this. Why me? Why not somebody else? Questions? There were a hundred questions swirling through my mind, but I didn't know how to articulate them. So when Laurie said, 'Is that it? Do you have any other questions?' I just shook my head.

'You'll be paid through the end of the month. You can leave as soon as you've gathered your things. And we'd appreciate your discretion for the time being. Please don't say anything to the others just yet.'

The phone started ringing. 'I should take this,' Laurie said, visibly relieved at the interruption. 'Could you close the door on your way out?'

I sat down at my desk. I heard the printer humming, the phone ringing in the lobby. The office was unchanged from a few minutes earlier, except for the silent bomb going off in my brain. A half-written e-mail floated on my computer screen. It was a summary of Laurie's expenses for the month of November, for accounting. A rote, routine e-mail. Anyone could do this after I left. But why not just finish it? All I had to do was attach the statement and click Send. I was numb.

It was as I started typing that it hit. My hands shook. I was aware of the smooth plastic keys against my fingertips, the too-loud clacking, the strange way the words emerged on the screen, like someone else was writing them. The last e-mail I'd ever write from this desk. Finally it exploded, flooding my mouth with a sickly iron-tinged flavor. I had just lost my job. I was unemployed. *Unemployed.* I turned off the computer, gathered my things – an extra pair of shoes, a coffee mug, a spare sweater, that was it – and waited for the elevator. Unemployed. Unemployed. It ran through my head like blinding ticker tape.

Outside, the snow was starting to thicken. Fat, lazy flakes drifted heavily through the air, coating the pavement in white. There was the sharp piney smell of Christmas trees for sale down the block. I tried calling Abby, but it went to voice mail. I tried my parents next, but they weren't there. Then I called Adam. He picked up right away.

'They fired me,' I said, my voice splitting in half, tears springing unbidden.

★

I used to wonder, those months I lived in New York, about the women I saw crying in public. Usually they were on the phone, sobbing into the mouthpiece. It was always women. What was it? I wondered. What bad news were they delivering or receiving? It was so disturbing, one red crumpled face in a sea of blank expressions. Did they know something that the rest of us didn't? Was this the first wave washing ashore with news of some global tragedy, something we'd all hear about in a matter of minutes? In this city, privacy was a luxury. You shared the sidewalks and subways with strangers, heard sirens through the windows, your neighbors through paper-thin plaster. What you did – what you *had* to do – was erect invisible walls to protect yourself. A stranger sobbing on the street, a dirty hand holding out a cup filled with change, an elbow digging into your back on a crowded train. The person in your bed whom you haven't really talked to in months. Look forward, breathe in, shut your mouth, think about other places. Think about anything except what's right in front of you. It's a way of staying sane in an unreasonable place. But at that moment, I saw the downside of this careful indifference. Even in the cab I wasn't alone, though I might as well have been. I hiccuped and cried, and the taxi driver kept his gaze straight ahead, the scratched plastic barrier between us.

Adam gave me the name of a hotel bar in midtown, said that he was on his way. I stopped in the bathroom to clean myself up. I looked awful. I splashed cold water on my face, dropped Visine into my eyes, reapplied lipstick and mascara. I missed Evan suddenly. He'd seen me like this before, crumpled and exhausted and freaked out: our fights in college, the moments of bad news, the disappointments, the long four years. He never cared how I looked. And he wouldn't try to stop it; he wouldn't tell me to snap out of it or calm down. He was quiet and steady, always ready with just the right thing to say. This vanity was stupid. It didn't matter how I looked. And yet there I was, fixing my hair and makeup like someone about to embark on a blind date.

Adam wasn't there yet, so I found a seat at the bar with a view of the TV in the corner. The bartender came over, and I ordered a vodka soda with lime. The TV was tuned to CNN. A reporter in Kabul was describing a recent spate of fatalities. I knew I ought to feel lucky. I could have been born in war-torn Afghanistan, every day fearing for my life, and instead my biggest problem was losing a job I didn't even like. I had no right to complain. This was my mother kicking in, her voice in my ear. *Don't be a brat, Julia.* I finished my drink and waved to the bartender for another. I was glad that my parents hadn't picked up the phone, actually. Their sympathy would be brief, and then they would immediately embark upon the project of Fixing My Life. But I wanted a few dark hours to dwell in my resentment. I wanted to get really, really drunk. I wanted Adam to fuck me and then hold me while I fell asleep. I didn't want to go back to my shitty apartment on the Upper East Side, my shitty life.

I realize now: that should have been another clue. I had just lost my job – I *hated* the sound of those words – but I didn't want the encouragement of my parents. I didn't want the genuine sympathy of Abby. Even though part of me wanted to call Evan, I didn't, I couldn't – I couldn't go back to that old life. I didn't want anything useful from the people who'd known me the longest. What I wanted was Adam. He offered me an escape. A new situation entirely. I couldn't see it at the time, but Adam was always the easiest way out.

When I was halfway through my second drink – where was he? – the CNN anchor switched to coverage of the Bernie Madoff scandal. Madoff had been arrested the day before. They interviewed one of his victims, a sad old man in Florida with eyes like a basset hound. I fiddled with my phone, wondering if I should call Adam. Abby had texted. Saw your call, what's up? I had started typing out a reply when I heard my name.

He ran over. He *ran*. That's how much he cared. I dissolved. 'Oh, Julia,' Adam said, kissing my forehead. 'Babe, babe. It's okay. I'm here.' He was the only one who understood. He put his arm around me and steered me toward a booth in the corner. I hadn't wanted to cry in front of him like this, but maybe it didn't matter. If Adam and I were going to be together, really together, I had to trust that he wouldn't care about a few tears. He went to the bar and returned with whiskey for him and a vodka soda for me, with a wedge of lime floating on top. A little part of me wondered whether he'd finally remembered my drink order or whether the bartender had corrected his mistake.

'Do you want to talk about it?' he asked. He held his glass up, clinking it against mine. 'Or should we just leave it at "Fuck them, they're idiots"?'

He wanted me to laugh. I did, and he smiled.

When I told him what happened, I found that a story emerged. A narrative with a satisfying arc. It was so obvious when I traced it from beginning to end: I was the victim. *I didn't deserve this.* So what if I'd hated the job? That wasn't the point. The point was that it was unfair. I had worked hard, never made a mistake. I'd been fucked over, and I was angry about it. I had every *right* to be angry. It had taken the firing for me to see that. I was angry at Laurie and the Fletchers and Evan and everyone who had been treating me like shit for the previous six months. The floodgates were opening.

'So wait a second,' Adam said. 'Laurie said that the Fletchers had to cancel their donation for financial reasons, right?'

'Yeah. Apparently they're having a bad year.' I thought of my father, on the phone with Henry Fletcher every day over Thanksgiving weekend. It made sense. The Fletchers were running out of money.

'Did she say specifically that they were strapped for cash?'

'I don't really remember. It happened so fast.' He was staring at me. 'Why? What is it?'

'It doesn't add up.' Adam pulled his phone out, typed something in, then handed it to me. 'Look at this.'

'What?'

'It's from today's *Journal*. Just read the first paragraph.'

ForeCloser, a company that tracks upcoming foreclosure auctions within a given geographic range, announced today that it has raised $20 million in Series B financing. The round was led by Fletcher Partners and included founding investor Henry Fletcher. ForeCloser will use the financing to aggressively increase the scope of its geographic coverage, which is currently limited to California, Washington and Oregon. In the announcement, the company outlined a goal of covering all 50 states by the end of 2009.

I looked up at him.

'Do you see what this means?' he said. 'The Fletchers are fine. They have plenty of money. Maybe they withdrew their donation, but it wasn't because they didn't have the cash for it.'

'So they still could have donated the – then what?'

'I'm sorry, babe. It isn't right.'

Something turned. Darkened. 'What the fuck, then? Why would they do that?'

'I don't know, Jules. These people play by a different set of rules. Henry Fletcher isn't thinking about what's fair or not. Maybe when things were flush, he was happy to toss a little aside to make his wife happy. You know, give her a charity to play with. But now that the market's bucking, he has to stay lean. You see what he's doing, don't you?'

Adam finished his drink, held up two fingers at the bartender. His eyes were hard, shining, in pursuit of something. I'd never seen them like that. Or at least that's what I thought, in the moment. I *had* seen that gleam before. I knew what it meant. But I'd suppressed that memory with remarkable success.

'I mean, look at this company he's investing in. People want to snap up these foreclosures while they're cheap, and Henry Fletcher is going to get rich by helping them do it faster. They'll make money flipping these properties, and he'll make money giving them access. These guys just drove the economy off a cliff, and now they're trying to suck more money from the corpses. They're actually profiting from all this. It's more than unfair. They should go to jail, if you ask me.'

The alcohol made everything swirl together. Evan always at work. Tossing aside the manila envelope, like it was nothing. The arrogance, the indifference. Why did no one ever care about right or wrong? Why did no one ever care about *me?* Adam slid a new drink in front of me.

'It's fucked up, right?' He held my hand tenderly. My mind was going fuzzy, the radio signal growing faint. 'They shouldn't be allowed to get away with these things. None of these guys should.'

★

The spark had been lit. I'd succeeded at one thing, at least: getting really, really drunk. I was aware, in a detached way, of the rising pitch of my voice, of my frustration releasing in a continuous vent. Everything came spilling out. Adam kept signaling to the bartender, never letting my glass sit empty. What was I saying? I lost my train of thought. He mentioned Evan's name. I shook my head. I hated Evan; I hated everything that Evan made me feel. Evan, who reminded me of everything that had gone wrong, of every disappointment.

I felt myself curling in at the edges, growing blacker. Evan. It spun together into one theme: Fletcher, Spire, Madoff, all of it. I grasped at it through the vodka, the point I was trying to make to Adam. How had I never seen it before, the way the world worked? I described the strange identification I'd felt with Madoff's sad, gray-haired victims on TV. We were casualties of the same greed-fueled catastrophe. Adam nodded vigorously. He understood. *Don't we have to do something about it? Don't we have a responsibility to stop these things?* He asked me about Evan again. What had I meant about Spire? What was going on there? *You don't have to protect him, Julia. You need to let these things out. You can't carry this around by yourself.*

The afternoon plunged into darkness.

At some point I got up to use the bathroom, wobbling in my heels. In the hotel lobby, people came and went. It was nighttime. My head spun as I sat down on the toilet. I propped myself up with one hand against the stall. Later, minutes later, hours later, in front of the bathroom mirror, I tried to fix my reflection in one place, but it danced and wavered no matter how hard I stared.

I spun around and stumbled back into the stall and threw up. The bile came in miserable waves. With one hand on the toilet, then one on the stall, I pushed myself up like a fever-weak patient. I rinsed my mouth in the sink and hunched over the basin, watching the water swirl around the white porcelain before vanishing down the drain, wishing I could follow it down there, away from all this.

———

In the time that has passed since that day, I've asked myself, over and over, whether I was aware of what I was doing. Aware of what I was setting in motion. Did I think it was the right thing to do? Did I know the impact it would have? I ask myself now: is guilt determined by outcome or by intent?

I woke up the next morning in Adam's bed, and I knew this wasn't a regular hangover. The headache and dizziness and dry mouth were compounded by a nagging awareness. I had done something wrong the night before, something not on a continuum with the cheating and the white lies. But, amazingly, I got up and went about my normal routine. I drank two glasses of water, took a long shower, dressed. I pushed the previous night to the back of my mind and I walked out the door. I didn't even say good-bye to Adam, who was sleeping soundly. Outside, the sidewalks were white from the blizzard. The doorman hailed me a cab, and we flew across the silent snowscape of Central Park. It was early, and the snow was pristine, unmarked by footprints and sled tracks. I had no idea – no conscious idea – of the turning point I had just passed. One chapter of my life over, another about to begin.

Time has made it worse. It isn't just regret for that afternoon, for the things I shouldn't have said to Adam. It's the bigger realization that the entire thing was a mistake. Last year is like a movie starring somebody else. It's a scene in time lapse, sped-up and frantic, everything moving too fast to grab hold of. That girl, the girl who existed from July to December – she wasn't the person I had been before. She tricked herself, twisting the reality around her into something different. She was looking at it all wrong: like it was a plan finally coming together. She should have known better. The signs were always there. But there was something narcotic about the fantasy I was living, the idea of becoming someone else. No one had told me that doing these things could feel so good. They could feel so good that they blocked out everything else. They put to sleep the part of me that should have been watching.

———————

The afternoon plunged into darkness.

'Jules, babe, it's okay. Shh.'

I was crying again.

'I'm sick of it. I'm sick of him. He told me all this like

284

it was *my* problem, too. He dumped it on me, and I've been carrying it around for weeks.'

'What is it? What did he tell you?'

'Spire. It's this deal they've been working on. It's messed up. It's rigged. They've been lying about it the whole time.'

'Who has? People at Spire?'

'His boss, Michael. Evan is part of it, too. He went along with it.'

'Michael Casey, you mean? Shh, Julia, it's okay. I'm here. I'm here.'

I was still crying, hot and angry tears.

'I'm so si-si – sick of him. He's an *asshole*.'

'Tell me what Evan told you. How was the deal rigged?'

'It's Michael. He knows people. Government officials in China. He bribed them to let them import from the Canadians, to get around the taxes.'

'How did he bribe them?'

Did I notice Adam reaching for the notepad in his pocket? Did I register his one-handed scribbles under the table? Did he even do this, or am I trying to rewrite the past, to insert a screaming siren for my former self, to make her sit up and notice what she was doing?

With his other hand he held mine, rubbing his thumb across my palm.

'Jules. Did Evan say how they bribed them?'

'Immigration. Canadian immigration paperwork. Spire and WestCorp helped the Chinese get their papers.

285

That's why they went to Vegas. I could kill him. He's such an idiot.'

'They got papers for the Chinese, is that what you're saying? In exchange for getting them visas, these officials are letting them export their lumber to China? Jules? That's what you're saying, right?'

'I hate him. Hate him.'

'Julia?'

———

Saturday, the day after. There was a feeling clinging to me that refused to be brushed away. A hammering in my heart. In the cab across Central Park, from Adam's apartment to mine, I texted Abby. My phone buzzed with her reply a minute later. Oh, Jules, I'm so sorry. Are you okay? Can you still make it tonight? I'm so sorry.

The cab let me out. I brushed the snow from our stoop and sat down. My dad picked up the phone. My mother was out, walking the dog. How was I? What was going on? I told him everything, including what Adam had said about Fletcher Partners' investment in the new start-up. When I finished, he sighed heavily. I could picture him in his study, the leather-bound books and diplomas lining the walls. Leaning into his elbow on the desk, rubbing the bridge of his nose where his glasses sat. Finally he said:

'Sweetheart, obviously I'm sorry to hear about this, but I hope you understand how complicated it is. The Fletchers have many factors to consider. It hasn't been an easy year for them. I'm sure they were very unhappy to have to do this.'

He'd used this voice on me before. A voice with an unbearable weight to it. My father wasn't someone to whom you talked back. His lawyerly gravity made you so painfully aware of your shortcomings: your irrational emotions, your unthinking reactions, your taking things personally when nothing was personal. The world wasn't against you. Stop indulging yourself. Why had I expected this time to be any different? But part of me had hoped for that, for some rare tenderness from my father, and I felt a doubling of the heaviness. A deflating of that hope and an awareness that I should have known better than to harbor it. He was taking the side of his client over his daughter. It shouldn't have surprised me.

An ache in my throat made it hard to swallow. 'I know, Dad.'

We hung up. The sky was clear blue, and the sunlight reflected off the snow. It was still early for the weekend, and Evan would probably be home, not having left for work yet. I could have lingered longer at Adam's, stayed for breakfast, but a voice in my head had propelled me out of his apartment. But now, at home, something kept me stuck to the stoop, just shy of the threshold. Evan probably wouldn't ask where I had been, or care. He'd keep assuming whatever he'd been assuming all along. But he would notice the redness in my eyes and know that I'd been crying. Over the previous few months, I'd built such a careful distance between us. He went to his office, I went to mine; he had his life, I had mine. I had Adam. There was barely anything left. But Evan would ask what was wrong, and I would start crying again, and I knew, just knew, that he would comfort me like he used to. He would remind me that everything would be okay, like the good boyfriend he always was in times of crisis. That careful distance would disappear, and I didn't know what would happen next. I wasn't sure I had the courage to find out.

When the door behind me opened with a suctioning whoosh, I stared straight ahead, ready to avoid eye contact with whichever neighbor was coming out. It would be easy; I knew no one in our building.

'Yup, yup, I'm on my way in now. I'll be there in ten minutes,' the familiar voice behind me said. I turned around.

'Julia.' Evan looked surprised. He bounced down the steps to the sidewalk, where he stood and faced me. 'Hey. I was just on my way to the office.'

I had to shield my eyes to block the sun. It was too bright. 'Hey.'

'That was Michael. He needs me to come in for something.'

'Oh. Okay.'

He seemed at a loss for words. 'Hey, are you going to Abby's party tonight?'

'I think so.'

We were a pair of strangers.

He looked closely at me. 'Is everything okay?'

'Oh, well . . .' I was so tired. I couldn't keep doing this. My voice cracked. 'It's work. I got laid off yesterday.'

He stood perfectly still. 'Shit. Julia. I'm sorry to hear that.'

My eyes hurt from the sun. I glanced down at the sidewalk for relief, at the snow and my salt-crusted boots, and then looked back up from under the hood of my palm. Evan was regarding me quietly, like a hunter watching a wild animal. Getting no closer than he had to. Eventually he reached out and put his hand on my shoulder, leaving it there for a moment. That was all he would give me.

'I'm sorry,' I started to choke out, the tears returning to my eyes. And I was – all of a sudden, I was sorry for everything. I wanted to rewind to six months earlier, when we stood on this stoop in the June humidity with our boxes, when we opened the door for the first time, when we hadn't yet started down this path.

But at that very same moment, he said, 'I have to get to work.' I don't know if he heard me. When he removed his hand, then removed himself and walked down the street toward an available cab, I felt the imprint of him linger on my skin, like a memory pressing itself to me one last time before it vanished forever.

# CHAPTER 13

## *Evan*

'Where the hell is he?' Chuck said, craning his neck toward the glass walls of the conference room. The meeting had been called for 9:00 a.m. sharp, and it was 9:06. 'He's keeping half the company waiting.'

Roger took a swig of coffee. 'I don't think Michael's real concerned about how busy the rest of us are.' He jiggled his knee, knocking against mine on purpose.

This was the weekly Monday status meeting, the last one before the end of the year. An empty chair awaited Michael at the head of the table. Roger and the other analysts and I sat around the perimeter of the room. Chuck, seated at the back end of the table, turned his chair around to talk with Roger. Most of the higher-ups at the table were in a sedate Monday mood, chatting about soccer practice and piano recitals, plans for Christmas in Aspen or Saint Barts. Chuck's wedding was fast approaching, and his fiancée spent most of her weekends in Connecticut ironing out the wedding details, which left Chuck by himself in the city, enjoying one final run of debauchery. Every Monday morning, he and Roger traded stories from the weekend.

'A model? I don't believe you,' Chuck was saying.

'For real. Apparently she's the next big thing out of Croatia.'

'Did you check your wallet before she left? Or maybe you just paid her up front. I know some of them won't have it any other way.'

'Fuck you, man. I'm not washed up like you. I don't have to pay for ass.'

'Bullshit. What about Vegas?'

'That's different. That's Vegas. Even *Evan* was paying for it in Vegas.'

Chuck raised an eyebrow. 'Evan?'

'Our first night there. He didn't come home until the morning.'

Chuck threw his head back and laughed. 'You think our little Evan was out with a *prostitute?*'

I felt the heat rising under my collar. I should have said something, changed the subject. But in the previous few weeks, I'd learned it was better not to draw attention to myself.

'Well, where was he, then?' Roger was acting like I wasn't right there.

'He crashed on our couch that night, in my and Brad's room. After you and your hooker locked him out.'

Brad, sitting across the table, glanced up at his name. He froze, thumbs hovering above his BlackBerry keyboard. He looked at Chuck, but Chuck had already moved on. Then Brad shifted his gaze to me. I could see the rapid realization in his stare.

The room went quiet. Roger's knee stopped jiggling. 'Finally,' Chuck muttered, spinning around to face the table.

'Morning, everyone,' Michael said, and the room murmured in response. He took his seat at the head of the table. 'Steve, why don't you start us off?' Steve nodded and launched into an update, doing his best to make the macro group's weak results sound palatable. Michael watched him with his hands steepled together, like a villain out of a movie. He did look the part: steely gray hair, a face carved with deep wrinkles, a skeptical squint. People still feared Michael, as they always had, but now the fear was earned. He was in charge; he'd saved the company. Things were going exactly as planned on the WestCorp deal. The rest of the world had noticed West-Corp's growing exports, and their stock was rising rapidly, just as predicted. There were whispers that Kleinman was going to stay in DC and angle for the top job at Treasury in the new administration. That would mean Michael was permanently in charge, and that my trajectory at Spire could continue unchecked. Michael hinted at a raise and a promotion on the horizon. I couldn't really believe how lucky I was.

But I had miscalculated what would happen after the deal went live. The rest of Spire didn't want to see that the firm's survival hinged on this one specific deal. The only thing they saw was their exclusion from it. We were the competition. Roger confirmed it for me a few days earlier. I bumped into him as I was leaving Michael's office. 'Shit, sorry,' I said, bending down to help gather the papers he'd dropped. While we were crouched, our faces close, Roger snarled: 'You think you're real hot shit, don't you?' People stared at me pointedly in the hallways – others, not just Roger, had noticed how much the newly powerful Michael had taken me under his wing.

I thought they'd be happy about the success. I thought I had finally proved that I belonged in this world, too. But I wouldn't make that mistake again.

A parallel had become clear to me. For a long time I'd hoped that things would get better, at home and at work. That the small daily miseries – jealous glares from co-workers, stiff silences from Julia – would eventually prove temporary, if I worked hard enough. But it was Julia, the previous weekend, who finally made me understand. I'd been hurrying out the door on Saturday morning, and Julia was sitting on the stoop, her eyes red and puffy. She told me that she'd been fired. I felt a pulse of sympathy for her, and then – nothing. I was struck less by the news than by my own lack of reaction. It was like hearing about a minor plane crash in a distant country. Sad, but not sad for me. On the way to work, I wondered whether it was a delayed response. Maybe the feeling would come later, the feeling of watching a loved one suffer. But it never did. I didn't love her anymore: that was the answer. Simple and clear. I was relieved to realize this, actually — it was about time. I shouldn't have kept loving Julia for so long after things had turned so bad. And I shouldn't have expected that Roger and the others at Spire would see me as anything but the competition. It wasn't worth it, caring about people who didn't care about you.

The droning at the front of the conference room stopped. Wanda was waiting for Michael in the doorway. He gestured at the person talking to continue. On the other side of the glass wall, Wanda fluttered her hands as they spoke. She looked nervous.

Michael stuck his head back in. 'I have to take this,' he said to the room. 'Finish without me.'

In the silence, Steve cleared his throat, said we might as well keep going. But I wasn't listening anymore. I leaned back to watch Michael and Wanda retreating down the hall toward his office. Michael was walking so fast that Wanda had to run to keep up.

Around noon, I passed by Michael's office for the ump-teenth time that day. The door was still closed. Wanda's chair was empty. I turned my back, pretending to exam-ine the papers in my hands. The hallway was quiet, and I strained to hear something, anything, through the door.

'Excuse me,' a woman said, pushing past me. It was our head of PR, a woman in a bright green dress and a crisp bob, her bracelets jangling as she knocked hurriedly on Michael's door. Her perfume had a distinctive musky scent, a trail she left whenever she barreled through the hallways to put out a fire. A smell I had come to associate with panic. She opened the door without waiting for a response. A loud conversation erupted through the opening before she slammed it shut again.

I walked back to my side of the floor, scanning faces and computer screens and conversations for clues. The floor was emptier than usual, but the lunch hour would explain that. A muted TV flashed silently in the lobby. Two analysts tossed a Nerf football back and forth from their opposing desks. The wind outside had picked up, and when I stood at the windows at the edge of the building, I could see black umbrellas popping up like mushrooms on the street far below. The last of the lingering snow would be gone by the afternoon.

At my desk, I hit the space bar a few times to wake my computer. I watched Roger nodding his head to the music in his earbuds, typing with emphatic keystrokes, looking perfectly normal, exactly like he looked every day.

But I knew, even if I didn't know what: something was wrong.

That night was supposed to be the Spire holiday party, an extravagant dinner at the Waldorf or the Pierre followed by a long night of drinking. It had been canceled this year. The recession made it impossible, both financially and optically. The secretaries felt bad for us, so they improvised. Tinsel was strung in the hallways, and miniature Christmas trees and menorahs decorated their desks. Around 6:00 p.m., someone went around offering beer and Champagne. There was a scrappy, festive mood that night. The year from hell was nearly over.

But I was restless. That afternoon, like something out of a dream, I found myself back at Michael's door, arm raised and fist clenched, ready to knock. *Stop,* I thought, and I shook my head. Whatever it was, Michael could handle it. I stayed at my desk the rest of the day, willing my mind to focus, trying not to obsess about things I couldn't control.

Roger was drinking a beer. He'd stolen the Nerf football from the other analysts and was tossing it up and down with one hand. He was in the middle of a running monologue about what to order for dinner.

'Hey, Evan,' Roger said, chucking the Nerf at my chest. It bounced to the floor before I had time to catch it. 'Listen. We need to decide. Italian or Chinese?' He burped. 'Let's get more beer, too. We can expense it, right? Anyway . . .'

Roger may have hated me, but he liked an audience more. He sounded out every mundane thought that passed through his head, narrating every part of his life. I was used to it by then. I let it wash over me without really listening.

'Y'know, though, there's a new Vietnamese place I think we should try, too. Shit – what's it called?' He sat down at his computer, his cheeks ruddy from the beer. 'You know, the one on Forty-fifth. Or is it –'

I heard a ping from Roger's computer, the sound of an e-mail arriving. He clicked, his monologue trailing off, then he went silent. His eyes were scanning the screen. I heard the same ping sounding on the computers around me, like a chorus of chirping birds.

'Holy shit,' Roger said. 'Holy shit.'

'What is it?' I tilted back in my chair, tossing the Nerf from one hand to the other.

Roger's face went pale. 'Check your e-mail. Right now.'

The message came with a bright red exclamation point. A news alert. I double-clicked to open it. My stomach plummeted as I read the headline:

### SPIRE UNDER SCRUTINY
Evidence of bribery sparks investigation

*No,* I thought. *No, no, this can't be happening.* But of course it was happening. It was the exact fear I'd been trying to suppress all day. I clicked through and began to read the article:

Federal authorities have initiated an investigation into whether Spire Management, a New York City–based hedge fund, bribed the Chinese government to obtain favorable terms on lumber imports.

The investigation was launched after the *Observer* contacted authorities for comment on Spire's practices in China. The paper learned, through confidential sources within the company, that Spire Management has bribed highly placed Chinese government officials in order to

arrange for tax-free imports of lumber to China from several
Canadian companies. Spire has taken an aggressive position on these companies, which includes the conglomerate
Pacific WestCorp, and stands to profit significantly from
their growth.

A review of WestCorp's most recent quarterly statement
shows that exports to China have increased substantially
over the third quarter, and the company expects continuing
significant growth in the next fiscal year . . .

The byline at the top of the story stood out in big,
bold letters. Adam McCard.

Roger was staring at me when I finished reading. The
floor had gone silent while everyone read the news.
The only sound was of the building's joints, creaking in
the high wind.

'Did you know about this?' Roger asked, in a charged
whisper.

Was I being paranoid again, or were people murmur-
ing as I passed? A numb panic spread through my body:
my limbs had gone leaden, but my mind was racing faster
and faster. I speedwalked over to Michael's office. All the
e-mails and phone calls back and forth with WestCorp.
The delivery to Chan in Las Vegas. Security footage from
the cameras in the hallways at the Venetian. Chan's cack-
ling demands. The $20,000 in cash, still sitting in my sock
drawer. There were a thousand different trip wires suddenly lying in wait.

Wanda was back at her desk. Her fingers flew across

the keyboard; ten different lines blinked red on the phone. A half-eaten salad lay forgotten at her elbow.

'I need to talk to him,' I said.

She looked bewildered for a second, then laughed. 'Are you kidding?'

'But it's about this story. The WestCorp story. Please, Wanda.'

'Evan. This is way above your pay grade, okay? Just go home, get some rest. It's the best thing for now. Trust me, hon. I'd help you if I could.'

When I got back to my desk, Roger stared at me with a mixture of pity and contempt, maybe even a little bit of awe. I turned off my computer, pocketed my phone, put on my coat. The elevator whisked me down to the ground floor. Outside, the night was consumed by a vicious rainstorm, dark and howling and damp. I walked to the subway at Times Square, dodging umbrellas and sprays of water from cars streaking by. One foot in front of the other. Just keep walking. I elbowed my way into the middle of the train for a seat and collapsed, my clothes dripping wet.

I thought of Brad, shouting and seething with anger that night in Las Vegas. It would have been nothing to him to pick up the phone and vent it all to a reporter. Michael had a fat bull's-eye painted on his back. Anyone who resented him, anyone who wanted him gone, any of those people would have happily spilled the news. And who knew how many people Brad could have told? Chuck, or Roger. Roger, his jealousy barely guarded by derision. He wasn't someone used to coming in second. On the roof that day in September, the day of the crash, he had been the one to summon forth Adam McCard's name. *I always read the* Observer. *Just for their finance guy. He's good.* Adam's silky touch might be exactly what Roger's wounded ego needed. Making Roger feel like he was doing the right thing. It explained Adam's pointed questioning when he ran into me at Thanksgiving. He'd been chasing the scent of the story. Roger had acted so surprised when the news broke.

Who would do this? *Why* would he do this? If someone really hated Michael, if he wanted him gone, there were other ways. Roger or Brad could have gone straight to David Kleinman, and Kleinman would have handled it – probably would have rewarded the whistle-blower, to boot. Instead, whoever did it had gone nuclear. Someone was willing to blow up the whole company because of some petty jealousy. I felt my blood rising. It stank of hypocrisy. Everything Spire did, every bet we made and trade we transacted, was dependent on some kind of asymmetry. We had better information, faster networks, a heavier footprint. We got rich to the detriment of some other party. That's how it always worked. For this particular deal to be singled out was completely arbitrary. How many hundreds of morally questionable deals had been made at Spire in years past? Who had the gall to decide that, here, a line had been crossed? Who had the *right?*

I knew how it would go. It would be a fucking

nightmare. The country had just been devastated, and it needed someone to pin the blame on. The SEC would come in with guns blazing. In the papers, on TV screens, broadcast over radio waves: people wanted blood. They bayed for revenge. The complexity of subprime mortgage products meant that the real bad guys might never face punishment. But this story, our story, was easy to understand. Rich guys bribe the Chinese in order to become richer. All while the rest of the country shrivels in a drought of our own creation. I saw it from the outside for the first time, just how bad this looked.

The train pulled into 77th Street. The crowd moved up the stairs in a slow trudge, each person pausing at the top to open an umbrella or pull up a hood. It was earlier than I usually came home, the tail end of rush hour still thick with commuters. My thoughts looped back to Adam. That slimy bastard. Preying on disgruntled employees to get his next story; converting other people's unhappiness into fuel for his ambition. I wondered what Julia ever could have seen in him, even as a friend.

Then it occurred to me, as I waited for the light to change on 3rd Avenue. Julia. Had she seen Adam lately? Had she mentioned his name? I sifted through my memory: no, she had never said anything. But this city wasn't very big. Even I had run into Adam, and what were the odds of that? And Julia kept in touch with everyone, even people she claimed to dislike, even the bitchy girls from prep school. But she hadn't uttered his name once since that rainy March night, sophomore year, when she'd disappeared upstairs with Adam during that party. I wasn't stupid. I could guess what had happened. But after that party, the fights tapered off. Things felt steadier, calmer. She went away to Paris, and, after that, we were happier than ever. We never spoke about it again. It had been left completely, resolutely in the past.

As I turned onto our block, I passed a group crowded under a bar awning, smoking cigarettes in soggy Santa hats and holiday sweaters. 'Rockin' Around the Christmas Tree' blasted out through the bar's open door. A girl wearing an elf costume stumbled into me as I pushed through the crowd. 'Whoa!' she said, sloppy and laughing. I mumbled an apology. She stuck out her tongue, swaying on her feet. 'Merry Christmas, grinch!' she shouted at my back.

The image materialized as I dug my keys out of my pocket. Julia, turning at the sound of her name. At a bar or a party, or some sidewalk in the city. Smiling at an old friend. Softening and bending toward him, like she had all those years before. A little lonely, bored in her job, with so many hours alone in that tiny apartment. So much restless energy. What might have happened between the two of them, reunited after so long? The conversations, hours and hours of conversation, saying everything she had to say. The things she was no longer saying to me. Julia always loved a good listener.

The apartment was dark when I opened the door. The light, when I flipped it on, illuminated a strange scene. The blanket was rumpled around a fresh-looking dent in the futon. A take-out container of soup sat on the coffee table, still steaming with heat. The dread swelled, a tinge in the back of my throat. Where was she? I spun around, surveying the room for clues. But the rest of the furniture was neat and in place. A bowl and mug sat on the drying rack next to the kitchen sink. The tea towels hung square from the oven door. The bed was smoothly made, the pillows plumped. A stupid phrase came to mind: *There was no sign of struggle*. Julia had just up and left moments earlier.

I pulled out my phone and called her. I belatedly realized that the ringing was louder than usual, coming not just from the speaker next to my ear but also from somewhere in the room. I followed the chime and buzz to the coffee table, where her phone was partially obscured by a stack of take-out napkins. I picked up her phone, which was glowing from my missed call.

The wallpaper on her iPhone screen, for a long time, had been a picture of the two of us taken during that summer in Europe. She had handed her phone to another tourist while we leaned against the railing that separated the rocky path from the bright blue sea below. She loved that picture. The two of us smiling and squinting, happy and tired and sunburned from an afternoon trekking through the Cinque Terre. After the digital shutter snapped, we relaxed our smiles, Julia thanked the tourist, and we walked back to our B and B in Monterosso. That night we drank wine on the terrace overlooking the Mediterranean. She pulled her hair loose from its bun and tilted her head back to look at the stars. I took her hand and led her back to our room under the attic rafters. We fell asleep curled together as the waves crashed far below. But that photo, that moment, that life was gone. In its place, on the phone screen, was a generic image of planet earth floating in space. That image wedged in my brain like a shard of glass. Erasure of our happiest memories. Evidence of just how far we had drifted.

But that's not what I was really looking at. I was reading, over and over again, the text message that appeared on the locked screen of the phone. Eight short words, but that was all it took. It became suddenly, painfully clear who was behind the revelations about Spire. Who had been drawing closer and slipping information to the person on the other side of the table.

Adam McCard, *thirty-two minutes ago*.

I'm sorry, babe. I had to do it.

# PART III

# CHAPTER 14

## *Julia*

Last week I was lying in bed, pretending to take a late afternoon nap but really just staring at the ceiling, when I heard a car pull up in the driveway.

My father wouldn't be back from work until dinner. My mother was busy all day with errands and meetings. I was home alone on that sunny May day. I pulled aside the curtain and saw my sister shutting the trunk of her silver Saab.

It was like Elizabeth had forgotten, for a moment, that I was living at home. A look rippled across her face as I appeared at the top of the stairs. There she was, fresh from her junior year at college, embarking on summer break with all its possibilities – and as I dragged myself down the stairs in ratty old leggings and a T-shirt, I was there to remind her of everything that could go wrong. Failure, heartbreak. A vector for a disease she might catch, too. But the look vanished in a second, and Elizabeth threw her arms around me in a hug.

We had seen each other at Christmas and when she

breezed through over spring break before hopping a flight to Belize. But those had been short, distracted visits, and the depths to which I was sinking weren't yet clear. It was evident enough now: months had passed, my excuses were running out, and I was still hiding inside with unwashed hair and worn-out clothes. After settling at the kitchen table, Elizabeth asked me how I was. The look on her face said she wanted the full answer.

I'm okay. That's what I've been saying all along, hoping that eventually I'll trick myself into making it true. It's been months now. I'm getting over it. I'm okay.

But I'm also, distinctly, not okay. I'm not getting over it. Sometimes I feel like I'm living on two planes: the present in Boston, which I move through physically like a hollow zombie, and that night in New York, where I'm stuck forever mentally, replaying the same disastrous sequence on a loop. The memory persists like a hot cavity. I shut my eyes, and I see Evan. I try to fall asleep, and I see Evan. And I see him as he was at the very end, his face written with disappointment. That's the worst part. It wasn't shock or anger. It was like he'd always known that it would come to this. Four years of my life disappeared into that expression. All the good things that had come before were negated by that pitch-black reminder of what I was capable of – of the person I had been all along.

I called my mother later that December night. I was jobless, single, with nowhere to live. But she was too busy to help, so I moved myself out. I shipped a box of books home. I took a taxi to Penn Station with two bulging suitcases in the trunk. A man in a Santa costume stood on the corner of 34th Street, ringing a bell, collecting for the Salvation Army. Tourists streamed down the sidewalks, eyes shining in the holiday lights, on their way to Radio City or the Rockefeller Center tree. It all receded so quickly. The train pulled out of the station, right on time for once, and a few hours later I was in Boston. As fast as that. My life in New York had ended.

It was like I'd been hit by a truck. My joints felt sore, my skin tender. I hibernated through the winter, confining my movements to the bedroom, the kitchen, the den. I slept too many hours every night – sleep was the only thing I wanted to do, the only way to make the time pass. Lately, though, I'm plagued by a different problem: insomnia. Maybe my body is trying to tell me to move on after the glut of the last several months, but my mind won't let me. So I'm awake late into the night. Nothing works: warm milk, hot baths, prescription pills. I spend hours going for drives through the darkened suburbs, past shuttered windows and empty parking lots, with only the radio for company. My mother hates my middle-of-the-night peregrinations and the way I sleep so late, wasting daylight hours. So now I'm presented with a double serving of guilt: for what I did last year in New York, and for the way I am constantly failing to get over it.

An hour after Elizabeth arrived, my mother got home from her errands, carrying a box from the local bakery.

She beamed when she saw Elizabeth sitting in the kitchen. She was the good daughter, the successful daughter. Elizabeth would never derail her own life, like I did. She was too smart for that. She was only home for a few days before moving to New York for the summer, where she was interning for a famous painter, Donald Gates, in his Tribeca studio.

Elizabeth had just turned twenty-one. We had her favorite meal that night: lasagna and garlic bread, then chocolate cake from the bakery for dessert. Elizabeth leaned forward and blew out the candles, their light pale and flickering in the spring twilight. She looked up at me a few minutes later, while I pushed a swab of frosting around my plate. 'Jules?' she said quietly, but I just shook my head. Evan's birthday had been last week. It was always twinned, in my mind, with Elizabeth's. I was melancholy not because I'd been thinking of him. I was melancholy because, despite my fixation on Evan, I'd forgotten about his birthday until that moment. Time was passing. I was forgetting things, the specific things. Evan was becoming an abstract longing. I was losing him all over again.

Elizabeth's college schedule complemented my insomnia, and we lay awake that night in her bed, the lamp in the corner casting exaggerated shadows across the walls. A cluster of glow-in-the-dark stars floated on the ceiling, a reminder of the lives we had lived in these bedrooms before going away and trying to become grown-ups.

'I wish I could stay longer,' she said. 'It's kind of nice, being home.'

'Me, too. It's so quiet here without you.'

She picked at the dark polish on her thumbnail. 'You could come visit.'

'New York?'

'My roommate is going to be gone most weekends. Her boyfriend lives in DC.'

'I haven't gone back since I moved out.'

'So? You're not banned from the city. It's not like they're going to turn you away at the border.'

'Very funny.'

'You have to meet Donald. He's so great.'

I made some noise of equivocation.

'Come on. What else are you doing up here? It could be good for you, you know – a distraction. Get out of the house.'

'You sound just like Mom.'

'Ugh. Shut up. You know what I mean. It'd be fun. We can go out together.'

'I'll think about it.'

She sighed. 'I'm not tired yet.'

'Welcome to my world.'

Elizabeth lifted a finger and delicately scratched the side of her nose. She was so deliberate, so economical in her gestures. The fidgety tendencies I'd noticed among girls our age – twisting their hair, touching their faces, biting their lips – Elizabeth was completely devoid of. When had she become so mature, so self-possessed? I had been so immersed in my own life the last five years that I had completely ignored hers. I wondered what else I'd missed.

'So Mom's being hard on you?' she said. 'I bet she's going crazy right now, with you hanging around all day. She probably hates it.'

I laughed. 'Yeah, you can tell?'

'Maybe it's good for her. This will teach her a lesson. Not everyone can have perfect children all the perfect time.' She paused. 'But she's always been hard on you. Did you ever notice that? They were both so tough. They set such high standards. I think I had it easier. They didn't pay as much attention to me.'

I propped myself up on my elbows, staring at her. 'Are you kidding me? *You?* You are one hundred percent the favorite.'

'I'm not saying that. It's just – I don't know. With you it's like they had to check every box. You were the first kid. Once you did everything you were supposed to do, they kind of let go of me. Don't get me wrong, it's been great for me. But I always felt kind of bad for you. Everything you did had to be a certain way. Like, do you remember the first time you brought Evan home?'

'Jesus,' I groaned. 'Poor Evan. That was such a disaster.'

It had been terrible. A weekend toward the end of freshman year, we took the train up to Boston for the first parental meet and greet. My dad spent the whole night on the phone with a client. Elizabeth had a friend over for dinner, and they did their best to distract us by chattering about high school gossip. But my mother's mood descended on the table like an unpleasant odor. She decided, instantly, that she didn't like Evan. That he was all wrong for me. That he would never, ever live up to Rob. Evan was sweating through his shirt during dinner.

*So your parents own a grocery store, I hear,* she said, eyebrow arched as she dragged her knife through her green beans.

*That's right,* Evan said. *It's doing really well. They've started stocking a lot more organics lately. It's catching on even in our little town.*

Elizabeth laughed at the memory. 'That was great, actually. She didn't have a *clue* what to say to him. I still remember the look on her face when you told her you were dating a Canadian hockey player. It was worth it just for that.'

Her laughter stopped as soon as the words escaped her. 'Oh, God. I'm sorry. I didn't mean – sorry.'

I shook my head. 'It's fine, Lizzie. Tell me more about Donald.'

The night crept by, the house silent around us except for the occasional chime of the hall clock downstairs. Around 3:00 a.m., Elizabeth finally started to yawn. She drifted off while telling me about a new photo series she was working on. I tucked the blanket around her and went back to my own room, to wait for sleep.

And it was the truth. It was, surprisingly, fine. It was the first time I had talked about Evan with anyone since the breakup. My parents pretended it had never happened. Elizabeth, I think, had pieced together most of it, but she had some of our mother in her – she didn't probe when the topic was too delicate. Whenever Abby brought Evan up, I tended to change the subject. She'd snapped at me once. 'Julia. Seriously. Enough of this repressive WASP bullshit. We *have* to talk about this at some point.' There was a long silence, then she sighed. 'I'm sorry. That was unfair.' But where could I begin?

'It's just . . .' I'd said. 'I just need more time.'

And so to finally say his name aloud was a relief. Like ice shattering. Evan. He existed. He still existed.

I thought I had rid myself of any feeling for him, so that when the break came, it would be clean and easy. Just like the switch from Rob to Evan four years earlier. Adam would be waiting, baton extended, and I would simply reach for it and keep going. But this wasn't to be. Adam wasn't there (how could I have ever thought he would be?), and, more important, Evan wasn't someone I could leave behind so painlessly. At this age perhaps we take change for granted: you can adopt and discard different identities as easily as Halloween costumes, and from that comes the arrogance of thinking that you can decide when, and how, you get to change. Evan had been one chapter of my life, I thought, but for the next – for Adam – I was going to become a new kind of person.

But when everything washed away in the ensuing mess, I was left with something not so easily discarded after all: the girl I had been before everything started. The girl who had loved Evan, who had finally understood that the past didn't have to determine what would come in the future; the girl who had learned to be happy. It seemed that I had her back now, but I worried it was too late. She doesn't fit in anymore. But this is me. This is the real me. I so desperately don't want to lose it, that tender flame of being.

---

I spent that December weekend trying very hard not to think about my outpouring to Adam. Through my pounding hangover that Saturday, I cleaned the apartment. I beat the rugs on the fire escape, washed the windows, scrubbed the bathtub until it shone. That night I went to Abby's holiday party. Her apartment was cheery and cozy, garlanded with lights and tinsel, mulled cider bubbling on the stove. I drank only water, still feeling sick from the night before. Evan had mentioned the party. I'd texted him to ask if he was coming, but he didn't respond. Whenever a wave of noise announced an arrival, I found myself hoping – for the first time in months – that it would be Evan walking through the door. I wanted something beyond our stilted interaction on the stoop that morning. I felt it dangling in the air, like a sharp blade, the danger of what we hadn't said.

By 2:00 a.m., as the party was emptying out, I gave up and left. Evan came home later and slept for a few hours before heading back to work early Sunday morning. I woke up nervous and jittery, needing distraction from my ballooning guilt. (But guilt over what, over which part? I still didn't quite know.) I went to the Met that afternoon, but I couldn't focus on the art. My lack of concentration seemed like a failure, and it gave the museum an oppressive air: another reminder of my inability to engage, to find a passion, to *figure it out*. A tour was wending past, and I clung to it, sheltering myself in the monologue of the leader. It was dark by the time I left the museum, and I went to bed early, falling into a shallow sleep. Evan got home past midnight, and I awoke wondering if I ought to turn on the light and try to talk to him, *actually* talk to him. To offer a real apology. But he lingered in the living room, and I fell asleep again.

Monday morning brought a new sting. Maybe I could pretend things were fine over the weekend, but on a weekday my unemployment was impossible to ignore. I went to the coffee shop down the block and looked online for job openings. I couldn't concentrate. The whirring and banging of the espresso machines, the tinny jazz, the yoga-toned mothers with their lattes. Distractions everywhere. I was waiting for something, but I didn't know what. Adam hadn't called or texted. He hadn't said a thing since Friday night. I reach back and try to remember what I was thinking about Adam at that moment, but I can't quite say. My memory of that time is so infected by what I feel now. Or perhaps it's that I was starting to realize the scope of my mistake. I wasn't fixated on Adam anymore, because Adam wasn't the person I'd have to reckon with. Evan was.

But that can't be entirely true. Later that Monday

night, after I ventured out into the rain to pick up dinner, some thought of Adam had driven me to open my computer. At home, I shook a packet of oyster crackers across my container of too-hot soup while I navigated to the *New York Observer*'s website. Maybe I was curious to see whether Adam had been working all weekend. Maybe I wanted to check the news after ignoring it for a few days. Or maybe an alarm bell was already ringing in my subconscious, finally forcing me to acknowledge the trigger on which I'd been resting my finger for months. I had only lifted one spoonful of soup to my mouth before I saw the headline strung across the top of the website in big, bold black letters for the whole world to see.

---

Last night I thought about calling Evan. It was near midnight, and I was driving down the empty roads in our neighborhood, killing time, the changing colors of the stoplights cascading and reflecting like a beat on the wet surface of the pavement. I pulled over, the car idling askew in a parking lot while I dialed his number. My pulse skittered. I wanted so badly to hear his voice. My finger was hovering over the button when my mind flashed to him, two hundred miles south in New York, his phone vibrating on the surface of his desk or on some bar. Lifting it to check the caller and grimacing at the sight of my name, silencing it without a second thought.

What could I say? What could I ever say that would

explain what I had done? I switched off my phone and turned back toward home.

———————

I read the article on my computer through blurring vision. What stood out the most was the byline at the top of the story. Adam McCard.

It was so obvious. I was so stupid. *Through confidential sources within the company*. Everything I'd chosen to ignore or dismiss or rationalize through the fall – every sign had been pointing to this outcome. Adam had been playing me all along.

I called Adam over and over. It rang before going to voice mail, then eventually it went straight to voice mail. Why bother answering? He knew exactly why I was calling. And I had served my purpose. I sent him a string of texts, my hands shaking. Call me back. WTF?? What the hell is this? I felt a hot bellow of anger at him, but especially at myself. I had done this. This was *my fault*.

I stared at my phone from across the room, wanting to smash it into a hundred pieces. I couldn't think straight. I needed to go somewhere, out, away. In my rush to leave, grabbing a raincoat and enough money to get myself a drink, I left my phone sitting on the coffee table. I realized my error belatedly, in a bar five blocks from home, halfway through my first drink. But I wonder now if I did it on purpose. Evan would have seen the article, would be searching for an explanation, wondering who the betrayer was. He deserved an answer. Maybe I wanted to give Evan the final pleasure of catching me in the act, and myself the punishment of finally being caught.

———

Yesterday Elizabeth waved good-bye through the open window of the taxi that was taking her to the station, for her train to New York. She insisted on taking a taxi, saying she was too old for a big scene at the train station. I was walking back up the stairs to the front porch when my phone rang.

I could picture Abby on the other end, taking a break from her usual Sunday run around the reservoir, hair pulled back in a ponytail, dodging strollers and dogs. I sank into the wicker chair that my parents' interior designer had artfully placed in the corner of the porch, where it caught the summer breeze and a view of the blooming hydrangea. The yard was brilliantly green. Abby had only a few weeks of teaching left in the school year, then a summer of freedom. She and Jake, who had finally quit his job, were planning a trip to Spain, maybe Morocco, maybe Greece – a wandering months-long itinerary.

Abby cleared her throat. 'I have to tell you something.'

I wondered for a flash if she and Jake were moving in together. I never would have predicted that she'd wind up with a preppy finance guy, but they just clicked. The rule book, as far as I could tell, had been thrown out the window. She was happy, and I was happy for her. I had decided, some months earlier, to bury the secret of me and Jake somewhere deep and unfindable. It was something I was glad to let go of.

'What's up?' I said.

'Jake's parents are getting a divorce.'

I wasn't surprised. Perhaps a little that I was hearing this from her – surely my parents had known? – but the Fletchers hadn't seemed happy for a long time.

'Oh, Abby, I'm sorry. That sucks. How's Jake doing?'

'He's okay. But that's not really – it's not just the divorce. It's – well. Dot found out Henry has been cheating on her.'

Of course. He and Eleanor weren't exactly subtle.

'What? Really? That's . . . that's horrible.'

'With your old coworker, actually. Eleanor. I guess it had been going on for a while. Apparently Dot always had her suspicions. There's been a whole string of women from the foundation who Henry's slept with.'

'That's awful.'

Abby was silent on her end. I could hear honking and traffic in the background, a barking dog, a faraway siren. The sounds of the city.

'You there?' I said.

'Okay, Jules, this is going to sound really weird. But I feel like I have to tell you.'

'What is it?'

'Promise you'll stay calm, okay? Deep breaths.'

'Abby? You're freaking me out.'

'So all these women Henry slept with, they were always girls who worked at the foundation. And they were usually – ugh – they were usually Laurie's assistants. I guess Laurie often hired friends of the family as a favor to the Fletchers. They were always the young, pretty ones. Henry's type, I guess. He went through them fast. Eleanor was the exception.'

'Creepy.'

'Dot found this out a while ago. Back in November or December, around the gala. Dot confronted him, and she made Laurie clean house. They fired Eleanor around Christmas. And – God, Jules. She made Laurie fire you, too.'

'Abby? What –'

'Dot's going to keep the foundation after the divorce. She'll have plenty of money to keep it running. But she wanted to get rid of anyone she suspected might have slept with Henry. Which included you. So she made Laurie fire you. The story about having financial problems was a cover.'

I barked out a hybrid cough-laugh-sob. 'Oh, my God.'

'I'm so sorry. I thought you should know.'

'Jesus.'

'Jules, for what it's worth, this is only Dot's paranoia. I told Jake that Julia Edwards is not like that. You just wouldn't do that. Never, ever. You're way too good a person. She's a total bitch for thinking that about you.'

I felt a sick pain in my stomach. Maybe at one point I had been a good person, but not anymore. I couldn't pretend to be offended or outraged at the insinuation. For so long I'd been able to cling to this purity, at least: my firing had been unjust. I was justified in my complaints – until now, suddenly, I wasn't. I *was* a liar. I *was* a cheater. Maybe Laurie had seen that about me all along. This explained her cold attitude all those months. The things she must have thought about me. The roses on my birthday. Sucking up to Dot at the gala. Another pliable, too-eager-to-please young woman making a fool of herself.

The whole time, I'd thought I was too good for that place. But at last I knew the truth, and while the suspicion was wrong, the underlying moral lapse wasn't. Abby was going on, trying to convince me it was going to be fine, fuck them, they're terrible for thinking that about me. The knife twisted. That was the worst part, the unearned sympathy. Abby, my best friend, the person who saw only the good in me, who believed I was innocent. I hung up before she could realize how hard I was crying.

---

The 2nd Avenue bar that rainy Monday night was nearly empty. The bartender saw my wet hair and distraught expression and gave me one on the house. I felt like I was in the last stage of a long race, pushing for the finish line, trying to outrun whatever was chasing me, but I realized – after my second or third vodka soda, I can't remember – that it was pointless. It was done. It was already over.

Evan was sitting on the futon when I opened the door, his head cradled in his hands, a weary cliché. My phone was sitting on the coffee table. He looked up.

'Julia. How could you do this to me?'

I was silent. I had no defense, no excuse. Only pathetic tears, invisible in the slick of rainwater that streamed down my face.

'How long?'

'Two months. Evan, I –'

He shook his head. It was almost like pity. He stood up, put on his coat, and picked up a duffel bag that was sitting by the door.

'I'm going to a hotel for the rest of the week. You can stay here, but you need to be out by Friday. I'm going to call the landlord and get you taken off the lease.'

I should have apologized. I should have at least tried to explain myself, should have thrown myself at his feet, but the expression on his face said he didn't want to hear it. He looked like a person who knew better than to waste any more emotion on something that had been dead for so long.

He paused, one foot propping the door open. A memory flashed – the day we moved in together, Evan turning to me before going down for the boxes that hot June morning. 'Julia,' he said finally. 'It's over. I don't want to see you again.'

---

'Mom? Dad?' My voice echoed in the front hall, the screen door slamming behind me. Abby's words were running through my head, loud and clamoring.

'We're in here,' my mom called from the living room.

She and my father were sitting on the couch, the Sunday paper spread out between them. My father looked at me over the top of his glasses. 'What's wrong?' he asked.

'Did you know the Fletchers were getting divorced? Did you know why?'

My mother glanced at my father, panic skipping across her face. 'Sweetie –'

My father interrupted. 'Why don't you sit down, Julia.'

'Do you want to know why I *really* got fired? Or did you know the whole time and you just didn't feel like telling me?'

He took off his glasses, placed them carefully in his pocket. 'Julia. You know I'm bound by attorney-client privilege. You know what that means.'

'I'm your *daughter*. Doesn't *that* mean something?'

'Of course it does,' my mother said. 'Honey, it just didn't seem like it was going to make it any better. You were already going through such a hard time. We didn't think –'

'What? You didn't think I deserved the truth?'

'Watch your tone,' my father said, his voice snapping into firmness.

'James, that isn't necessary.'

'Nina, don't *coddle* her. And Julia, for God's sake, this isn't all about you.' This was the voice I'd overheard through the years, during so many fights and arguments. His end-of-the-rope voice. I'd never before been on the receiving end. I'd never dared. But a new anger was bubbling up in me. My parents, all that time, listening to me complain about my firing, letting me humiliate myself with every retelling of the story, choosing to keep quiet about the truth. The knife twisted again.

'So you were fine with it,' I said. 'You were fine with them thinking I was some stupid slut. I guess that's more important to you, right? I mean, God forbid you *defend* me. You would never want to stir anything up with the beloved *Fletchers*.'

'*Enough.*' He stood up and pointed at the stairs. 'That's enough. Go to your room.'

My mother looked like she was on the verge of tears. She started to open her mouth. My father barked, '*Nina, don't. She needs to get control of herself.*'

I scoffed. I knew he would hate it, this show of insubordination. 'I'm not a kid anymore. You don't get to talk to me like that.'

'You are. You're a child, you're our child, and you'll listen to me.'

'I'm a person,' I shouted. 'I'm a fucking *person*, Dad.'

My mother came upstairs, knocking light as a butterfly on my door. She sat on the edge of my bed. I was curled up, facing the wall. I had stopped crying an hour earlier, but my pillow was still damp with tears.

'I don't want to talk about it,' I mumbled.

She reached over and laid her palm on my forehead, like she was checking for a fever. 'Honey. I'm sorry about your father. He shouldn't have lost his temper like that.'

Why were we always apologizing for the wrong things? My father and his temper, Dot and her paranoia, my betrayal of Spire's secrets. They were all proxies for the real problem. We talked in circles to avoid what we didn't want to admit. My father, the chauvinist. My selfishness, my complete lack of empathy. But I feared my problems were anchored by even deeper roots than that. I didn't know what it was to love. I had never known. All I had to do was look at my parents. My heart had grown a hard shell a long time ago, long before I had ever thought of boyfriends or lovers or careers or a life of my own. Maybe, under other circumstances, that shell would have made me impervious to heartbreak. But it was only a brittle barrier, and with enough pressure it had shattered and left me exposed.

A month later. Spring unfurls into summer with a string of sunny days. I scan job listings and compose halfhearted cover letters, but each attempt sinks like a stone. I hear about other classmates getting laid off, too many to count, classmates who have also moved back home or applied to the shelter of grad school. I ought to find solace in this company, in the collective misery of the country, but it does nothing to mitigate the specific pain – it's like taking painkillers that flood the body when you have a big, throbbing splinter in your thumb.

There is a certain comfort to bottoming out. To knowing what you're capable of enduring. These past months at home, I kept waiting for things to improve, for the upward swing to arrive. There was one more thing left, though. The last piece of the puzzle. A memory, one I had tried so hard to forget, that finally helped me understand why things had gone so wrong last year.

---

The night of the day when I found out the truth from Abby, after my mother left me alone in my room, I found I couldn't stop thinking about it. What, really, was wrong with me? Why had I done the terrible things I'd done? The nasty voice that had started dogging me the summer after graduation, the doubts and insecurities: it seemed clear where that came from. I had always been the girl who did everything right, who had followed the rules and checked every box. The problem emerged from my failure to continue that trajectory. I had grown too unsure about everything. I hesitated, I wavered. I needed someone to tell me what to do next.

There was the clink of cutlery downstairs. My parents were going to eat dinner like it was any normal night, pretend that fight hadn't just happened, like we'd been pretending all along. Then I heard a soft tap on the door. 'Julia?' my mother said. 'I made you a sandwich. I'm going to leave it here, okay?' Silence, but I could tell she hadn't walked away. 'Sweetheart. We were only trying to protect you because we love you so much.'

I took a long shower. I meant to leave the sandwich untouched in protest, but I was hungry, and my mother's words had softened me. And while I ate, I started thinking. What if I was wrong? What if I hadn't needed someone to tell me what to do next? Last year, after graduation, I'd had no idea what I was supposed to do with my life, and I wanted an answer. But what if the point was the question, not the answer?

It's so tempting. Being told: this is who you are. This is how your life will go. This is what will make you happy. You will go to the right school, find the right job, marry the right man. You'll do those things, and even if they feel wrong, you'll keep doing them. Even if it breaks your heart, this is the way it's done.

That night sophomore year. The memory I had been trying not to think about for so long. After Adam invited me into his room, upstairs at his party, he stepped close and backed me up against the wall. He leaned in and kissed me. For the first time all night – all year – I stopped thinking. I stopped thinking about everything confusing and difficult and uncertain. Doubts about my relationship, about friendships, about what I should major in. The sickening look of disappointment on Evan's face, downstairs. The feeling of having too much space and not ever knowing what I was supposed to do with it. It vanished. Adam was such a good kisser. My mind was finally at peace, focused on only one thing: the person in front of me.

Then a bang sounded from the party below, a speaker blowing out, the music stopping abruptly. We pulled apart, and Adam looked at the door. A loud chorus of booing filled the void. And then, a second later, the music started again. Adam, satisfied that the problem had been fixed, turned back to me. There was a gleam in his eyes, a hunger for something he knew he was about to consume.

But I was frightened of myself, of what I was doing. I'd been this person before – a cheater, a liar – but I didn't want to be that person again. I wanted to be better. Adam slipped his hands to my waist. The clash between temptation and resistance made me nauseous. I wanted this; I didn't want this; I'd been daydreaming about this for months. He kissed me harder and started sliding his hands under the hem of my dress.

'No,' I said, turning so his lips grazed my cheek. 'No, Adam, I can't do this.'

'Yes, you can,' he muttered, kissing me on the collarbone.

'No,' I said, more forcefully this time. 'No, I can't. Please stop.'

I pushed him away. He looked confused. 'You're joking, right?'

'No, Adam. I have a boyfriend. You know that.'

'You're serious?'

I started for the door, but he grabbed my hand. 'Let me go,' I said.

'What the hell, Julia? This is exactly what you wanted.'

'No, it's not. Adam, *stop*.' I tried to wrest my hand free.

He laughed. 'You are such a fucking tease.'

'I'm not – I'm sorry if I led you on. I thought we were just friends.'

'You're *sorry*? Julia, what the fuck do you want? You really want to go back to Evan? Like he's going to make you happy?' He laughed again. 'He's *never* going to make you happy. Anyone can see that.'

I shook my head. 'You're wrong.'

'I'm not wrong, Jules. I mean, you guys are going to break up sooner or later. It's so obvious. So what's the problem here?'

'You don't know him. You don't know anything about it.'

'I know exactly who Evan is. And I know who you are. You're bored. You want more, don't you? You want something better. I know you do.'

He was waiting for me to say something. When I didn't, he stepped closer, his hands against the wall on either side of me. He leaned in so his mouth was next to my ear.

'Let me tell you how this is going to go,' he said in a low voice. I closed my eyes. 'You're going to forget about Evan. Forget about everything else. It's just you and me, right now. Isn't that what you wanted?' I could feel the damp heat of his breath against my neck. 'I know you, Julia. The real you. I know what you want. You're going to stay here with me.' I was thinking: *Is he right?* Does he know the real me? Is that so impossible to imagine? 'You're going to take that dress off. And then you're going to –'

'I'm leaving,' I said, ducking under his arm. He didn't know me. I'd been so stupid, letting my boredom

330

disguise such an obviously bad idea as a good one. I wanted to be better than I had been before. I *was* better. Adam didn't know the real me. He was wrong.

But he grabbed my hand and yanked me back. He pinned me against the wall with his weight and used one hand to pull up my dress, the other to unbutton his jeans.

'What the fuck are you doing?' I squirmed away from his hands.

'Come on, babe,' he said, trying to kiss me. He pressed against me, harder.

'Let me go. Adam, *stop!*'

Finally I got my hands onto his shoulders and used the leverage of the wall behind me to shove him away. He stumbled backwards, tripping.

'Fucking *asshole,*' I said, gasping for air.

He stared at me, his cheeks flaming red, then cooling. Then, after what felt like an eternity, he shrugged. 'You know what, babe? I feel bad for you. I was just trying to help you out.'

I straightened my dress and wiped his spit away from my mouth. 'Your loss,' he called as I slammed the door shut.

He graduated two months later. It took more than two years before he finally acknowledged what had happened that night. And by then – as awful as that night had been – the scar tissue had hardened so much that I couldn't even feel the original wound underneath. I saw Adam again, and I didn't remember what had come before. I didn't want to remember. From the moment

Adam came back into my life, I grew restless and unhappy and yearned for something new. I thought he was the answer. I never stopped to think that Adam was the source of my unhappiness. I thought my life was the illness and Adam was the cure. But the more time we spent together, the deeper my dissatisfaction grew. His presence was the only thing that could distract me from it. And so I kept returning to the well, drinking deeper and deeper.

Maybe that's why, even though I've spent so much time thinking about last year, I don't think about Adam that much. In the end, what we had went no deeper than the quick hit of a drug. All those dinners, those bottles of wine, those nights in his bed – they add up to nothing. The lie I told myself collapsed in one shattering moment, and now I can only start from scratch.

———————

In the past month, I've carved out a new, careful routine for myself. I wake up early. I've started running again in the mornings, before the heat sets in. I take Pepper on long walks through the woods, throwing sticks for him until my arm is sore. I come home and eat lunch, leftovers or sandwiches, cleaning up after myself like a guest. My father is always at work, and my mother is always at her meetings and committees. Most days it's just me and Jasmine, the housekeeper. We move on our separate tracks, nodding when we pass each other.

I have a stack of books from the local library. I'm

filling the holes in my education, all those English classes I never took because I thought I hated the subject. Austen, Dickens, Brontë. Ovid and Homer, Woolf and Joyce. I have a vague plan to work my way up to the present. Some of the books make me laugh, some make me cry, some bore me to death, some I suspect I am utterly missing the point of. It doesn't really matter. It's the act of concentration that I need to relearn. I am trying to be present. Some afternoons I go to the Boston MFA, where I spend hours sitting in the galleries, losing myself in the artwork, grasping at the feeling I had in Paris.

In the mornings, I scan the news for a mention of Spire. The coverage has lessened as the months have gone by. In the beginning, the story was everywhere: the investigations, the plummeting of WestCorp's shares, the promises of full cooperation with the authorities. Michael Casey ducking and covering his head whenever the cameras chased him. In those early weeks, every ringing phone or approaching car put me on edge. I was certain it had caught up to me. An officer at the door, ready to serve me with a subpoena, ready to haul me off and take my statement.

But that's not what anyone cared about. The leak paled in comparison to the laws that had been broken, and Spire and the feds had bigger fish to fry. What mattered was the crime, not the telling. And I bet no one suspected Evan of being connected to it. Evan was chosen precisely because he would never run his mouth. I studied every picture in the paper and every clip on TV for a glimpse of his face, for evidence of what had happened to him. But there was nothing. The cameras were focused solely on Michael Casey, the one whose head the public demanded. Once or twice I saw Adam on TV, commenting on the latest update in the Spire story, grinning broadly under the hot studio lights. He's finally as famous as I always thought he would be.

———————

My mother, meanwhile, has been watching from a wary distance.

Most days she's out the door before I've even left for my run, on her way to one of her appointments or Pilates classes, but the other morning she lingered at the kitchen table. I looked up from the paper and found she had a rare gaze of contentment.

'Julia.' She reached for my hand. 'Sweetie, I'm proud of you. I'm so glad you're feeling better. I can't tell you how happy it makes me.'

'Thanks, Mom.'

She stood up. Sentiment over. While she fussed for her purse and car keys, she kept talking.

'You know who I ran into at the coffee shop yesterday? Rob's mother. She didn't know you were back.'

'Oh. That's nice.' I hadn't told Rob, or anyone, that I was back. I couldn't find a way to mention it without inciting cloying pity.

'Rob's coming out from Cambridge for dinner on Friday night. His mother's invited you over, too. I think it would be really nice if you went. She seemed a little hurt that you hadn't been by to see them. She's always loved you.'

'I don't know. I'm not –'

'She's not going to take no for an answer. *I'm* not going to take no for an answer. Call her and tell her you'll see her on Friday. It will be good for everyone. Okay?' She kissed the top of my head, rearranging a few rogue strands of hair before she left.

Friday evening, I knocked on Rob's parents' door. In the past, I would have let myself in.

Rob opened the door. He grinned and kissed me on the cheek. 'Come in,' he said, gesturing me into the front hall. 'They can't wait to see you.'

Rob's parents weren't so different from my parents – this was true for all my friends except Evan – and the flow and contour of the conversation made me feel at home. It was instantly comfortable in a way I hadn't quite expected: the same worn wood of their kitchen table, the familiar view of their backyard through the window. Rob's father was a lawyer, and his mother had a successful career as a cookbook ghostwriter. She was an excellent cook. The wine, the chicken Marbella, the fragrant basket of bread and the yellow butter – the flavors were unchanged. His mother had a deep, lusty laugh I had always loved. His father still liked a Cognac after dinner. For a moment, it felt like the last four or five years had been a mere skip of the record.

After we finished dessert, a homemade pear tart, Rob and I stood to help his parents clear the table. His mother shook her head. 'No – you two go on. I'm sure you want to catch up.' I wondered if she was in cahoots with my mother.

Rob held the front door open. 'Let's go for a walk. It's a nice night.'

He filled me in on everything that had happened since Thanksgiving, when I'd seen him last. He had been accepted at Harvard Medical School. He'd also been accepted at Johns Hopkins, Stanford, and Columbia, but he'd decided on Harvard. He wanted to be a neurosurgeon eventually.

'So you're staying here? I mean, in Cambridge?'

'Yup. Hey, you remember Mindy? From biology senior year?'

'Yeah, why?'

'She's going to be in my class at Harvard.'

'The girl who threw up when we dissected the pig? Mindy wants to be a *doctor*?'

He laughed. 'I wonder how she's going to handle anatomy.'

We walked in silence for a stretch. I was tempted to take his hand; it only felt natural to do what we'd done so many times before. I stole a glance at him when we got to the park near his house. His face was illuminated by the far-off floodlights on the tennis court. I was trying to decide if he was different. He looked almost the same as he had in high school. Maybe a fraction taller, more stubble in his beard. But he was still, mostly, the person I'd fallen for when I was sixteen years old. What I was wondering was whether I was mostly the same person, too.

'What about you?' he said after we stopped and sat on a bench. 'Are you going to stay?'

'Here? I don't know.'

'How is it, living at home?'

'You know what my mom's like.'

He held up his hands. 'I plead the Fifth.'

'It's fine, actually. It's not so bad. They pretty much leave me alone. I guess I need to figure out what I actually want to do next. You know. Where I want to go.'

'Why not here? I know one reason for you to stay.'

The trees made a rushing sound when the night breeze blew through them, a sound like rain falling. The park was empty except for the two of us. I pulled my sweater tighter around me. I slid my feet free of my sandals and felt the cold, spongy grass between my toes. I used to play tennis in this park. The past, my past, was everywhere in this town. When I turned back to Rob, he was looking at me. He'd stated it as a fact, and he was right. He *was* one reason for me to stay.

I shrugged. 'I'm not in any hurry. Just taking it one day at a time.'

'Do you want to come back to Cambridge tonight?'

'Not till the third date, buddy,' I said with a laugh.

'No, not like that. My roommates are having people over. A party.'

'It's kind of late.'

'It's, like, ten o'clock, grandma.'

'Well, I told my parents I'd walk the dog before bed.'

He offered a hand to help me up. 'So living at home does have its downside.'

'Free food, though. Unlimited laundry.'

When we got back, his house was dark. I had parked at the bottom of the driveway, borrowing the Volvo for the night, and Rob's old green Jeep was parked in front of it. It was the same junky car he'd driven in high school. On winter weekends in boarding school, we'd sometimes drive out to the beach on the North Shore. I'd dared him to go swimming once, on a frozen and windy January day, and before I could tell him I was kidding he had stripped to his boxers and run into the steel-gray Atlantic. Rob gave me a thumbs-up, his chest chapping red in the wind, then ducked beneath a crashing wave. We were alone, the only people on the beach. A moment passed. Another moment. Rob didn't emerge back up. Five seconds, at least. Ten seconds. That was way too long. Just as I started sprinting for the water, he popped back up, grinning like a jack-in-the-box. 'You're insane!' I shouted over the roar of the wind. He'd done it just to get a rise out of me. To be able to say, later, that I'd been so worried about him I'd almost gone in myself. He was covered in goose bumps, lips turning blue, but he laughed the whole way back. Rob was like that.

I didn't know what we were doing. Rob took my

hands and pulled me toward him. I kept my gaze fixed to his shoulder.

'How about next week?' he was saying.

'What about it?'

'We should hang out again. Lunch?'

'Okay.' Thinking. Lunch was innocuous enough.

'Tuesday work for you?'

'Well, I'll have to check my calendar. I'm a busy woman.'

'Good. Tuesday it is.' He tugged me in and kissed me on the cheek before letting go. As I drove away, he waved good-bye from the bottom of the driveway, and I watched him shrinking into the night in the rearview mirror.

Elizabeth had been calling in her spare moments to tell me about New York, doing her best to distract me. She was always rushing, always late to something.

'What about this weekend?' she said. It was Monday, the day before I was going to meet Rob for lunch. 'My roommate's going to be gone. I already cleared it with her. You can stay in her room.'

'I don't know, Lizzie.'

'You know I live in Chinatown, right? It's really far from the Upper East Side. You won't run into him. You're going to have to set foot in New York at some point.'

'Yeah, it's just that –'

'Donald is throwing a party this weekend. In his loft.

It's going to be amazing. Jules, come on. You need to get out of that house. Shake it up a little.'

Rob was waiting for me when I arrived the next day. The Thai restaurant he'd picked was cool and dark inside, a bamboo fan spinning lazily on the ceiling. The restaurant was empty at the lunch hour, most people coming for takeout.

'It's not fancy,' Rob said, drinking his beer. 'But I like it.'

'So how much longer are you working at the lab?'

'The end of July, I think. It's sort of arbitrary. It's not like I'm really leaving. I'm staying in the same apartment next year.'

'You didn't want to take time off before school?'

'I did. I took this year.' He reached across the table to try my noodles. 'Hey, we're going out to the Cape this weekend. One of my buddies rented a place for the summer. You should come.'

'You and your roommates? A bunch of dudes?'

'The girls are coming, too. It's going to be awesome. It's right on the beach.'

I took a small sip of beer. Elizabeth, urging me to New York. Rob, inviting me to the Cape. I knew this point would come eventually, my hibernation forced to an end. The weekend on the Cape would be fun. I could picture it: the burgers sizzling on the grill, the Frisbee floating back and forth. But I also had the feeling that if I were to do it – to go with Rob for the weekend, to be with him again – the previous four years really would vanish without a trace. Every way in which I thought I'd changed would be wiped out by the easy backslide into his arms. It was tempting, to so cleanly erase the messiness of the past. Adam, Evan, all the mistakes I'd made. The man was going to be a *brain surgeon*. Our life together could be a good one.

But I shrugged. 'I might go stay with Elizabeth in New York this weekend.'

'I need to know by tonight, so I can save you a place in the car.'

'I'm not sure.'

He stared at me, quizzical. 'I'm not going to wait around forever, Jules.'

We emerged from the cool darkness of the restaurant onto the too-bright sidewalk. I was squinting, disoriented, my vision spotty from the sunshine, and when Rob said good-bye he kissed me square on the mouth. His lips were still spicy from the noodles. 'Let me know by tonight, okay?'

# CHAPTER 15

## *Evan*

There were thunderstorms over New York that December night, earsplitting booms and low rumbles that would have kept me awake if I hadn't been already. I lay fully dressed on top of the covers in the midtown hotel room, counting down the hours until it was time to go back in.

David Kleinman had been stuck in DC because of the storm. The thwack of helicopter blades overhead greeted me as I hurried into the lobby on Tuesday morning. I arrived on the floor just as he did. Kleinman walked through the silent hallways without meeting anyone's eyes. He went straight to his office, dusty from the previous few months, and slammed the door behind him.

Roger plopped down across from me with a wolfish smile. 'How'd you sleep, my friend?'

I stared at my steaming coffee, willing it to cool so I could start drinking it.

'Listen, you lawyered up yet? Huh? Hey, I'm talking to you here.'

'No, Roger. I haven't.'

'You *haven't?* Shit, Peck, what are you waiting for? You know they're gonna be after your ass.'

'Knock it off.'

'Whoa, whoa. So hostile. I'm just trying to help.'

'It's none of your business.'

He snorted. 'You're kidding, right? You don't think you and Michael made it my business when you decided to fuck everything up for the rest of us? When you broke the *law?*' Roger shook his head. 'You could have said something, you know. Why didn't you go to Kleinman?'

He waited, but I didn't have an answer.

I went past Michael's office that morning, but it was empty and dark. Wanda's desk was vacant, too. Rumors raced like wildfire: Michael had hired a security detail to protect him and his wife. He'd fled to Europe. He'd lawyered up and was refusing to talk. He'd come in at dawn via the freight elevator and cleared out his things. No one knew what was true and what was false. It wasn't like the market crash back in September. We weren't in this thing together. This time, everyone fractured into distinct modes of panic, scrambling for seats on invisible lifeboats. Some claimed they'd seen it coming. Others were already on the phone with headhunters. I came around a corner in the hallway and heard a pair of angry voices, one of them saying he couldn't *believe* what Michael had done. But when the pair saw me, they shut up. That's how it went that day. Conversations halted when I came too close. I was persona non grata.

Kleinman gathered everyone that afternoon in the

same conference room where he'd addressed us on the day he left for Washington. The mood was more somber this time. He once again emphasized that this crisis – a new crisis, one of our own making – would not be the undoing of Spire. This was an aberration, one rogue actor. A man who didn't stand for what Spire was. Spire would be cooperating fully with authorities. The rest of the firm was clean. Kleinman wasn't going to let this destroy us. *Us*. Us. That's what I focused on. I was still there, still part of the team.

A hand touched my elbow as I filed out. David Kleinman's secretary, giving me a sympathetic look. 'Evan? He'd like to see you.'

Kleinman was waiting inside his office. A grandfather clock ticking in the corner marked the silence. He watched me sit, fiddle with my cuffs, shift in my chair, like he was waiting for a truth to reveal itself. Or did he want me to speak first?

At last he said, 'I hear you were the one working with Michael on this deal.'

'Yes, sir.'

'You'll have access to a lawyer, one of ours. From now on you shouldn't say a single thing about this without your lawyer present. Okay? Complete silence unless the lawyer is there. Not to your mom, your friends. Your girlfriend, whatever.' I swallowed; my mouth went dry. 'But right now is the exception. Right now I need you to be totally straight with me. What did you know and when did you know it?'

After I told him everything – the beginning of the deal, what I'd overheard in Vegas, the briefcase for Chan, the $20,000 in cash from Michael – he nodded and dismissed me. Kleinman didn't say anything about where Michael was, or what was going to happen to him. Maybe it would have been stating the obvious. On the walk back to my desk, I noticed a team of strange men in dark suits in the conference room. Files and stacks of paper and laptops covered the table. The blinds were lowered on the windows. They looked like they were setting up for war.

The SEC took over one conference room, and our lawyers took over another. The nameplate outside Michael's office had been pried off by the end of the first week.

Kleinman's speech his first day back didn't do much good. The death spiral began immediately. Investors pulled their money. No one bought what Kleinman was selling – that this was a contained crisis, the mistake of one greedy egomaniac. Michael had been the acting CEO. His fingerprints were on everything. Any deal conducted during his tenure was tainted. Every last skeleton was going to be dragged out of every last closet. We were getting hammered.

'Michael *fucking* Casey. I could murder this fucking guy,' one trader said to another in the kitchen. People had stopped bothering with silence around me. They didn't care anymore, or maybe they'd already forgotten who I was.

The other guy laughed bitterly. 'You're gonna have to get in line.'

I felt my throat tighten as I stirred milk into my coffee.

'Fine. I'd settle for just pissing on his corpse if I had to.'

By that point, it was clear to me that Michael was almost certainly going to jail. And the odd thing was, I felt pity for him. If we hadn't been caught, those same guys would have declared him a hero. They would have admired his brilliance and ballsiness for pulling it off. But in this game, you didn't score points with hypotheticals. Execution was the only thing that mattered.

Christmas snuck up on me. It was just another day to get through: reruns, takeout, a quiet apartment. My parents called, and so did Arthur. They had seen the news when it broke a few weeks earlier. They knew the outlines of what had happened, but I let the calls go to voice mail. I didn't feel like talking about it, not yet. There was too much that I hadn't made sense of. How was I supposed to feel? Guilty, contrite, apologetic? What was I supposed to say? I understood, intellectually, how bad it looked to other people. To people like Arthur and my parents. Normal people. But there was some of me that still saw the upside in what Michael had done. I felt guilt over the wrong thing – over the role I'd played in making the news public. The deal had been working. It was going to make Spire an enormous amount of money. I wasn't ready to let go of that yet.

*

After the holidays, I was sitting at my desk when I felt a tap on my shoulder. A man with a crew cut and an ill-fitting suit told me to follow him. We went into the conference room, where another man who looked just like him sat at the table. One was named John, the other Kurt, both of them from the SEC. I immediately forgot who was who.

'Have a seat,' one of them said. 'Help yourself to water or coffee or whatever.'

'Thanks,' I said, although their hospitality seemed pretentious when it was our conference room they were occupying.

'You have a good holiday?' one of them asked.

'Um, yeah. It was fine.'

John looked over at Kurt, or vice versa. 'Did I tell you I had to drive all the way to Short Hills on Christmas Eve? For that new Elmo doll. Jesus.' He rolled his eyes, then said to me, 'Don't ever get married, okay?'

I laughed. At that moment, the door to the conference room opened. A blond woman in a skirt suit came in, brandishing a briefcase in one hand and a large Starbucks in the other. She stopped, froze. 'What did you say to them?' she said, her eyes wide.

'We were just shooting the shit,' John or Kurt said. 'Don't worry.'

'*Never* talk to him without me here. Understood? That goes for you, too,' she said to me. 'You really should know better, Evan.'

But I didn't even know why I needed a lawyer. The

questions that John and Kurt asked were easy, straight-forward. I nodded, confirmed, clarified, helped them establish the particulars of the deal: the timeline, the players. As the week went on, my fear started to dissipate. They were treating me like I had done nothing wrong. Maybe I'd be okay. Maybe all wasn't lost just yet.

'Hold that?'

I pushed the Door Open button. Roger hurried into the elevator. 'Oh,' he said, catching his breath. 'Thanks, Evan.' I think it was the only time he'd ever thanked me for anything. It was definitely the only time he'd ever used my first name.

'Good weekend?' I asked.

He glanced away, staring instead at the ticking floor numbers as we zoomed up the skyscraper. 'Yeah. What about you?'

'Fine,' I lied. The weekends felt endless without the distraction of work. I went through a case of beer without even trying. I had no idea what to do with the time.

We were silent for the rest of the ride up. Both of us were in early. Roger was working on some big new deal with Steve. And I'd been coming in early because I knew that appearances mattered. I needed to prove that I was ready to hit the ground running when this mess was over. I'd been removed from every project, every e-mail distro, but things would be back to normal soon enough.

As Roger and I approached our desks, I saw an

unfamiliar woman standing near my chair. A spark of hope: maybe she was there to give me a new assignment.

'Evan Peck?' she said, and I nodded. 'Could you come with me, please?'

She led me to the other side of the floor and stopped in front of what I'd always assumed was a supply closet, tucked in the building's core, far away from the windows. She balanced a stack of binders in one arm while she shuffled through a ring of keys with the other hand. 'Do you mind?' she said with a smile, handing me the binders. She was kind of cute.

'Here we go,' she said, finally finding the key. She opened the door and flipped the light switch. It was a small, windowless office. A bare desk, a computer, a chair. It smelled like paint. Yes, I realized, I had in fact seen the janitor opening and closing this door just the other week. 'This is nicer, isn't it?' Her voice had gone up an octave. 'Your very own office.'

'I'm supposed to work here?'

'You know, I've never heard of an analyst getting his own office before.'

'But why? Why are you moving me?'

She turned on the computer, swept her hand across the desk, nodded at the whole array. 'It's nice in here, actually. Nice and clean and quiet. Don't you think?'

'So I just . . . are people going to know where to find me?'

'Well, it sounds like you've been spending most days in deposition with the SEC. While you're tied up with that, we figured we'd move you in here so we could free up your old desk.'

'Free it up for who?'

'I'm really just here to help you get settled. Actually, I have to go. I have a nine o'clock on another floor. Here's the key. The door locks automatically.'

There was a forgotten industrial-size bottle of window cleaner in the corner. I used that to prop open the door while I settled in. A minute later, I looked up to see that the door was pushing the heavy bottle across the carpet, gradually trying to close itself against the outside world.

The following week, when I walked into the conference room for our usual 9:30 start time with the SEC, something had changed. I couldn't put my finger on it at first. Then, as I poured myself a cup of coffee from the setup at the side of the room, I realized that John and Kurt were both silent. My heart started beating faster. They were staring purposefully at the papers in front of them instead of engaging in their usual stupid banter.

My lawyer arrived, and John or Kurt turned on the recorder. 'So Evan. We have new testimony from Michael that we need to ask you about.'

'Okay,' I said, glancing over at my lawyer. She nodded.

'You've stated that you were unaware of Michael's relationship with the Chinese officials until the night of' – he looked down at his papers – 'November thirteenth, 2008.'

'Right. The first night in Las Vegas.'

'Now, Michael has testified that you were aware of his relationship with the Chinese officials from the beginning. Since' – he looked down again – 'August eighth, 2008.'

'No. I didn't know anything until Vegas. I wasn't even supposed to hear that. They didn't know I was –'

'Michael stated that you were aware of his trip to China, taken in August, to facilitate the initial meeting with the officials.'

'No. I mean, yes, I knew about the trip, but I didn't know what it was for.'

'Michael stated that you did.'

'I didn't! He didn't say anything about it, except that he was going to China.'

'Michael said, and I'm quoting here, "Evan knew exactly what we were doing."'

'Can we have a minute, please?' my lawyer said.

We stepped out into the hallway. Her high heels brought her up to my eye level. 'Evan. Point-blank, is there anything you haven't told me? I don't like surprises.'

'No. Nothing. Why would Michael say that?' My heart was beating even faster.

'It could be part of his strategy. Make it seem like you had more responsibility than you actually did. So he's not the only one who looks bad.'

'Do you think I look bad?' My voice cracked.

She cocked an eyebrow. 'It doesn't matter how I think you look. It matters that I protect you. Understood?'

We went back into the conference room. I could feel John and Kurt staring as I took a small sip of coffee. The scratching of pen against paper, the buzz of the fluorescent light above. A dull ache throbbing through my temple.

'Are we good?'

'Go ahead,' my lawyer said.

'Evan, you turned over the twenty thousand dollars that Michael gave you on November twenty-fourth, 2008. You had said, in previous testimony, that Michael gave you this money as a – I'm quoting here – a token of his appreciation. Is that correct?'

'Yes. That's what he said.'

'But you didn't deposit or spend any of the money.'

'Right,' I said, relieved. 'It's all there.'

'Why didn't you spend any of it? What were you waiting for?'

'I'm sorry – what?'

'Twenty thousand dollars is a lot of money. Is there a reason you were so hesitant to touch it?'

'Is this really relevant?' my lawyer said.

'Do you think you deserved that money?'

'I – I didn't ask for it. Michael just gave it to me.'

'But you didn't turn it down. You didn't give it back. Clearly you thought you were entitled to that money in some respect. Except that you didn't spend any of it. See, that's what doesn't make sense to me, Evan. You make it seem like you were just a low-level player. But Michael Casey wouldn't be giving you a twenty-thousand-dollar payoff unless you were intimately involved with this deal.'

'It wasn't a payoff!'

'Then what was it?'

'A . . . a bonus. It was a bonus.'

'Spire didn't give out bonuses last year.'

'Can we move on?' my lawyer said. 'I don't see that we're getting anywhere with this.'

'Fine,' John or Kurt said. 'The next thing we'd like to ask you about is Wenjian Chan. Has he been in touch with you since you saw him in Las Vegas?'

'I already told you. No. I never heard from him.'

'Well, it's possible he might have reached out to you since we took your testimony the other week. Has he?'

'Why would he do that? He knows we're being investigated.'

'Maybe he wanted to find out what exactly you were telling us. Maybe he wanted to make you an offer for your cooperation.'

I felt like I was going to throw up. 'Don't you think that I would have told you? That I would have told you if I'd heard anything from him?'

'Come on, Evan,' John or Kurt said. 'You don't exactly have a great track record with that. That's the whole reason we're here.'

'What the fuck does that mean?'

'Evan,' my lawyer said, in a warning tone.

'It means you kept this deal a secret long after you knew the truth. It means you chose to keep silent about Michael's plan even though you knew it was wrong. It means we can't trust you to give us the full picture unless we ask.'

'I didn't keep it a secret!'

'Then who did you tell about it?'

'Okay,' my lawyer said, shutting her briefcase with a firm click. 'I think that's enough. Let's take a break.'

My lawyer and I had lunch together that day at the Indian place on 9th Avenue. Roger and the other analysts were at another table in the restaurant. I hadn't been invited to lunch with them in months.

My lawyer spent most of the meal on her BlackBerry. 'Sorry,' she said. 'My nanny has the flu. We had to use the backup. Now the kids are sick, too. It's a fucking nightmare.' She noticed my untouched food. 'Hey. You okay?'

'No.'

She put her phone down. 'You know it's not personal, right? The things they were saying back there. They really don't give a shit about you.'

'It doesn't feel like that. It feels like they're after me.'

'They're only trying to get as much out of you as they can. So they can nail Michael and the Chinese. You've got the testimony they need. But you're small fish, Evan. I mean that in a good way.'

Roger and the others walked past on the way out.

354

Roger bumped into my chair. 'Oops. Didn't see you there, Peck,' he said, grinning. 'Hot date, huh?'

After we finished eating, after she paid and we stood up to put on our coats, she asked: 'What did you mean before? When you said that you didn't keep it a secret?'

'Oh.' I was hoping she had forgotten about that. 'I didn't really mean anything. Just that, um, I didn't *consciously* keep it a secret.'

When we returned to the conference room, John and Kurt looked up in unison. 'Actually, we're done,' one of them said. 'For now, at least. We don't need anything else. You can go back to work.'

'That's it?' I said.

'We might need to call you back for a few things as they crop up. But yeah, that's it. You're done. Thanks for your help.'

'You must be relieved,' my lawyer said, walking me back to my office-slash-closet. 'Now you can go back to normal, right?'

'I guess.' I did feel relieved – that weak but good feeling that comes after you've finally thrown up – but I also felt confused. Shortchanged somehow. What would come next? What was going to happen to me?

We stopped outside my door. 'Well,' she said. 'Good luck, Evan.'

---

My life went soft at the edges. The same feeling permeated the hours at work, the hours at home: emptiness, futility, like a bucket with a hole in the bottom. The SEC investigation had been my last vestige of purpose. For a few weeks I continued to arrive early, stay late, and keep my closet door propped open so that anyone walking past might imagine me hard at work. Then I left a little earlier. Arrived a little later. Started shutting my door at lunch so I could watch the postgame highlights with the sound on. January became February, then February became March. Eventually I gave in to it. I punched in and out. I ate dinner; I drank. I'd go entire weekends without speaking, so that my voice felt scratchy and strange when I greeted the security guards on Monday mornings. I arrived hungover and shut my door for long stretches to take naps on the coarse industrial carpet, letting time pass like high clouds drifting through the upper atmosphere.

I realized at a certain point that I'd been celibate for nearly three months. It was the longest by far I'd gone without having sex. In high school, it was only ever a few weeks at a time, and in college, too, and after that came Julia. It was like a portal to an earlier time. The texture of this frustration was identical to what I'd felt as a virginal teenager. It was almost as if, by going so long without sex, I had become my younger self again. I felt confused and melancholy in a way I hadn't in a decade. I could have gone out to a bar and ended the celibate streak with a one-night stand easily enough. But in a way, I liked being alone with my former self. I indulged it. I liked recalling how it felt when adulthood was still a distant mystery.

When the concrete details – an apartment in Manhattan, a high-paying job – would have been sufficient by themselves. I hadn't realized, back then, how messy it actually was. I wanted to go back and hide inside that ignorance.

I kept waiting for the SEC to come knocking, to ask the question I'd never answered. *What did you mean, you didn't keep it a secret?* I had blurted it out without thinking, and they treated it like a throwaway. A pathetic, confused, nonsense lie. But it was the truth; I *hadn't* kept it a secret. I was the whole reason the SEC was there, shining a bright light on the dirty deal. No one ever asked about the leak. Maybe they always assumed it was me, the young analyst gone nervous and blabby, or maybe they just didn't care. It was a paltry defense in any case. I *had* told somebody, but not the right somebody.

One day in March I lay down for a nap after lunch, intending to sleep off another hangover. When I woke up, it was late – past 8:00 p.m. I'd slept for almost five hours. On my way to the elevator, I passed the other analysts, gathered near Roger's desk.

'Steve's riding you that hard?' one of them was saying to him.

'Go without me,' Roger said. 'I've got at least six hours left here.'

Roger's face was puffy and pale, exhaustion and caffeine lending a nervous twitch to his features. But when he noticed me approach, he grinned like his old self. 'Look,' he said. 'Peck can take my place. Make him pick up the tab. He's rich.'

Everyone had heard about the $20,000. They knew I had to turn it over, but it was fodder nonetheless. Roger laughed. 'Still can't take a joke, huh, Peck?'

'You can come along if you want,' one of the other analysts mumbled, a residual politeness kicking in. The group walked slow, including but not quite acknowledging my presence. No one knew what to say to me. I glanced back over my shoulder at Roger. He was staring so closely at his screen that it looked like he was going to tip over. Just as I must have looked, so many nights during the previous year. It was like coming across a photograph of myself that I didn't remember being taken.

*When had I become so invisible?* I thought as the elevator descended and the analysts traded stories I knew nothing about. When had I become an afterthought? Other people made mistakes and were forgiven. I didn't know how much longer I could endure this. I knew it was fucked up, but I missed Michael. Or maybe it was more that I missed the way Michael made me feel. Like I was part of something bigger.

The neon sign for McGuigan's glowed ahead of us in the darkness. It was the same as always – the stale beer smell, the jukebox, the crack of cue against billiard ball, the rattle of ice. But before I could follow my coworkers to the usual booth in the back, my eye caught another familiar sight.

'Evan?' she said. Her eyes wide, uncertain. Almost regretting it.

Then she smiled.

★

I nursed my Guinness. It wasn't until late, long after my coworkers had gone, leaving bills stuck to the damp table, that Maria came and sat next to me.

'Do you want another?' she asked, pointing at my empty glass.

'I'm okay.' For the first time in a while, I didn't feel like getting drunk.

'Sorry. I meant to come over earlier. It was a crazy night. How are things?'

'Good, I guess.'

*Good?* I missed the way things had been between us in the fall, but I didn't know how to go back to that. I doubted it was possible.

'I have to say something,' Maria said at last. 'I should have said this a long time ago. I'm sorry things got kind of weird when I started dating Wyeth. That was bitchy, bringing him in like that. I should have told you.'

'Oh,' I said. 'That. That's fine. You didn't owe me an explanation.'

'That's not true. I really liked you, Evan.' Her voice wavered. 'I just – I kept waiting. You know? I kept waiting for you to make a move or do something or say something. Eventually it seemed like you didn't want anything like that. And Wyeth was cute, and he asked me out. So I said yes.'

She shrugged. 'You seemed pissed afterward. Then you didn't come around for a long time. But you're back now, and – I don't know what I'm trying to say. I don't know what's going on in your life or why you're back,

359

but I want us to be friends again. I'd like that. If you want to.'

I stared down at the bar, blinking, willing the seams to hold together.

'Are you okay?' she asked in a soft voice.

I shook my head. 'God, Maria. I'm sorry. I'm a jerk.'

'No, Evan. I shouldn't have put you in that position. I —'

'No. I'm an asshole. I didn't make a move last year because I had a girlfriend.'

'A girlfriend?'

'I should have said something. I'm sorry.'

'Oh, my God. That makes so much sense. A girlfriend!' She laughed, then stopped. 'Wait. Did you say "had"?'

'Yeah. We broke up a while ago.'

'Oh.'

'It was complicated. It's better that it's over.' Was that true? Was that what I really thought? 'It had been dragging itself out for a long time.'

'What happened?'

'Well,' I said. 'How much time do you have?'

The next morning, as I passed Roger's desk, I noticed that he was wearing the same clothes as the day before. Shirt wrinkled, tie stained with oil, smelling and looking like he hadn't slept in days. It was the first morning in a long time that I had woken without a hangover. I'd picked up breakfast, which I never did, the toasted bagel radiating heat through the white bag. I stopped next to Roger's desk.

'Want breakfast?' I said, extending the bag toward him. He raised an eyebrow. 'They messed up my order,' I lied. 'I asked for sesame but they gave me an everything. So they did it over, but they gave me both.'

'Um. Okay. Thanks,' he said warily, taking the bag.

'You're welcome,' I said. Then, before I lost my nerve: 'Do you need any help?'

He tore off a bite of the bagel. 'Help?'

'With whatever you're working on. It looks like you're slammed.'

He stared for a beat. 'You're joking, right?'

'Nope. Not joking. I've got time to pitch in.'

Then he laughed. 'Well, yeah. Duh. They can't staff you on anything. The investors would freak out.'

My stomach turned at the smell of the warm cream cheese.

'They told us not to talk about any live deals in front of you,' Roger continued. 'It's a liability. You're going to be gone soon, anyway.'

'A liability?'

Roger's expression softened. 'Look,' he said quietly. 'I'm not trying to be a dick. Do you want my advice? Just cash your checks and ride this out. Then you can move on to another firm. Start fresh. Somewhere else, they won't even care.'

Down the hall, the other employees were arriving for the day. Roger rearranged his face back into its usual smug grin. 'Thanks for the bagel, but just get out of here, okay?' he said under his breath. 'I shouldn't be talking to you.'

I went back to McGuigan's that night, and the next, and the next. I drank Coke, and I watched whatever was on the TV – a Yankees game, *Jeopardy!*, the local news – killing time, waiting for the bar to quiet down enough for Maria to take a break. She was the only person I had talked to in months. I couldn't lose her again.

That first night, I told her the whole story: Michael, the bribery, the trip to Las Vegas. The Julia part, too. I figured it was fine. The investigation was nearly finished, and the findings were going to be public soon enough. Maria stared at me, rapt.

'Have you heard from her since you broke up?' she asked at the end.

'Nope.'

'But you haven't called her, either?'

'There's nothing to say.' I jabbed at a melting ice cube with my straw. 'She checked out a long time ago. I don't think she was ever going to come back.'

'Why are you still here, then?'

'What do you mean?'

'Why stay? I mean, you must be miserable at Spire, right? And you always said you weren't that crazy about New York. You could go somewhere totally different. Don't you want to start over? Leave it all behind?'

But where would I go? How could I explain? I couldn't

leave, because for the first time, New York finally felt like home. Last year the city was a backdrop separate from my life, something I was only borrowing. But the shift had happened not long ago, when I realized that I had changed. That the city had been witness to different versions of myself. It gave me a new claim over this place. I had tried, failed, collapsed, but I was still here. The city was still here. The scale of the place had become newly comforting. It had a way of shrinking my pain to a bearable smallness. It was nothing compared to the towering skyscrapers or the teeming crowds. Any given day, in any given subway car, there were people who were happier than I, people who were sadder than I. People who had erred and people who had forgiven. I was mortal, imperfect, just like everyone else. It was good to be reminded of that.

But that mortality also made me old. I felt like I might vanish in a second. I realized – knowledge that arrived all at once – how much the world would continue to change after I was gone. Someday, people would look back on this era in the same way I had looked back on the settlers of the New World or the cowboys of the West in the slippery pages of my schoolbooks, strangers whose lives were distilled down to a few paragraphs and color illustrations. They would shake their heads, not believing that we could have known so little. It was nearly impossible to imagine the continuity. Then they would turn away from the past and continue their lives in a world transformed by technology or disease or war. By rising oceans or collapsing economies or by something that we – we soon-to-be relics – couldn't even imagine.

But I wanted to. I wanted to imagine, and then to see. I clung to the time I'd been given. I didn't want to leave.

On my fourth night in a row at McGuigan's, Maria said, 'I'm off early tonight. You want to get dinner? I can cook.'

A cat was purring atop the refrigerator when she opened the door to her studio apartment, up in the northern reaches of Morningside Heights. 'Make yourself at home,' she said, turning on the stove with the click and hiss of gas igniting. She handed me a beer, and I wandered around. I liked her apartment right away. She had houseplants on the windowsill, a rag rug, a desk covered with textbooks and notes from law school, a refrigerator layered with family pictures and yellowed recipes. I stood at the other side of the room and watched Maria at the stove – apron tied around her waist, humming along to the radio – and I remembered the night I came home to Julia cooking in our tiny kitchen. How she had glowed from a happiness that I thought belonged to both of us. That was the worst part: I'd been misreading it all along. It was why I couldn't bear to think about Julia, not even the good parts, because I couldn't be sure that there ever were good parts.

After dinner, after sex that was surprisingly intimate for a first time, we lay in Maria's bed, which was tucked in the corner next to an open window. I was half asleep when she climbed out of bed, wrapped herself in a robe, and turned on the desk lamp. 'Stay there,' she said. 'I'm going to study for a few hours.' She was taking the bar exam that summer. Her cat had been asleep on top of Maria's stack of textbooks. The cat unfurled and stretched, purring regally as she hopped down to the floor and made way for her owner.

The next morning, Maria kissed me good-bye, and we made plans for dinner the following night. It was while I was shaving in front of the bathroom mirror back at home that I felt it. I'd told someone the truth. The actual, whole truth. And it was okay.

Was it that Maria had finally given me the thing I had craved for so long? Acceptance and forgiveness; grace? I thought so at first, but I realized that wasn't it, because she wasn't the one whose forgiveness I needed. What Maria had given me was simply a reminder that the lone-liness didn't have to last forever. I didn't have to know what came next in order to have hope.

---

One morning in early May, Kleinman summoned me to his office.

'Peck. Have a seat. You're aware that we're approaching a settlement with the SEC in the WestCorp case.'

'I had guessed as much, sir.'

'And you probably know about the compromised state of the firm right now. We've taken a lot of hits in the last few months. We're starting a round of layoffs later today. Someone from HR will be calling you around eleven to go over your package. But I wanted to give you a personal heads-up.'

I had been expecting this for a long time, but it was still strange to hear the words actually spoken. Kleinman smiled at me.

'You know, I can see why Michael liked you so much. You're loyal, and that goes a long way. In another life, you probably would have had a great career ahead of you here. But you understand why we can't keep you on.'

I nodded. 'Yes, sir.'

'You're Michael's guy. He made you his guy. If I kept you around while laying off a bunch of people who had nothing to do with this – you know how bad that would look. People would hate you, to be frank. And then they'd hate me. You'd just remind everyone of what came before. What we need here is a fresh start. We're going to be a lot smaller, but we'll rebuild eventually.'

Kleinman stood up and extended his hand. 'Well. Best of luck, Peck. Thank you for your cooperation these last few months.'

The HR woman fetched me shortly afterward. It was the same woman who had moved me into my windowless closet office. I wondered whether she felt guilty about her earlier deception; she must have known, even then, that she'd have to deliver this news eventually. There was a piece of paper that listed my severance package: several months' salary, a one-time payment in exchange for my signing a nondisparagement agreement. It was a lot of money. She cleared her throat delicately.

'Mr Peck, I should also remind you that your visa will run out eventually, given that you're no longer employed by Spire. You can, of course, obtain sponsorship from your next employer. We have excellent contacts at other firms in the city and in Connecticut. Mr Kleinman has offered to write a glowing reference. We're confident you'll find a good home. Would you like a –'

'No, thank you,' I said loudly. Then I stood up. 'Is that everything?'

She looked startled. 'Yes. That's it. Just turn in your badge at reception.'

I had purposely avoided thinking too much about what came next. But now that the time had arrived, I knew one thing for sure. This wasn't what I was meant to do. Five minutes later, I turned off the computer and shut the door for the last time, leaving the keys dangling in the lock for the janitor.

'So should we celebrate?' she said when I walked into McGuigan's at midday.

'Celebrate me getting fired?'

She grinned. 'I can't think of a better reason.'

Maria got someone to cover the rest of her shift. We bought tallboys of beer in paper bags and picked up Sabrett hot dogs and ate them in Columbus Circle. I thought of Julia, the night we had spent out here, drinking wine and watching the traffic swirl. That moment felt distant and immediate all at once. The city was like that, layered with memories that existed in multiple tenses. Ever since I had started sleeping with Maria, five weeks earlier, I had been thinking about Julia more. Memories of her were creeping back in. But Julia only existed as that, I reminded myself – as a memory, as the past.

'Was it weird? Finally saying good-bye to that place?'

'A little. Mostly it's a relief.' I shook my head. 'It's sort of surreal, you know? I can't believe all that shit actually happened. I can't believe I just went along with it.'

'Well,' she said, crumpling up her ketchup-stained napkin. 'It's amazing what people can rationalize. Humans are a delusional bunch.'

'You're gonna have to tone down that sympathy when you start prosecuting the bad guys instead of serving them their drinks.'

She laughed. 'You criminals are humans, too.'

The previous week, Maria had gotten a job offer at the district attorney's office. The pay was miserly, the hours long, but it was work that actually made a difference. I envied her sense of purpose, her accomplishment, but it was easy to forget the years of hard work that had led her to this point. I put my arm around her and pulled her in for a kiss.

'Actually,' she said. 'That reminds me. I'm getting together with my new coworkers tomorrow night, so I won't be able to do dinner after all.'

'No problem. I can come over afterward?'

'Sure, if you want.'

She leaned back against the stone steps and tilted her head up toward the sun. Already it was slipping away. The bar exam was in a few months. Her start date at work was soon after. Maria had carved out a life for herself in this city long before I arrived. I knew she liked me, liked what we shared, but the need was one-directional. Maria brought me back into the real world, but I was seeing that it stemmed from compassion rather than love. She asked nothing of me; there was nothing I could give her that she didn't already possess. And maybe I didn't need love right then. Being with Maria was the first time I felt remotely like a grown-up. Like a person capable of surviving on my own.

She stood up. 'Do you want to walk home?' Her home, not mine: she never once set foot in my apartment. 'It's a beautiful day.'

There were several guys from the hockey team also living in the city, Sebi and Paul and a few others. Most of them worked in finance. When we got together for drinks a few days after my firing, they were envious of my situation.

'You are fucking lucky, man,' Sebi said. Late on a weeknight at a bar in Murray Hill, which was so similar to McGuigan's that if you squinted you couldn't tell them apart. 'I would quit my job in a second if I got that kind of package.'

'What are you gonna do next?' Paul asked.

'Don't really know. I thought about joining a league, just for fun.'

'You should,' Sebi said. 'Actually, one of my buddies plays up in Westchester, in a midnight league. They're always looking for players. I'll give you his number.'

Which was how I found myself lacing up rental skates one night the following week. The other players were men mostly older than me, fathers going gray and potbellied, but I was rusty from so many months off, and we were evenly matched. The team I was on for the scrimmage lost, but it still felt good. After the game, just as I'd cracked a Coors in the locker room, one of the guys on the team came over to me.

'Evan Peck?' He extended his hand. 'I'm Frank Donovan. Call me Donny. Sebi told me about you. I heard you might be looking for work.'

'Oh,' I said. 'Yeah. Well, yes, sort of.'

'I've got something to offer you for the next few months, if you're interested in hearing about it.'

A few weeks later, I was back on a train to Westchester. I had to call my parents and get them to ship my hockey stuff back to New York. I was going to work as an assistant coach at a summer hockey camp for middle schoolers up in Westchester. Donny needed someone to help with his program, running drills and reffing games. I got to the rink early on the first day, before any of the campers arrived. After the first lap around the glassy ice, I felt dizzy and short of breath. I had to pause and lean against the boards. The sound of my blades against the ice, the smell of the cold air, the mustiness of the rink – it was almost too much to bear. Hockey had always been more than a sport to me. It had been the thing that rescued me from the suffocation of a small town, and when I escaped it, it was the thing that I clung to in a strange new world. But I realized – chest heaving, heart aching, my breath escaping in curls of white fog – that it wouldn't work this time. I couldn't hitch my dreams to it anymore. I couldn't love it the way I used to.

Donny dropped me off at the train station at the end of the first day. We chatted during the drive about the kids and how the day had gone. I had to stifle a yawn when we said good-bye – I hadn't worked so hard in months. Before I closed the car door, he asked, 'You gonna be back tomorrow?'

I laughed. 'Wouldn't miss it.'

The week went fast. That Friday night, I called Maria.

'Hey, stranger.'

'Hey, I know. I'm sorry.' All week I'd been coming home, making dinner, and going straight to bed. My new routine was already digging grooves: apartment, Metro-North station at 125th Street, grocery store. McGuigan's felt like another universe.

'Yeah, I know how it goes. First week on the job and all.'

'Can I see you tonight?'

'I'm off at midnight. Come over then?'

A few hours later we lay in her bed after having sex,

the sounds of the street floating in through the open window. Maria had turned on the fan, which rotated toward us every few seconds. There was something different that night. The way she lay there with her eyes open, when normally by then she'd be drifting off, or back at her desk. Her silence had an alert quality. I could sense her thinking.

'Hey,' I said, running my hand along her arm. 'Is everything okay?'

She turned to face me, resting her chin on my chest. A serious gaze.

'Evan, you know, we don't need to keep pretending for no good reason.'

'Maria.' I swallowed. A lump formed in my throat.

'This has been fun. I'm going to miss you,' she said.

Something within me was finally falling. My fingers were being pried away when I wasn't ready to let go.

'Can't we just . . .' I said. 'We don't have to do this right now, do we?'

She propped herself up on one elbow, rested her hand on my chest. Her palm covered my heart. 'It's time.'

Maria stood up and padded into the bathroom. I heard the sound of the bath running. Her cat was atop the refrigerator, purring loudly in her sleep. I got dressed and hovered outside the bathroom door, my hand almost touching the doorknob. I could smell the candle she liked to burn while she was in the bath. And then I stopped. I withdrew my hand. I let myself out, looking around the apartment one last time to make sure I hadn't forgotten anything.

Arthur was passing through the city the following weekend. He had been accepted to all the top law schools in the country – no surprise there – and was making up his mind about where to go. He was in town to visit NYU and Columbia before swinging up to see Harvard and Yale, and he was staying with me for the night.

'This is weirdly good,' Arthur said. 'I had no idea you knew how to cook.'

'I'm learning.' Enchiladas, nothing special. It was Friday night, a week since I'd last seen Maria. I thought about her, but only occasionally. She had been right. Arthur and I sat on the futon, plates balanced on our knees. 'So you're really up for spending another three years in New Haven?'

'There are worse things. I don't think it would be anything like undergrad. It would probably feel like a totally different place. Different people. You know what I mean?'

'Yeah, I think I do.'

'You going to be ready to go in a minute?' he asked. Arthur's phone kept buzzing. A friend from college was throwing a party that night in her Williamsburg apartment. Really more Arthur's friend than my friend. He had a lot of people to see during his short visit to the city. 'What's the best way to get there?'

'The six to the L, I think.'

When we got to the party, I recognized a few people from school. I asked one guy what he'd been up to since graduation, and he cocked his head. 'Same thing as before, man,' he said, taking a long draw from his beer. His tone was odd, almost offended. And then I fuzzily recalled: it was *this* guy. I'd talked to him at a party not so different from this one, several months earlier. Back when I was still at Spire and still with Julia. 'Sorry,' I said, shaking my head. 'Shit. Sorry. I knew that. I have a bad memory.'

My memory was fine. But memory was beside the point when I wasn't even noticing things in the first place. The thing that kept me going through the months at Spire – it was the same thing that had kept me alive through playoffs and postseason intensity in the past. An adrenalized tunnel vision, everything else dropping away into background noise. And maybe that was okay in short bursts, but there was a danger when it went on for too long. For months at a time. It was like a hole in my brain. There was an entire section missing.

A little later, I felt a hand on my elbow. I turned around and saw Abby.

'Evan,' she said after we hugged. 'Wow. It's so nice to see you.'

'Been a while, huh? How are things?'

I didn't really have to ask. Her happiness was obvious.

'Well, I'm in the home stretch.'

'School's almost done for the year?'

'Praise the Lord.' She laughed.

People came in and out, rearranging our corner of the room. Abby and I didn't get to talk for much longer. I caught her eye a few times and started to move toward her, but then someone else would get in the way. Her gaze said the same thing – we were both thinking about the one thing missing from this night. The hip-hop on the stereo, the keg in the bathtub, the Solo cups scattered across the kitchen counters. It was almost like college. Almost, but not quite.

'Hey,' Arthur said, coming over. 'Ready to go? I've got an early train.'

I glanced back over at Abby, stuck in conversation with some close talker. I took a deep breath. I wanted to interrupt. This merited interruption, didn't it? A chance for news of the person I had spent four years of my life with and hadn't heard from in months? But Arthur was already holding the door open, waiting for me.

We took the subway back to the Upper East Side. 'Pizza?' Arthur pointed at the neon sign of the slice joint on Lexington. It was just like old times. Two pepperoni for me, one cheese for him.

'Was it weird?' he said on the walk back to the apartment. 'Seeing Abby?'

'Kind of.'

'You don't talk about her much, you know.'

'Who? Julia?'

'No, the Mona Lisa. Yes, dummy. Julia. The girl you used to live with?'

I shrugged. 'What is there to say?'

'Well, you don't have to be so stoic. You can admit that you're upset. Or mad or whatever. You don't have to pretend like nothing happened. It's kind of strange.'

'I'm not. I'm just . . .' I shrugged again. 'I've learned to live with it.'

We walked for a while. By silent agreement we sat down on the stoop outside my building, finishing our pizza. I felt a click, the temperature rising a notch. 'Why?' I said. 'Did you want to say something about Julia? Do you have something you need to say?'

'What do you mean?'

'Come on. You're not tempted to say "I told you so"? That you could have seen this coming all along?'

'I'd never say that.'

'Aren't you the one who called her self-centered? Don't you remember?'

'Yes,' he said, picking at his pizza crust. 'But I didn't mean like that.'

'What did you mean, then?'

Arthur was silent for a long time. Finally he cleared his throat. 'Okay. Yeah, maybe I thought you guys shouldn't have lived together. That wasn't a great idea. I'll stand by that. But it doesn't mean I don't *like* her. It doesn't mean I think she's some terrible person, that you should never think about her or talk to her again. I mean, she made some pretty big mistakes. But so did you, right? You guys both screwed up. I just don't think it does anyone any good if you keep hanging on to it. If you don't let your-self move past it.'

'You think I'm hanging on to it?'

'Aren't you?'

It was almost exactly a year earlier that Arthur and I had our big fight. A night just like this: late walk home, pizza, warm air. Part of me was itching for a redo. To shout until my throat was raw. To scream even if no one was listening. But there was a difference, a big one. Last year, I hadn't been able to hear what Arthur was saying. I was so focused on the idea of what came next. On the idea of packing up the last of my boxes and putting them in the U-Haul with Julia's and arriving later that week at our apartment in New York, beginning the next chapter of our life together. That's all that had mattered, the continuation of the present into the future, the unin-terruption of that dream.

'Do you see what I mean?' Arthur said. Arthur knew the whole truth of what had happened by then, but this was the first time he'd voiced the other side. That I'd screwed up. That as much as Julia had betrayed me, I had betrayed her, too.

'I'm just saying,' he continued. 'Don't act like it's noth-ing. But don't be so hard on yourself. And don't be so hard on her. I don't know. Maybe it wouldn't be such a bad idea to give her a call. I can tell you're still thinking about her.'

'How?' I said. Was it that obvious? In the previous few

weeks, she'd come back into my mind, memories growing stronger and stronger. That was the real reason I couldn't leave. I needed to know whether the Julia I had known and loved was the real Julia; whether that Julia would ever come back. I had no idea how long I'd have to wait.

He shrugged. 'I'm your friend, Evan. I just can.'

# Chapter 16

## *Julia*

The loft was in an old building in Tribeca. There was a freight elevator, which he used sometimes for moving his oversize canvases, but we took the narrow metal staircase. He had the whole second floor – half for his living space, half for his studio.

I started to knock on the unmarked metal door, but Elizabeth said, 'Don't bother. No one can hear you.' She pulled a jangling ring of keys from her purse.

Saturday night, the night of the big party. She'd shown me pictures of Donald Gates, and he looked exactly the same in real life: unkempt gray hair, paint-stained cargo shorts and plastic Crocs, a belly that strained against his T-shirt. But his voice was deep and booming, and even from a distance, I could see the brightness in his eyes. He had a pipe clamped between his teeth. He looked like the king of his small kingdom.

'Donald,' she said. 'This is my sister, Julia.'

'Julia. Lovely. Elizabeth talks about you all the time.'

'Did the frames arrive this afternoon?' she asked.

He sighed. 'They got the order wrong. We have to send them back.'

The apartment was one big undivided space, vast and pleasantly chaotic. A kitchen in one corner, with a metal sink as big as a bathtub. A long wooden table in the middle of the room covered in dripping, flickering candles. A massive living area with mismatched couches and armchairs grouped around rugs and coffee tables. A thick slab of a sliding wooden door, standing partially ajar, opened into the studio.

'I'll show you the studio later,' Elizabeth said, pouring us each a glass of wine at the island in the kitchen. 'It's pretty spectacular.'

'So this is where you work?'

'Most days. He's getting ready to mount a new show at a gallery in Chelsea, so we're over there sometimes, prepping the space. Here. You should meet the others.'

Donald Gates had several assistants working for him. Some, like Elizabeth, were on summer break from college. Others were closer to my age, young artists pursuing their own careers in their spare time. They were sitting at the long wooden table watching a skinny Asian boy roll a joint. 'Hey, guys, this is my sister, Julia. She's visiting for a while,' Elizabeth said as we slid next to them on the bench. The others looked up and said hello in unison.

I'd been skeptical about tagging along. It made me feel so old, the idea of following my younger sister to this downtown loft. Elizabeth is cooler than me, I'd always known that, but I wasn't sure if I was ready to have it rubbed in. She already seemed to know the city better than I ever had. But I was skeptical for another reason, too. Those orbiting the great Donald Gates would surely resort to insufferable pretension when they got together. The thought made me cringe: lofty theories and showy name-dropping, a posture of sophistication, conjuring – for me, at least – the ugly ghost of previous seductions.

But as I sipped my wine and listened to their patter, I found I was wrong. They talked about their work with a weary professionalism, like union members down at the local. The walls in the Chelsea gallery weren't right for the kind of mounting they usually used. Pearl Paint was out of Donald's preferred brush. Donald wanted to finish a big series, and they were all going to have to work late to get it done. The work wasn't about pretension. It was about humble logistics. Theirs was a mild sort of complaint, and I could tell that Elizabeth and her coworkers actually took pleasure in it. It was the breaking down of something big into a series of finely grained tasks, like glass melting into sand, something you could sift through your fingers.

The skinny Asian boy handed me the joint. I took a small toke before passing it. I didn't want to get too high or too drunk. I'd gotten to New York a day earlier, on a sweltering Friday afternoon, and that was overwhelming enough on its own. I tilted my head up. The ceiling of the loft was so high that I could barely see it. Donald had bought the space in the 1970s, when the city was teetering on the edge of bankruptcy. I tried to imagine what it would be like to live in one place for so long. Keeping your head turned to the light, letting the seasons change and the decades pass, doing your work.

A little later, when we stood to get another drink, Elizabeth led me to the wooden door. 'Don't tell anyone,' she said. 'We're not really supposed to bring other people back here.' She made sure no one was watching, then we slipped through the opening.

The noise of the party vanished behind us. The studio was even bigger than the living space. The dim light that filtered through the windows gave just enough illumination to see by. The room had the patina of long use: paint-splattered floor, walls spidered with cracks, empty tubes and crusty brushes. But the artwork hovered above and separate from the ordinary mess of the room. Donald Gates was known for his big, aggressive, abstract canvases, a throwback to an earlier era. 'You can get closer,' Elizabeth said, nudging me forward. I felt drawn to the paintings like a magnet to iron. The thick and tactile smears of paint. The blend and contrast of colors. They were so beautiful, but so ordinary, too. It was just paint, applied by the human hand. They glowed, gently, through the darkness. I couldn't believe that something that revealed itself to be so simple, when seen up close, had the power to move me so much.

'It's amazing, isn't it?' Elizabeth said. 'It's hard to turn away.'

'Exactly.'

'He's just a guy. He sleeps, eats, breathes just like the rest of us. Gets grumpy, makes stupid jokes. But then he does *this*, and I realize I have no idea what's going on inside his head. How he comes up with it.'

'It's so beautiful.'

'I know.' A beat later: 'We should get back to the party.'

The night continued. Guests arrived bearing bottles of wine and gifts of food. Some were young, like us, but many were closer to Donald's age. The gathering felt like an assortment of friendships collected over a long period of time, like a plant shooting off vines in radius. As the hours passed, the room gradually quieted until it was only the lingerers with their empty glasses. Donald was holding forth from a high-backed velvet chair, a shaggy mutt curled at his feet. Elizabeth stood up, stretched, and yawned. 'I'll say good-bye, and then we can go, okay?'

Despite the late hour, in bed back at Elizabeth's apartment, I couldn't sleep. I kept remembering how Elizabeth had looked, when she said good-bye to Donald. The dog awoke, his tail thumping the floor when Elizabeth reached down to scratch his ears. Donald patted Elizabeth on the shoulder. Together they looked like a version of home. Elizabeth had found the tiny nook in the world that was shaped just for her. She possessed a sense of belonging that seemed so rare to me in this city. But I'd encountered it before; a path that I'd been too foolish to pursue. I turned on the bedside lamp. My wallet was sitting on the dresser, and inside it was the business card I'd been hanging on to all these months. I took it out and stared at it for a long time.

In the morning, the card fell loose when I stood from the bed. I double-checked the time – well past noon on a Sunday. A perfectly reasonable time to call. I took a deep breath and dialed.

I hadn't been planning to stay longer than the weekend. My tote bag held a few changes of clothing, my phone charger, a book, and that was it. I took the train down midday on Friday, and I had a return ticket for Monday morning. Rob sounded nonchalant when I called. 'Okay,' he said. 'No worries. I gotta go. See you around, Julia.'

Elizabeth met me at her apartment on Friday after-noon. 'If you want to shower, the shower's weird,' she said, showing me around. 'The faucet is on backwards. Let's see . . . help yourself to whatever's in the fridge. You can use my computer if you want. I have to go back to the studio for a few more hours, but maybe we can get take-out or something for dinner. Oh, and I already changed the sheets on the bed for you. You're welcome.'

I smiled. Despite the grubby Chinatown setting and Elizabeth's budding artistic pursuits, her habits were reflexive – the manners of a good hostess, which our mother had instilled in us. The apartment was small, but it was sunny and clean, the window propped open to let in the breeze. A bouquet of bodega carnations sat on the bookshelf. Her roommate's bed, where I'd be sleeping, was neatly made with hospital corners. I'd taken a nice bottle of wine from my parents' collection and stuck it in my bag as a housewarming gift. We'd drink it later, on the roof, with our cheap dinner.

I had an e-mail on my phone from Abby. She and Jake were in Barcelona. We'd promised each other that we'd Skype at least once a week while she was on her European jaunt. Her e-mail asked if I wanted to talk that afternoon around 4:00 p.m., their nighttime in Spain. It was 3:52. I opened Elizabeth's computer and logged on, and soon the computer chimed with the sound of an incoming call.

'Abby?'

'Buenas noches, amiga!'

'Hey, you're practically fluent!'

She laughed, her voice echoing as it traveled the span of the Atlantic.

'Are you guys having fun?'

She sighed, or I think she sighed. I couldn't tell with the lousy audio connection. 'Holy shit, Jules, it's amazing. I'm quitting my job and never leaving.'

'How long are you there?'

'Barcelona for another two nights. Then Valencia next week, then Málaga, then we're going over to Morocco.'

'Where's Jake? How is he?'

'Too much wine at dinner. He passed out. He's good. We're' – she smiled, glancing down – 'I'm really happy. Things are really good.'

'Oh, my God, you're *blushing*. When's the wedding?'

'Shut up.'

'You know, I'm the reason you guys met. Dibs on maid of honor, right?'

'All right, all right. Hey, what about you? Where are you? I don't recognize it.'

'In New York. I'm staying at Lizzie's.'

'Jules! You had to wait until I was gone, huh?'

'It's just for a few days. I'm going home on Monday.'

'Why such a rush?'

'Well,' I said, looking around the tiny apartment. 'For one, I don't live here anymore. And I'm staying in Lizzie's roommate's bed. She's back on Monday.'

'You should stay longer. You can stay at my place. It's just sitting there.'

'You didn't find a subletter?'

She shrugged. 'Too much of a hassle. My rent is cheap. Jules, I'm serious. You should stay there. What else are you going to do? Aren't you bored to death up in Boston?'

'But your roommate –'

'Cat won't care. You know she practically lives with her boyfriend.'

It seemed too crazy, too all-at-once. 'I don't know. Let me think about it.'

'I'm going to e-mail Cat now. I'm gonna say that you'll call her tomorrow and get the keys, okay? I'll send you her number and stuff. Hey, have you talked to Evan lately?'

'Evan?' His name felt funny when I said it out loud. 'No. Why?'

'Well, are you going to see him? Now that you're back?'

'I doubt it. We haven't talked since December.'

Abby was quiet on the other end. I thought the video had frozen, but I could see the flicker of her eyes. Part of me was tempted to change the subject, avoid the Evan minefield, but I remembered what Abby had said on the phone. *Enough of this repressive WASP bullshit*. She was right. 'Okay, spill. What's up?'

'I saw him. The other week. At a party.'

'You saw Evan? How is he?'

'Are you sure you want to hear?'

My stomach dropped. He was with another girl. Or he'd launched into a tirade against me. Or both. But I needed to know, all of a sudden. Evan. The thought of him filled me with an aching curiosity. 'Yeah. Tell me.'

'He's good, actually. He has a new job. Spire let him go. They let a bunch of people go. It sounded like things were pretty rough for a while.'

'Where's he working?'

'Brace yourself. He's a hockey coach.'

'You're joking.'

'At some summer program up in Westchester. It's sort of temporary while he figures out what he's going to do. I guess he got a bunch of severance from Spire. He seems to like it, though. He said the kids are great.'

'Is he still living in our old place?'

'I think so. Jules, listen. You should call him. Or at least let him know you're back in town. Don't you think that's only fair?'

Fair. I was glad for the shitty video connection,

disguising the hot beginnings of tears. I could only think of that night, Evan making it so clear that he didn't want to see me again. Fair wasn't a factor.

'I don't know,' I said. 'Abby. Did he . . . um, did Evan –'

'Did he ask about you?' She shook her head. 'I think he wanted to. I mean, you know Evan. He's so Canadian. He probably didn't want to be rude and put me on the spot. But so what? Call him. Life is too short. Hey, so I'm sending you Cat's number. Go get the keys from her. Deal?'

'Deal.' I smiled. 'I miss you.'

'I miss you, too. I'm glad you're back.'

That night, on the sticky tar roof of her apartment building, I told Elizabeth about Abby's idea. Part of me was hoping for one last exit ramp, for Elizabeth to raise her eyebrows and say it was crazy. But instead she exclaimed that it was a brilliant idea, and she clinked her plastic cup of wine against mine. I wondered how my parents were going to take the news. I'd have to ask my mother to send down a box of clothes.

'This is great, Jules,' Elizabeth said, crumpling the wrappers from our banh mi into a tight, waxy ball. 'It's going to be a great summer.'

On Sunday, Cat opened the door. We'd met a few times, through Abby.

'That's all you have?' she said.

I shifted my tote bag on my shoulder. 'Yup. For now.'

She showed me around their West Harlem apartment quickly, apologizing for her abruptness, but she was on her way downtown to meet friends for dinner. 'That's the thing about this neighborhood,' she said, responding to a text, slipping on her sandals, tying her hair back in a bun, a flurry of motion. 'I love it, but it's so far from everything. Anyway, I sleep at Paolo's most nights. He's in the East Village. It's just easier.'

I spent a lot of time walking that first week. I had nothing else to do. I woke up in the morning, and it was always the first thing I realized: there was nothing I had to do that day. But this was different from how I'd felt in Boston. Then, the emptiness of the day stretched before me like a punishment. The discipline of my routine was a way of combating the loneliness, the reading and running and walking the dog like beads on a rosary. But at Abby's I woke to an empty apartment, and the emptiness actually felt good. Peaceful. Every morning was different. Sometimes I'd make coffee in the kitchen, drinking from Abby and Cat's mismatched mugs. Other mornings I'd go to the diner on the corner, watching the sidewalk traffic over eggs and bacon. Or I'd set out on a long walk to some unknown destination and pick up things on the way. Coffee from a Cuban restaurant, milky and sweet. A hot, spicy samosa for breakfast at 11:00 a.m., because I could do whatever I wanted.

Was it that the city had changed since I left? Was it such a different place, altered by the events of the previous year – the collapse of the economy, the election of a new president? Maybe it was, in small ways. The quieted construction sites, halted until the money started flowing again. The real estate listings, marked down further and further. The miasma of worry that hovered in the subway cars, nervous and desperate job seekers, commuters distractedly thinking of their 401(k)s. But mostly, life went on. Before long, it would be back to normal. The market would rebound. Apartment prices would pause, catch their breath, then resume their relentless climb.

But my city, my New York, was different. It was empty of the people I had known, of the associations I had clung to before. Abby was gone, on another continent for the summer. Evan was living his own life. Adam had surely moved on to another girl. Elizabeth was busy with work. This, too, was different from what I'd felt the summer before: neglected, and bored, and constantly waiting. Waiting for Evan to get home, waiting for his attention to refocus on me, waiting for him to fill whatever this vacuum was. Waiting, and wanting, for someone else to solve my problems.

I walked down Frederick Douglass Boulevard, near Abby's apartment, or through the twisting blocks of the West Village, or down the Bowery, or along the Battery. One day I walked across the Brooklyn Bridge and along the promenade in Brooklyn Heights, looking at the city from a new angle. The skyscrapers glittered in the late afternoon sun; the harbor was dotted with the white slashes of sailboats; the spray from a Jet Ski refracted the light. I could pick out Jake's apartment building, the balcony where Abby and I had stood during his party the previous summer.

Through it all, I began to see how badly I'd gotten things wrong. I kept looking for salvation in other people. I kept waiting for something else to come along. But that was never going to be the solution. The solution wasn't going to be Rob, either. It wasn't going to be staying at home, listening to my parents. I was lonely because I was alone – because everyone was, and no one could solve that for me. I could only learn to solve it for myself. For once, that knowledge didn't feel oppressive. I walked through the dusk back across the bridge to Manhattan. I didn't know where that realization pointed me. But for the moment, I let myself be content with it, with knowledge divorced from action.

I saw Elizabeth for dinner every couple of days. We'd eat something cheap and easy in her apartment, pasta with butter or scrambled eggs with cheese. I ate a lot of my meals alone, on bar stools or park benches. I liked the way it felt. I was free to observe the city, uninhibited because no one was observing me. I'd been slow to appreciate the invisibility New York grants. No one cares what you do, and that's a good thing. I felt more alive that week than I'd felt since graduation. Or maybe even further back, since that summer in Europe. In the middle of that first week, my mother sent a box of clothes to Abby's apartment. In among the T-shirts and sundresses she had tucked a note, written in her delicate script on a sheet of her mono-grammed stationery. *Jasmine was cleaning out the kitchen drawers, and she found this old disposable camera. She got the pictures developed — I thought you might want them. We miss you. It's very quiet here without you. xxx, Mom.*

I walked, and I walked. I walked down the West Side a lot. I could pass Adam's apartment building on Riverside Drive, and it was surprisingly easy — I felt nothing. I finally acknowledged what I'd been carrying around for so long, and I had started to make my peace with it. But the one neighborhood I avoided was the Upper East Side. I didn't even like to cross the invisible midline of Central Park. I worried about what might happen if I ever ran into Evan. What scared me was the possibility that I could inflict more hurt. That there was more damage to be done. That Evan and I might bump into each other, and I would say or do something that only made things worse.

I knew what was on that camera that Jasmine had found. I kept the unopened envelope of pictures on the desk in Abby's room. Over the following few days, it gradually disappeared underneath an accumulation of receipts and spare change. I didn't forget about it. I would open it eventually. But I wanted to take my time.

Sara Yamashita was waiting for me in a booth at the back when I walked into Balthazar at 12:30 on Wednesday. She stood up and kissed me on the cheek, smelling like mint and cigarettes. It had taken her a moment to place my name when I'd called, the Sunday before. A pause, then recognition. 'Julia! Of course. Adam's friend. I always wondered what happened to you.'

The room was buzzing, the mirrored walls reflecting a sea of attractive faces. 'Have you been here before?' she asked, stirring a packet of sugar into her iced tea. 'I'm getting the cheeseburger. You can't go wrong with that.'

'I'll do the same,' I said, closing my menu.

'So you went back to Boston? What happened?'

'It's a long story.'

'Well,' she said, spreading her arms. 'That's why we're here, isn't it?'

I had never really told anyone the full truth. Adam knew, and Evan knew. Abby, my parents, other friends — they knew about the breakup, but they didn't know what had triggered it. No one searched for a precise, time-stamped reason amid the rubble. But Sara was different. She knew about me and Adam. I wouldn't be able to leave him out of the story. It was why I forced myself to stick to the plan, even when gripped with nausea on the walk to lunch. If I didn't take this chance, I wasn't sure I ever would.

'Was it something to do with Adam?' Sara asked. 'You're not still seeing him, are you?'

'Yes. And no. We're not still seeing each other. Adam is part of the reason I left last year.' I took a deep breath and told her the whole story. My relationship with Evan. The things that started going wrong. Adam's reappearance in my life at exactly the right time. Everything Evan confided in me and the way I'd repeated it. And then, eventually, the implosion. By then our food had arrived. Sara listened attentively, nodding and asking a question every now and then. She didn't dispense excessive sympathy or judgment or outrage. She just listened until I was finished.

'Wow,' she said. 'Holy shit. You must be hungry after that.'

I nodded and picked up my burger. I was hungry. Starving, actually.

'You seem like you're doing okay, though. All things considered.'

'I am. I think so, at least.'

'God. I wish I could say I was surprised.'

'You're not? Has he –'

'Has he done stuff like this before? Yes. Unfortunately.'

I swallowed a bite of my burger. 'To you?'

'Maybe never as bad as this. But he's just *shady,* you know? We were dating freshman year, and I applied to an internship in the city for the summer. I asked him to read my cover letter – you know, proofread it, edit it. He took a long time to give it back to me. Like, a week, two weeks. He kept saying he was busy, but he'd get to it. When I finally gave up and went ahead and applied, I found that they'd already filled the position. Another Yale student.'

'Adam?'

'He was like, why are you pissed? He acted like I was totally nuts. Then he broke up with me two days later. But you know what? This shit's going to catch up with him eventually. I've seen him around a few times since the Spire story. He's insufferable. But he knows this was a fluke. His editors are already asking for more. They want their genius reporter boy to keep working his source. Which is you, I guess.'

I pictured Adam squirming in his editor's office. Sara smiled.

'Yeah,' she said. 'Exactly. I'm sure he's spinning the bullshit for them as fast as he can.' She dragged a french fry through a hill of ketchup. 'But you came back, huh? Do you know what you want to do?'

'I'm not sure,' I said. This stretch, as nice as it was, wasn't going to last forever. Within the hour, most people in this restaurant would push back from their tables and return to their offices, where they'd continue carrying out whatever slight rearrangement of the world their jobs demanded of them. But they were doing it. They were in it. They had found a way to fit themselves into the flow of time. I poked at the remains of my burger. 'I'm still figuring it out,' I said. 'I'm staying at a friend's place for a while. I guess I'll start applying to jobs soon.'

Sara cleared her throat. 'Can I give you some advice?'

'Of course.'

'I'm an only child. I never had an older brother or sister or anything like that. You're the oldest?' I nodded. 'Right, so you can understand. I always wished someone had warned me about what it was like after college. How weird things are. And I had it really easy. My parents are connected. I got a job right after I graduated. I had *nothing* to complain about. But I still felt like shit. No one told me how hard it was going to be. It sounds like you went through this last year, too. You can relate.'

She leaned back, letting the waiter clear our plates. 'Dessert? Coffee?' he asked, glancing toward Sara. 'Two coffees?' she said. Then she continued.

'What I mean is there's nothing *wrong* with you. You had a shitty job, a shitty guy who messed things up for you. But that happens. You can't really avoid that stuff. It's not easy, figuring out what you want. It's really hard. And I mean what *you* want, not what your friends want, not what someone else wants.'

I was quiet. She paused. 'Is this making sense?'

'Yeah,' I said. 'I guess I just – I know what you're saying, but I don't know . . . how do you actually do it? I mean, how do you figure that out?'

'Well,' she said, sitting up straight. Then she laughed. 'This is kind of silly. I'm, like, two years older than you. Tell me if I'm being obnoxious.'

'No, not at all.'

'Well, I don't know. It takes a while. It's trial and error. But you just have to start doing it. And you have to trust yourself, to know what matters to you. You're a smart girl. You're going to be fine. Don't let other people think they know better.'

The waiter set the coffees in front of us, two china cups quivering in their saucers. Sara tore open three sugar packets at once and emptied them into her coffee. 'I have such a sweet tooth,' she said, shaking her head. 'It's terrible.'

Time seemed to slow down – the dissolve of the milk

into my coffee, the clink of the spoon against the cup, the breeze from the door opening at the front of the restaurant, the grains of sugar falling from between Sara's fingertips into the black liquid. I thought about what Sara had said. I thought about the canvases, hovering, in Donald Gates's studio. I thought about the unopened envelope of photos back at Abby's apartment. I thought about the loneliness of the spring, which had recently transformed into something else. A purer, simpler feeling. Like the satisfied, heavy-limbed awakening that follows a long night of sleep.

I looked up. Sara wrapped her hands around her coffee cup, waiting for me to speak.

'Thank you for that. It's really good advice.'

'Is it? I'm not sure it would have actually helped if someone told me that after college. Honestly, I probably wouldn't have listened.'

'Can I ask you something?'

'Please.'

'Why did you ask me to lunch? I mean, last year at the party. I'm grateful, really, but why do all this?'

'You seemed smart. You seemed better than the situation you were in.' She shrugged. 'Also, you seemed better than that asshole Adam. I can relate to that. I only wish you had called sooner. We had a job opening a few months ago that would have been great for you.'

My stomach dropped. I had been in Boston, I reminded myself. I hadn't been planning to move back to New York. 'You filled it?'

'I did. I'm sorry, Julia. I wish I had something to offer you now. But things come up. I hear about things through friends. You *are* looking for a job here, right? You're staying in New York?'

'Yes. Yes, I'm staying.'

'Good,' Sara said, smiling.

I saw Cat every few days when she returned to the apartment for a change of clothes or, occasionally, to spend the night. She had tattoos and cool thrift-store outfits, and when I first learned she was a musician, I thought, *That makes sense*. Then she clarified that she was a cellist, studying at Juilliard. Her boyfriend, Paolo, was the lead singer in an indie band. It was a Thursday night. Cat was standing in the kitchen, eating a bowl of cereal before she headed back downtown.

'You sure you don't want to come along?' she asked, rinsing her bowl in the sink, opening the fridge. Cat's visits to the apartment were always crammed with action, a determination to squeeze as much utility as she could from her trip uptown. 'They're playing at the Bowery Electric. It'll be a great crowd. We're going out afterward.'

'I think I'm going to stay in. Thanks, though.'

'Text me if you change your mind.' She paused amid her flurry and looked at me. 'You know, the drummer – he's single, and you are totally his type.'

I laughed. 'Go, I'll be fine.' Cat waved as she walked out the door, and then the apartment was quiet again. Cat had lived in this apartment for four years, since she had started at Juilliard, and the place carried the sediment of permanent life: framed posters, painted walls. I could see why she didn't want to give it up. There was an elaborate sound system in the living room. Cat sometimes plugged in her stereo headphones and listened to recordings of her work, head nodding and eyes scrunched closed, opening only when she paused to scribble down notes.

A towering stack of CDs sat next to the speakers. I don't know what inspired me that night, after Cat left, to crouch down and examine them for the first time. She had gestured at them before, telling me to play them whenever I liked. A familiar title stood out in the stack. *Kind of Blue,* which Adam used to play for me. I slid the CD into the tray. A moment later, the music began, filling the apartment. The twinned initial steps of piano and bass, the soft invocation, the shimmering light of percussion, the eventual pierce of the trumpet. Adam liked to put things before me, novels or albums or movies, and when he told me of their greatness I'd nod along, feigning comprehension, letting his gestures guide my response. I must have heard this album a dozen times at his apartment, but that night was the first time I actually listened to it. I let it fill me, like water rising in a glass.

I'd finally opened the envelope of photos that afternoon. I felt myself on the verge of something. My mother would have opened the photos after Jasmine had them developed; it was the only way for her to have known they were mine. I imagined her pulling the first one from the stack, her hand twitching instinctively toward the trash bin. No one would have been the wiser. But instead she had sent them to me. I felt grateful to her in that moment, when I took out the photos for the first time. At least she was letting me decide this for myself.

My digital camera had broken while we were in Rome, two summers earlier. The battery fritzed, refusing to hold a charge. I bought a disposable camera in the train station on our way to La Spezia. We were spending the last week of the trip in the Cinque Terre. The first photo I'd taken, the photo at the top of the stack, was of Evan in Riomaggiore. He was standing on a stone boat ramp that led to the sea, his back to the water, the afternoon light casting his long shadow before him. The boats around him were painted like wooden candy, bright blues and greens and pinks. Evan had resisted when I told him to go stand for the picture. 'Come on, Jules, let me take one of you,' he said with a laugh. 'You're the good-looking one in this relationship.' But I shook my head. 'This picture is for me,' I said. 'I want this for when we get back.'

The magic had faded so quickly. I must have misplaced the camera when I was back at home, unpacking from the summer and repacking for senior year. That by itself wasn't so remarkable, but I felt a surge of sadness when I sat back onto Abby's bed and looked at the pictures for the first time. Why hadn't I missed these? Why had I never thought of that August afternoon on the edge of the Mediterranean, and let that lingering memory spark the recollection of the camera I'd misplaced? I'd never even bothered to miss it. I'd never bothered to appreciate what we had.

Evan looked so peaceful in that picture. His smile was wide and unselfconscious. He had a backpack slung over one shoulder, a cone of gelato in his other hand. The vividness of that afternoon: raising the camera to look through the plastic viewfinder and pausing for a moment. Evan was backlit by the lowering sun, his sandy hair sprayed with golden light. 'What is it?' he called over the noise of the motorboats puttering out to sea. A family walked between us, parents trying to corral their children, and I paused for a moment, letting the frame clear. He smiled at me – the smile of someone who knew exactly how lucky he was, in this postcard village more than four thousand miles from home. Finally I pressed the button, and the shutter snapped with a satisfying pop, and I returned the camera to my purse.

The music kept playing, filling the apartment with its mellow swells. I took out the photos again and spread them across the carpet in the living room. I was surprised to find that I remembered almost every single one of them: dinner on the terrace of our B and B in Monterosso; our sunburned faces after a hike one blistering afternoon; on the steps of the Duomo on our last night in Florence. It was Evan's first time abroad. He was a boy from the middle of nowhere who had decided he wanted more. Who wasn't satisfied with the path laid before him. I saw, for the first time, the bravery it had taken for him to do all of this.

I had obsessed over it all through the spring, that awful night, the idea of taking back what I had done. But maybe it was time to let that go. Maybe I was seeking an answer to a question that didn't matter, because it had already happened, because the undoing was impossible. Sara was right. It was a messy, difficult, shitty process — growing up, figuring out what you wanted. Some were lucky enough to figure it out on their own. I could see Elizabeth doing it already. Others were lucky enough to find a partner in the process, someone to expand their narrow views of the world. Abby and Jake, as unlikely as it seemed, were doing just that. But maybe there would always be people like me. Those for whom figuring it out came with a steep cost. I could feel it happening, slowly, in the smallest of steps. The future getting brighter. Where I was that day was in fact better than where I had been a year earlier. But the painful part was admitting what had happened to get me there. The implosion of two lives so that I might one day rebuild mine.

I saw it before I felt it, the darkened spots on the carpet, the drops of water on the glossy surface of the photos. I was crying, but this was different. It wasn't like the helpless spasms of guilt that had followed the breakup or the crushing anger I'd felt after learning the truth about the Fletchers. I wasn't crying for Evan or for what I had done to him. I was crying for the person I had been before. That night, the music on the speakers, the night air through the window, the prickle of the carpet against the back of my legs: what washed over me was the realization that I was finally letting go of that girl. The girl who clung desperately to a hope that it would all work out, that everything would make sense if she just waited a little longer, if she just tried a little harder. I let myself cry for a long time. Until, gradually, the spotlight faded to black. The curtain lowered slowly, a silent pooling of fabric against the floor. The hush that followed. The stillness that felt as long as a eulogy.

And then the house lights coming up. The room blinking back to life. And me, alone, surrounded by a sea of empty seats. I stood up and opened the door.

---

The next morning, I had an e-mail from Sara. We had promised to stay in touch after our lunch.

> Julia – so great to see you on Wednesday. A friend of mine is looking to hire an intern for her gallery. It's part-time, doesn't pay much, but she needs someone to start ASAP. I told her she should hire you. Can you call her today at the number below? I think you will hit it off. Yours, S.

I left a message for her friend, one of the associate directors at an art gallery in Chelsea. She returned my call an hour later, while I was trying to focus on the crossword puzzle and not stare at my phone too obsessively. Sara's friend seemed impressed by the Fletcher Foundation on my résumé – 'They do really important work. I'm a big admirer of their president, Laurie Silver' (who knew?) – and five minutes later, I was hired. 'You can start on Monday?' she asked, and I said yes. 'Great. I have your e-mail from Sara. I'll send you all the details.'

We hung up. I was gratified by how quickly it had happened, but my reaction was more tempered than it had been when Laurie had hired me a year ago. This wasn't going to be the only answer. The internship didn't pay much, and I'd have to find another part-time job, or maybe two, to make a livable wage. The gallery didn't offer health insurance. I'd have to work nights and weekends on occasion. But interns sometimes turned into full-time employees. It was hard work, a fast-paced and demanding job, but if I liked it and could prove myself, there was room to move up. And if I didn't, if it wasn't for me, then I could leave with no hard feelings.

It was another beautiful June day. A blue, cloudless sky. I'd e-mail Sara to thank her. I'd tell Elizabeth the good news, and Abby, and my parents – but later. I wanted to be alone with it for a while. I wanted to let the idea sink in. It was past noon when I left the apartment. I bought an ice cream cone for lunch. Eventually I found myself walking through the western edge of Central Park, looping around the edge of the reservoir, down toward the Great Lawn. I lay down on the grass, pulling out the book I'd brought along. I read for a while, then closed my eyes against the brightness. Friday afternoon sounds. People talking into their cell phones as they walked home. A girl reading aloud a magazine quiz to her friend. A couple debating what to have for dinner. I dozed off, and when I woke up the sun had moved toward the Upper West Side. My watch said it was close to 4:00 p.m. As I brushed the blades of grass from my shorts, I found that I had crossed into the eastern half of the park. Past the invisible midline that I'd always been careful not to violate. When I started walking again, I was walking east. I let my feet lead me without focusing on the destination.

They had taken down the scaffolding at the corner of 3rd Avenue. The approach to our block looked different, bare and vulnerable. But our building was the same – the glass door tattooed with handprints, a FedEx slip taped at eye level. I sat down on a stoop on the other side of the street, facing our old entrance. I didn't really have a plan. I just wanted to look, for a while, at the place I used to call home.

The foot traffic on the street thickened as the hour passed, people coming home from work, their arms laden with dry cleaning or groceries or gym bags. I wondered if Evan was on the train right then, riding back from Westchester. I had talked to Abby on Skype that week. She and Jake had moved on to Morocco, her tan deepening. She asked me whether I had been in touch with Evan. 'No,' I said. 'I will, eventually. I'm just waiting for the right time.'

'What do you mean? Just do it, Jules. It's not going to get any easier. Rip the Band-Aid off.'

'I don't know. I just don't think he wants to hear from me.'

'Do you want to see him? Do you miss him?'

I nodded. 'Yeah. Kind of. I do.'

'Then call him! It's not that complicated. I'm telling you, I saw him, and he's okay. Jules, he's *fine*. Better, in fact. He hated his old job. You know that.'

The afternoon was slipping into evening. Evan was probably going to be home soon. Maybe Abby didn't know the full truth of why I was so nervous about calling him, but I could see she had a point, no matter what. It wasn't going to get easier. If I wanted to see him, if I wanted a chance to stand before him and let him look at me, let myself look at him, I just had to do it. I had to live with whatever the consequences might be.

The light changed on 3rd Avenue. A stream of pedestrians crossed the intersection. Some turned up the avenue, and some turned down. As the crowd thinned, I saw him emerge, like an image sliding into focus. He was wearing jeans and a T-shirt, the old baseball hat he'd often worn in college. He held a bag of groceries in one hand. I remembered the morning he'd returned from Las Vegas, the eeriness of seeing him down the block. How unfamiliar he had seemed, contorted by his situation into a person I didn't recognize. I sat on the stoop, perfectly still, and watched Evan walk down the block toward our old apartment – toward *his* apartment. He still lived there, I reminded myself. I saw what Abby meant. He seemed okay. Happy, even. It was evident, something in the way he slung the grocery bag from one hand to the next with an easy gesture, digging for his keys in his pocket. Evan had a new life, a life he managed to rebuild without me. This was nothing like the morning he'd returned from Las Vegas. The Evan I was watching was the Evan I had always known. The person I had fallen in love with years ago.

He was standing outside the door. He dug deeper into his pocket and wrinkled his brow. Set down his grocery bag and swung his backpack from his shoulders. He unzipped the front pocket, and after a moment of blind groping, he pulled out his keys. He slung his backpack over his shoulder again, and picked up his grocery bag. He must have learned how to cook. I found myself over-whelmed with so much curiosity that I almost shouted his name. There was so much I wanted to know. What he was going to have for dinner that night. What his new job was like. How his day had been. Whether he ever thought about me. Every tiny, mundane detail of his life, every glittering grain of sand that made up the person he had become.

I stood up and started to make my way down the stairs, but Evan had already opened the front door. I had waited too long. He was about to disappear. I was at the curb, about to hurry across, when a cab blasted past, roaring down the block. It slammed on its brakes with a sharp squeal. The driver, stopped, continued to blast his horn at the cars ahead of him. I noticed that Evan, too, had paused because of the noise. One foot propping open the door, the other still outside.

And then he turned, surveying the street. Maybe he

was curious whether this minor rip in the neighborhood fabric had been noticed by anyone else. Whether it would be remarked on, acknowledged by a shared shrug with a neighbor. Or whether it was just another passing mishap of city life, fading into oblivion almost as soon as it happened, a tree falling in a forest with no listeners. That's when he saw me.

'Julia?' he called, raising one hand to shield his eyes from the sun. This was the Evan I had always known, and I could see it on his face already – the recognition of who I was. The understanding of everything that had come before and everything that would come after.

I didn't know what to say. Not yet. It would take a while, I knew. Maybe a long time. But I crossed the street and climbed the steps. What he said next made me realize that we would get there, eventually.

'Julia,' he said. His steady, light-colored eyes, the eyes that had managed to see the parts of me that I hadn't known existed. 'You came back.'

# ACKNOWLEDGMENTS

Thank you to Allison Hunter for her guidance, fierce wisdom, and unmatched savvy. Thank you to Carina Guiterman, who saw what this book could be and then made it a thousand times better with her deft and brilliant edits. I am lucky to have you both in my corner.

Thank you to Lee Boudreaux for taking a chance on me. Thank you to everyone at Little, Brown for giving me such a good home.

One of the reasons I became interested in the world of finance and hedge funds is Michael Lewis's writing, particularly *Liar's Poker* and *The Big Short*. I will forever be a grateful admirer. I also found invaluable illumination in *More Money Than God* by Sebastian Mallaby, *Too Big to Fail* by Andrew Ross Sorkin, and *Hedge Hogs* by Barbara Dreyfuss. And an enormous thank-you to my friends Cal Leveen and Lee West, who provided sharp-eyed feedback.

Thank you to Kate Medina, who has taught me so much about books, writing, reading, and life.

Thank you to my parents, Ed and Kate. Thank you to my sister, Nellie. Thank you for making me laugh, for laughing at me, for reading and rereading so many drafts of this book, and for always believing in me.

Last but not least, thank you to Andrew, whose love has made me a better person.